THE *SONG* BENEATH THE *ICE*

THE
SONG
BENEATH
THE
ICE

a novel

JOE FIORITO

M&S

National Library of Canada Cataloguing in Publication

Fiorito, Joe, 1948-
   The song beneath the ice / Joe Fiorito.

ISBN 0-7710-3231-5

   I. Title.

PS8561.I59S6 2002   C813'.6   C2002-903117-6
PR9199.4.F55S6 2002

"If You've Got the Money (I've Got the Time)" by Lefty Frizzell and Jim Beck.
Copyright © 1950 Peer International Corporation. International Copyright
secured. All rights reserved. Used by Permission.

Lines from "Ellesmereland," from *Selected Poems* by Earle Birney. Used by permission, McClelland & Stewart Ltd., *The Canadian Publishers*

We acknowledge the financial support of the Government of Canada through
the Book Publishing Industry Development Program for our publishing activ-
ities. We further acknowledge the support of the Canada Council for the Arts
and the Ontario Arts Council for our publishing program.

This is a work of fiction, and the characters in it are solely the creation of the
author. Any resemblence to actual persons – with the exception of references to
public figures, past and present – is entirely coincidental.

Typeset in Sabon by Sharon Foster Design
Printed and bound in Canada

This book is printed on acid-free paper that is 100% ancient-forest friendly
(100% post-consumer recycled).

McClelland & Stewart Ltd.
The Canadian Publishers
481 University Avenue
Toronto, Ontario
M5G 2E9

1   2   3   4   5   06   05   04   03   02

In memory of
T. F.
27 July 1954 – 22 October 2000

ACKNOWLEDGEMENTS

Thanks to Charles Foran for introducing me to Charlie Wilson. Thanks to Dinah Forbes for her sharp ear and her bright eye. Thanks to Karen Alliston for such a close read. Thanks to Susan Mahoney for everything else – and I do mean everything else.

Art is a means of communication with people, not an end in itself.

– Modest Musorgsky

Passionate subjects must be dealt with in cold blood.

– Hector Berlioz

If people could see into my heart I should feel almost ashamed. To me everything is cold – cold as ice.

– Wolfgang Amadeus Mozart

YOU MAY RECALL THIS STORY from the newspapers:

A year or so ago, during a recital of *Pictures at an Exhibition*, the concert pianist Dominic Amoruso stopped, got up from the piano, turned to the audience, paused – and walked away without a word. Just like that, he disappeared.

There were suggestions at the time of an attack of stage fright; the onset of some sudden illness; a temperamental reaction to some careless noise in the audience; perhaps a nervous breakdown. I was there that night. I saw what happened. I'm still not sure I understand.

He was performing in the Walker Court of the Art Gallery of Ontario. He was playing the piece with which he launched his career, and with which he is most closely associated. He'd begun with his usual brilliance. There was no hint of anything unusual.

He plays the Musorgsky as written – more powerful, perhaps more jagged than you are used to hearing it. Closer to

Richter than Horowitz; closer to Ashkenazy than Richter; but all Musorgsky. Or so I am told. I am not a music critic. But I do have particular knowledge of Amoruso. I have known him since childhood. He has the nerves of a burglar. He often joked that he could play *Pictures* in his sleep, that he played it better in his dreams. That night, however, he became progressively more tentative as he made his way through the music and, towards the end, his hands began to jerk back from the piano as if he feared the keys might bite him.

He appeared puzzled. Then frightened. He grimaced. He fought himself. He froze. He sat for a moment with his hands raised high in front of him, unable or unwilling to move. The image was that of a child shielding his face from the attentions of a large black dog.

In the audience: silence, whispers, murmurs, gasps. Men and women shifting in their seats. A few rows behind me, a man began to clap and a shrill, two-fingered whistle pierced the rising murmur. Someone hissed at the rudeness; then, as if to explain that the hiss was meant to admonish the whistler and not the pianist, the crowd broke into earnest, almost apologetic applause.

Dominic let his hands fall. His shoulders sagged. He pushed himself up from the piano bench and faced us as if he were about to speak. I held my breath; we all did. He made a useless gesture with his hands. No words came. He looked up and flinched as if he thought something might fall on him. He turned on his heel and walked away, without so much as a sideways glance.

The director of the gallery tried to catch his elbow.

Thomas Carter is a small slim grey-haired man who favours a crisp black suit and an impeccable white shirt. Amoruso brushed past him.

Carter took centre stage and apologized briskly on Dominic's behalf. Said he was sure it was nothing serious. Efforts were being made to take care of him, there was indeed a doctor in the house – a remark that caused a titter. There were plenty of them in the house.

And then, with a confident smile, Carter made a few remarks about the evening's exhibition, about which more in a moment. He invited us to join him for a glass of champagne, after which he said we might like to take a stroll through the gallery.

I caught up with Carter and asked if I could help in any way. He directed me to a makeshift green room off to the side of Walker Court. Dominic was nowhere to be seen. No one could tell me where he was. And so I resolved to find him.

I left the gallery and went to look for him in his usual post-performance haunts. I went to Pho Pasteur, Dai Nam – his favourite noodle shops in Chinatown: *No, sorry, we haven't seen him, not tonight, we don't know where he is.*

I went to the Fran's on College St. *No, dear, he hasn't been in. At least not this evening. If he drops by later, is there a message?* I took the subway to the Fran's on St. Clair, the one near his apartment; the same response. I walked to his apartment building and rang his buzzer. Nothing doing. The doorman said he hadn't seen him that evening, although I was sure this was an act of loyalty.

I was stumped.

As nearly as I can determine, he made three phone calls that evening: first, to Claire Weller – they were intimate; second, to his agent, the elderly but formidable Anne Langelier. And there was a brief and simple message on my machine when I finally got home: *It's me. I'm sorry. Don't worry. I'll be in touch.* His voice sounded altogether serene.

It seems to me that when someone does something quite out of character, says "Don't worry," and then drops out of sight, it is prudent to worry in earnest. I tried to return his call. I was not the only one – his phone rang busy all night long. Eventually I gave up – either several of us were trying to get through all at once and we were blocking the line, or he had taken his phone off the hook.

I finally got through the next morning.

His voice mail kicked in after half a dozen rings. His mailbox was full and would no longer accept new messages.

It didn't add up.

In spite of what the morning papers reported, he had never been bothered by stage fright. He had jitters before a performance, but that was normal. He was rarely bothered by noise from the audience – or so he let on. "It's part of being human: we cough, we fidget, we sneeze, we fall asleep, and we snore. It puts the so-called glory of art in perspective."

Of course, I have also seen him glare at whisperers, fidgeters, and those who insist on folding and unfolding the pages of their programs. He once said concert programs ought to be made of silk, an idea borrowed from the pianist Paderewski.

He is supremely confident in his hands, his knowledge of the repertoire, his memory, his touch. He is no *artiste* with a repertoire of sighs and swoons. When he speaks in public about the act of performance, he likes to paraphrase the Zen: "Eat your rice, wash your bowl. Sit at the piano, play the score."

I spoke to two of the music critics who were in the audience that night and who had intended to review the recital; all they knew was what I'd seen and heard myself – up until the moment he faltered he had been, as one of them put it, uniformly and unremarkably excellent.

Carter, when I called him the following morning, declined to comment. He knows I am a journalist. He was reluctant to say anything. He told me that no one had seen Amoruso leave.

Madame Langelier was somewhat more forthcoming. She said Dom had phoned her late in the evening – or rather, early in the morning. He'd got her out of bed. She was cryptic about their conversation. She hadn't been at the performance, and insisted that I tell her what I'd seen.

I don't know her very well, but I am fond of her because she is so clearly fond of Dom. She thinks of him as a son. I gave her the précis, which was by now too familiar. She confessed to being in the dark about what might have gone wrong. But you can never take an agent at her word when it comes to the protection of her client. I suppose I'd have kept mum in her place, too.

As for Claire Weller, although she and Dominic are intimate, I don't think they are close. It's a delicate thing. She is married to a prominent businessman. On the society pages, she is usually described as a patron of the arts. Her affair with Dom is an open secret in some circles. It is a curious relationship. She is older than he is by a good ten years. They meet discreetly once a week. She brings Asian takeout to his apartment and stays the afternoon. They speak frequently on the telephone. He'd hate the reference, but Dom, like Glenn Gould, is an insomniac. He makes frequent calls to friends at all hours of the night when rehearsing or preparing to record.

Claire was not in when I called.

I was given a private number by the maid. Claire sounded tired on the phone. Said she was under the weather, and had been unable to attend. Like Mme Langelier, she insisted that I tell her what I'd seen, and so I filled her in.

She had nothing to say. She confirmed that he'd called her that evening. Airily, she refused to elaborate. I was given to understand that he told her what he'd told me: *Don't worry, I'll be in touch.*

Mme Langelier called me back. No word from Dom, as I'd hoped – she simply wanted to know if I thought she should call the police. She was genuinely agitated and unsure of herself. I said it was early days, but I gave her the name of a cop I knew in Missing Persons.

At first, the police said there wasn't much to do but wait – a missing person isn't missing until sufficient time has passed, or if there are indications of foul play.

But Mme Langelier, in spite of her birdlike appearance, is formidable when seized with a task. She had connections, markers to call in, and strings to pull. So did Claire Weller, of course. Within a day or two, the police had questions for everyone.

They searched Dom's apartment.

He – or someone – had cleaned the pills from his medicine cabinet. There were several vials of painkillers and sedatives lying around the apartment, all of them empty. The police concluded from this that he might have been suicidal. I did what I could to dispel that notion.

Dom has frequent migraines. They have bothered him since childhood. He has also complained of a variety of other ailments, real or imaginary: pain in his joints, shortness of breath, dizziness, soreness in his ears and tingling in his extremities, swollen hands, mood swings, and so on, and so on. He goes nowhere without a pocket full of pills. Not even to the park.

Drugs had been taken from his apartment. I was certain it meant two things: He had come home after the recital, and he had packed what he needed to be away for any length of time.

The cops shrugged. They are slow to conclude and they do not like conclusions drawn for them. Especially by amateurs.

Apart from the missing meds – and the usual mess left by a bachelor who relies on the weekly ministrations of a cleaning lady – there was nothing remarkable about the apartment. Except for the eloquence of his piano, which stood lid-up, mute in his studio. A black linen shirt hung from the topstick. Tellingly, I thought, there was no note. Suicides, as a rule, tend to leave them. He'd have left his on the Steinway.

More shrugs from the cops.

I have covered the police beat on occasion. I made a call or two later in the day and learned that tracker dogs would be sent to sniff through the ravines. When the police understood that I knew Dom well and could be trusted not to get in the way, I was given permission to tag along.

And so we explored the nearest reaches of the city wilderness: under a dusting of early snow, the cold remains of the campfires of the homeless; the dry white skull of a dog long dead; lifeless sleeping bags in empty pup tents, the occupants gone begging; and the usual litter of the ravines – empty bottles, empty tins and jars, empty rusted shopping carts.

In the thick underbrush of the Don Valley we came upon three sculptures made of dried vines, scraps of metal, twists of scavenged copper wire. The sculptor, one of the more talented of the bush hermits, had fashioned a life-sized horse, a giant bird with spreading wings, and a twig-man who stood pointing with one arm at the Bloor St. Viaduct. We walked with the dogs along the base of it. Dom had not jumped. Or at least, as the cops noted dryly, he had not jumped there.

The Harbour Police were instructed to patrol the shore of the lake from Sunnyside to the Beach; nothing. The tugboat captains who worked the Cherry St. slip were asked to keep their eyes open; now and then, as they churn the shallow water of the inner harbour, they disturb a body. *Not much traffic on the lakes right now, but I'll call if anything turns up!* said one of the captains, a joker.

The hospital emergency rooms had of course been checked, as had the cheap hotels and the shelters – because Dom could be lost and wandering, because he could be at risk. And so it was that the ill, the mad, the homeless, and the art and music crowds – everyone in Toronto – were aware that Dominic Amoruso, concert pianist, had walked off stage and disappeared, could not be found, had left no note, was gone.

The headlines in the papers: VIRTUOSO VANISHES, *Globe and Mail*. PIANIST TAKES A POWDER, *Toronto Star*. DIS-CONCERTED, *Toronto Sun*.

After a few days, the story was left to the weeklies. Out of sight is out of mind in a town where the news agenda on the city desk is set by crack whores who slit the throats of horny pensioners, and women who drown their babes in tubs of scalding water, and bored cops who gun down rabid cats in the dark halls of public housing. Forgive me if I'm cynical about the press. I make a living as a freelance journalist.

There was something about his disappearance that nagged at me. He might have had a breakdown of some sort, but I never believed for a minute that he'd killed himself. He wasn't – isn't – the type. Yes, I know; there is no type. But there was no reason

I could see for him to disappear: His critical reputation was solid. He had a small circle of close friends. He never missed a performance. He was intelligent. He enjoyed his life. He travelled often. He had no debts; he was, in fact, well off. The only real fly in his ointment was his migraines.

How to explain his disappearance? I could not.

I have written about him once or twice – profiles and so on. He and I have worked together now and again on collaborative interviews. I've given him editorial advice a few times concerning things he'd written – articles, criticism, pastiches on various musical subjects similar to those cobbled together by Glenn Gould in the old days.

Dom had a thing about Gould. A mania, really. He never quite explained why, but I think he was jealous of GG's gift, despised the liberties Gould took with scores, was scornful of his retreat to the recording studio, and above all could not bear the legendary quirks – the famous little boy's chair, the overcoat and gloves at the height of summer's heat, the naive belief in chiropractic and homeopathic remedies – *Imaginary cures for imagined ailments!*

Most of all, he refused to accept the view that Gould's recordings were a high-water mark in the history of the piano. *A high-water mark in the history of neurosis, more like it.*

My friend is a man of views.

I don't think he liked the pressure, which was constant. I also think he is more like Gould than he knows.

Now and then, late at night, some prankster would attach a fat red rubber clown's nose to the statue of Gould outside the studios of the CBC. I always suspected Dom of doing it. Or causing it to be done. He always denied it. And he always laughed heartily after the denial.

A month or so after his disappearance, I wrote a short appreciation for one of the papers, for no other reason than to remind people that he still had not been heard from. Eventually, however, it became apparent that there was nothing new to say. The story of the missing pianist faded; even I had to set his absence aside and continue with my own affairs.

Three weeks ago, I returned from an out-of-town assignment.

I'd been researching a feature on the lives of the homeless across the country. I'd hit the streets in half a dozen cities, slept on grates, ate stale bland mashed food, and bunked in louse-ridden shelters. The story? TB on the rise; the diseases of malnutrition on the rise; despair on the rise; death by exposure, etc., from one end of the country to the other.

I came back late at night, cold and tired, exhausted and depressed, with a troublesome cough and a dreary story. I dumped my bags and opened my windows to let in some fresh air. I poured a drink and was sorting through the sheaf of built-up mail – bills and cheques, more of the former than the latter – when I found notice of a parcel waiting at the post office. I had not ordered anything. My birthday was months away. I had no inside sources in the habit of slipping me documents.

I set the card aside, ran a bath and fell asleep in it, woke shrivelled and shivering, had another drink and went to sleep, this time in my bed.

In the morning I walked to a diner on Roncesvalles Ave. and took a place at the counter beside two of the neighbourhood old boys. They were watching television, nursing cigarettes, and drinking breakfast beers. I ordered coffee and a plate of ham and eggs with hash browns and brown toast. The coffee thin, the ham tough and salty, the eggs over easy, and the toast limp with butter. At least I didn't have to make it.

I don't smoke, not any more, but while I ate I wanted to. This, the result of three weeks living on the street and in the shelters. Cigarettes are to the homeless what vitamins are to you and me.

When I had cleaned the yolk from my plate with the last soft corner of toast, I walked to the post office in the drugstore on the corner. The woman behind the counter is young and pretty, blonde and formal, shy in my presence. She thinks journalism is important work. I do not disabuse her of the notion. She batted her eyes and asked me, please, for one piece of identification. The frown on my driver's licence photo sent her scurrying into a back room. She returned a moment later, rushing, blushing, and pushed a box across the counter at me.

The box was wrapped in brown paper and decorated with a row of cancelled stamps, as handsome as the medals won by old men in foreign wars. It was neatly tied and knotted with waxed cord. Who ties a package with cord these days, except old people and immigrants? I know plenty of both, none of whom had the means or the motive to send me gifts. There was no return address.

I carried the mystery package back to my apartment and set it on the table in the dining room. I was in no hurry to open it. You never know what sort of surprises a surprise package might contain. Jacks jump out of boxes and lives are changed of a sudden.

Instead, I looked for my briefcase, and spent some minutes sorting through my receipts. I thought about calling the office. My deadline was a long way off, but I thought I'd let my editor know I'd come back in one piece. And then I thought to hell with him.

I made a pot of coffee stronger than the diner's. And I sat and slit the package open.

The contents – a clutter of cassettes, a stack of small black notebooks – meant nothing to me until, at the bottom of the box, I saw the tape recorder. I recognized it instantly: Japanese, brushed aluminum, the size of a slim paperback, pleasing to hold in its fat leather case. No doubt about it. Dom took it with him everywhere he went. Until now, that is.

I set it aside and rummaged through the box again, spilling everything onto the table, looking for a note, an explanation, anything that might tell me what I wanted to know. No clues. I looked carefully at both sides of the brown paper: no letter, no instructions, no return address, nothing.

It was obvious Dom had sent the package. And then a second possibility occurred – he might have left instructions for it to be sent. And there was a third possibility, along with its logical corollary – someone other than Dom had sent the package, and had done so with or without his knowledge or permission.

While it was not exactly a plain brown envelope slipped under the door, it amounted to the same thing. I was onto something. Surely it would clear up the mystery of his disappearance.

I thought for a moment of calling . . . who? His agent? One of the papers? And say . . . what, exactly? I slowed myself and tried to think. No matter who had mailed the package, or why it had been mailed to me, the point was that it had been mailed to me. Which meant I was supposed to do something with it. What and why?

I was overwhelmed with caution. Dominic had been gone for almost a year. He seemed to have fallen off the face of the earth. It was still unclear if he'd jumped or had been pushed, if he was alive or dead, if he intended to return or preferred to remain in hiding. What to do?

I can be a bit thick at times. It took me another cup of coffee and the better part of ten minutes to reach the obvious conclusion: Notebooks are meant to be read. Tapes are meant to be played.

I swept my dining table clear of clippings, files, magazines, old newspapers, etc. And checked myself again. If it wasn't Dom who'd sent the package . . . if I was going to have to call the police . . . if there were fingerprints on the cassettes or the recorder, and I spoiled them. . . .

I went to the closet and found a box of surgical gloves. I'd swiped it from a hospital once, while doing a story on emergency room surgery. I felt a bit foolish, but I snugged on a pair and bagged the tape recorder. I took my own from the closet shelf. It is a thing I rarely use in my work. I prefer to listen closely and take notes as I go. My recorder is old and nowhere near as good as Dom's, but it would do. And so I went at the tapes with all the patience of a child on Christmas morning. And once again, I fell back before I could get started.

I'd been sent the pieces of a puzzle. If I was going to fit them together without the benefit of a picture to work from, then I would need some sort of structure, an organizing principle. It was likely the tapes meant nothing without the notebooks, just as the notebooks – at a glance they were full of observations, descriptions, and so on – would increase their meaning when read along with the tapes.

Nothing else to do – I would pair up the notebooks with the corresponding tapes, and begin the tedious task of making transcriptions. Dom was meticulous about dates and times. There were fifty-two notebooks and thirty-six cassettes – the last of these apparently completed two weeks before the package was put in the mail. And two more cassettes, undated, in a separate envelope.

I examined the package one last time.

The box had held jars of caviar from the Soviet Union. I unfolded the brown paper wrapping and spread it out carefully one more time. My address had been block-lettered with a blood-red china marker; not Dominic's handwriting. A clue? Maybe so, but the postmark – Wolf Cove, Northwest Territories – was a non sequitur.

I set up my laptop, took a breath, cleared my head.

As a general rule, an hour of tape involves a day of redaction. Others may work faster than that, but I have to listen and listen again in order to get the sense of what I'm hearing; then I listen a third time and only then do I transcribe. A phrase at a time. Two steps forward, one step back; play and rewind, make notes and play again.

I loaded fresh batteries in my tape recorder.

There was only one place to begin: at the end.

The most recent tape, dated June 23, seemed to hold nothing but the whisper of white noise. I fast-forwarded until I found a discernible sound – footsteps on gravel, then the call and response of two barking dogs, the busy drone of an approaching all-terrain vehicle, a heavy door opening and closing with a pneumatic sigh; a sniffle, a cough, and a laboured breath – his? Presumably.

I got the impression it was evening. I'm not sure why I thought so. Perhaps because day is busy and night tends not to be. After the opening of the door, there was a shift in ambience. I imagined I was looking down a long corridor. Then I heard a single voice, rising and falling in the distance, punctuated by the echo of a hammer on wood – one hollow blow, another and another. Dom – it could only have been him, who else could it have been? – moved quickly.

The sound of the hammer blows grew nearer. I heard a voice quite clearly; not his. The language was guttural, coughed up from the back of the throat, the base of the nostrils, the pit of the stomach. If the tapes had been made in Wolf Cove, it was no leap of logic to assume the language was Inuktitut. There was a shout – Dom's voice – "*No!*" And then an inarticulate, other-worldly syllable of anguish, a crash and a wail, as if . . .

I stopped the tape. It made no sense.

If I was going to learn anything – if I was hearing what I thought I heard – then I'd need to begin at the beginning.

After several false starts, I have decided to adopt the following conventions: To distinguish my own notes and observations, and for the purpose of clarification, I have used italics.

Dom occasionally used the tape recorder like a dictaphone – his narration and conversation will appear in plain text.

The descriptions of taped actuality, wild sound and so on, occur inside square brackets.

I have also tried to match the notes to the tapes as closely as possible. It seems only obvious to do so, since he records and makes notes at the same time. I have taken the liberty of ampli-fying certain references made on tape or in the notebooks. And I have added supplementary notes with the help of a music spe-cialist on the information desk at the Metro Toronto Reference Library. Margie Warriner was able to shed generous light on much of the text, for which I am grateful.

He had the habit of wordplay. Anagrams appear with a whimsical frequency.

One last thing: It may be pleasurable to watch a silent movie, but a soundtrack with no visual cues is tedious to the point of tears. If you don't believe me, stand on any street corner. Close your eyes to the ebb and flow and describe what you hear. Ten minutes of the sound of footsteps on a city sidewalk is nine minutes and fifty seconds more than most of us want or need to know about the click, the limp, the drag, the skip, and the scuff of heels on pavement.

And so, we begin.

Tape, August 14:

Note: This is two months prior to the recital.

[A snatch of pop music – *if you change your mind, take a chance on me* – leaking from the doorway of a shop. A man's hoarse voice in passing: *Spare change for food? Nice day. Spare change for food? Nice day. Spare change for food? Nice day.* The laughter of girls and the hiss of drawn breath, his. A siren in the distance, far and near and far. The push of a door, and a change of ambience – the sound of the street is replaced by a rising rattle of cutlery and crockery and the murmur of low conversation. He is – we are, I am – in a restaurant. He clears his throat and takes a seat.

Dom, his taped narration *sotto voce:*]

Fran's, St. Clair, the corner booth happily free. For me, the beginnings of a post-performance headache. The tip of a familiar needle in my best eye, the left eye, the needle making its familiar way to the back of my head. Um, another – not a needle but a long sharp knife – pushed up from the base of my jaw. Where needle and knife intersect, a node of white light. It is time for my drugs. Except that whenever it occurs to me that it's time for drugs, it's too late for drugs. I am fighting a rearguard action. And I'd better keep my voice down.

[Short thick squeaks as his leather jacket is unzipped and shucked, and three sharp slaps as he folds his daily paper.]

Note: The jacket was a tic, a quirk; he performed in it whenever he could. He was known as the Punk Pianist in some of the papers, some of the time. So much for the papers.

He read them in spite of himself.

He always did the cryptic crossword in the Globe.

As for the migraines, you'd make money if you bet he had one. He invariably had one after he performed in public, as if music were a cause, as if, upon emptying his head of music, there was room for nothing but pain. He said the headaches made him sensitive to light, taste, touch, smell, and – worst of all – overly susceptible to sound.

He thought they were the result of adrenalin – or rather, the lack of it, post-performance. To complicate matters, the medication he took to ward off the onset of a migraine – or to kill one that was fully developed – contained a compound of drugs that dulled his reaction time, clouded his perception, and made him furiously vague. Or vaguely furious.

Tape, August 14, cont'd:

The light in here tonight is the colour of lemons. There is something in the air – I don't know if I'm picking this up or not – I hear what sounds like a mumbled chorus in the background: *Oh no, not now. Oh no, not now.* Oh no not now. I get it now. An overhead fan, the blade off-balance and –

"Hello, dear, what will it be tonight?"

"A glass of ice water. And, um, a slice of pie."

"I have apple, raisin, cherry, peach –"

"It really doesn't. I don't, I can't. You choose."

"Are you sure? If I bring something you don't want and –"

"No, it's fine, really. Pie is fine. Any pie will do."

"Was that a cup of tea with that as well?"

"Just ice water. Lots of ice, easy on the water."

Notebook, August 14:

Why doesn't anyone think you're serious unless you exercise the right to choose? Why didn't I hear her coming by the sound of her footsteps and the smell of her perfume?

White Shoulders: Eludes His Throw.

As if the fate of human history rests on my knowing what sort of pie I require. I am not here for pie. I am here for . . . ice. The illusion of a little company. A place to rest. A search for clues. A glass of water for my pretty blue drugs.

What else: eels thaw.

There is this: the hiss of the coffee dripping on the burner; the scratch of a match lit for a cigarette; oh no not now; and two girls giggling. There is also a guy in a blue uniform sitting at the counter: a security guard filling his belly before clocking in at midnight? His plate is piled high with slabs of something brown.

Meat loaf: tame foal.

Potatoes: stoop, eat.

His lips work in and out, like those of a fish out of water. His fork rises, he cocks his head to the side and opens his mouth, inhaling the food as he eats. I'll bet he has a bad tooth.

I have, at this moment, a needle in my eye.

An eye for a tooth. A fair trade: a far tirade.

Depending on the state of the eye and the state of the tooth. Would he trade mine for his? I can hear him chewing, even if the sound doesn't make it onto this machine. How can you not choke, inhaling as you eat?

I bet I could set his dinner to music: stab of fork and slice of knife; knife laid down and food sucked in; the chewing and the swallowing; a slurp of coffee followed by the succulence of the swallowing; the scrape of fork and knife on the plate again. There is no repeated action that cannot be made musical.

Oh no, not now. A useful phrase. I am a genius.

What was it that Szell said – "That nut's a genius."

He did not say, "That genius is a nut."

He put the nut first.

Note: *White Shoulders: Eludes His Throw. Meat loaf: tame foal. Like I said, he fiddled with anagrams constantly.*

As for the Szell reference, it prompted the first quick call to Margie Warriner. She and I have a bit of history. We once worked at the Montreal Gazette, she in the library and me reviewing movies and theatre for the arts pages. We went out briefly, not long enough to learn to dislike each other. She, clever girl, quit the paper when the quitting was good. Moved here to take a job at the Metro Toronto Reference Library. We have drinks on occasion. We compare now to then, and here to there, like all good former Montrealers. She called back in half an hour to tell me that Szell was a conductor; his nut crack was a reference to Glenn Gould.

Dominic is, as I said, haunted by Gould; what good pianist in Toronto isn't? It's as if there has ever only been one player here. I imagine it is like being a painter in Picasso's hometown.

Gould also ate at Fran's on occasion, at least he did before he died. Dom told me he felt obliged to eat there after he played because "the food is bland but I'm still here and that nut's not." That's how he spoke, speaks. In rapid strokes, in strophes. He said there was no sense ducking the place.

He also said he was not above picking that nut's pocket – by which he meant his own use of the tape recorder. Tape led Gould from the stage into the studio in search of perfection. Dom was skeptical of that, and considered it an excuse – he thought cutting and splicing was an exercise in sterility. That obviously didn't stop him from toying with recording technology for his own purposes.

He collected wild sound the way some people buy records – each shuffle step, each snatch of music and overheard remark contained the seed of something musical.

One further observation: Dominic used conventional and lapel microphones when it suited his purpose, but he had a two-piece mike, the kind used by documentarists for stereo recording. The latest clever thing, it is worn in the ears and is easily mistaken for earphones. When he wore it, he appeared to be listening to a Walkman, and not making a recording. As a result, he could tape himself, and whatever was going on around him, without being noticed; a felicitous subterfuge.

Tape, August 14, cont'd:

"Here you are, dear, lemon meringue; enjoy. And one large ice water. There you go. Will there be anything else?"

"That's fine, that'll be . . . oh, damn it to –"

"Oh, my. I'm sorry, let me –"

"No, I'm fine, it's not – please just –"

"Here, let me – I'll bring another."

"It isn't worth the bother."

"It's no bother at all."

"Oh, no, not now."

"You're sure –"

"For the love of – I have never been surer."

[Her tired sigh, the rustle of her uniform, the squeak in the sole of one of her retreating shoes; the slow purr of his zippered jacket pocket, and the retrieval of a notebook; his licked finger and the turning of pages, the sound as soft as a flame in a gas fireplace; a china plate pushed across his table, and the wet thin scratch of his fountain pen.]

Notebook, August 14, cont'd:

I drop pen, nib hits plate, pen flips in air – how could I be startled by the appearance of a waitress with a slice of pie? I pin the blame on post-play jitters, adrenalin decay, not to mention fatigue, inattention, and ennui – On who? On we! – and the onset: stone of another bad head – above all, not enough sleep, never enough sleep. I would like to sleep a week.

I have never not wanted this.

[The tape recorder remains on; the ice in his water glass makes a sound as delicately veined as wind chimes; the lewd wetness of his gulps, the intimacy of his swallowed breath.]

Notebook, August 14, cont'd:

Pills kicking in; nicely, warmly. But there are limits to technology: that bead of ink in its airy arc – its slow-motion rise. It fell like a blue pearl into a trough between the waves of tan meringue. There must have been the merest whisper of ink in the air and the tiniest of splashes – since all movement equals sound. Is it on tape? Could the tape be amplified? Can such a sound be isolated and retrieved? Can one sound be subtracted from another?

A man on the street is peering in through the far window. He stares at me and mimics the movements of my head. He looks familiar. I sense that he has no use for my needled eye, and judging from the curl of his lip he is repelled by my boredom and my clumsiness. He has a wide thin mouth, high cheeks, a long straight nose, and thick black hair slicked back and distinguished by a widow's peak; he seems pop-eyed, skittish, as if about to bolt –

I am startled by my reflection.

And I understand how I startle others.

In the booth in front of me, a pair of chatty teenagers: geese rant. Private school girls in tartan skirts, white shirts, the collars open, their ties undone, leaning over fountain sodas, their foreheads nearly touching. Nothing startles them: They are oblivious to the waitress and the man with the meat loaf at the counter and most certainly they are oblivious to me, the blue pearl on my pie, and the trace of my ink in the air.

Where is there a trace of what I played tonight?

Tape, August 14, cont'd:

"... in the yard after school. This old guy rolls down the street in a convertible with the top down, giving me the eye. He's like, 'Hey, baby!' I'm like, 'No way!'"

"And then what happened?"

"He drives off real slow, but I can see he's looking back at me. Like he thinks he might be getting some. As if. I blew a bubble at him with my gum and raised my skirt. Mrs. Johnson came walking over. He took off, real fast."

[Their bubbling giggles, the scratch-itch of a butane lighter. If you listen carefully, you can hear the dry suck of lips on filter tips, the exhalation of salty blue smoke, and the gurgle of straws in the bottoms of glasses.]

Note: Dominic was single. He had – has – From now on, I'll stick to the present tense until I hear otherwise – he has, as far as I know, normal appetites. He slept with Claire, among others; several others, in fact. But he is not, as far as I know, attracted to schoolgirls. At least no more than normally so for a single man in the prime of life. But he is an inveterate eavesdropper.

Notebook, August 14, cont'd:

The fuck-you of her pleated skirt.

This is lasciviously real. I can hear what they say – I can see it as soon as they say it – the voice of the blonde contains a streak of white, a smudge of red, a swirl of something yellow: ow, yell. The pain in my temples pulsing.

In the air tonight: the smell of sugar and vanilla; weak coffee and browned butter; white vinegar and tobacco; thick-skinned

lemons and – oh, precious child! she waves a hand as she talks –
the dry sweet scent of her stubbled underarms.

Tape, August 14, cont'd:
   [A hollow clatter on the table.]
   "Oh for chrissake . . .

*Note: I've played this part three times. It sounds as if he's
dropped his pen again. I have a mental picture of the lacquer
barrel of his black Mont Blanc rolling in a wide arc across a
white formica tabletop, but there is another sound, or sounds:
rat-a-tat-tat. His pills – some white, some red, some blue and
white, also his little orange tablets with quadrant grooves. What
else could it be but pills? They are brittle colours, a brittle
sound, spilling from his silver pill box – a gift, he told me once,
from his music teacher, Carlo Lupo. I wonder where he gets his
pills now? Is there a pharmacy in Wolf Cove? Is there a doctor,
a clinic, a hospital? Is he there now?*

Notebook, August 14, cont'd:
   The architecture of chlorine. I can taste the structure of the
molecules in the back of my mouth. The brunette faces me as I
mutter into the mike. Perhaps she thinks I am one of those guys
who moves his lips when he reads. Oh shit. She. Just. Licked.
Her. Thumb. Stuck it in her mouth and sucked and looked at me
while sucking. Flicked the tip of her thumb with her tongue. Oh
Christ. My head is about to burst and there is a hot stick poking
into the iris of my jellied eye and my thin skull is about to split
and I am stirred like a cup of coffee by her thumb.
   I am never not surprised by my capacity to be stirred. I
expect to be stirred on my deathbed if there is a nurse nearby

and she looks at me the way that girl did, and licks her thumb. I think I would be stirred while my fingernails were being yanked out with rusty pliers, if the yanker were her and I could peek down the front of her blouse while she was doing the yanking: Any king would feel like me. Oh, no, not now.

Blondie hasn't washed her neck in a week. If I could lean forward and sniff her, just below her pierced ear where the smell is sweet and stale and waxy. If I could taste her pulse in my mouth. She rocks her head, swivels it from side to side, squirms in her seat and pulls at her left lobe – three studs in it, each one round and silver. The top stud newer than the others, judging by the redness that surrounds it. Her bitten nails, unpolished, the colour of erasers.

Girls' giggles, water falling, pure sound, nothing else.

I hear the waitress leafing through her magazine; the spindle of the tape recorder; the whispering of the girls; the man eating softly, inhaling his food from his fork; the metronome of his cutlery as he sits at the counter: recount: our cent: torn cue: cot rune: core nut: cunt ore. . . .

Oh no, not now.

Note: I assume that the complete musician hears music in all things. It was sometimes difficult and sometimes amusing to be in Dom's company. He'd often become, if not distracted, then focused on something else apparent only to him. Like a dog hearing the high notes, now and then he'd stop what he was doing – no matter what or where – and scribble a note. Now and then he'd simply walk away without a word.

Although he never made reference to the reasons, I think he bought the tape recorder, not to keep up with Gould, but to keep track of what he heard – to capture sound as he heard it, when he heard it. Having listened to a fraction of what there is to hear so far, I also wonder if he heard something else on his mind besides Musorgsky as he was playing his final – rather, his most recent – recital.

Tape, August 14, cont'd:
    ". . . the matter with you, you pervert! You're taping me? You're fucking taping me. That's so fucking sick. I ought to call the cops!"
    "I didn't. I'm not. It isn't. You don't –"
    "I ought to call the fucking cops."
    "Oh, for chrissakes, no. If you think –"
    "He fucking is!"

Note: The tape stops abruptly; just as abruptly it restarts, as follows:

[Thump and hiss of hastily pushed door; his footsteps are a counterpoint to his laboured breathing; a car horn and a groan, a curtain of voices fluttering, fading in and falling off as he walks. In passing: "If she wants to stay in a relationship like that, I personally don't think . . ." And then Dom's voice, high and rising, strained and pained:]

Tape, August 14, cont'd:
    Too fucking perfect. For reference. I was checking. The tape. To see if I'd picked up. What the schoolgirls had to say. Hit rewind. Playback. Too loud, too loud. Too far back and too fucking loud. They heard it. And they turned on me. The blonde. I think it was the blonde. "That's so fucking sick I ought to call the cops." Her contempt, almost iambic. The strap of her bra. "He's

like, hey baby, I'm like, no way." *Honi soit qui mal y pense*. She couldn't possibly know what that means. Double or nothing she doesn't care. The brunette. Another story. Two-thirds of *Three's Company*. Music only hints at this. There ought to be more. There will be when it's scored.

Note: His hysteria is audible, almost visible. Dom did not compose, or so I thought. He never spoke of composition. According to Margie, there were never any references to his ambitions as a composer in the music press. This is news.

Tape, August 14, cont'd:

[A minute or two of street noise, the sort of thing you hear at night: sirens wailing nearer and moving away, cars speeding up and slowing down, the click of a dog's nails and a woman's heels on the sidewalk. He may not be aware the tape is still running. He greets his doorman, waits for the elevator, breathes in, holds his breath, breathes out, and clears his throat as the elevator swallows him, lifts him fourteen storeys high and spits him smoothly out. The key in the lock, a chunky sound; his door closes with a sigh and the click of the lock. Then this: *Oh, no, not now.*]

~

Notebook, August 15:

Slept in; grateful for having done so.

I seem to have had a rather large handful of pills since playing. I am not sure what I took in total. I shall mark it down as two of each – blues, oranges – with no mention of having any reds. I am not supposed to increase the dose and I am certainly not to mix things up – you are not to be taking your red with your blue, says doc, because your red and your blue will make you green – her little joke.

She has never had a headache in her life. I suspect her of taking tisanes and sprinkling herbs in her bath – now there's a vision – splashing her ducky, breathing deeply of medicinal vapours, and so on.

What followed was what was hoped for: deep and dreamless sleep. I am now, as usual post-head, vaguely doped and making these notes in bed, puffy-eyed, unwashed, and coffeeless. It would be simpler to live in the Windsor Arms, with a standing order for room service and someone else to change the sweaty sheets.

I don't think I moved all night.

In truth, I don't feel much like moving now. It's a wonder I have strength to scribble, let alone the inclination, because I feel the familiar weakness in my arms and shoulders. Given the way I make a living – not that it's much of a living – any such weakness is troublesome. There is, as usual, something else – the sense of something missing. As if I had played some previously unknown music while I slept and the flurry or slurry of notes, on spilling from my hands, vanished into the air. What I dreamed I played is gone for good.

As with any dreams, I have only the dimmest sense of this. But I am sure that what I played – rather, what I have the impression of having played – exists. I'd recognize it in an instant if I heard it again. The trouble is I have no idea where to look or whose music it might be. Not mine; a snatch of Ravel? If it ever was, it is not now. If only I could record the sound I hear in dreams – I must plant the notion: In the next dream there will be a recorder with a tape in it.

The vagueness of the present moment is not entirely unwelcome. It is a slothful pleasure to be in the thrall of helplessness, pinned down by the weight of the sheets. I hold my hands in front of me – a tremor?

No one else would notice.

Note: That's enough redaction for one day.

The street is dark, my apartment is darker. I have done nothing but listen to the sound of his voice and read his notes – at least he has a neat hand – for the past eight hours. I am hungry. My eyes are tired. My ears hurt from the earphones. My back is sore. It is too late for supper. I ought to get a headset.

I knew he made tapes on occasion, but I had no idea that he kept diaries as extensive as this. I cannot escape the feeling that I am eavesdropping. His voice is just as I remember: pleasing to hear, direct, precise, intimate, unselfconscious. He might have been talking to me. I think that's one of the things that made him successful as a pianist. He found a way to reach each listener. He ought to have had a radio program.

The content of the tapes and the notes are almost shocking in their intimacy. I hit playback and there he is, living and breathing, clearing his throat, talking the way he used to talk to me. A sense of dislocation.

The stink of my last shelter is still smeared inside my nostrils. The tapes can wait for the moment. My apartment is unfamiliar. I need an open window and a pot of coffee on the stove. No. I need a drink.

(Later) A rough night. Every time I return from a trip I have to learn how to sleep in my own bed all over again. I have not been in beds these past few weeks – I have been on cots,

slabs of foam, sheets of cardboard, heaps of blankets, and in one instance in a sleeping bag beneath a heating duct in an alley behind a hotel. I feel bruised, as if I'd fallen down a flight of stairs.

The best remedy for which is a cup of coffee and a modest breakfast. No one knows I'm back, except for Ari who overed my eggs easily at the diner; the young woman at the post office who fetched the parcel; and Margie. No one else need know.

But as much as I would like to take a break, I had better work.

An odd sensation – on my way to the kitchen a moment ago, I saw the box, the notes and tapes. They startled me. I was under the impression I'd seen them in a dream. Dom plays me the way he plays his piano.

Why is it that the real virtuosi always live on the edge?

There are, of course, exceptions. Anton Kuerti, for example, seems downright normal. Dom is many things. Normal is not one of them.

I have sorted the cassettes into rows as neat as packs of cards.

For the record, he favours a French notebook the size of a small missal, the kind you could stick into a jacket and take to church on Sunday if you were so inclined. It has a thick black cover, an elastic to hold the page, and the paper is lightly graphed and soft as onion skin.

The temptation is to riffle through the notebooks and listen to the tapes at random. But I'm a plodder, not a gambler. And I am wasting time.

Tape, August 15:

[Water hissing thinly from a tap; six sticky steps – his bare feet on the kitchen tile? A cup and saucer being carried, shakily;

spillage of coffee beans into an electric grinder; the fall and rise of the whirr from coarse to fine. He has a stovetop espresso pot. Pot clunked on burner. *Tic-tic-tic*, then the pop of the gas flame and the dither and blather of all-news radio. He retrieves the newspapers from the front door and talks to himself – quite consciously, I think – in sleepy sing-song rhymes: *The scent of this orange peel is bright and thick; thank god, it does not make me sick. It does the trick. The girls think I'm a prick. The night recedes in a rising tide of light. Tra-lee, tra-la, la, tra-lady-o, I listen to the radio. And read the capers in the papers.*

The rattle of knives in a drawer, a slice of bread dumped in the toaster's clutch, and the turning of the pages of the papers – he took three dailies, not for the news but for the puzzles.]

Notebook, August, 15, cont'd:

It occurs to me to call a carpenter and have shelves built. I have a spate of tapes to paste. Not now. *Oh, no, not now.* The pain in my head is not quite dead. Pain is as it does. Not as vivid as it was. I'll err on the side of optimism, if I may. No drugs today: undo stray dog. Falling off a log.

A pretty program last night. Scriabin, Satie, and the little Fauré – hip, hip, hauré. Nothing too good for the senior students at the conservatory; the recital well-attended because free; generally reviewed because me.

I could write the reviews myself: *Amoruso unveils his usual effortless technique: a silvery sound, a fluid ornamental line. Italian by inclination and by nature, he is the virtuoso imagined by the composer. . . .*

But I was not reviewed this morning. Should I care?

I have a gift – some gift; it is no more extraordinary than the colour of my hair – that dazzles those who do not know how much work it takes to appear effortless. And I have – I almost hesitate to note it this morning – nerve; neither the stage nor the repertoire holds any fear.

But I want to scream: Any fool can play. Giu, if he weren't so lazy, could play. He pretends to have a tin ear, but he has a feel for music and he has eclectic tastes. He likes the right music for the right reasons, and he writes well about the arts for one who is not a critic.

Note: He means me. Joe Serafino. He calls me Giu, or Pino or Peppino. It is an affectionate prod. We are both of the third generation. He speaks Italian, but I do not.

It's odd to see a reference to oneself self in a private diary.

He is not here and is therefore unable to stop me from this correction: I couldn't carry a tune in a bucket if the bucket had a handle.

Notebook, August 15, cont'd:

I have had the privilege of excellent teachers.

Lupo, dead a year next month: *My dear boy, the audience is a woman or a cat. Either will purr when stroked, and either will scratch if you rub the wrong way.*

If you want the truth this morning – and this is the underpinning of a larger argument – I often wish I did not have to play. My dear old Lupo, one mustn't let the cat out of the bag. The real art is to keep them purring without too much effort. Let me paraphrase the poet, what's his name? The minute some poor sap tells me he was moved by what I played, I can't help but feel I've picked his pocket.

It's a con game.

Note: Something is familiar here. A quick phone call. According to Margie, he is paraphrasing Auden. Fortunately, she not only reads widely, she remembers what she's read. Like Dominic and unlike me.

She seemed surprised I called again so soon. So much so that she did not stop to chat, she did what she'd have done if I were a regular customer – she dug up the answer right away and did not ask why I'd asked the question in the first place. She will ask soon. She's too smart not to.

Notebook, August 15, cont'd:

There is no mystery; there is discipline. And here is a libretto for a sunny morning:

The Leafs, the fleas, make a trade
My toast pops when brownly made.
A bank of grey cloud dulls the horizon.
No need to impale my eyes on
Such spears of light as these.

I have faith in the sports pages – in the box scores, that is – and no faith in any opinions other than my own, nor any faith in the merits of a libretto that mentions hockey. Nothing about last night's recital. No matter. The nonsense that passes for criticism in this town is much the same as the nonsense written about wine and food, a mucky slather of adjectives and arrogance.

Note: I can't seem to concentrate on Dom this morning.

I might as well digress. Certain Toronto newspaper columnists, musical and otherwise, could not resist remarking on Dom's late-night habits; they were intrigued by the notion of a classical pianist with a working-class stance on the subject of culture, and an utter lack of fear when it came to prowling the streets. He made good copy. He therefore had reason to read the papers with caution.

Journalists are not easily amused, but we are easily diverted. Dom was a game some played when there was none better. On a slow day, he was the equivalent of a shiny object for a magpie writer. I am not proud of this, it's the nature of the business.

He made an easy target. There were rumours – he didn't discourage them – of drugs harder than those required to kill his headaches, calm his nerves, soothe his stomach, steady his hand. I used to think, uncharitably, that some of these drugs were placebos. In any case, the rumours fit the image he chose to cultivate. On stage, whenever he could get away with it, he wore old black work-boots, black jeans, a black shirt, and a motorcycle jacket – also black. The effect was punk; in reality the shirt was tailored linen from Milan. But from a distance it carried the scent of danger.

Dick Lodge, an arts columnist for the Globe – a tall twee prick with sandy hair and wire-rimmed glasses who has never recovered from the misfortune of his private school education – reported that he'd seen Dom in a strip club in conversation with two women. He described the strippers as abundantly naked; he wondered if they were music lovers, or if Dominic had taken an interest in the dance. Of course, Lodge didn't bother to say what he himself was doing in a strip club.

Dom called me in a rage. I think he held me responsible for everything he read in the press; it took me a while to calm him down. He eventually told me the women had season's tickets to Massey Hall; on the evening in question, they'd stopped at the College St. Fran's for tea. Dominic had come in, as usual, to decompress. They recognized him, and asked if he'd sign their programs. He did so. One of the women said she'd taken piano *lessons as a girl and the other invited him to their show at the Filmore – they apparently did some sort of bathtub act.*

I told him he ought to call the assignment desk and write a follow-up piece himself; after all, a pair of strippers with season's tickets to Massey Hall made a better story than a pianist in a strip club. He declined. "Why should I help them sell their lousy paper?" Of course, it's also possible the strippers tipped Lodge to come down that night.

The Star once ran a picture of Dom standing in the entrance to a soup kitchen as part of a "City at Night" photo series. The image was grainy, and had been taken with a telephoto lens; it showed an old man wagging a finger in Dom's face. As usual, he called me.

The old man had stopped him in his tracks by clucking. As Dom drew near, the old man shouted: "I, too, am living in the House on Hen's Legs!" He was an emigré, Russian, well-educated, down on his luck, quite possibly deranged; but he knew his Musorgsky backwards and forwards. He claimed to be related to the architect Hoffmann, and was familiar with the nuances of Dom's recording and the details of his career. I tracked the old man down and wrote about him for Toronto Life: the homeless man related to the architect who had drawn the pictures that, at the exhibition, inspired Musorgsky. He may have been dissembling; old men, on occasion, do.

Not to be left out of the game, a photographer from the Sun once shadowed Dom after a late rehearsal. On the way, Dom fell in with the crew of a garbage truck. The genius who supplied the cutline under the photo wondered if modern music was garbage, or if Toronto's garbage was the stuff of symphonies. Never mind that Dom rarely played with an orchestra.

*None of these so-called journalists bothered to ask him what
he was doing. To presume eccentricity is the easiest, most obvious
thing to do. This is a town that spawned the overcoat-in-summer
oddness of Glenn Gould. You'd think eccentricity was delivered
by the drop in the municipal tap water of prodigies. Had he
been asked, Dom would have refused to explain. But neither the
photographers nor the columnists were paying close enough
attention. He was recording.*

*I wanted to write about it. He preferred to keep it quiet,
didn't want people to know. He said there were clues to the
source of all music in rhythm, from the beat of the human heart
to the ebb and flow of the city: police sirens, the hydraulic snort
of trucks, the cacophony of the noodle shops in Chinatown, the
thick wet coughs of the wine gang, the rustle of the paper
wrapped around the sandwiches of the salesclerks sitting by the
fountain in the park, and so on.*

*Gershwin was not wrong, nor was Ellington, and if Liszt
could transcribe larks. . . .*

Clang went the trolley.

*It has been a useless morning. I have not made much pro-
gress. I am trapped in memory. So I am going to have lunch.*

Notebook, August 15, cont'd:

Ashkenazy, on the radio as I dressed, tossing off scraps of
Scriabin; Quatre Morceaux, op. 73. I've played it often enough.
The music is pretty, if you are willing to admit that an aluminum
stepladder, falling down a set of stairs, makes a pretty, bright
sound instead of a clatter.

I am reminded of the nude descending the staircase, or one
of those NFB shorts in which the movement of the dance unfolds

one frame at a time. Normally, this music is silver in structure; at least, that's what I see when I am at the piano.

It's hard to explain. It is as if there were colours stored in my forearms, a spectrum of potential energy, waiting to be summoned from the sinews, ready to pour from my forearms and spurt like so much blood through the tips of my fingers onto the keys as I play . . . except it is not blood. More like thermometer mercury: my cure.

I ought to have had a sense of colour as I listened, but for some reason I could summon not a sliver of silver. I am not frightened by that, but I am curious. Perhaps I am frightened that I am curious – it ought to have been automatic.

Tape, August 15, cont'd:

[The studio door opens and closes with a suck of air; a softness afoot, his three deep breaths and then –]

Note: A word about Dominic's apartment:

The studio is central. Every other room is peripheral. He bought it as it was being built, intercepted the architect, and paid a large sum to alter the plans. He wanted a soundproof studio and the other rooms around it. It is a useful lesson: Money doesn't open doors, it builds them to your specifications. The acoustics are as good as those in any professional studio. He showed me once. He stood at the door, pulled it open and said, "The sucking of the air as it breaks the sound lock never fails to please. It's as if the piano inhales my entrance."

Pains were taken to deaden the ceiling and dampen the floor. No matter how loudly or softly he plays, no études leak out, no sonatas float up into the apartment overhead, no rhapsody drips through the floor. Not at 3:00 a.m. Never. You can stand outside the studio door when he is playing and not hear a note.

Yet if he does nothing more than trip a single key as gently as he could, there is a reward in that closed room. The sound is light as a feather in the air, pure and bright as running water. It is as if the room itself were an instrument. Speaking of which: His piano is a D-model Steinway grand, sixty years old, and as handsome an instrument as was ever made. He rarely lets anyone see it. When the top is raised, it resembles a raven's wing in flight. He found it in Rome and had some difficulty bringing it over because the white keys were ivory. It took him quite some time to obtain the necessary permissions and approvals. He had to prove it had been made before the ban.

Tape, August 15, cont'd:
   [He rattles off the Quatre Morceaux three times in succession. The music is delicate, tentative, subtle and, to my ear, slight. At the end of each performance, he makes a guttural sound – an expression of disgust? The music, as far as I can tell, is perfect. I have no idea what he means when he says he can't sense colour – he certainly reproduces it.]

Notebook, August 15, cont'd:
   I am, for some reason, unable to throw the ladder downstairs. My head is empty, my arms are heavy, my hands are tired, and I lack the nerve to abandon myself completely. Instead, I will abandon music.
   From the front window, the long black vein of Yonge St. pulses with late-morning traffic. In the space between the tall buildings there are a dozen gulls, random and graceful in the air

as the scraps of paper swirling on the sidewalk below. On one of the scraps, in my handwriting: *pho, sheet music, fiorinal.*

Note: *Fiorinal, a codeine-caffeine painkiller, is his medicine of choice. I played a hunch off this and made an appointment to see his doctor, Alena Capek. Which is to say, I called her office and left a message with her assistant. The message was simplicity itself: Dom's name.*

Dr. Capek called back within minutes. Originally from Czechoslovakia, she is a short, handsome woman with steely grey hair, a quiet manner, and a short list of patients – for the most part actors, painters, and musicians. She agreed to see me if I could come down right away.

I had no idea what she told the police a year ago. I knew Dom had a standing order at the pharmacy – refills of the various migraine medicines as he required them, plus a few minor stimulants, sleeping pills, vitamins, supplements, and so on.

Had she had any recent contact?

It was not the question she was expecting. And so began a game of chess. Instead of answering, she asked me what I'd heard. In turn, I asked about his health at the time of the disappearance. She said – hedging just a bit – that his health was generally good. She offered nothing more. I said I knew he complained from time to time of a lack of energy, insomnia, loss of strength in his shoulders, weakness in his forearms, the occasional numbness in his fingers. This, as I'm sure she knows, is his usual post-migraine state.

She said that, in the year since he'd been away – that's how she put it; as if he were on tour – new drugs had come on the market that she wanted him to try, drugs that might solve his problems without the danger of side effects. I asked her again if

he'd been in touch, if he'd made arrangements to have his med-
ications forwarded, if he'd called to have a prescription filled.
She frowned. It was as if I'd closed a door. She scribbled a note
on her memo pad. She said she appreciated my concern and
muttered a word about how sure she was that I, as a journalist,
understood the nature of patient confidentiality. She added that
the situation was one of some delicacy, escorted me to the door,
and summoned her next patient. I took this to mean that she was
forwarding his meds.
So, he is still alive.

Notebook, August 15, cont'd:
   I could and should write an ode to codeine: nice ode.
   The purchase of a new supply never fails to fills me with joy
– I feel as if I am plunging my hands in a treasure chest filled
with blue-and-white jewels.

Note: My ears hurt. I have two choices. I can find a headset. Or I
can hunt up some patch cords and hook the cassette to my stereo.
   Who knew I'd be listening to tapes again? He knew.

(Later) I can hear a man and woman walking up the stairs and
along the hall outside my apartment. Sound carries clearly in the
stillness. Their voices are cinched tight as belts. A door slams, a
lock turns, and the voices are cut off. I am left with the white hiss
of water running through the pipes and the one-note hum of the
computer. And this:

Notebook, August 15, cont'd:
   I admire most of all the composure derived from competence
– in its truest form, it rests on repetition; you see this in athletes,

tradesmen, nurses, secretaries. There never was a carpenter who was frightened of his tools. You do not always see this in musicians.

An arrogant man refuses to acknowledge the possibility of the unexpected. A wise man expects the unexpected at every turn.

Look around, look up, look out, look away.

Find a path between.

Note: I am reminded of an old cartoon, the punchline long forgotten: A man is walking along a street of tall buildings. He glances up, and sees a piano about to land on his head. Is this what happened to Dom that night? Did he sense a piano, falling?

Notebook, August 15, cont'd:

Jessye Norman: the tear that trickled down her cheek and left a scar. There is no art in nature, which is artless. That is not to say there is no beauty. Who or what caused her to weep a tear of acid?

The sounds of nature – thunder, water rushing over rocks, etc. – have no meaning unless you happen to find yourself caught in a storm, or if you are fording a creek; taken out of context, they are as beautiful as a cliché painting of the cold mountain lake with the noble stag alert for danger in the clearing by the shore: horse. You cannot use nature in place of music. Not unless you are Harry Somers with the wit to treat the loon and the lake as instruments.

Nature's day is done, is over before it's begun.

Note: This next is printed on a yellowed piece of paper cut to fit and pasted to the page:

gg: Any favourites among the younger pianists?

GG: I prefer moral judgments to aesthetic ones, but if you insist –

gg: I insist upon insisting.

GG: Then allow me to limit the damage and confine myself to the northern half of this continent. Kuerti – how appropriate for a man who makes his living at a keyboard – Kuerti, qwerty. He is much better than a typist. Perhaps Amoruso.

gg: Perhaps?

GG: Too soon to tell. He is young and he has that buttery Italian touch, but I dislike the leather jacket; it gets in the way. Or perhaps it does not get in the way enough. Now, if he were to ride a motorcycle on stage . . .

Note: *This scrap of paper – my guess, it was clipped from an article in* Saturday Night *magazine – is undated. But it is old. He has been saving it for some time. It obviously predates Gould's death. And so, another call to Margie Warriner.*

I have always taken pleasure in the sound of her voice over the phone. She pulled up several of Gould's self-interviews but couldn't find this passage. She said I could call her any time I needed help, then threw in an aside: Gould loved his little pranks. In addition to the motorcycle idea, he is supposed to have suggested that Dom hire a couple of heavy-set men in pinstriped suits, furnish them with violin cases and have them guard the entrance whenever he played – an obvious Mafia reference. The great neurotic once suggested something similar to Kuerti – that he place two armed men on stage when he played, in response to some imagined cold war threat.

To whom did he suggest this first?

I don't suppose it's ever wrong to give an audience an enhanced notion of risk. Art is, or ought to be, the most daring risk. But Gould, of all people, ought to have known what was at stake in simply walking on stage and sitting in front of a keyboard. It's clear he never thought the idea through.

"Mr. Amoruso, what is the threat?"

"No threat, really."

"Then why the men with machine guns?"

"It seemed like a good idea at the time."

You see my point. The press would have eaten him alive. Dom would have been a laughingstock. And Gould would have laughed up his sleeve.

Margie couldn't find the article in any publication.

I have a hunch the offending passage never made it out of galleys. Which means an editor must have cut it, and may have forwarded the cut to Dom as a prod, a goad, a spur, and a souvenir. Editors are a cruel breed. The good ones are.

Tape, August 15, cont'd:

[A heavy door opens on a pair of well-oiled hinges, keys and coins rattle in a pocket, a sharp cough, idle humming. The elevator closes. He improvises the largo of the New World Symphony. Or the spiritual "Going Home." Take your pick. I opt for the spiritual.]

"Nice day, Mr. Amoruso."

"Yeah, nice day, Abdi, nice day to you."

[A doorbell's tingaling. I know the one – the store at St. Clair and Yonge, the northwest corner – I recognize the triple ring. He strolls down an aisle, riffles the pages of magazines. Then the soft flutter of paper money plucked from a billfold.]

"Long time no see, Mr. Amoruso. How's the music going?"
"Good, Johnny. The music is going good."
"That's good then. There you go. Nice day."
"Nice day."

[Footsteps stitched into the fabric of the corner traffic; his descent into the St. Clair subway – the tunnel is cavernous, boomy, unmistakable – you have to hear it only once to know the sound of underground.]

Note: He did not record the ride downtown. My guess is that he has made and taped that trip often enough. He may be an obsessive, but one recording of the journey would be sufficient for anyone's obsession. If he were really trying to keep a record of the sound of the world and him in it, he'd obviously solved the philosophical problem – he apparently had no wish to record himself recording himself while he recorded himself. I suppose, if you fell into that trap, you'd need an infinity of tape recorders. You'd spend your time pressing "Play" and "Record" on the first recorder, the second recorder, the third – you'd never get out of the house. There aren't enough tape recorders in the world for that sort of thing. And I'm wasting time now.

Tape, August 15, cont'd:
[Unexpected, gradually increasing in volume, there is the see-saw sound of an accordion and its reedy-weedy echo. I am impressed with the microphone; the sound it picks up is remarkably faithful. Entry of subway train from left to right: the double-rubber snort of hydraulics, the discharge of passengers, those three falling notes that signal the closing of the doors. The shuffling of the herd, the silvery chink-tink of tossed coins.]

Note: Dom is not and never was shy about the use of a tape recorder – I presume it is because of his experience as a performer, and because of his familiarity with tape – it was a necessary tool.

And then there is this: The self-conscious man betrays himself. That's very nearly a maxim. He was completely unselfconscious in what he did. As he has already noted, no carpenter was ever shy about using his hammer. And I am wasting time again.

Based on what follows, it's also clear he is unafraid to be seen talking to himself in public. I suppose, with bud mics in his ears, people would assume he was listening to a song and mouthing the lyrics to himself – not unusual on a subway platform.

How does his purpose – these tapes, this sound – meet mine? I don't quite understand. Not yet.

Tape, August 15, cont'd:

Bloor station, noon: No big city ought to be without an underground; it is a kind of long and skinny village that gives us an opportunity to rub shoulders with the other villagers – subterranean milkmaids, drovers, cattle on the hoof, and wandering minstrels.

[End of tune, clatter of coins, smattering of applause.]

The polka is an expression of pure urge, and the accordion is an instrument of yearning: step lively, step lightly, come now, come. It is irresistible and utterly anti-modern. Did the instrument give rise to this music, or did the need to express this music give rise to the instrument? Neither, I suppose – or both. Is there an answer in folklore? Did it come from Italy through Europe by way of the gypsies? Who gives a flying? Not this old man in his Cossack shirt – puffy sleeves, white ruffles, embroidered flowers; Ukrainian or Polish? I can't tell the difference.

He doesn't care what I can or cannot tell. He sits on a camp chair near the platform. I will never camp and I'll bet he has never been camping – but he knows his chairs. His is light, strong, portable. On his feet, black leather boots, knee-high, his trousers tucked into the tops. Gold rings on his fat fingers, silver stubble on his chin, one soft gold tooth on the left side of his grin. A backwards baseball cap. A clown at heart. Aren't we all?

Notebook, August 15, cont'd:

Bellows of the accordion below me in the belly of the city.

Under the polka I heard the footsteps of the herd, and the tick-tack-tick of a woman's heels. She came upon me from behind, her hips brushed mine as she edged past. A handsome woman, middle-aged, with a yellow scarf at her throat. Her coat belted at the waist. Tiny ten-pin legs, and tiny fat feet in tiny pointed shoes. Her heels not just high but spiky – a bit too suggestive for business. Depends on the business.

Apart from her shoes, she is nothing less than prim and clearly on her way to work. Or a dental appointment. I have a hunch there's a girdle on her too, too solid waist. Who knew women still wore girdles? I'd also bet on garters. A pity you can't ask.

She has short practical nails and sturdy hands which I'm guessing have kneaded bread and men alike. Like me, she finds the music irresistible. An intersection of tastes at the intersection of Bloor and Yonge. Exotic; the polka is not a local dance. At least, not east of Roncesvalles.

Note: Dom's handwriting is almost illegible – these notes clearly made on the fly. Roncesvalles: a west-end, working-class neighbourhood of Toronto – Little Poland, where I live. Think of sugar-dusted pastries, fat sausages in the windows of the butcher shops, glum old men, and a golden statue of the Polish pope outside the Polish church. The architecture of the street is low, cheap, and dispiriting but there is a forlorn prosperity in the air. Warsaw might have this feeling, were it not for two world wars.

Notebook, August 15, cont'd:

I sensed her, smelled her, saw her at the same time as the accordionist sensed her, saw her, sniffed, and smiled at her. Instinctive: A musician observes his audience, without whom – even if it is an audience of one – there is no performance. That's a minim – not big enough to be a maxim.

She looked neither up nor down nor to the side, unaware of me or the rest of the throng; she paused, poised and self-aware. The music held her, hemmed her in, pinned her in place. She clutched her purse as if music were a thief. Of course it is.

She clearly didn't want to dance – noon is not the time of day for dancing – but she was ready to kick up her heels. She was waiting to be, wanting to be, swung. And impatient with herself for wanting it. In another village at another time of day I might have grabbed her myself. Although for some reason – this is lodged deep in my poor brain – I find dancing so frankly explicit that it is impossible for me to dance without blushing. Heat, scent, and the gestures of coupling. Whereas, I do not blush when I . . .

The accordion player saw me look at her. He winked at me and closed his eyes and let his head fall back. His gold tooth gleamed, the brightest thing of all in the dim light of the Bloor station. He doubled his tempo. And had this been a wedding, she'd have reached for the nearest man if the nearest man did not reach for her, and the accordion player would have made a game of seeing how fast he could make them spin. He played harder now, elbows pumping, stabbing the keys and unbuttoning the rows of pearls, rocking forward and backward on his camp chair, his fat legs spread – trying to squeeze a reaction, any reaction from her. She stood still, stood coiled, wanting and waiting.

A test of wills, broken when the train pulled in. The doors of the nearest car opened and her thigh twitched; the first step of the dance – that long flinch of muscle and the susurrance of her nylons against the lining of her skirt – inaudible, imaginable, suggestive.

Could the finest instrument detect it on this tape? Could I suggest as little, or as much, in performance?

She slipped the old Cossack a dollar – or perhaps you could say he stole it from her. He nodded, smiled at the money; winked again at me. She stepped into the subway car. As did I.

Note: Dom has an eye and an ear for a scene.

There are no ums and ahs on tape – at least not yet. And there are no words scratched out in his notebook – at least not yet. His instincts are spontaneous, assured. He gives the impression of accuracy.

I have yet to write a sentence that I wouldn't like another crack at but I get the same sense when I read him as I do when I listen to him talk, or when I hear him play. He does it; it stays done. Deft, precise, the lightness of his touch. A pickpocket's skills.

Notebook, August 15, cont'd:

She entered the car ahead of me. She stood. I sat and watched her as she, on tiptoes, held on to the overhead rail. She swayed with the movement of the train. A disappointment now – her face impassive, her mind elsewhere, the music has evaporated. As music does. Without a trace.

A hunch: Was the old man playing something cribbed from Chopin, or was he playing something Chopin cribbed? As for technique, I am reminded of Antonin Kubalek – something the same in his phrasing, a hint of the Steppes. One passage lingers, the colours red and black, the shapes similar to wrought-iron, not unlike the notation of embroidery on the busker's shirt.

Tape, August 15, cont'd:

[D., whistling on the street, a chipper theme and its chipper variations – even I can tell it's improvised from the sound of the accordion. Then, in a doorway, the whistle is replaced by the quicksilver sound of a piano:]

"Don't just stand there, boychik, you're letting the flies in."

"Buddy! Tell me how the hell did I get here?"

Note: Bohdan Kenk. Buddy to his friends, and Daniel Keane to almost everyone else. His father changed the family name when Bohdan was a child. He is an old friend of Dominic's. Trim, neatly composed, in his early forties, with twenty-eight years of concert piano under his belt. He no longer plays.

Shortly after he won his first major competition, his father died. Buddy quit performing. "It was his dream, not mine." He took a job in a record store. He now makes a living selling compact discs, sheet music, and Broadway scores. He takes the occasional student.

This is what I don't understand: With a skill of the highest order – whether in the arts or sports or the trades – why would you walk away?

Buddy reminds me in some ways of my brother. A tool and

die maker, you can see his work in the TTC *subway cars if you know where to look. He managed, over the course of a couple of years of increasingly belligerent behaviour, to get himself fired. He doesn't talk about it. But I have a hunch he was frightened by his ability to make a perfect thing. He now drives a cab. Is it the terror of perfection? Does Buddy have the key to Dom?*

Tape, August 15, cont'd:

"How the hell did you get here? On foot is my guess, Amoruso. You don't drive a car and you're too cheap to take a cab."

"Don't get smart with me, you little kulak. I was caught up in – I can't remember where I – never mind. Who are you listening to?"

"To whom do I listen? Kissin, as in cousin. Wouldn't I like to. I'm surprised you didn't recognize him. Dom, either you keep up with the Russians, or you do not. I thought you did. You've let the side down. What can I do for –? Oh, wait a minute. You've come up for air. You played last night."

"And you didn't hear me. Prick."

"Keep your voice down, dearest, and let's leave my prick out of this. Turn that tape recorder off. I had, shall we say, prior commitments. What time is it? Let me tidy up here. You can buy me lunch and tell me how it went, although I am sure –"

Note: Buddy Keane is genuinely pleased to see Dom.

The next sounds are of lunch, at Pho Hung, presumably. It's the nearest soup joint to the store. Which means they have walked west on Bloor from Bay, past the Park Plaza Hotel, in the direction of the Remenyi piano shop, the conservatory, Dr. Capek's office, and the Konop pharmacy: This is the heart of Amoruso country.

Pho Hung is one of the places I'd gone looking for him the night he disappeared. It is a temple of kitsch. Red paper lanterns hang from the ceiling. Formica tables and plastic chairs. An altar laden with joss sticks and oranges near the entrance. On the walls are grey silk fans painted with scenes of bamboo leaves in the breeze, carp in reedy ponds, and white cranes flying over distant mountains.

Notebook, August 15, cont'd:

The usual lunch: pho ga, lemon soda, and two of the lacquered blue pills to ward off – whatever. I had planned to take none but I do so like a little preventive medicine – the blue, the same colour as what they ward off. Taking them makes me feel I've done something healthy and useful. I was staring out the window at the grey stone lions on the lawn of the museum when it occurred to me – grey is not a colour of the spectrum.

This morning's Scriabin was also off the spectrum. Scriabin, synesthete, would have smirked. What happened while I listened, while I played? Fault of me, or fault of the music? Or fault of the fact that I've played that piece a thousand times?

Perhaps, if I had played it once more, I'd have seen – what? Stepladders? Running water? Icicles? Bicycles? I was still staring at the lions when Buddy nudged me under the table with the toe of his shoe. The waiter had come and gone and left two bowls of soup.

Buddy allowed me to record.

Tape, August 15, cont'd:

". . . a little, let's say, preoccupied; what's up?"

"Nothing much. The usual. I have no idea any more. Maybe it is unusual. I played the Satie last night at the conservatory, that variation on the four-hander, you know the one I mean. My party piece."

"You mean your parlour trick. And?"

"And nothing. I played well enough. Jealous students afterwards. 'How lovely.' Blah, blah blah. Little brats getting ready to elbow me out of the way when their day comes. I had a bad head after it was over. I swear I get these damned migraines because I play. I think it must be some form of post-traumatic stress. It's getting worse. Every two days now. Not tonight, maestro, I have a headache. Only my doctor knows for sure and she's not telling. Not that I care, as long as she's prescribing. Did you see the reviews this morning?"

"You don't still read reviews, do you? I didn't then and I don't now. If you believe them when they're good, then you have to believe them when they're bad. You've simply got to stop – oh, I forgot – do you want spring rolls?"

"Not for me. Go ahead, my treat. That's not the point. I'll tell you why you didn't read the reviews this morning. There were none. If the newspapers are going to have critics, then the critics ought to listen when music is played, and the papers ought to print the goddamn reviews. Such as they are."

"Watch your tongue, dear, you'll upset the other diners. Tran, an order of cha gio when you get the chance."

"Not that any of the critics in this town can write. They care more about my leather jacket than about what I do at the keyboard. What I mean is this – if music is played, it ought to be heard. But it won't be heard tomorrow if it isn't reviewed today."

"Yes, yes, yes. Now eat your soup before it gets cold."

[Plastic spoons splashing and clicking in the depths of the broth, trickles of tea in tiny cups, tick-tock of chopsticks, slurp of noodles, and adjacent conversations as other orders are taken: *"Okay, you are number twelve small beef soup with tendon and you are number seven large chicken soup. You want some imperial roll with that? No? Okay, be right back."*]

"Where was I? Oh, yeah. This morning I was listening to the radio. Ashkenazy having a go at Scriabin. The little Quatre Morceaux. The strangest thing. Every note sounded the same. I thought I was losing my – I went into the studio and ran straight through it three times, top to bottom. I'm sure it was okay. The way I played it. Do me a favour, would you – take this home and pop it in your machine and give it a listen. I swear I can't tell one note from another. It frightens me. It sounds like a handful of nails dropped on a sheet of tin. I don't know why I play."

"You're tired, that's all. I've heard you do that piece. I'll listen at home tonight. I'm sure it's fine. You could play it if you were deaf. You could play it in your sleep. You could play it with one hand behind your back. You could play it –"

"Quit greasing me. Maybe I should take up the accordion. I heard this guy on the way over. In the Bloor –"

"I know. You have it on tape. What's the goal here –"

"Don't interrupt. Bloor station, the platform by the magazine stand. It's him I was whistling when I walked into the store. You may have seen him. Guy looks like he just stepped off the Steppes –"

"I know him. He's an asshole."

"Why do you say –? Sorry, I won't interfere in your ethnic squabbles. All I'm saying is, I think it's simple for those subway guys. Didn't you ever want to do that? Stake out a station and play? He draws an honest reaction, he doesn't need reviews, he can measure his performance by the amount of money in his hat when he's done; on top of which, I'll bet more people heard him today than heard me last night."

Notebook, August 15, cont'd:

Buddy bent over his bowl, cool in the face of my little rant, spooning his broth and slurping his noodles. He is a good friend who ignores me dutifully when I'm in a state: sat, ate. He is a Ukrainian peasant who eats his pho like a Vietnamese peasant. Quite the little conjunction. Did the Ukrainians even know about the Vietnamese two hundred years ago?

Tape, August 15, cont'd:

"Get over it, Domino. Last week, there were two guys on the corner just outside the shop. Not the usual bunch. Have you heard that woman with the clarinet who plays the first four bars of 'Hey, Jude'? Or the blind guy who tinkles out some never-ending nonsense on children's vibes? These, I should say, were not those. The keyboard player was very good, more than competent. But the violin was first-rate. My guess is they're refugees from some Soviet state orchestra somewhere. Technique dripping from their fingertips. Bound for freedom and playing for quarters. The streets are alive with the sound of mujiks. No reviews for them, apart from all those tax-free coins. Maybe one person in a hundred stopped to listen, but that's a high-volume corner and the ones who stopped, including me, were – is it transformed or transfixed? I can never remember the difference. Can one be both? If so, I was."

[D. snorts, grunts, slurps. A longish pause. Buddy resumes:]

"You might do that, you know. Oh, Jesus, try a pepper. Oh, hot. Oh, my. Every time I. Never again. Let me just. Oh, I forget how hot these are. You should try one. Oh, Jesus, it will give you something else to think about than the critics, or their absence. There, better. You might sneak out of town, you know. Just turn up somewhere unannounced and play. Montreal is the only other city I can think of in this two-bit country with a metro. Doesn't have to be underground. Any big-city corner will do. I can see it now. You and your little keyboard, wowing the locals. They know a bit about music in Montreal. Nobody would guess who you were. You could wear a hat and a fake beard as part of your act. Pull in two hundred bucks a day is my guess. Learn a few of those Gilles Vigneault tunes, dress them up. I'm only half kidding. It would certainly shake up your senses. You really should try a pepper."

[No response. Buddy was clearly expecting one.]

"Or not. Look, if you really want to cleanse your palate, why don't you, forgive the expression, pull a Gould."

"What do you mean? Butcher a bit of Beethoven? Sue a piano tuner? Or wander around town in an overcoat and gloves in June?"

[Laughter, snorts, and soup noises.]

Note: I've always been put off by the sound of others eating; it is much too intimate for earphones. But let it pass. I am surprised by the freshness of D.'s sarcasm. Gould has been gone for years. The incident of the piano tuner he refers to is ancient history: He sued a Steinway man who had the gall to slap him on the back.

Tape, August 15, cont'd:

"No, silly. I mean, spend some time in the studio. Shuck your leather jacket and enjoy yourself. Not that it isn't a very nice jacket. Even if it is a bit butch. Take a few months off and write something. You're taping this now, aren't you? What's the point of taping unless you use what you've taped? You've got what, a wall of tape? You are a tapeworm. Score the whole thing and call it 'The Toronto Symphony.' I personally suggest you incorporate the sound of the streetcar. I am quite fond of the way they slide by each other on the rails, with the drivers in their little uniforms ringing their little bells at each other. Now shut that off and pay attention to your soup."

Notebook, August 15, cont'd:

Buddy says I should do something with the tapes. On the street after soup, I asked him to send me a package of sheet music and the new Kissin, and to tack it onto my bill. We shook hands. He said it again: *Make something from the tapes.*

I waved as I passed the window of the piano shop, just in case any of the Remenyi boys saw me go by and thought me *poco pretenzioso* for not stopping. I have used up all my piano talk today.

Make something from the tapes.

Maybe it's time. The question is – what am I on the verge of making? Glenn Gould's – or Joe Gould's – Secret?

Make something of the tapes: a step?

Note: I claim some influence here.

Two years ago, I gave Dom a copy of Joseph Mitchell's book, Up In The Old Hotel. *Mitchell, a feature writer for the* New Yorker, *met a Greenwich Village eccentric – Joe Gould – who claimed to speak the language of seagulls. Over the course of several months, Joe Gould indicated that he was scribbling what he called "An Oral History of Our Time." Mitchell believed him and wrote a feature story. But, there was no Oral History. I suspect the old man played Mitchell for a sucker. Or maybe Mitchell hoodwinked himself; it happens. A good story is hard to resist.*

On learning that Gould had not exactly told the truth – there were bits and scraps of notes, but there was no Oral History – Mitchell wrote a wind-up piece, "Joe Gould's Secret." He published it in 1964. And then he stopped writing. He remained on staff at the New Yorker *until his death in 1996. He never filed another story. In effect, he stood up and – at a loss for words – he walked away.*

Opinions about this are a dime a dozen, but I think Mitchell lost confidence in his public self. The same way the other Gould – Glenn – lost his. But I don't care about Joe Mitchell, or Joe Gould, or Glenn Gould.

What the hell is Dom up to?

Notebook, August 15, cont'd:

Messages after lunch: Anne called twice and asked if I would be so kind as to give her *"un coup de téléphone."* She refuses to say "telephone call." It is part of her charm, and she knows it. There was one hang-up, which I assume was Claire – she refuses to respond to an answering machine. This I find less charming. Her imperial manner; my imperial roll in the hay.

And Tony Roberts of the *Globe*.

Note: Anne Langelier is a deceptive force, as the police found out when she trumped their reluctance to begin a search for Dom. She is an iron sparrow of a certain age. Her hair is lacquered and bobbed. She squints at the world from behind over-

*sized black-rimmed glasses. Is never seen in public without hat,
gloves, pearls. Looks frail but leaves younger people in her wake;
shows up early, stays late, can hold her liquor. She also smokes
hand-rolled cigarettes, or rather she affects them. Dom says she
never inhales.*

*He is loyal to her, as he ought to be. She made him very rich,
very quickly. She signed him as a teen, after he won the Kiwanis
competition. A year later, she put him in the Tchaikovsky and
he won again. The leather jacket was a draw, a novelty. She
arranged a whirlwind series of concerts in Europe, booked him
into Berlin, whisked him into Carnegie Hall, negotiated a contract for three quick and successful recordings, including his
famous Musorgsky. She advised him to make a couple of shrewd
real-estate investments. These days, she is winding down her
career. She, too, is wealthy. Dominic is her only client.*

Notebook, August 15, cont'd:

Three calls from people who had better reasons than most
to come to the recital last night. Two of whom did not. Should I
be keeping score? It's probably better that Mme. stayed away.
She is impossible when she is cranky and she will not give up her
cigarettes and they will not let her smoke in the conservatory.

As for Claire –

Tape, August 15, cont'd:

[One ring, and a second ring, interrupted. He has the tape
recorder hooked up to his phone. It is disconcerting – I think back
to the various conversations I had with him; are they also on tape?
Did I say anything smart? What, so to speak, is the score?]

"Hello."

"*Ciao, Anna.*"

"Dominic, *la, la.* I am so glad you have called me. Listen carefully now. I have a leading question: When was the last time you played the *Pictures at an Exhibition*?"

"You know as well as I do, my dear. But you might begin by asking how I played last night. I played very well, thank you. Even though you were not there to hear me. I came home with a bad head and I tried to sleep it off and I –"

"Did you get something to eat today?"

"Yes, I –"

"What did you have?"

"I had a bowl of Vietnamese soup."

"You should still look after yourself better than that. That's all you eat is that soup. Someone should come to take care of you. Are you feeling very well?"

"*Parlez piano, piano.* I'm not quite up to speed. Not yet. The Musorgsky. It's been a while since – Apart from me, who bothers with it any more? Why? What's up?"

"The Art Gallery of Ontario is, as you say, up. They are planning a new show for later this fall – paintings and drawings with musical themes and so on. They have rounded up all they could find. I have no idea why anyone has not done this before. I don't yet have the whole of the story. But listen to me. There will be a tiny fête to open the show. They have managed to obtain – never mind, it should come to you as a surprise. I've said too much already."

"You haven't said –"

"*Mais, non.* No more. Please to call Monsieur Carter and –"

"Anna, *bella,* I'm not sure I want the work."

"Work? But this is not work. How is this work? It is money in the bank. You go, you play, afterwards you have a nice glass of not very good champagne. You look at some paintings, you let the ladies flatter you, you smile at their husbands and you get a nice fat envelope of money. In any case, this is now for you a defensive move. They insist only to hear *Pictures*. No one plays it as well as you. You could sleepwalk from here to the Kiev gate, if that was your wish. These new boys, Hamelin, LaPlante, they are very flashy. Even your old friend, Monsieur Kuerti. If they were to play, there will be questions; questions of the kind you do not need. In any case, please to do me a favour and call the director."

"His name, again?"

"Thomas Carter. A foursquare handle, no? Not like yours or mine. A suggestion – find yourself a nice girl who can make you some split pea soup and give you a lot of little Amorusos, and perhaps –"

"Children are the death of music, Madame. A high price to pay for, what's the term, the revenge of the cradle, don't you think?"

"I find at times, dear boy, you are quite completely wrong. A lack of children is the death of music. You would be a fair parent, I think. Not good, but fair, which is better than most. Alas, it is too late for me. I had my chance. Never mind. I think you'll like what Monsieur Carter has hiding in his sleeve. It is a gimmick, yes, but a good one. And your friend Weller intends to supplement the fee. He helped them to achieve this show and he wants it to get a good start. He is making an inducement. A supplementary to the fee. Pick his pocket. You have already picked his *chambre de coucher*. Well, I'm an old woman. I should no longer be shocked by your arrangements. But he is pleasant for a wealthy man, don't you find? He phoned me personally and –"

Note: At the mention of Weller's name, caution seeps into Dominic's voice. Understandable, given his relationship with Claire. A bit of explanation:

Edward Weller is the brains behind Weller Fidelity, a small, exclusive mutual fund that regularly outperforms the others on Bay St. He is balding but not unhandsome, and far too rich. He takes manicures. He revels in creature comforts and always makes the best-dressed list. Once, at a shareholders' meeting, he bragged that his suit had been tailored from the wool of unborn lambs. The caption under his photo in the business section of the Globe *the next day was "The Golden Fleece."*

He and Dominic have a complicated relationship. They met three years ago when Weller booked Dom to perform a benefit in aid of Seaton House. The concert has become an annual sop to Weller's conscience. Every autumn, when the streets are littered with yellow leaves and the shelters are overflowing, Weller has his staff round up a gang of homeless men – addicts, alcoholics, and so on. The men are cleaned up and furnished with Armani suits, Turnbull and Asser shirts, and Versace ties from Harry Rosen. Once dressed, the bums are whisked away to seats at the conference tables of the big banks and the investment firms around town. Photos of the men – their faces grizzled, grinning, and wildly out of place – are used in Weller Fidelity's newspaper and billboard ads. The men earn a handsome fee for posing. After the photo session, the men wear their flash duds to a benefit concert, the proceeds of which Weller donates to Seaton House.

That first concert was a great success. Dominic played the Satie he referred to earlier, the Aperçus Désagréables. *He'd rescored them, taking them from four hands to two, upping the tempo here and there and rearranging them in such a way that the music sounded as if it might have been played, not merely by four hands, but by four hands at two pianos. Splashy and showy, a tour de force.*

The concert was held at Massey Hall. The bums were in the balcony. It was a bit of cheeky fun.

Later that evening Weller introduced Dominic to Claire. He left them alone, and Claire took him in hand. Not literally. He disliked being touched on days when he played. She introduced him to brokers and philanthropists. He followed her with his hands behind his back.

When he began to grow uncomfortable, she offered him a ride home. Asked to see his piano. Wondered if he'd make her a cup of tea. Curled up on his couch. And, if it wasn't too forward, would he mind rubbing her feet because they were killing her after a day in heels, etc. A bit of calculated boldness. His hands, her feet; the fetish his or hers?

The next thing Dom knew, he was sleeping with her once a week. If Weller knew – it was hard to imagine that he didn't; everyone in town knew of their affair – he seemed not to mind. If he didn't mind, it meant he wasn't worried, there was an arrangement.

Tape, August 15, cont'd:

"He phoned me personally and –"

"Of course he phoned you personally, Anne. He is required to call you in order to reach me. He cannot phone you impersonally. He certainly can't ask Claire for my number. That would be a bit much, even for him."

"My boy, may I be frank? I have never quite understood what you see in La Weller. Never mind. She is none of my business. You are my business. And you should consider this job very seriously. Think of it as a daily double – you have the money, and the girl who is married to the money."

"If I didn't know you, I wouldn't love you. You make it sound a bit commercial."

"Ah, well, it is best when it is so. Commerce pays the rent. A dollar is neither clean nor dirty. And if there is such a thing as dirty money, then you are free to spend some of it on soap. Call Carter. See him soon. You will like what he has to say."

"When does the show open?"

"That's the problem. It's not a problem. They just got the final piece of the puzzle. It's coming up soon. October or some such. He apologized for the last minute. But I told him you had nothing scheduled."

"You are very naughty. All right. I'll call. You might find out if the CBC is willing to consider a live broadcast; maybe there's a way to maximize our profits. Although they may not want to bother. If I remember correctly, the acoustics in the Walker Court stink. In any case, if the CBC isn't interested in recording, I might want to use their Bosendorfer. Will you see if it's available?"

"When shall I tell Carter you'll call?"

"No need to tell him anything. I'll call him. Today or tomorrow. I will. I'll call."

"Good boy; I already said you would."

"*Ciao*, Anne."

Note: There is no break in the tape.

He hangs up and dials again. It's answered on the fourth ring. Tony Roberts at the Globe. *I know him, after a fashion. The newspaper world is a small one. We keep jealous eyes on one another. Roberts has no enemies but other critics. He writes with more intelligence and fewer adjectives than most. He is that rare bird, the fair reviewer. He has been bracingly accurate but never unkind to Dom. He plays the flute in a small quartet. On weekend mornings, he hosts a program of thematic, eclectic music on the CBC – music performed by left-handed players, the music of composers born in June, that sort of thing.*

Tape, August 15, cont'd:

"Mr. Amoruso, Dominic, it's been a while. Thank you for getting back to me so soon. I caught your performance last night. The paper may or may not run a review tomorrow. It would have made today's but I got bumped for a rather large photo of a rather young girl with rather big breasts. I have no control over the arts section which, as you know, is rather small. But that's not why I'm calling. I hear you've been asked to play *Pictures at an Exhibition* at the Art Gallery of Ontario. Am I right? Is it true? Will you play?"

[A discernible pause. Dom has just heard the news himself. At this point, as far as he knows, only he and Anne Langelier and Thomas Carter are aware that an approach has been made. His tone is guarded.]

"You were at the conservatory last night? I didn't see you."

"I came in a few moments late, took a seat at the back, and slipped out a bit early so I could file. Is it true? I mean about the Musorgsky?"

"Tony, I've heard the rumours; why don't you call the exhibitionists and ask them yourself? Let me know what you find out; I've always wanted an informant. You can be my own personal Deep Throat."

"Come on, Dominic, you can –"

"Nothing doing. Call the AGO. You know Carter. If there is a show, if he's planning some sort of recital, then it's his baby and not mine. Seriously: You find out what's in the works, then call me back and fill me in. I'm just a pair of hands for hire – not that mine have been."

[He hangs up, muttering: "What is going on here? Why am I the last to know?" He dials another number. There is no response; after seven rings he hangs up.]

Note: *And now it's time for a break.*

The difficulty comes when I try to imagine what I hear.

I haven't seen Dom for roughly a year. I remember his face. The expressiveness. His squint, his grimace. The way he cocks his head to the side when he talks. The way he covers his mouth with his hand when he laughs. The gaps in his conversation. I am trying to fill in the largest gap of all. In a way, I am trying to become him.

Is this why I was sent the tapes? At this point I don't quite know what I'm supposed to understand – which means I can't discriminate in the way I listen. I have to listen to everything. At this rate, it will take forever to finish. Attention must be paid.

It is exhilarating. It is exhausting.

(Later) I slept late – a fitful night of half-formed dreams – and took my time over coffee this morning. I could not bear the thought of returning to the tapes. Before I knew it the morning was gone.

Instead of transcribing, I went to Song & Script. Buddy Keane was nowhere to be seen. Where is he now and where has he been?

Buddy. Dom's buddy. Buddydom. Enough wordplay. I've

decided to keep the tapes to myself. I wouldn't tip my hand before I play it. I wanted to see what Buddy knows. Maybe he'd tip me.

Dom's wordplay is affecting me.

At the counter was a new clerk, a dangerously slim aesthete with a pencil-thin moustache and thinning, slicked-back hair. A neatly pressed red tartan shirt. A black velvet string tie. John Waters of Green Gables.

I asked to speak to Mr. Keane. By way of an answer, I received an indifferent lift of one eyebrow. He licked a tobacco-stained forefinger and turned the page of his magazine without a word. Fuck, as it were, you.

I decided to wait and browsed through the discs, amusing myself by pairing artists for imaginary duets: Lefty Frizzell and The Georgia Sea Islanders. Annie Lennox and Emma Shapplin. Hank Williams and Frank Sinatra. Vera Lynn and Björk. I was very nearly tempted to pick up something by the little berserker when I felt a hand on my elbow and a whisper in my ear:

"She'd eat you alive."

"There are worse fates. Hi, Buddy."

"What brings you here?"

"Have you got a minute?"

"I have an hour; I'm taking a late lunch today."

"What do you say to a bowl of soup?"

"Pho Hung? I'm gung ho."

We took a table near the window. I made a point of taking a seat facing the street. I wanted to see it from Dom's point of view. I stared at the stone lions on the lawn of the Royal Ontario Museum. They didn't look much like lions today; they'd been wrapped in blue plastic and tied with yellow cord for the winter.

Blue plastic tarpaulin, yellow cord, grey stone lions – in another setting, it might have been another kind of art.

I put it to Buddy as soon as we'd ordered: Had he and Dom talked here a year or so ago, just before the disappearance? If so, in retrospect, did he recall anything that might –

"I remember very well. I was taken by surprise. He expressed dissatisfaction with his playing. I thought he was just tired. Little did I know how tired he really was. He'd played the night before. At the conservatory. A recital. This was prior to the famous performance by a month or two. He said he didn't think there was a point. To music. No point. Any longer. I think that's what he said. Perhaps not exactly. But as I recall, it's certainly what he meant."

"And you said?"

"I said, 'Of course there is no point.' Which, for me, is the point. Music exists for its own sake. The minute you go looking for a reason, reason disappears. I think he was simply tired. He and I go back a long way. Not that way. You know him as well as I do. He's as straight as they come. Although I don't know why he insists on – insisted on – sleeping with that Weller woman. Do you know Claire? Then you know what I mean. I attended the conservatory recital. I came late; he never saw me. I ducked out before he finished. Because, forgive me, if you want the truth, he stank. His playing was all over the map. If I didn't know better, I'd have said he was stoned."

"Stoned?"

The waiter interrupted with our soup.

Buddy tore up a few leaves of fresh basil, scattered them over his broth, added a fistful of bean sprouts, squirted a short ribbon of chili paste, and squeezed his wedge of lime. He armed himself with chopsticks and a spoon, and began to untangle the nest of noodles in the bowl.

Dom was right. Buddy slurped like a peasant – wetly, inhaling broth and noodles at the same time. Although he did not splash his shirt. A trick, with pho, I have yet to manage.

"I've never known him to hit wrong notes. I mean, we all do. It's accepted. And it can be charming. But he simply does not hit wrong notes. That night, he didn't just hit them, he hammered them home. His touch was gone. The tempo was also weird. Almost deliberately so. As if he were tampering. Not unlike Gould. I don't think very many noticed. Not the kids; he was playing stuff that was over their heads. If they hadn't heard the piece before, they wouldn't have known. Roberts was there, from the Globe. You know him? In any case he arrived after me. We left at the same time. He looked at me. I looked at him. He shrugged. Thank goodness there was no review."

"As bad as that?"

"Perhaps I exaggerate. No, I do not. He was well off his game. It happens. There was an odour of – I'm not sure if I know how to . . . do you play an instrument?"

"No."

"I was very good as a boy, in a limited way, but he always played in another league. Let me put it this way. There are certain things you don't have to think about when you are a superior performer and you've done the work. You play the way a tennis player does – without thinking. You have the sense of what you must do well before you need to do it. The tennis player sees the ball, senses the direction, gauges the speed, notes the position of his opponent, whether he's moving this way or that. And he does what needs doing as he moves to meet the ball. He's done it before he's thought about it. If you get my drift. Stop to think and you're dead. Dom seemed to me to be thinking that night. Tell me something. Is he dead?"

He waited for my answer. He looked down and prodded his bowl, inhaled another mouthful of noodles. He took a spoonful of soup, snatched a bit of spring roll with his fingers, dunked it in the broth, popped it in his mouth and swallowed it without seeming to chew, dabbed his chin, wiped his fingers. Still waiting. I said I thought he was alive.

At that moment, I wasn't sure.

I added that I didn't think it would be easy for anyone, let alone someone who was well-known, to drop off the face of the earth and stay dropped off. In any case, I had no idea why he'd want to.

Buddy said, "I think if a man like Dom doesn't want to be found he will remain lost to everyone but himself. He is not, as you know, without resources. There are places where – I remember saying I thought he ought to go to Montreal, busk in the subway, or do something equally left-field. I was trying to distract him, trying to get him out of his rut. He needed shaking up. There are lots of cities in the world with subways, where they have an ear for music. London, Berlin, Rome. If he grew a beard, who'd know it was him? You'd have to be very good to recognize him by his sound."

I suppose it's true. Even as close to home as Montreal, Amoruso with a beard would be a busker, albeit better than most. And Mme Langelier has a host of connections there. But the package had not been sent from Montreal. Or Berlin or Rome. I was confused.

Buddy said, "I'm not really worried. At least I wasn't at the time."

I took the subway to St. Clair and walked around Dom's neighbourhood, looking for – what? I had no idea. It had grown *dark and there was a chill. I found myself walking past the vacuum cleaner stores, two of them side by side – the owners, competing to see who could set more vacuums on the sidewalk by day, and whose sign glowed brighter by night. Past the flower shop whose owner had famously flirted with Frank Sinatra. Finally, I was sitting at a table in the Tre Mari, with an espresso and a meatball sandwich, when it hit me –*

The remains of that sandwich, half-eaten, are at this moment wrapped in a sack on the dining room table because I didn't finish eating. I couldn't taste a thing, couldn't stop thinking about the notebooks and the tapes. The where of them, the why. And the why me. And then I swore – dio porco! – loud enough that the woman behind the counter, who was slapping together an order of sausages and peppers to go, looked up and glared.

I am supposed to be a journalist. I have been trained to observe, record, deduct, investigate, conclude, and report. And I was suddenly struck by the obvious, a real forehead slapper, something that should have occurred to me immediately.

Wherever he was, he'd have a phone.

The waitress wrapped my sandwich and put it in a bag. I paid the bill. Took a cab back to my apartment. Dialled directory assistance for Nunavut. Was given a choice of service in English, French, or Inuktitut. The operator giggled and said she could find no listing for anyone named Dominic Amoruso in Wolf Cove. Nor in the nearest community, Iqaluit. I sweet-talked her into making a bit of a search – but there was no listing anywhere in the Arctic.

I should have thought of this first.

And so, with disappointment, back to the cassettes.

Tape, August 19:

[Dom is talking to himself as he makes his way around what must be his apartment. His voice is cheerful, but the sound is vague – impossible to make out what he's saying. As for what he is doing, there is a slapping of magazines, a rustling of papers, an idle whistle, an exploratory humming. He's interrupted by the buzzer – three short, and one emphatic long. Is this a code? His voice is now clearer, as if closer to a microphone.

His sing-song tremolo: "Hello-o-o."

Her gay declaration: "It's me. Open up or I'll shoot."

Some ninety seconds of white noise. I must be patient, I am looking for clues. I cannot tell you how tedious white noise is. Dom is my friend, but the man who records his every moment on the earth, including his belches, his grunts and moans, his tidying up – that man is an egoist. Finally, he opens the door. There is a rustle of packages.]

"Clara, *carissima*!"

"Never mind the Claire, dear. Take these . . ."

"Here, let me. What have we here?"

"The same thing we always have here. If you'll just. There's your barbecued pork, your sticky rice, bok choy –"

"No duck?"

"Yes, duck. For heaven's sake. Watch the – here, take this. Let me get my coat off."

[A crossing of footsteps, his and hers; several minutes of unidentified noise and chit-chat; apparently, he never bothered to hide a microphone in the kitchen, or else he has not bothered to switch it on; there is some infectious pop music in the background.]

"I hear you've agreed to play."

"Play what? At the moment, I am agreeing to eat."

"I mean *Pictures*. At the gallery. In the fall."

"Who told you? How do you know what?"

"Don't be thick. Edward tells me things."

"It never fucking fails. Everyone in town knows about this fucking recital except me."

"I should think you'd be pleased. Don't say fucking."

"Do I detect your hand in this?"

"I've had a hand in many things. You've been glad of it on occasion. What difference does it make? The paintings have to do with music, it's an intimate setting, and who better than you?"

"That's more or less what Anne said. The idea is a trifle obvious, that's all."

"Don't be stubborn! It's a chance to play. What does it matter? Would you rather the work went to Kuerti?"

Note: Margie with a quick sketch: Anton Kuerti, b. Vienna 21 July 1938. Began to play at the age of four. Moved with his parents to the U.S. in 1944. Resident of Toronto since 1965. Prickly, brilliant, a man of convictions, unwilling to suffer fools. He ran for the New Democrats in the federal election of 1988. Prickly brilliance and conviction are fine qualities in an artist, but not necessarily attractive to the electorate. He lost handily.

Gould befriended him early on. Kuerti – how was he to know? – once made a famous error at a lunch with the great neurotic: He ordered a plate of calf's brains. Gould fled the table with his hand over his mouth.

Kuerti's greater misfortune, apart from brains – and a dish of brains – was that he played Beethoven brilliantly. In this town, even now, that meant taking a back seat to you know who. Anywhere else – France, Italy, Spain, Germany – the presence of two such gifted pianists in one city would have been seen as reason to celebrate; but not here. Such riches are considered unseemly. Gould was ours; Kuerti came from away. There was not enough room for two.

Kuerti once noted the presence of fifteen books devoted to Gould in the Metro library – more than those about any other pianist, including Horowitz. His point was that this says much about Toronto. According to Margie, it says more about Kuerti, who clearly took the time to count. Presumably, K. chose to ignore the hometown factor.

Notebook, August 19:

I handed Claire a bottle of wine. She dropped the corkscrew while I was setting the table. Had it been me, I'd have cursed. If I drop a thing, it startles, or it disappoints – it usually means I've been interrupted in the midst of an idea. Claire, instead of cursing, fumed.

Perhaps it was the music. I was playing an old Sugar Cubes CD – brisk, Icelandic, an acquired taste – the girl singer in her skirt and crinolines. I was right to predict big things for my little Björk.

[Squeak of cork released from neck of bottle, slip-slap of noodles on plates, crisp snap of chopsticks split apart; she makes succulent, smacking sounds as she eats.]

Notebook, August 19, cont'd:

I have no idea why she gets so easily upset. It isn't as if she has to perform for people who have too much money and not enough time or taste to enjoy it. What am I saying? Claire also has too much money.

In any case, I chivvied her – pull the cjörk, pass the pjörk, are you tired of chopsticks, would you like a fjörk. She did not bite.

I tried again to engage her. I have sneaked peeks at newsstand *Teen Beats* – Björk's parents were hippies. Odd – perhaps not odd – how the least powerful nations cling hardest to notions of peace and love long after that stuff lost its currency here.

The sixties lasted until the Chinese invaded Vietnam. After which, it's all about shopping.

In any case, the Gudmundsdottirs raised their little Björklet on a diet of Hendrix, incense, and innocence. The influence is apparent: She sings "Njall's Song" by way of "The Wind Cried Mary." She is a geyser of heated kerosene, scalding anyone close enough to listen; she scalds me.

Not a word from Claire. Might have been worse. She might have seen my Björk and raised me Glenn's Petula.

Petula: up late.

Tape, August 19, cont'd:

"Would you like hot sauce?"

"Mmm. You know she doesn't like you very much."

"Who doesn't?"

"My agent thinks you are a distraction. Where was I? You see, you distract me now. You with your mouth full."

"It's what I do. You're a big boy. Take the money. Play the concert."

"Yeah, sure. Maybe I could pull an Andy Kaufman."

"What do you mean, pull an Andy Kaufman? Who is Andy Kaufman? Does he play?"

"Does he play? He is a comedian. Was a comedian. He's dead now. Try some of this bok choy. He had a bit where he'd come on stage with a portable record player, drop the needle and lip-synch to some song. Any song. The cornier the better. Just stand there kind of wide-eyed. In a plaid jacket with a bow tie and a stupid little grin. Say thank you very much when it was over. Performance art or something. I could do the same. Put on my bow tie. Stand next to the piano. Put my tape machine on the lid. Smile and press 'Play.' "

"You don't own a bow tie. Would you rather the work went to –? Honestly, sometimes I wonder. Seriously – if that old fossil Langelier doesn't lock you into this, I'll stuff her into her own purse and toss her in the harbour. But you don't have to decide at this very moment. Eat your duck. You know you can't bear it when your duck is cold."

"Duck off, dearest."

Note: I'd forgotten. Dom will not eat duck – or any other fowl, or beef or pork – unless it is smoking hot; in restaurants around town, he was famously in the habit of sending plates of half-eaten food back to the kitchen for reheating.

[Brittle clatter. "Fuck!" "Yikes!" Her fuck, his yikes.]

Notebook, August 19, cont'd:

I asked Claire for more wine. She, lost in thought, was startled. Dropped her chopsticks and sent them flying across the floor. Knocked her glass over while reaching. Corkscrew, now chopsticks. She, who so rarely swears, swore; worse, spilled wine on me.

"Fuck!" she fumed, off her game: hem rage.

Perhaps it was my reluctance to commit to the recital. Or perhaps it was the Sugar Cubes.

Note: Petula did not come out of the blue. Margie reminded me without hesitation that Glenn Gould had championed both

Petula Clark and Barbra Streisand in separate articles written for High Fidelity *magazine more than thirty years ago. A case of high-culture slumming if there ever was one.*

GG is supposed to have written the Petula Clark piece while staying in the hotel in Marathon. I have been to Marathon. It stinks, thanks to the paper mill, which bathes its workers in the smell of rotting eggs. Dom was born there a year after the Petula piece was written. A coincidence, surely; there was never any suggestion that GG had ever bred. But wouldn't it be funny if . . .

It is the stuff of novels.

Funny, what the tapes trigger: Claire is said to have tried to seduce Gould when she was in high school. He had been enticed into speaking to her class on graduation day; she is supposed to have lured him into an empty classroom on the pretext of showing him the school piano and asking him for some advice about a piece of Beethoven. She is reckoned to have been rebuffed rather awkwardly. Gould may have liked Pet, but there was little evidence of him wanting to pet.

Did it happen? It was implausible enough to be plausible. Claire is, in the estimation of the socialites, a predator, a counter of coups, a carver of notches. Perhaps she had an early start. If she had set her cap on Gould, it would certainly have been a long shot. He was a delicate creature in the forest of his own imagination – he spooked far too easily for his own good.

Did Claire have a thing for pianists? Had she dared herself to try? Dominic never had the nerve to ask; he did, however, put me up to asking. He had a cocktail party at his apartment to celebrate his most recent recording. She arrived, sans Weller. Dom whispered in my ear: "You're a journalist, that's what you do. Go ahead and ask her."

I did. She slapped my face. A good answer.

Tape, August 19, cont'd:

[A disappointing segment: thirty more minutes of wine being dribbled into and sucked from wineglasses, chopsticks clicking and pecking, duck bones being licked to the tune of muffled rock 'n' roll, and a slow stream of soft, low, idle talk. Had she draped her jacket over the pick-up? Had he forgotten to turn off the machine? I can't believe he had any practical use for this noise. His version of a diary?]

Notebook, August 19, cont'd:

Björk vs. Petula?

B. – no need to go through pseudo-intellectual hoops – sings rings around P. Also rings around GG's other pop star, Streisand: tries sand. Björk is better than the pair of them, one at a time or – here's a thought – hooked up in sequence.

In any case, it wouldn't have made a difference to Claire. It is a matter of taste. Speaking of which: Pink Pearl takeout – the duck fatty and gamy, tough and much too sweet; the noodles salty and satisfying – although an odd aftertaste, something like baking soda – and the pork and vegetables too slippery. Never again from there.

I drank most of the wine.

After supper, Claire put a tea towel around her waist and knotted it behind her back. I have the instincts of a touch typist. I have played the piano with my back turned to the keys. Once, when I was young and wanted to show off at Tanglewood, I crawled on top of a grand piano, lay on my belly, leaned forward and – right hand secundo, left hand primo, black keys near and white keys far – rattled off the Bach "Arioso." It made my head spin, I had a headache afterwards, but I did it oh-so-air-ily. Tying an apron behind my back, however, is beyond me.

I offered help with dishes – it is, after all, my kitchen – but she shooed me away (she mu-shu'd me away! ha ha) and filled the sink with suds rather than put everything in the dishwasher: hard wishes.

Does she do the washing up at home? I don't think so. It seems to me she has a daily maid. She busied herself with the vigour of someone intent on instructing the help. She rinsed each glass and wiped it dry with a distracted fury. This – pay attention now! – is how it ought to be done!

A brittle image: shards and tendons.

I shivered and thought briefly about engaging her in conversation, but she was paying attention to something other than dishes, or me. She cleaned the sink, dried her hands, folded the tea towel, hung it by the stove, and led me to my bed.

Tape, August 19, cont'd:

[Murmur, yawn, sigh, sniffle – hers, his, hers and hers. The impression is one of haste spent, underlined by the flat of a hand – my guess, hers – on a post-coital pillow.]

Note: I think I am beginning to understand why he records the ebb and flow of a conversation:

There are rhythms in the sound of repeated gestures, and there are patterns in the human voice, and so on. But I am puzzled. He and Claire have clearly just made love and the most elemental rhythms of all are unrecorded. Surely – if he prized chatter, traffic noise, bone-sucking suppers, church bells, phone calls, hydraulic snorts, squeaks of chairs, the rip of zippers, subway accordions – he would have recorded the sounds he made when he was . . .

Did C. object to being taped? Or did she like it? She must have known what he was doing. He had a wall of cassettes, all

clearly labelled, and a studio full of dubbing and editing gear.
She had to have known. Maybe he erased the love-making as a
courtesy to her. Or maybe he declined to record the sounds they
made as a consequence of his own modesty.

Tape, August 19, cont'd:
  "Can I get you anything?"
  "Nothing. Let me lie here. Hold still. I'm going to bite you."
  "Jesus no, please, dammit, don't you –"
  "There, there. You weren't complaining a moment ago."
  "That was then. Stop or I'll . . . Move your . . . No, move
over."
  [The recording stops.]

———

Note: I watched television until midnight. I don't remember what
I watched. Which, after all, is the purpose of television. If you
can't remember what you've seen, you will keep watching reruns.

I slept on the couch and awoke sticky and gummy and sore.
The apartment is too hot this morning. There is no point in getting
dressed. There is no point in shaving. I'm not going anywhere.

I now have a pot of coffee, a place at the dining room table.
I have now eaten an egg and an orange and some toast. I have
now turned the pages of the morning papers dutifully. I can't
remember what I read, and the pictures have not registered. Not
that it matters. The newspapers have nothing to do with the task
at hand.

The curtains are open wide. The apartment is filled with
yellow light. It's cold outside and warm inside. I have fresh

batteries. The computer hums with confidence. Let us begin the day with text:

Notebook, August 21:

And so to the gallery: largely.

To see Thomas Carter: chart some rat.

Unusually hot today, even for August. The air is as thick as the breath of a sick animal. All shirts stick to warm backs.

How glum we are on public transit in this town.

We are, I suppose, so many slave labourers, our shoulders slumped, our eyes downcast, our selves at half mast. No point in talking to our fellow slaves. I suppose it's understandable: the price of mortgages, inflated rents, miserable wages, lousy food, the high cost of the high holidays and the thought – it hangs in the air like a whiff of burnt hair – that some of our fellow travellers are psychotic.

Who wouldn't be sullen, who wouldn't be mute? And who wouldn't want to leap onto the tracks of the subway the way we do, at the rate of two or three a month? On a good day, this place is enough to drive anyone mad – and to leave any jumper sadder and madder since, according to Serafino, only one in ten succeeds.

Note: The reference is to a piece I wrote last year about an incident in the Spadina subway station: A mother, well-educated and well-to-do, in the midst of postpartum depression, spent two hours walking back and forth on the platform, with her baby in her arms. No one paid her any mind. She was working up the nerve to jump. She found the nerve. The child died and she lived for a few days and then she died, too. Luckily, I suppose.

*The TTC driver saw her face at the instant she made the deci-
sion. Nothing he could do. She was his fourth jumper. He is still
in therapy. That Dom should remember this is curious.*

Notebook, August 21, cont'd:

Above the inner entrance of the AGO, a Moore sculpture: a
woman in white, on her elbow, on her side, knees slightly parted.
Draped Reclining Woman. Whatever his intent, Moore might
just as easily have called it *Claire, Afterwards.* As if he had her
hips in mind.

We'll see what Carter has in his.

Tape, August 21:

"Can you tell me where I might find the director's office?"

"The director's office is not accessible to the public."

"I didn't ask if it was accessible. I asked where it was."

"Excuse me, sir, but if you want to see the director, you'll
have to call in advance and make an appointment."

"I have one."

"Who might you be?"

"My card."

"Sir, if I may –"

"No, you may not. You may call Mr. Carter. He is the one
who made the appointment. You may tell him I am here."

*Note: Dom's voice is flat, and perhaps more menacing than war-
ranted. I've seen his baleful eye. Better men than the haughty
receptionist have trembled. I suppose, given Dom's usual appearance – the slick hair, the leather jacket, the stubble on his cheek,
and his scowl, not to mention the deceptive microphones in his
ears – the poor clerk must have thought he was looking at a*

*punk who'd gotten lost on his way to the Second Cup on the
corner. His mistake.*

[A drumming of fingers. Dom's idle humming – my guess, some
little snippet of the Musorgsky. An intense pause while the clerk
turns away.]

*Note: I don't know why, but I still can't get used to the idea that
I am spying, even though I have his – or someone's – permission
to invade his privacy. I am also invading the privacy of others.
Notably, Claire's. And now that of the buffoon receptionist.*

*Permission to do this is conferred, in a way, by possession of
the tapes. But I still feel like a sneak.*

*That aside, I am yet again impressed by the sense of direc-
tion on the tape – it seems the receptionist is turning to Dom's
left – the way his voice moves as he speaks. Is there a companion
word for voyeur? Eavesdropper is too plain, and I've yet to see a
modern building with open windows and eaves from which to
drop. I, auditeur?*

Tape, August 21, cont'd:
[Voice of receptionist:] "Isabelle, I have a Mr. Am-o-ru-so at
the desk. Yes. Amor-uso. Yes. He says he is here to see the director. I don't know. I don't know. I don't know. So he says. Yes,
I'll hold."
[humming, drumming]
"I see. Very well. Thank you. Yes, I will. Ahem. I will tell
him. Yes. Sir. You are ten minutes early. In ten minutes, someone
from Administration will come and escort you to Mr. Carter's
office. You may wait here, if you wish, or you may choose to
visit the gift shop and I will send them to fetch you."

[D. walks away, muttering:]

"Is it the proximity to art that turns some people into asses? I ought to let Carter find himself another piano player. Let them fetch me if they can. Whoever they are. Whenever they – what do we have here? Christmas cards, no, thank you. Old posters, no thank you. Coasters and Kandinsky. Pencils and Jackson Pollock. Memo pad, dog-eared, half-price, with a fat pink nude on the cover. Huh. What sort of memo would a Rubens nude prompt? Breast of chicken for supper. Hello. What's Leinsdorf doing here?

[Pages flipping. He reads:]

"Just as an audience that coughs its way through a soft passage can quickly demoralize the most professional performer . . .

"He got that right. The cough is the performer's coffin. Richter's *Pictures* was an exercise in self-defence. He played, not to get through the piece, but to protect himself from the coughs, the candy wrappers, the sneezes and the snuffles of the good burghers, the good Bulgars of Sofia. Now, what does Leinsdorf have to say about . . . ?"

[Suck of tooth, riffle of pages, sniffle, and explosive curse.]

"Oh for the love of Jesus!"

"Um. Excuse me, sir. Um. If you'd care to follow –"

"Forgive me for swearing. I take it you are, um, fetching."

"Excuse me?"

"You are the fetcher. That little prig at reception said someone would fetch me. I am the fetchee and you are fetching – in the act of fetching me, I mean. I babble. I was just looking at this. I have a tendency to swear when I am taken by surprise. I don't mean by you. Have you read this? Leinsdorf, nobody's fool, says Gould was, and I quote, a pianist of the first rank, kind and gentle. He's not wrong about the pianist part, but

Gould was neither kind nor gentle. He was addled. And I am subtracted. I must read the rest of this. Is it possible to take it? I wonder if I might –"

"Please. Pay for it on the way out. This way, if you will."

[Her tick-tock steps stitch his soft stride.]

Note: Another call to Margie, to track down the Leinsdorf reference. "You never call, and then you can't stop calling. I'd say it was my perfume. In which case you have a good memory and a remarkable telephone. What is it now? And be careful how you answer – I'll make you pay for this."

I said she could name her price.

It took her ten minutes: Erich Leinsdorf, b. Vienna 1912. Conductor of symphonies in Cleveland, Boston, the Met. One of those rare musicians whose ability to write matched his musical intelligence. Author of three books. From On Music, *this is what prompted D.'s outburst:*

"Glenn Gould, perhaps one of the all-time greatest (and in my view perhaps also the kindest and gentlest) artists, preferred to do his playing in a recording studio."

"So you're working on something to do with the punk pianist."

"I couldn't say."

"You don't have to. I read you like a cheap novel, buddy boy. Here's something else. It is Leinsdorf's view that stage fright derives from an insufficient obligation to one's talent – he said talent is a gift, as well as a debt to be repaid – an obligation that provokes a certain discomfort in some people. Speaking of obligations, this adds up to a rather nice supper. You won't forget. I'm keeping track."

We left it there. I said I'd call.

Perhaps Gould had been kind and gentle. Given the bequest of his estate – he lavished his money on the Humane Society and the Salvation Army – it would be easy to argue towards a kind of kindness. You could at the very least say he had a soft spot for strays. But dogs don't play piano, and old alkies – at least, those of my recent acquaintance – tend to be out of tune with their surroundings. I think Gould was wary of the obligation of his talent. "Look at me, stop looking at me." Quick to cut those he disagreed with, and quicker to cut those who disagreed with him.

The hired help – tuners, technicians, and so on – were useful until they weren't, and then they, too, were dropped.

Kind and gentle? More like high-strung, febrile, arrogant.

As for preferring the recording studio. . . .

When you flee the stage in fear, can you be said to prefer flight? Gould's was one of the most significant cases of stage fright in modern times. Did this strike a resonant chord in Dom?

Tape, August 21, cont'd:

"Have you worked here long?"

"I'm just new. I started six months ago."

"Art school grad?"

"Yes, actually. Well, no. I have a degree in the restoration of art."

"Would that you could restore it to its proper place."

"I don't. I'm not sure if. Here we are."

[A flurry of voices; a fuss being made.]

"May I take your coat?"

"May I get you a cup of coffee?"

[And the voice of the confident Carter:]

"Welcome to the gallery, sir. It's a pleasure, um, to meet you. Forgive me, but I'm never sure whether to shake the hand of a concert pianist. I have, um, enjoyed your performances for a long time now."

"How do you do. I don't generally shake hands on the day of a performance, nor do I do so after having played – there are always one or two bonecrushers in the crowd who think they can – well, who knows what some people think. Otherwise, my hands are put to the usual uses. I prune the roses on my balcony, I change the washers in my tap. Well, actually I call the superintendent about the plumbing."

Note: Thomas Carter, b. Toronto 1941. Ivy League education. Affluent, bilingual, suave; former director of the Musée des Beaux-Arts in Montreal. Previously with art galleries in Boston, Philadelphia, Chicago. Dubbed "The Canadian Hoving" by the arts crowd. He has maintained a discreet silence concerning events on the night of the recital.

Perhaps there's something more I can pry out of him. . . .

Tape, August 21, cont'd:

"Won't you please come into my, um, office? Forgive me, but word is leaking out already. As I'm sure you know. We can't, um, seem to keep a lid on anything any more. The press is voracious. Let me come straight to the point. We have. Um. Sally, thank you, on the desk please. Help yourself to cream and sugar, Mr. Amoruso.

"Let me start again. As you may know, the AGO is one of the major museums in the world. We are members of a rather select club, if you will; membership consisting of other large galleries and museums. There are roughly fifty of us altogether. We share expertise, we cooperate with one another regarding scheduling, publications, licensing, and so on. From time to time, we share work from our collections. Um, if you'll allow me, I'll come right to the point. We have just finished negotiations, and we are about to launch a major show this year: 'The Art of Music.'"

"I had heard as much, yes."

"Yes. We put it together. Rather I, um, did. Work from the Tate, the Hermitage, the Guggenheim, and so on – paintings that portray musicians, or that serve to illustrate music in some way. I'm sure you know most of these. Lichtenstein's *Girl at Piano*. Picasso's *Old Guitarist*. That habitant picture, the name of which escapes me – the painting of the boy blowing into the harmonica after he's had his soup and bread."

"Ozias Leduc. *Le Musicien*."

"Very good. You know it, then."

"I have always thought it a bad idea to play the harmonica after eating a meal of soup and bread."

"Just so. Of course, we also have all the usual stuff coming in – men with flutes, girls with lutes. One or two things that I'm sure will interest you. Some beautifully printed manuscripts of ancient music – Hildegarde von Bingen, and so on; gold leaf, spectacular stuff, the work of monks. This show is intended to be a money maker. It will travel. But we do have to earn our, um, keep. There will be a catalogue. A CD if we can clear the rights to certain selections of music. Perhaps we can include. But let's – I'm getting ahead of myself. The reason I've asked you here is this: We have obtained the Hartmann drawings."

[A pause; spoons circle cups, spoons tap saucers.]

Dom: "I haven't seen them for some time."

Note: This is the surprise hinted at by Mme Langelier.

Hartmann, Viktor. Russian architect; b. 1834, d. 1873. A close friend and contemporary of Musorgsky, he died quite

*unexpectedly of an aneurysm. Musorgsky was distraught. A show
of Hartmann's work was arranged a year or so after his death.
Why it took so long is anybody's guess, but this was the exhibition – and these were the pictures – that inspired Musorgsky.*

*Although as many as four hundred architectural drawings,
sketches, and watercolours existed at the time, fewer than a
hundred of these works survive today; of the ten pictures from
which Musorgsky drew inspiration, only six remain.*

Tape, August 21, cont'd:

"You have the Hartmanns here?"

"They are not due to arrive until – well. Let's say they should
be here soon. We have only just concluded our negotiations.
These things take time. We have confirmed *The Hut on Hen's
Legs*, and those charming unhatched chicks; also *The Catacombs*;
one of the portraits of the old Jewish men, you know the ones I
mean, the long dark beards and so on. And the Kiev gate. You
know the value of this work, of course. Art that inspires great art
is somehow more remarkable for having done so."

"How did you manage to – ?"

"Oh, it took no end of persuasion. Discussions went on for
months. The art world does not move, um, swiftly. I'm sure the
world of classical music is the same. It's, um, delicate. A work
never leaves a museum and returns in the same condition it was
in when it was sent. Works on paper are especially fragile.
Assurance must be made. But in the end, I must say the Russians
were quite, um, generous. And you helped us indirectly, without
even – you see, they know your work."

"They should. I won one of their competitions. I play their
repertoire. I'm very glad to have helped, even though I had no
idea I was helping."

"Naturally we had to make certain guarantees. The Russians have expressed an interest in the Group of Seven. Now. This is why I asked you here. I hope you will consider playing on the evening of the members' preview. It would be a privilege for us – after all, you are most closely associated with *Pictures at an Exhibition*. It seems a natural fit. Your agent said it would be –"

"Let me interrupt. On the wall behind your desk –"

[Dom's tone of voice is direct. I'd say he has made up his mind to play at this moment, but is buying himself a little time.]

"You have a good eye. We are planning a small show of young photographers in the New Works Gallery. I intend to liven this place up a bit. Fresh air, and all that. These were taken by a young woman named Carol Paterson. One of the privileges of office – I get to hang things here before they go up out there. Gives me a feel for the artist."

"I can't help noticing the old man at the piano."

"I'm not surprised."

"Who is he?"

"No idea, I'm afraid. Is he someone I should know? You'll have to ask the photographer."

"He reminds me of – never mind. Explain the preview, please."

"A private viewing for patrons. Something we, um, put on prior to the opening of each show. One of those things we have to do. A way of acknowledging our donors, the major sponsors, and so on."

"I presume you have a piano."

"We have two. A newer Yamaha grand and an older, slightly smaller Steinway. A Model L, I think it is. I have no idea, really. Not my, um, field of expertise. I'm sorry to say I have no idea if they are good or not. I will leave that for you to decide. I'd be happy to show them to you –"

"Where will I play, if I play?"

"The Walker Court. I must apologize for, um. It isn't the finest concert hall in town. But it's really the only room we have available for use. If you agree to play, and we would love it if you would, then we'd be more than happy to arrange for the delivery of your own piano. Or, if you prefer, we could bring one in from Remenyi or –"

"That won't be necessary."

"Does that mean you'll play?

"I won't say no; not yet. But I don't make the deals. I leave that for my agent. I'm sure you understand. Call Mme. Langelier next week. She and I will have talked it over and come to some decision. As for pianos, I'm not fussy unless it's for a recording. I might want the CBC's piano. A Bosendorfer. But if I can't cut a deal with the CBC, then a piano is a piano. It's pretty much like driving a car. You hop in and off you go. Unless yours is a lemon. There are lemon Steinways. Not many, but some. Who is your tuner?"

"We use a man named Frank Mazur. Do you know him? I can give you his number if you'd like to call him."

Note: Here's how I read this: If this were poker, you'd figure Carter has three of a kind. He's playing with confidence. He knows the value of his cards. But there is a "tell" in his voice – he's eager. Dominic, on the other hand, doesn't care one way or the other what anyone else is holding. He has the nut flush.

Tape, August 21, cont'd:

"Let me have a look at Walker Court first, please."

"If you'll come with me. Sally, would you please dig out Frank Mazur's phone number? And bring along Mr. Amoruso's jacket, if you wouldn't mind."

[The tape picks up again with three loud handclaps, one after the other – the noise of one clap overlapping the others – then a pause, followed by three more claps from elsewhere in the room.]

"You hear how the sound echoes in here?"

Note: This is a statement, not a question. The sound is boomy, muddy, atrocious. Dom claps his hands a dozen times in quick succession as he walks from one side of the court to the other – his clapping is as brisk as the fanning of a deck of cards.

Tape, August 21, cont'd:

"You hear the way it bounces off the walls? As the sound returns it practically cancels whatever comes next. There is a perpetual – let me put it this way. It's like seeing yourself in facing mirrors – a repetition of smaller images all the way to infinity until there is nothing left."

"I'm afraid I know what you mean. We have used this room before with, I'll be frank, mixed results. Anton Kuerti has played here on occasion. You know him? I must say his reception was, um, rather warm. But he was, um, less than thrilled. Well, as I said, it is the only room we have. Is there anything we can do? Hang baffles, perhaps. To make it more suitable?"

"Don't bother. More effort than it's. I wouldn't. It doesn't really matter what you. I'm not the one who has to. I merely have to play. But the softer sounds will be hard for anyone to hear, I think, with any clarity. And when I play with volume – as I said, the room is –"

[Their footsteps cease; D. holds his breath, releases it with a short, almost violent sigh. He sounds almost helpless. Like an animal in a trap.]

"Excuse me, are you? Is there something wrong?"

"A migraine. I get them. On occasion. Am getting one now. They arrive, as you see. Unbidden. Forgive me but. I need air. And to get out of here. What was I talking about?"

"Please, never mind that now. You have gone quite pale. Come with me. Shall I, um, have someone call you a taxi? The exit is just around the – We can discuss this later. Call my secretary when you feel up to it. She can arrange for you to see the pianos. I can have them brought up any time you'd like and you can, um, can try them at your convenience. The door is. Are you sure you're all right? Is there anything I can do?"

"Not unless you have a pocket full of codeine. I feel a bit . . . It's not as bad as . . . Mr. Carter, that room is a cavern. I don't imagine that matters much to patrons. I know about patrons. If I play, they will get their . . . money's worth. As will you. Excuse me, but I have to. Please."

[A wash of white noise like the crashing of slow waves rolling in on a low and sloping beach; then the jingle of his hand fumbling among the keys and the coins in his pocket. Then the tape is switched off.]

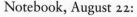

Notebook, August 22:

I took more pills four hours ago.

I have slept and the pain is swaddled: add welds. It has not disappeared, it is simply wrapped in the cotton wool of my lovely drugs. Now and then, if I am not careful, one of these heads will take a hairpin turn and I will find myself right back where I started – me with a needle in my eye, me cringing from the light, me hammered into submission by the loudness of my heartbeat, me unable to walk a straight line, me frightened by the ringing in my ears, me overwhelmed with the urge to vomit.

My fear: It's not a migraine but a blood vessel swelling awkwardly. An aneurysm fragile as a balloon. The good doctor Capek has sent me for tests from time to time. She thinks I am a hypochondriac. She tells me not to be dramatic. I don't remember what it's like not to feel this way.

If I didn't feel like this –

I'd miss it.

I turned left on leaving the gallery.

Past the video stores; past the neon signs in the windows of the rub shops; past the discreet offices of the benevolent societies of the largest and most powerful Chinese families; past the windows of the restaurants with their tea-smoked ducks; past the crispy sides of roasted suckling pigs that hang dripping fatly from iron hooks – the sight filled me with nausea. The smell of star anise drifting onto the street.

I walked past cardboard barrels mounded with lotus seeds, salted plums, dried shrimp, thin roots as dry and white as bone and thick roots shaped like dark and hairy men; tree fungus fragile as communion wafers; dried fish as delicate as starched silk. I walked past jade bracelets heaped in wicker trays and jumbles of tiny green Buddhas with swollen bellies; past baskets of worthless coins and red-wrapped sheaves of worthless paper money.

Pain heightens my vision.

An acid light –

I have to be careful of what I look at.

I, helpless, bumped into an old woman, almost tripped, almost toppled her. She had been shuffling along with four white plastic shopping sacks, two in each hand, overflowing with stalks and fronds. She spat and muttered something to me. Or about me – I imagine she said I was too big and therefore too clumsy, and a danger to the normal people.

That's what I would have said if I were her.

I backed away, apologizing all the way, and bumped into a vegetable stand stacked high with bok choy. The crowd carried me along. I was surrounded, a human stone in the human stream.

I saw a man sitting on the curb, half-gloves on his hands, lifting noodles with his deft chopsticks, steam rising from his bowl. A carter, not a gallery man but a hauler of vegetables, an unloader of boxes of crabs, shrimp, and spiny lobsters. He was watching me with amusement.

His clothes were the colour of clay, of sand, of mud. You could cast him as a cadre on the Long March to . . . Toronto. He smiled as he shovelled his food into his mouth. For an instant, it seemed as if he wore a dragon's beard of hot white noodles. If I closed my eyes and opened them again. . . . Duck, you're in Peking.

It occurred to me that no one in this crowd, including the old lady and the carter, knew anything about Musorgsky. On the other hand, I know next to nothing of Chinese music. And you can never tell who knows what, e.g., my two Filmore strippers.

I walked until it occurred to me that I couldn't hear a thing.

Not a car. Not the cries of gulls overhead nor the boy trimming celery and joking with his mother. A silent movie unspooling, a sea of mute heads bobbing. The light stabbed my eye.

Ashkenazy at his piano . . .

Not a note.

In the eddy by the entrance to the bank at the corner, a salaryman in a summerweight suit – poplin, pale green, improbable; what sort of business? – stood holding the hand of his son; the boy with his shorts pulled down around his ankles and a pair of blue plastic sandals on his feet. Barely old enough to walk. Lips pursed. Underpants soiled. Shit, yellow and runny, leaking down the backs of his legs. The look on his face: *Don't laugh, it's funny that I shit myself like this. But it's not my fault, please don't laugh at me, I had to go, I couldn't stop.*

A woman in a tight bright red silk dress knelt by the boy, wiping his bottom with a tissue and wrinkling her nose.

It occurred to me that I was walking in the wrong direction. I was squinting, vision blurry. I remember stopping at Pho Pasteur – "Hello, mister, how are you doing, haven't seen you in a long time, chicken soup is very good today as usual, small two spring rolls, one iced tea, that's what you like, right? Please sit here or you can sit where you like!"

I reached into my pocket. . . . No pills. I'd changed my pants and left the little silver box at home. It happens now and then, when I am distracted. The thought of seeing Carter had been a distraction. Which in itself ought to have been a clue – distraction is as good a sign as any that I need to remember to bring my pills. And now I had none.

My eyes were blurry, tearful: flat rue.

The smell of soup hit my nose – salty, oily, almost rancid. There were, I knew, two large cauldrons in the kitchen, spring onions floating like seaweed in the broth: throb.

I leaned on the counter to keep from falling down.

"Mister. Why don't you sit down? What's the matter? You're not well? Can I get you something?"

I drank a glass of water and walked out and hailed a taxi. In the balky traffic, I sat back. My hearing returned. Acutely. Car horns hard as hammers. The raw scrape of my breath. The smell of gas and diesel fumes, stale tobacco, the stench of the sewers. I closed my eyes: Moore's woman, on her side, draped in folds of stone; the scent of Claire; barrels bulging with dried sea creatures; a table of bok choy; a boy with a shitty bare bottom. Gulls in the air, as indolent as fish.

11:30 p.m. I took a bottle of mineral water from the fridge. The hiss of the unscrewed cap – *frizzante* – a word that ought to be part of the lexicon of musical notation. How stupid of me not to have pills on my person: or pens.

I have pills in the kitchen cupboard; I have them in the drawer of the night table; in a glass ashtray in the piano room; in bottles in the medicine chest in the bathroom; and in a mortar on the shelf near my stereo. I ought to sew them in the lining of my pockets.

Useless to have pills, unless you have them at hand.

A little codeine never hurt. A lot of codeine hurts less. And the prospect of careless dreams has never hurt at all. A blue jewel, and one candy-pink, and a couple of red and yellow antibiotics, for no good reason. For good measure. For sleep.

2:30 a.m. Can't sleep.

Thomas Carter: hot car master. Swifter than he looks.

There isn't a hall in the world that does not benefit from the addition of stuffed shirts; you have to count cash. The coughers enrich the coffers. As for the chords of the "Gate at Kiev" – when I close it, the Gate will remain closed until I open it again.

Note: I mistrust coincidence; nevertheless, I was just on the College car, on the way to Little Italy to lay in a store of fresh supplies – juice, coffee, apples, a sack of mints (instead of cigarettes).

As I rode along I was haunted by the sound of his disembodied voice and the intimacy of a life overheard. I had the clues to solve a mystery, but I needed batteries. No, I didn't need them, but I wanted them. I was afraid of running out of them. I work better when I am comforted by an abundance of supplies – me and my batteries, he and his pills.

I got off at Grace St., and as I walked along College I was startled by a snatch of piano, the music spilling from an open window overhead. The music was a beginner's exercise, a simple phrase from a learner's hand, the music halting and repetitive. I stood still, listening. I do not know if it is the accident of music overheard or the self-conscious optimism of the diligent learner – more likely, it's a combination of these things – but the sound of music in rehearsal never fails to stop me in my tracks. I was reminded of Dominic as a child.

Scales before school. I could hear him play as I came up the walk to knock on his door in the morning. Practise after lunch. He was so skinny I think he sometimes skipped lunch altogether in order to work on his lessons. He played after supper and before bed, he played on Saturday mornings, he played at church, and he played daily during the summer holidays, especially in the morning when the air was cool.

He stopped playing baseball. He began to spend his summers away. And when he was gone there was no music in the neighbourhood. There were radios playing in backyards on Mondays when the laundry was hung on the line; there were pop songs drifting up from basement windows in the early evenings as the high school kids yearned and burned and learned; but there was no music.

He was ours. And there was an unspoken longing when he went away. You could see it on the face of the postman – a smile as he walked past Dominic's house. The memory of that sound.

The absence of his gift.

I lingered on the sidewalk for a moment before moving along. I stopped in front of Balfour Books and went in on a whim to prowl the shelves and pass the time. And I noticed, in one of the remainder bins, The Virtuoso Pianist by C.L. Hanon. It looked out of place because it is not a book. It resembles an old scribbler, soft, dog-eared, brittle. There's a signature in the top right corner, made with a sharp-nibbed fountain pen: Theresa Sturgeon, whoever she is. The date, also in ink: 1932, whenever that was.

The year of Gould's birth.

"For the acquirement of Flexibility, Strength, Independence and perfect Evenness of the Fingers as well as Suppleness of the Wrist."

I suppose today we'd say Acquisition, not Acquirement. I knew Dominic had studied the Hanon canon – there were several volumes for the piano. I cannot read music – the whole idea of notation is incomprehensible – but I came to recognize the sound *of those exercises for the third, fourth, and fifth fingers of the left hand. Dom practised them endlessly. I can still, in idle moments, whistle them. That was what I'd heard on the sidewalk.*

At the foot of the title page, in a small paragraph of fine print, the publisher touted another of its titles:

" 'The Musical Times' of August, 1931, says of 'The Modern Piano Student' by Boris Berlin and Ernest MacMillan: 'There is a wealth of excellent material provided in this well-planned and comprehensive work, all three volumes of which should prove useful to teachers of any "School." ' "

Another coincidence: Berlin plays a small role in Dom's story. He had heard a recital, years ago when he was old and Dom was new. Rather than take the prodigy as a pupil, Berlin pulled a few strings, called in a few favours, and arranged a modest scholarship. Shortly thereafter, Dominic was sent to study with Berlin's colleague, Carlo Lupo, in Siena.

Again, from the introduction:

"The study of the piano is practically universal at the present time, and good pianists are so numerous that mediocrity on this instrument is no longer tolerated, the result being that some feel it is necessary to study the piano eight or ten years before attempting to play a piece of moderate difficulty, even before amateurs.

"How few people are able to devote so many years to the study of this instrument! It often happens that for want of sufficient practice the execution is uneven or faulty; the left hand is impeded by many of the more difficult passages; the 4th and 5th fingers are almost useless, for want of special exercises, these fingers being always weaker than the others. . . ."

My own experience of the use of those fingers has nothing to do with music. Sister Marcella – we called her Moose – taught us touch-typing in high school. She would disapprove of the way I am typing now, with the first two fingers of each hand. She was Dominic's first serious piano teacher – a fact that amused him no end. She used a ruler on my knuckles when I typed badly. I learned to type, and I learned when to jerk my hands back. Every good boy deserves whacks.

Did she strike Dom?

"For many years we have been seeking to obviate this stage of things by trying to collect, in one work, special exercises which will enable the pupils to complete their pianistic studies in a much shorter time.

"To attain this object, it was necessary to solve the following problem: If the five fingers of each hand were equally developed they would be able to execute anything that has been written for the piano, and the only remaining difficulty would be that of the fingering, which could be overcome readily."

Included in The Virtuoso Pianist *– its pages, creamy as old ivory – were various exercises that, although they are music, resemble nothing so much as calisthenics. For the passing of the thumb. Trill exercises for all five fingers. The quadruple trill in thirds. Sustained octaves with the accompaniment of detached notes. The notation is thick and reminiscent, in a way, of those page-long blocks of typing exercises –*

frf juj frf juj frf juj
frf juj frf juj frf juj
frf juj frf juj frf juj

Which we chanted in unison in class – eff-are-eff-space, jay-you-jay-space – hammering the letters into our Underwood uprights – uprights! Had you heard us in passing, you would have thought we were trying to smash the keys.

I bought the booklet. And after a quick espresso, I picked up my groceries – prosciutto, pecorino, olives, oil, and sausages

from Fratelli Porco; a few soft rolls from the Portuguese bakery;
some oranges and a head of lettuce from the grocer; a package
of batteries.

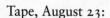

Tape, August 23:

"Hello, whaddya know?"

"Have you called Carter?"

"Claire. I'll bet you know the answer. What's your guess?"

"Will you play?"

"Wait a moment."

[He sets the phone down and walks over to the studio. The tape picks up, faintly, both the inhalation of the doorway airlock and the scrape of the bench on the floor. And then he plays – as loudly as possible – "The Catacombs." It is the thirteenth piece of the exhibition. The way he plays, it is an act of aggression. He stops playing. Scrapes the bench backwards. The door sighs shut. His footsteps rise in volume and he picks up the phone.]

"Did you hear that?"

"You'll play?"

"Not for Carter. Nor for Weller. Not for me. For you."

"Are you home?"

"Now?"

"Yes."

"Would you like some company?"

"What do you think?"

Note: This section of tape ends and the next begins sharply. There
are two possibilities: He has a sophisticated remote, and can start

*and stop a tape without being noticed – although it is unlikely he
could do this while next to her and get away with it; and highly
unlikely that she would be complicit. Or he could be dubbing
and editing. In fact, I'd bet on the latter. It's always the simplest
explanation. No sense looking for a zebra in a herd of ponies.*

Tape, August 23, cont'd:

"You look pleased with yourself."

"Seven with one blow."

"Don't be crude. Why don't you put some music on?
Something other than that Icelandic brat."

"Careful, Björk is my current favourite. I would crawl over
broken glass all winter long just to say hello to her in the spring.
Although I could probably get Madame Langelier to make
arrangements for me. That's what agents do. I've always wanted
to visit Iceland. I could record with Björk."

"You've never played with anyone else in your life."

"Not true. I play with you. Or is it you who plays with me?"

[A very long, comfortably post-coital silence, after which
Dominic begins to hum.]

"What's that?"

"This humming? Nothing, really. An impromptu for the flow
of traffic. I've become attuned to the timing of the lights and the
movement of the cars. I sometimes feel as if I can compose it on
the spot. A kind of automatic music. Auto-matic music. There
are days when I'd like to put a piano at the intersection – play in
traffic, so to speak. Amplify the hell out of – oh, well, you know,
hot town, Somers in the city. Harry Somers. You're not laughing.
What's the matter?"

"What would you do if I got sick and died. Tell me right now
– the first thing!" [pause]

"Is there something you're not – ?"

"Not fair. You're stalling. Tell me now."

Notebook, August 23:

A threat: at heart. Her mistake. I dislike illness. I equate it with weakness. If that's inconsistent, so be it. I am cruel, unfair, inconsiderate: send ice ration.

Also repelled, reflexively, by the illnesses of women: blotchy skin and runny noses, self-pity and crumpled tissues, compounded by the terrible promise that illness implies – the sourness of hospital sickrooms, wobbly trolleys of cheap blue sheets in corridors next to dirty buckets and dank mops, and – worst of all – the boredom of cleaners and housekeepers, indistinguishable from the boredom of doctors and nurses.

I stared at the birthmark on her thigh – a smudged star, blood-red, the only flaw on her otherwise perfect skin – and searched for what I hoped would be a playful response.

Not as easy as it sounds.

At first, I thought I'd give her the usual answer, if there is a usual answer: To Fran's, for a slice of lemon meringue. I'd mourn her with pie because there is something about the smell of lemon that reminds me of the taste of her. The best lies lie closest to the truth.

She tastes sour and sweet and I like sitting in Fran's, jumpy from adrenalin and codeine, with a grilled cheese sandwich, a cup of tea, and my wobbly yellow pie wedge. Un-Ravel-ing. I would mourn her in the corner booth with my back to the wall, staring at the wild man in the window. I could have said that to Claire. I could have carried it off. I might even, hypothetically, do it.

There was another possibility.

If she were to die – a stupid notion, she's in the pink – but if she did, I'd be more likely to call someone to come over. There are, after all, others. I'd ring someone and we would lie in bed a little tipsy, inhaling each other's breath and licking each other's sweat. And I would think of Claire until one ache dulled the other.

Would I do it? Not fair to, but fairness is useless in bed.

Her question was sharply toothed; no matter what I said, she was sure to find something wrong. She was, in fact, finding something wrong even as I stalled: last led, I lobbed an answer in the direction of the probable.

Tape, August 23, cont'd:

"I'd compose a requiem."

"Bastard."

Notebook, August 23, cont'd:

She swore at me; perhaps she really is ill. It was clearly not the right answer. I charged ahead before she could challenge me.

Tape, August 23, cont'd:

"Not a bastard. I knew both my parents. I admit to being a shit. But you'd like this. It would be worth dying for. 'Requiem for the Woman with the Star on Her Knee.' In C minor, C for Claire. I'd begin with your forehead, musically speaking, and work my way down and up again – lingering here and there – especially there. 'Dirty Pictures at an Exhibition.' I'd end with a portrait of you with your eyes raised and your arms spread – cross Claire on the cross. Why do you ask? You don't look ill to me. Come on now, don't be like that."

Notebook, August 23, cont'd:

She refused to say if something was wrong. If there is something wrong – Weller knows and I do not.

A flash of jealousy –

How unlike me.

Note: I took a chance and called Claire. Would she consent to one or two questions about Dominic?

She agreed to meet me at the bar in the Four Seasons. Made me wait three-quarters of an hour, then swept in wearing a short, tight navy blue suit and a matching hat pierced with a small white feather.

Claire Weller is tall and thin, with wide hips and plain features. She is not classically beautiful, but she has poise and presence. She is a woman capable of command.

She sat on the edge of her seat, her spine straight, her long legs crossed at the ankles. She pulled off her gloves and waited for me to begin. Before I could say a word the waitress, unbidden, set a martini in front of her and disappeared with a wordless smile.

I asked if there had been anything between her and Dominic prior to the recital that might have – that's as far as I got. She cut me off.

"You're writing gossip now? I'd have thought that was beneath you."

"I'm working on a piece about him, not about you and him. It's nearly a year since he's been gone. I don't think your private life has any bearing on what I'm doing, if that's what you're worried about. I have no wish to cause you any discomfort. But I need to know."

"I'm not worried about anything. You're wasting your time. It's really, as you say, none of your business."

"Let me try this another way. Have you heard from him? Recently, I mean. Or is that also none of my business?"

She reached in her handbag for a pack of cigarettes. A young woman in a cocktail dress began to play the bar piano. "Smoke Gets in Your Eyes." Claire drew a cigarette from the package. She didn't bother to light it. I noticed her hands: well-proportioned, the fingers long and slender, her nails lacquered with clear polish. I thought of her, drying the wineglasses in Dom's kitchen.

I lit her cigarette.

"What's this about, really?"

"No one has heard a word from him since the night of the recital. Or at least no one is admitting to having heard. Some people think he may have harmed himself. There's no evidence to suggest it. But that's the trouble. There's no evidence of any kind. It takes work to stay hidden. It requires the help of others. I prefer to think that's what he's doing. Staying out of sight. But I don't know where. Or why. No one does."

She plucked the olive from her martini, shook off a drop of gin, put the olive in her mouth, dabbed her lips with a handkerchief. She made mouth-sounds greedily, unselfconsciously. I knew more about her than she could possibly know. I had heard her eating barbecued duck. I had heard her in bed with my friend.

The piano segued into "All of Me."

It took me a verse and chorus to get it. Olive, me.

She said, "I don't know any more than you do. As you are aware – and you must be, if you're such a good friend as you say – he'd been having increasing trouble with his migraines. He was adjusting his medication. I think he wasn't feeling well. Perhaps it has to do with that."

"And you think it had nothing to do with – ?"

I let it hang. A useful tactic on occasion – to draw a blank and let the other rush to fill it in.

"I don't know why I'm talking to you. It's none of your business. I did not attend the recital that evening. As I think I told you when you phoned me."

"I don't quite remember, what was –"

"Perhaps he would have preferred it if I'd been there. If I had been, he might not have – oh, this is ridiculous. I was not there. Who knows what he might or might not have done."

I couldn't get any more out of her. She left without finishing her drink. She is a woman with places to go; she is not one to linger.

At home, later: I hear a man and woman in the hall, their voices low and hard and certain. Are they the same couple I heard the other night?

I've tried, and set aside, the tapes. I don't have the ear for it tonight. If there is an answer, it is not here, not now, not yet. I am oversensitive to sound. I hear the clock. My breath. The drip from the tap in the kitchen. The knocking of the water in the radiator. The wry squeak of the floorboards. The noise of others.

～

Notebook, August 24:

A full day in front of the piano, and this thought occurs:

Once, near the end of my stay in Siena, Lupo said I needed a week away from my studies. He gave me a fat envelope filled with money, handed me a train ticket, and sent me to Barcelona.

I think he wanted me out of town during the Palio, so he could rent my room for a fortune to some tourist.

At the station, he embraced me and kissed me roughly on both cheeks, gave me a fistful of gnarled black Toscas to smoke on the way, said I ought to drink a lot of Spanish wine and look at the Gaudi cathedral while I was there because, even though it was unfinished – perhaps because it was unfinished – there were lessons to be learned from Gaudi about structure. I should, he said, be careful. We would talk, he said, when I returned: run, deter.

And so I went off on my own.

I spent the first evening in Barcelona in a nearly empty hotel, too frightened to go anywhere. I spent my second evening walking along the Ramblas, sitting happily in the bars, pointing at the trays of tapas and drinking beer. Italian is not dissimilar to Spanish. I knew enough say *un poco mas, por favor – almendras, mandorlas* – more shrimp, more olives, more of those oily little fish.

By the end of the evening I was not quite drunk, but I was not sober either. I remember leaving a bar and being startled by a row of televisions in a shop window. The screens held blinking images of Ronald Reagan. I decided – those were the days – that the best thing I could do would be to return to the bars and see if I could find some hash. I got drunker, bolder, wandered from bar to bar, searching for someone who might have dope to sell.

I shudder now to think of it. Those were the times.

He wore a suit the colour of the ceiling in an Italian cathedral; the pants skin tight; a white porkpie hat with a red band on his head. He was black, almost purple; there was a scar and a sneer on his lip. He kept his jacket buttoned and his hands in the side pockets; a dandy. He scanned the bar.

I figured a hipster would speak English.

I walked over, put a tipsy hand on his shoulder, stared him in the eye, and asked if he had any hash. "Man, are you crazy? Get the fuck away from me!" Under his breath: "You talk like that, you'll get us both arrested. You want dope? Shut up, be cool, wait here. Give me two minutes, then come out. Turn left. You will see me at the corner; follow at a distance. Not too close, you hear?"

I was disoriented as soon as we turned the first corner. He kept half a block ahead of me, looking back, turning corners, gesturing at me to keep my distance. I was about to give up the chase when I turned one last corner and bumped into him.

"Wait here."

He entered an apartment building and returned a few minutes later.

"Let's go."

When I caught up with him and he was certain we weren't being followed, he handed me a small foil square, the size and shape of a bouillon cube. I peeled it open, sniffed it deeply.

"The fuck, man, you don't trust me? You talk about dope in front of strangers, you don't know who's police and who is not police, you put me in fucking jeopardy, and now you don't trust me?" I was dizzy drunk. He had a point.

"How much?"

"Not now. You follow me. We'll go someplace a bit more safe. We'll sit and have a drink like friends."

The little square was in my pocket now and I was lost: wits also. Eventually, we stopped at a dance club in which no one was dancing. He led me to a table of his friends. He ordered drinks. I paid. He told me the hash was fifty bucks American. I looked at him as if to say I thought that was steep; he looked at me as if to say I could take it or leave it. I didn't have the nerve to haggle.

I paid him, downed my cerveza, and stood. "Where you

going, man? You just got here. Who do you know in this town? You got another friend besides me?"

The others at the table watched quietly.

It occurred to me – a little late – that they'd seen how much money I had in my pocket. And I was in over my head. I said, "No, man, really, that's okay, I have to go, I've got to get up early."

Or something equally lame. Not tonight I have a headache.

I found myself on the curb in the cool darkness, amid the tall stone buildings, with no idea where I was or how to get back to the hotel. There were no cars. And no people, save the four men who were now standing in the doorway of the bar, each of them looking anywhere else but at me. My so-called friend nowhere in sight.

I thought I saw the glint of a knife from a jacket pocket. And I heard a car at the end of the street. A cab. I was safe until it passed, but it was speeding, the roof light was off, the driver had no plans to stop. Could I stop it? And if I couldn't . . .

It's better to be hit by a cab on a dark street than it is to have your throat cut in an alley. I waved both hands high and leapt onto the pavement. The driver braked a foot in front of me. I don't know what he said to me when I hopped in, but it might as well have been: "Dat a nice jump you got, too." Because I jump at least as well as old Birney.

The driver took me back to my hotel. I tipped him as much as I'd paid for the dope, and decided not to go to my room. No use sleeping. I was too tired to sleep.

Near the hotel, down by the water's edge, was a column on top of which stood Christopher Columbus staring at the sea, one hand pointing vaguely towards Reagan and America.

I sat on a bench beneath the palms and watched the ships come in and the sun rise across the water.

I was eighteen, a boy pianist on the edge of a career.

On my way to the Gaudi cathedral, I passed a row of shops. In front of a shoe store – "Spa-neesh boots of Spa-neesh leath-errr!" – an old woman, big-hipped and gap-toothed, knelt scrubbing the cobbles with a soapy brush. Next to her, a haughty girl was cleaning the windows, pouting and checking her make-up in the glass.

I can still see her breasts, the way she raised her arm to wipe the window dry. The old woman saw me stare, caught my eye, held a finger to her lips, dipped her scrub brush in the bucket. With thumb and forefinger, she slowly raised the back of the young woman's dress and – careful, now – she flicked cold soapy water upwards.

Miss Catalonia shrieked and jumped up.

She was about to wipe between her thighs when she saw me staring, smiling. She blushed, glared at the old woman, and as the washwater trickled down her legs, she swore.

Claire swore the same way.

———

Tape, August 26:

"Look, I'm sorry I hung up."

"I hope it doesn't. I hope you don't think –"

"I don't know what to think. I wish there was something I could do."

"You can play well."

[A longish pause, followed by his humming of thirteen single notes, the opening of *Pictures at an Exhibition*. Oddly, I can't tell if the voice is his or hers. Another pause.]

"I'll call."

Note: And I called Margie Warriner and asked her to check the reference – "Dat a nice jump you got, too." Was it Birney, Earle? A left-field question. M. seemed puzzled. "Do you mind telling me what this is about? If I didn't know better, I'd say you were taking advantage of me."

"I'm not sure I know what I'm doing. At least, not yet. I just need a little help putting answers to strange questions. As for knowing better, there was a time when you didn't mind if I took advantage of you."

"Wise guy. Wait a minute, I'll call you back."

It took her ten minutes to track it down.

It is the last line of a poem, "Meeting of Strangers." Earle Birney, on the verge of a mugging in Port-of-Spain, saves himself by jumping in front of a taxi. As Dom had done in Spain.

So: In addition to all his other gifts he remembers everything he ever read, and can cite what he needs, whenever he wants to. And I am not much wiser; never mind, at least I am amused. As was Margie.

Note: There is a month-long jump in the tapes. At first I was puzzled. But now I have decided, instead, to be relieved since, if this were a daily account, it would take me years to finish. I presume he's sent what he wants me to see – what he wants me to hear. Did he go on vacation? Was he at one of the summer music camps? It's too soon to tell if this matters, or how much it matters. And so I press on. Literally. I press "On."

Notebook, September 29:

And so, the preliminaries: ripe liars mine the beginnings of this undertaking. Carter is a smooth man with excellent manners; smooth men with excellent manners serve a purpose (often their own, but let it pass). He gets what he wants. He has me. A good choice on his part.

He gives me what I want. A good decision on his part.

The matter at hand: Offered a choice between a bad and a mediocre piano, it is my policy to prefer the bad one – it is much harder to blame the pianist for the result. In any case, however, you do what you can with what you are given. But a lousy hall always makes lousy music.

I remain uneasy in Carter's presence. I can't shake the feeling that he would hang me from a hook on one of his walls if he could. I suspect that he will spin our first conversation – and the circumstances of its ending – into an anecdote that he will dust off, reframe, and rehang with every telling.

But I owe an obligation to Hartmann. Rather, to the Hartmanns.

Tape, September 29:

[The brisk dry-rubbing of palms, a triplet of cracked knuckles, a cough, the scrape and rescrape of a chair on the floor, a sniff, a cough, an audible swallow, a double-clearing of the throat, a pause, and then a cascade of dense scales and warmup exercises, a waterfall of music up and down the keyboard. After which a sigh, the shifting of the chair, a repetition of the knuckle-cracking, the palm-rubbing, the throat-clearing, and the pause, and then the same brisk exercises in the same order, the same cascade of water.]

Note: I *would not have fast-forwarded through this, not for all the money in the world. There is something compelling in the way he plays, even if he isn't doing anything more than getting familiar with the pianos.*

I have no idea which instrument he played first. I can't tell them apart. They sound fine, and very much the same, to me. He reminds me of a race driver during a practice lap – now and then he propels his instrument as if it were a high-performance car catapulting out of a turn – you can almost feel the gravitational force of the music.

And then he changes his approach. It's not just that he downshifts. He changes sports. He becomes a fighter in the early rounds – he feints and steps back, dips a shoulder, seeming to jab at the score as if he were feeling it out. Presumably he is searching for nuances in action, subtle differences in touch, in tone, in pedal, and so on. As if I can tell what he's doing.

For no reason other than curiosity, I ran a stopwatch over both sets of exercises. The first he played in fourteen minutes, twenty-two seconds. The repeat on the second piano, fourteen minutes, twenty-three seconds.

Tape, September 29, cont'd:

"Excuse me, I couldn't help hearing, I was drawn by the . . . I'm sorry, I don't mean to . . . may I introduce myself?"

"You may. You are?"

"I heard the music, and I thought – I hope we weren't making too much noise. I just wanted to let you know we're almost done for the night. I don't mean to interrupt. I was hanging a show down the hall. Photographs, mine. A show down the hall. I'm Carol Paterson."

"And I am Dominic Amoruso. I play the piano. I suppose that's obvious. Here are two pianos, and here I am at one of them. In any case, you stopped what you were doing, so perhaps I was disturbing you."

"Oh, goodness, not at all, I was –"

"You were hammering nails, and I was hammering keys. You are the one who took the photographs in Carter's office."

"You've seen them? Isn't he a strange little man? He said he wanted to live with them a while before they were hung. I suppose I should be flattered. But the way he said it, he made it sound a bit *droit de seigneur*. If you ask me."

Note: The circle gets smaller.

I know Carol Paterson. She won the National Newspaper Award for feature photography a couple of years ago, for a series of photos documenting the work of a public health nurse on the streets of Toronto.

She is nervy, smart, not unattractive, in her thirties, still single – and there are the usual rumours about why that might be so. Rumours spread by the hacks she wouldn't sleep with.

She took the photos for a piece I wrote last year – a brief essay about the last of the little neighbourhood barber shops. She is clever, professional, and has a point of view. Funny to hear her voice on tape. As if she were in the room with me.

I almost said hello.

Tape, September 29, cont'd:

"Are you interested in music – I'm sorry, is it Paterson?"

"Yes. Carol, please. I'm interested the way everyone else is, I suppose. I mean, I like to have music when I'm – um, having people for dinner. Or if I'm working in the darkroom. I like to listen then. Not always to classical music. But I have your CD. One of them. *Pictures at an Exhibition.* Well, who doesn't in this town? It's only brilliant."

"I hope this doesn't sound immodest, but it is. I had one of those – you must have them – days when everything works for the good. I couldn't put a finger wrong. It's rare when that happens, given the number of things that can go wrong. The same in your business, I suppose."

"In fact –"

"Let me ask you a question. When I see a photograph I try to imagine what sound is present at the moment the photo was taken. A habit of mine – sound: intended, accidental, overheard. A way to flesh out the narrative. Photos are narrative, are they not? In any case, it's a habit. Do you hear what you see? Or do you see what you hear?"

"Most times, when I'm taking a picture, I don't hear a thing."

"Nothing at all?"

"I'm deaf when I work. After the click of the shutter – I always hear the shutter, it's the period at the end of a sentence – that's when the sound floods in."

"I may drop by for a look when I've finished. Will you be around? You can tell me more about that old man at the piano."

"I'd love to but I actually have an engagement. An assignment. I have to. I'm late. Let me just. My card. And my home number. The piano player. He's a good story. Feel free to call. I'll tell you what I can."

Note: There is a lightness, an anticipation in her voice.

I'm not jealous. Not true. I am. It took him all of a minute to get her phone number. Whereas I have worked with her. I saw her a few days after Dom disappeared. I took the time to

*see her show. We spoke once or twice after that. And I never got
her number. Of course I never really came right out and asked.
She was probably unaware I was interested.*

Notebook, September 29, cont'd:

Alertness, the best sign of intelligence.

There are many kinds of intelligence. Paterson, Carol. Red
hair in bangs, torn camouflage T-shirt. Tan freckles on her shoulders, bracelets and tattoos on her upper arms, and combat boots.
There is a barbed-wire tattoo circling her right wrist. On her it
looks, etc.

The thing about a tattoo: What will it look like when your
skin is no longer plump and supple?

If you set aside, for a moment, the subject matter of her photos
– men in rags, women with shopping bags, the usual scenes of
home- and hope-lessness – I'd say she aims right between the eyes.

As for the photo in Carter's office, I have a hunch he hung it
for my benefit: my fine bet. A black man at a Heintzman.

There is something more than familiar about him. The way
his fingers are arched, his hands half-hidden in a cloud of cigarette smoke, his eyes closed and his mouth open, his head bent
low, almost touching the keys. The ribbon of smoke rising airily,
as if from one ear – earily, eerily, a metaphor for the listener. I
will call her. I have to know. And I will use the Steinway.

Not a peach but not a lemon – Lupo. The action is fluid, the
tone is adequate, the touch is pleasing. It reminds me of the one
in Berlin. In the Kleiner Sendesaal. My first serious performance
after the Tchaikovsky. The Germans loved my leather jacket but
they loved my Schubert more.

This one has a fat down-weight – it gives me a bit of room
on the soft side – is surprisingly light at the back of the keys. It

will serve my purpose well enough. It's better than the Yamaha, and it is of course a brand name; old money likes brand names. I have a hunch Carter doesn't give a damn which one I use.

In any case, there's no point bothering to move mine into Walker Court. WC: apt, it is a bathroom, acoustically speaking.

Pho Tau Bay on the way home. Useful to spread one's custom. I made idle conversation with the owner. She is one of those women who looked thirty when she was fifteen and will look thirty-five when she is sixty. I have no idea how old she really is but she is always made up smartly in the high Viet style: full wet red lips; eyebrows thinly pencilled and finely arched; long white nails; a shiny blue dress with a cadet – or is it cadre? – collar. Spiky satin-blue heels, fat red toenails; her hair, a lacquered beehive. She might as well be wrapped in plastic and tied with ribbon and given to the man who hit the bull's-eye.

She has no idea what I do for a living. So much the better. We talked movies; I am not sure who raised the subject or why, but I asked her if she'd seen *Titanic*. She made a face.

"I was a boat person, mister. We left Vietnam. The boat was full. We had a storm three days in a row. Many people fell into the water. Friends of mine, they died. I could see them in the water. They hold on to the side of the boat until they can't hold on any longer. And they get tired and let go. Just like that, gone. Why do I want to look at another ship with a lot of people drowning?"

Note: This is becoming an exercise in faith.

I have to trust that I have been sent as many pieces of the puzzle as I require to fit it together. But I can't see the picture, not yet.

I am a blind puzzler, the pieces in my hand. . . .

Notebook, September 30:

There was no need for me to go to the gallery this evening –
I don't need to practise any more – but I like the feel of the place
at night. And I don't mind playing for the amusement of the
paintings.

I went on the prowl after I'd put in an hour. Thought I'd look
at the Group of Seven by myself. Set off an alarm. My minder –
I have a minder – minded that.

He is a Bulgarian with a degree in art history and a delightful
manner of speaking: "Excuse me, sir, but you must not without
permission freely wander. There are, as you have just found out,
alarms. Do not be alarmed. I am at your service. I can help you to
go where you like. You only have to say."

He added that many people in Sofia are familiar with my
playing; it was his opinion that my *Pictures* was a superior recording to that of Richter's. The clever delicacy of that phrasing – not
that my playing was better; the recording was superior.

I think he bears watching. He thinks I bear watching.

Bear with us.

He said he would tell me a story one day about the Richter
recital, if I would like it. I would like it very much. . . . He is not
to let me prowl on my own, but if I wish to go exploring, he will
take care of the alarms.

The perfect first step for an art thief – learn to play the piano.

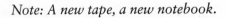

Note: A new tape, a new notebook.

Notebook, October 1:

I found Carol Paterson's card in my jacket. I took her up on her offer. Called her at home. Invited her for coffee. I sensed a hesitation – prints to develop, a new commission, she had to work on some photos of her elderly mother who is, it seems, about to die – there is nothing to be done, she is in her eighties and her health is not very good, the end is both longed for and inevitable.

But she agreed to meet me in a coffee shop near her studio.

She asked for a glass of water. Her eyes are alert as an animal's. I ordered an espresso.

Tape, October 1:

[The rattle, hiss, and hum of a coffee shop interior:]

"She looks like she's on the verge of saying something."

"Christmas Mary. They call her that because of the way she dresses. Red lips, green earrings. Her turban is red and green, almost lizardly. I mean iridescent. If Santa Claus were a cross between a gypsy and an iguana, she'd be his wife. Don't let her smile fool you. As I was taking this shot, she was telling me to stuff my camera somewhere quite uncomfortable."

"Charming. Why do you shoot in black and white?"

"Colour doesn't interest me as much as composition."

"A simple answer. It must take nerve. I mean, to point the lens. It's an aggressive act. You point. You shoot. Like a gun."

"There is aggression, and there is complicity. Most people understand. I try not to be rude. If I think there might be trouble,

I ask permission. It's all in the way you present yourself. If I sense there might be a problem, I usually start a conversation. Or I shoot anyway, and then I offer to send a copy of the photo. People are generous, for the most part. I get turned down, sometimes. People tell me to fuck off. It helps that I'm a woman. Most people think twice before telling a woman to fuck off. I wouldn't say it was hard, what I do. I don't know if I could do what you do. Play in public. That's hard."

"Do you play?"

"Lessons as a child. I stopped when I got my first camera."

"What I do does take nerve. But you learn to trust the equation. No one else plays like me. I'm not boasting. I mean it the way I mean no one sounds like me when I speak. I trust that the audience has come to hear me and not some other player. When I play, you hear it as I play it on that occasion. There is the salt of immediacy. That, at least, is the hope. You must make the same assumption – that people want to see what you have seen. Otherwise, why do it? The photo Carter had on his wall. The piano player. You said there was a story."

"I was walking past the Scott Mission one afternoon. Last summer. July. On my way somewhere, it doesn't matter. I had my camera. I always do. The doors were open. As I passed by I heard the most . . . Piano is not the first thing you expect from a shelter. I kept going. I took four steps, stopped cold, and walked back. Stuck my nose in the door. I don't remember what he was playing. It was abstract; a bit like Keith Jarrett, not classical but not exactly jazz. I thought I should check it out. No one paid me any mind. I think crazy people just assume everyone is crazy, or else powerful in some normal kind of way. So they keep their distance. Until they know what, or who, they're dealing with. I tried to appear harmless. I shot this with available light. I didn't want to spook him. I have an old Leica, it has a quiet release. I thought about asking but you never know about some of these men. Their meds, or if they're drinking. It was clear he'd been trained to play. He wasn't paying any attention to anything. See the way his head is bent –"

Note: I saw Carol's show just before it came down. Here, I'd bet they are discussing the photo of an old man hunched over at an upright piano, the shot from a low angle. A ribbon of smoke seems to rise from the old man's ear. There is no ashtray visible on the keybed. The cigarette is probably parked on the edge. It is not the first or last piano with cigarette burns. The old man appears to be swooning. His head is turned to the side; he faces towards the camera, eyes closed, mouth open, toothless.

Tape, October 1, cont'd:
    "Do you know his name?
    "Maisela Singer."
    [A sharp inhalation. Dom, on the edge of interrupting, holds his breath. She continues without missing a beat.]
    "He shows up at the end of the month to pick up his pension cheque; a lot of these guys use the Mission as a mailing address. I don't know how good he is. I suspect he was good once. It's clear he's had training. He's obviously used to performing in public – when he finished, he stood and put his hand on the lid of the piano. Held himself just so. He didn't bow. Not exactly. He looked into the middle distance, half-closed his eyes and nodded once. And then he turned on his heel and walked away. I got half a dozen shots. This was the best. You really should go and listen. You could play for these old men. They certainly liked what they heard from this guy. No one applauded but you could see them pay attention. Smiled, dug each other in the ribs when

he was done. For some reason, there are three pianos. You could take your pick."

"Let me buy you another glass of water. And let me tell you a bit about Maisela Singer."

"You know him?"

"He studied with my teacher."

[A break in the tape.]

Note: Mention of Singer means a call to Margie.

I could hear her frown. "Singer, Singer. He may well have studied with Lupo, there's something familiar about the name, but if he didn't have a career. . . . Not everyone who studies at that level goes on to fame and glory, you know. Is there anything else to go on? Shall I abandon all my duties to do your bidding, buddy boy?" If you would be so kind. . . .

I am not optimistic.

Notebook, October 1, cont'd:

I don't think he'd remember.

She thought it a coincidence.

If Lupo were still alive. . . .

She left abruptly – work to do – develop the photos of her mother, start a new commission. A complete lack of sentiment. I like that in a woman. She mentioned supper some night, somewhere. We'll see.

Her photos have force and subtlety. She uses opposites, constructs a spectrum using shades of grey. A gaunt Christ caught taking a smoke break during the Good Friday parade – his crown of thorns, the driblets of blood on his cheek, the cigarette dangling from his lips. The expression on his face: "Please don't.

Please don't take my photo while I'm smoking. Please don't nail me to this cross. Please get this over quickly."

Before she left I asked what she looked at when she was not shooting; she said she was always shooting, went nowhere without her camera, and lobbed the question back to me: To what do I listen when I am not playing? Not an easy question.

I couldn't tell her that I lately seem to have lost the sense of colour in what I hear. That I am spending more and more time listening to other sounds than music. In other sounds, some colour still remains.

I told her of The Idea of Here: A neighbour's window, winching open, is the colour of beach sand. Footsteps on the sidewalk are soft black beats, not unlike notation. Morning and evening traffic: an orange haze shot through with streaks of white, of blue, of red. The rattle of construction, the hum of commerce, the whistle of the birds in the trees in the park in the morning: yellow, silver, green. I did not say I hear, therefore I see.

But if I do not see . . . I therefore am not.

Music is a clipped hedge on the grounds of an asylum. It provides a refuge: It is an ordered, bordered beauty. And I am a gardener. I work according to the rhythm of my shears. As I clip, I hear the howls of the inmates.

They hear the crying of the leaves.

Note: *They hear the crying of the leaves.*

If this were a book, you'd mark that passage and dog-ear the page. He went home and sat in his studio and listened to a tape of what he'd played at the AGO. He did not tape himself listening to the tape – thank god, or I'd never be done – but he did play and record the same exercises on his own piano.

He also played – I know this because I let Margie listen to it over the phone – the Scarlatti L. 430 Sonata in E Major.

Margie said, "Amoruso."

She said it like an adjective.

No dice with Singer; she continues to search.

I don't know why this strikes me now: Dom has little use for high art or pretension.

He is well-read, dresses carefully, has good manners, and so on, but he has never left the working class. One of the reasons why he wore a leather jacket and jeans when he played is that he found the tux off-putting. He said it made him feel like a class traitor and wore it only when he was obliged to do so by contract. With apologies to him, and to Gould, it's a good gimmick. I'm not sure about this colour blindness. . . . It sounds panicky.

The creation of a work of art, he once said in a radio interview, is no different from the creation of any other object. I'm not sure he was being difficult. I think he believes it to be true. I'm sure the interviewer – one of those overmodulated idiots – thought he was putting on an act. Dom cut him off. Said the secret of good performance is not a secret at all – to play well, you must apply yourself to the bench. It's not much different from typing. He added that the piano, like the typewriter, did not care if it was struck with his finger or the tip of his umbrella. The interviewer gasped.

"Hindemith," said Margie.

Once, in an interview we did together for the anniversary issue of The Canadian Pianist, *I asked Dom if he was in the least bit superstitious; if, apart from the leather jacket, he had some sort of talisman, the way certain athletes do, a pair of lucky socks.*

He snorted. He had a routine, of course. On the day of a performance, he soaked in a warm bath, ate lightly, had an early nap; an hour or two before he was to play, he stood in a cold shower, jolting himself into consciousness. But there was no talisman, and apart from the nap and the shower, he had no fixed habits. "Why complicate one routine by making it dependent on another?" He claimed, waggishly, to have Richter's lobster.

May I speak to Ms. Warriner, please?

Sviatoslav Richter: a sacred monster and a neurotic. Aren't they all, she said. For a time, he had a plastic lobster and refused to play without it parked on his piano. Richter is, for Margie, the pianist of the century.

A few details: R. disliked flying. He once asked his doctor to put him under so he could board a plane and wake up at his destination; his doctor declined. Unwilling to fly, he once drove across Russia to Japan, stopping to give more than a hundred performances on the way, almost a Canadian thing to do, come to think of it.

She had no idea if R. was any good behind the wheel. GG apparently drove like a poet – easily distracted. Dom never drove at all.

Margie could not turn up anything else about the lobster, who gave it to him or how long he kept it. Dom may have been pulling my leg. All he'd say, cryptically, was that it was given to him by someone who'd been given it by Richter. A good story, I suppose. Of course, I once heard Allen Ginsberg say in an interview that he'd been had by a guy who'd been had by Walt Whitman. I was curious. I wanted names. Dom declined to elaborate.

According to Margie, R.'s is the definitive Pictures. The one recorded in Sofia, 1958, and championed so tactfully by Dom's *minder. It is the truest to Musorgsky's score, she says. After which she favours the Horowitz at Carnegie Hall in 1951, all flash and glitter, and a fistful of splashy added notes at the end; a show-stopper. Then came Dom.*

Still nothing about Singer.

Notebook, October 1, cont'd:

Paul Valéry: Seeing is forgetting the name of the thing one sees.

Me: Hearing is forgetting that one has heard.

I played tonight until I was barely aware of playing. And then I was aware of an overwhelming thirst and the usual other ghostly friends – stiffness in the shoulder; tightness in the fingers of both hands, a tingling in the second joint of my right thumb; a sore back; and this miserable business of seeing things in black and white alone.

Can I play in black and white like the photographer? Is the structure of the composition sufficient? Am beginning to think I need a full-time therapist. Like that scrawny hothouse orchid who nourished himself in the warm wet loam of his quirks, his phobias, and his fears.

Must be careful; can't fall into traps.

I recall the rumour: GG – or was it gg? – tried to diminish the mass of his shoulder muscles with the application of sound waves.

Note: I can't resist. Margie: "You interrupt me too often. If I didn't know you better. . . . Luckily for you, it's a slow day and I find your lack of musical knowledge charming. So, I forgive you. Now, pay attention: Alberto Guerrero was Gould's most impor-tant teacher. He is supposed to have worked on the development of the young Gould's muscles by pressing down on his shoulders and having Glenn resist. Isometrics, I suppose. As for the sound waves, if it's true, it's Freudian. Talk about erasing the father figure! Gould was quite weird, but you are a complete shit. No calls for three months, and then you call me every day. What's the story with the punk pianist? Have you found him?"

"I wish you wouldn't call him that. I don't know what the story is. Not yet. Can't I just ask questions?"

"You could fill me in."

"I can't. Let's just say I'm working on a highly specialized piece about the piano. Some preliminary work. In a general way. I don't know who for yet. Think of it as work on spec."

"You know we have a piano here."

"I didn't."

"People come and play."

"Who plays?"

"Anybody who has no piano at home. People who live in apartments. We have a soundproof room. You call to make an appointment. Singer comes."

"A lot of people come?"

"Some days, yes; some days, no."

"Can anyone just come and listen?"

"Well, you can't just –"

"Wait a minute. You said Singer comes?"

"Slow on the uptake, aren't we? I don't know if he's your man, but his name is Singer, he's black, and he's ever so gently off his rocker. I never put two and two together until I noticed the appointment book today. You can come listen to him if you're nice to me. I have a headset in my office. And you should. Be nice to me. He's booked in at 4:30 this afternoon. After you've listened, you can take me out and buy me supper."

Margie pointed out the regulars: at a desk, hands clasped in front of her, a woman in her thirties with a ponytail and a book of Broadway songs; an older man with thinning hair and stubble on his cheeks, prowling the stacks with a frown; a thin, wan Asian boy wearing a blue suit, white shirt, and no tie, who favours Chopin; a plump young woman who plays once a week at her church. Margie led me into a small room in the back, furnished with a cheap metal desk, piles of newspapers, file cabinets, plastic bags, and stacks of unshelved books. I caught a glimpse of the piano room as I passed by – the walls beige, the overhead light antiseptic; not a poster, not a notice, nothing on the walls but a large clock. Empty save for a piano, a bench, and Singer.

"I'd get into trouble if anybody knew you were listening. If anybody comes in here, whip that headset off. You can say you're looking through these." She handed me some magazines and let me be.

The volume was set to max; ouch.

He was playing big fat notes by the fistful; disjointed, the most private kind of music. None of it made musical sense, although now and then he'd slip in something familiar, a chord or two flitting in front of him like a curtain at an open window. I peeked. He swayed, hovering over the keys, wagging his head from side to side like one of those toy dogs in the rear window of the car ahead of you. Oblivious to everything except what he played.

"Is he it?"

"Have you found out anything more?"

"Just that he comes in every other day. And that he's, um, reality-challenged, but he seems completely harmless. If you're

right about his studying with Lupo, then your man has shaken hands with Beethoven."

"Huh?"

"Follow the trail: Lupo studied with Artur Schnabel, who was a student of Leszetycki, who studied with Czerny, who was a student of the mighty Ludwig Van. Three or four lives overlap and there you are, hollering into an ear trumpet. But if you detect a shred of the Ninth in that little room, you have better ears than I do."

As I was leaving, Margie told me another anecdote from the Leinsdorf book – not about Gould, but about a contemporary acquaintance, the chronic concert-canceller Arturo Michelangeli.

He apparently requested two pianos for use during a recital in Zurich; on arrival at the hall, M. noted that one of the pianos had "caught a cold" in transit . . . and since the other piano was useful only for the second half of the recital, obviously there was no point in playing at all – no loaf better than half a loaf, or some such nonsense.

Leinsdorf implies that Michelangeli was threatened into fulfilling the contract to perform. Margie said she thought there was a famous conductor who once said, "Michelangeli, Gould – where do you people find these weirdos?" Did I want her to hunt the reference down?

We went for supper instead.

———— ⤛ ————

Notebook, October 4:

This is the kind of thing that happens when you are holed up: If you do not go out, it becomes increasingly harder to face going out. There are days when I have to force myself to leave the apartment. Perhaps that's why GG essayed north, or, let's say northerly.

I'd love to have heard him discussing the problems of travel arrangements with Richter. But Richter had first-hand knowledge of the size of the Soviet Union, whereas I don't think GG knew just how much North there was beyond his Idea of it.

A vagueness tonight; I felt dizzy when I stood up to close the lid of the piano – a glimmer of something, a flicker of movement – nothing I could touch, nothing I could identify. The halo of a migraine, the continuing echo of the one I thought I'd fought off a day or so ago, or have been fighting off for weeks. Obviously I am not fighting it off well enough.

From the piano to the kitchen: In the refrigerator: fire got rarer – half a bottle of – forgive me – dago red. And a couple of tins of ginger ale and the legs and wings of a Portuguese chicken. I ignored the green olives, the heel of a salami, my parmigiano, a plastic bag of rusty lettuce, the stray halves of various onions and lemons, a quart of orange juice, and three hard green apples. I love lists, the compilation of – the images and the sound of the words are the rhythms of composition. I reached for the wine.

Alcohol, happily, has a particular effect on certain of my medications. A stiff red: fired fast – I have never bothered to mention this to my doctor – gives the fiorinal a head start. Or so I have found. In addition to which, it steadies my hand and makes me warm.

I poured a tumbler, drained it, shuddered. It tasted thin and sour, past its best-before date. I poured half a glass more, because it was a shame to waste the whole thing. Without thinking, I retrieved the ginger ale, popped the tab, and topped up the wine as if that was the most natural thing in the world to do. Drank it straight off with two fiorinal and a brace of pills for the sake of the tendinitis. As if that, too, was most natural.

And then I was overcome by a great wave of unhappiness:

My late brother's christening: The house was filled with hatted aunts and flowered dresses, girdled; my big-bellied uncles in white shirts, suspendered. Uncles with sleeves rolled up, collars undone, ties loose, smelling of Old Spice, clapping each other on the back and pouring drinks. Aunts with eggplant and lasagna. The usual gaggle of scrubbed and restless cousins, ducking and scattering from room to room.

For the toast to the newborn, I was given a tumbler of red wine cut with ginger ale – a kids' drink, it made me dizzy, happy, and silly. I sat at the piano and picked out a couple of pop tunes from memory. Perry Como, Nat King Cole. My newly christened brother howled; someone laughed and said what was the point of the lessons if I couldn't get the songs right, I should quit, I was scaring the baby.

I could have played any of the songs note-perfectly if I'd had the sheet music; I almost said as much. I held my breath. My vision blurred. I was ready to burst into tears. I hadn't studied any of the music – the nuns disliked the sound of anything current. I was playing purely from memory – the memory of what I'd heard on the radio. I'd been showing off.

My mother noticed – I saw her look at me – but she kept quiet, and paid the incident no mind. My father laughed as loud as the rest of the fools. I marked it as the first betrayal. And I decided there was no point in crying.

My older brother punched me in the shoulder.

Note: I know that piano. I remember it very well. I was aware of it before I was aware of Dom. And here, I might as well record my first memory of him and it: We had just moved into an old house in the west end of Fort William. I was not quite eight years old.

The house next door was much like ours, with peeling paint, a sagging porch, and fake-brick siding, but with a large front yard and a big vegetable garden in the back. We were settling in on our first night. My parents, for once, were not squabbling; there were too many things to distract them: where to put the sofa, when to expect the man to hook up the gas stove, and so on.

The boxes with the bedding remained hidden behind other boxes. I slept lightly that first night under an old coat. I was awakened in the early hours of the morning by a noise – the acci- dental blurt of a horn, the idling of a truck, the laughter and curses of men outside my window. I looked out and saw a man – Dom's father, as I learned later; I had no idea who he was at the time – standing in the back of a half-ton truck on the front lawn, a few feet from my bedroom window. He was wearing a sleeve- less T-shirt and, with his hands on his hips and his head thrown back, he was laughing helplessly. Two other men, also amiably drunk, stood convulsed against an improbably upright piano.

"Teresa, come out here and give us a tune!"

A middle-aged woman in a nightdress and curlers stepped barefoot onto the porch. The man in the T-shirt dropped the tail- gate with a careless thunk and then opened the piano and dragged his forefinger along the keys. Even in the dim light I could see there was a crack in the wood on the side of the upright.

"Teresa, get up. Come out here and meet your new piano. I won it with a pair of treys. We'll put it in the living room. A Steinway – what do you think of that?"

I don't know what she thought of that, but I was curious. I couldn't imagine how a pair of TV trays could be worth a piano, even if the trays were new and the piano was cracked.

I peeked through the curtain again.

Mrs. Amoruso folded her fat arms over her chest. "For pete's sake, Frank, you'll wake the neighbours."

The man – Dom's father – jumped out of the truck onto the porch and planted a kiss on his wife's neck. She pushed him away with a frowning smile, and the men began to move the piano into the house.

The next day, I met Dominic on the way to school.

He was a year younger. He smiled. I smiled back. I asked him about the piano. He told me he'd slept through the noise, and woke up only after it had been shoved through the front door and pushed across the living room floor. He got out of bed when he heard his mother playing chopsticks. He said the piano didn't sound right. He did not know his mother could play.

Dom and I became friends. It was only natural: We were more or less the same age, we lived next door, we walked to school together every day, and even though I was a year older, we were in the same grade. He'd skipped a year.

Now and then, he'd invite me to supper. I went happily. His mother was a bad cook; mine was worse.

The Steinway had pride of place in their living room. Its long flat top held his mother's houseplants on their plates, her fancy lamp, and her porcelain figurines.

The side with the crack had been butted up against a wall. Now and then she would sit down and play stiff old tunes from memory. The look on her face revealed a kind of shyness; lost time.

On occasion, if the cover happened to have been left open, one of the Amoruso cats – there were three – would stroll up and down the keyboard. One night, Dom's father awoke convinced

*the cat had somehow taught itself to play. Or that someone had
left the radio in the kitchen on. He got up to look.*

*There was Dominic, sitting in his pyjama bottoms at the
piano bench, carefully playing the skeleton of a tune, pinning it
down one note at a time. What happened next: He recalled the
dialogue as if it were a lesson from the catechism:*

"Who taught you how to play?"

"No one taught me how to play."

"How the hell did you learn?"

"I didn't learn. I'm playing what I hear."

"Where did you hear that?"

"In church."

*He was playing a boilerplate Catholic arrangement of "Agnus
Dei." He could not explain why the Lamb of God who taketh
away the sins of the world would bother to lead him to a piano
in the middle of the night. All he said – this, years later – was
that, while sleepwalking, he found himself in front of the piano
in the living room in the darkness; the melody in his head was
also somehow in his hands; without thinking, he sat at the keyboard and retrieved the music from his fingers.*

Notebook, October 4, cont'd:

The park is dark; there are no drug deals going down tonight,
at least none that I can see. The lights of downtown blink in the
distance. The crowns of the trees are dark green, almost black
beside the pale green neon of Fran's.

On the radio, Prokofiev. I have no idea who is playing. The
Sonata no. 7. My money is on Richter. I can see the score with my
eyes closed.

The score, mind. Not the colour of the notes.

I know how many bars remain before it will end. I can count the measures until the announcer will open his microphone and drool over the music and the performance, as if he heard things more purely and felt them more keenly than anyone, including his listeners. As if anyone who listened to Prokofiev needed to be told.

If a listener needs to be told, it is useless to tell him.

I can play it, I can't see it.

Memory; bubbles rising in a glass.

Not long after my father won the piano and the cat walked across the keys and I discovered that I knew how to find a tune, my parents were curious to know if the nuns would take me as a student.

My father phoned the orphanage one night before supper and was told to bring me around. He was cocky walking down the block. As if to say, This is my boy; because of me and my bad habits, I discovered that he has a gift. I may have wasted a lot of nights drinking at the card table and you may think ill of me, but by God it's been worth it just for this. I have wasted all my chances just to give him his.

On the steps of the orphanage, his confidence wavered. The strut went out of him. He was in a fix. Because – and this is in retrospect; he's dead and I can no longer ask him – I think it occurred to him that, once we got inside, he'd have to beg. He knew how to bluff, but he didn't know how to beg.

The housekeeper admitted us, looked us up and down – I have ever since despised the haughtiness of the servile – and told us to wait on the bench in the corridor.

In the half-dark, my father took off his hat. It was early evening, just after supper in the summer. The sky was blue and the tops of the trees were still full of light, but night had fallen early in the orphanage; every door was closed, the halls were dark, every window was shuttered.

The smell of cheap soap and boiled vegetables.

Thirty children lived there, more or less. You'd never have known there were any. There were no broken toys on the floor, no sweaters hung on doorknobs, no books piled on the window ledges; there was no cat's dish in the corner, no radio on a side table, no laughter from behind any door. There was darkness and there was silence.

Most of the children were not orphans. The majority were Ojibwa children sent from the reserves north of town because they were bright, or at least bright enough to have futures if they could be protected from drink or drugs or the fumes of glue or gasoline; and so they were cast out of their families and sent off to be educated, not for their own good but for the good of their reserves.

Some of the children, white and native, really were orphans. Their lives had been turned to ash by house fires, the gay carelessness of drunk drivers, the random appetites of the various cancers, or by – don't say it – suicide; their relatives, if they had relatives, would not or could not take them in. These were children whose futures had been snatched away.

We avoided them, we pitied and we shunned them.

A couple of the real orphans were in my class. They kept their heads down most of the time, and advertised who they were by the poverty of their clothes, which were patched and pressed and spotless, handed down and down again inside the orphanage. They were also marked by the uniformity of their hair: shaved heads for the boys, plain braids for the girls. And if they misbehaved, they were punished doubly; they had to live with the disapproval of the nuns at home, as well as the nuns in class. No one sought their friendship. Asked them questions. Invited them to play. As if the death of parents were a communicable disease.

The housekeeper returned and showed my father and me into an unmarked office. I can still see it when I close my eyes: an obligatory crucifix on the wall, the cross made of cheap wood dyed and varnished to look hard as mahogany.

The skinny Christ had been cast in some soft metal. There were tears of painted blood on his brow, dripping from the crown of thorns, trickling from the nails driven into the palms of his hands, and leaking from the wound in his side; there was blood oozing from his feet like so many tiny rubies.

A flesh-and-blood Mother Superior in her black robes was seated at the desk. Her wimple was white as the ledger in front of her and her habit, darkness personified. She capped her fountain pen and clasped her hands.

"So," she said, "this is the young man who wants to play the piano."

I nearly bolted. The way she said it made it seem as if wanting anything was a sin. The truth was, I knew I could play. I could breathe, I could run, I could hear, I could see, I could taste my food, I could drink water in the summer from the garden hose, I could pitch a rock and hit a post. And I could play. I was unsure of what might happen if this nun got her hands on the thing that allowed me not just to hear music, but to retrieve it from the keys of the old upright.

There was a discussion of money. Not much of a discussion. We had none and she knew it. Lessons were cheap but five dollars a week was more than my father could afford. I was surprised to hear him plead.

"Sister, he has a gift." Surprising because my father did not believe in God or gifts – in addition to which he either ignored or despised the clergy, according to his mood. It suited him to do so. He rarely went to Mass, except for funerals. Early mornings interfered with his late-night poker games. But when he was bound by the holy days of obligation or the weight of my mother's disapproval, he eased his discomfort by cursing the priests *sotto voce* on the steps of the church after Mass. His whispered views could not have been more widely known if he had shouted them out loud. The nun said, "We'll see who has a gift."

She removed her glasses, pinched her nostrils and considered. "I understand you are a gambling man." My father was startled. She was turning the tables. He was not going to beg. She was going to gamble.

She offered him a deal: If I showed any promise at all, she would accept a token payment for lessons, whatever we could afford. In return for which I would be required to attend the priest at morning Mass during the week. My father weighed the matter as he pinched the crown of his hat – it would be hard to walk away from a bet that wouldn't cost him anything; I was a small stack of chips. She had him, she had me, and he knew it.

My father never said a word; he nodded and he smiled and they shook hands. She stood and rang the little bell on her desk. Wordless, another nun appeared. "Sister Marcella, take this young man upstairs and lead him through some simple exercises. Find out for me if he can do what his father says he can."

I followed her up the wide steps to the second floor of the orphanage. As we climbed the stairs, I caught a glimpse of her ankles beneath the hem of her black habit – under the dark stockings, her skin was pale as milk. I thought of the way my father tied strings around the lettuce in the garden furrows so that, hidden from the sun, the leaves grew pale white instead of red.

I followed her heavy foot, the dark swish of her skirts, and the ticking black beads that dangled from her waist. She paused before the only open door in the hallway, waiting for me to catch up. I hesitated. She hurried me into a small white room. It contained nothing but a bench and a dull black piano with the fallboard down.

"Open it," she said. Here was an instrument pure and plain, the keys white and unchipped, the body polished and the lid unmarked by cigarette butts or the ghosts of stains left by empty liquor glasses. Any sound it made would be clean and pure and clear. "Sit here."

I hoisted myself onto the stool. The height was unfamiliar and I nearly slid off. She took me by the shoulder and spun me around, soundless and perfect, until I was at the right height. Dizzy, but at the right height. She placed a beginner's book on the music stand and squared my shoulders sharply with her hands.

Her breath smelled like chalk. I looked at the book. It was the same one I had at home, tucked in the well of the piano bench. "Mary Had a Little Lamb," and so on. I bent my head and leaned forward to hear the notes. That was how I played. With my ear near the keyboard. I was about to play when she grabbed my hair and pulled hard. "Not like that, sunny Jim. You sit up straight. You will never learn to play the piano properly if you cannot learn to sit up." She pinned my shoulders back. Took my arms, positioned my elbows and showed me how to hold my hands. "As if you were palming an orange!"

I had never palmed an orange. She showed me how to break my wrists a fraction so that my fingers curled slightly over the keys. A small Christ stared down at me; the metronome began to tick. I did not move. The distance was unfamiliar. How was I supposed to show how well I could play if I had to sit like this? I waggled my fingers and moved my elbows, my feet dangled. I felt like a small bird, heart beating, unable to escape the net.

"Now."

I played. She seemed surprised.

"Who taught you to read music, young man?"

"I taught myself."

"We'll see."

She instructed me to begin again. It was almost too easy. I began to play in double time, to get it over with, to show her what I could do when I really let loose. She cracked my knuckles with a pointer.

"You said you could read music. Play it as it is written."

When the lesson was over – I played three little songs, and she showed me another, I forget what it was – I felt a kind of despair, because it was so unfamiliar. Suppose I couldn't play? Suppose I was nothing more than a mimic? She led me, word-less, from the little room. I followed her into the hall and down the corridor.

As we neared the stairs, a door opened slightly. From behind it peeked a girl, my age; she had dark hair and skin that, no matter how hard she scrubbed it, would always be copper-coloured. She looked at me, and opened her mouth as if to whisper something. Before she could say anything, I blurted, "I don't have to be here!"

I meant there had been no tragedy, I meant my parents had not died. But she heard something else. She heard that I was somehow better than her, that I did not have to be there, but she did. And she was stung. She ducked behind the door and pulled it softly closed.

The nun, who had not seen the exchange, said, "If you want to learn how to play the piano properly, young man, you most certainly do have to be here!"

My father was waiting at the foot of the stairs.

The two nuns conferred. Mother Superior said, "He seems to be able to sight-read. This is a bit unusual. We are not sure if he has a gift, as you put it. He does seem to have potential. Send him to us on Tuesdays and Fridays at 7:30 in the evening. He may begin next week. In return for which, he can serve the Wednesday and the Saturday morning masses. If he has talent, we will find it and discover how best he can put it to use."

To me she said, "Take this book home and look at the first exercise. If you can read music as well as you think you can, learn it by heart and be prepared to play it – at the proper tempo – when you return. If you cannot play it, then we will teach you. But remember to play it as written. Music is not a race to the finish line."

She touched my hair. I flinched.

6:30 a.m. Startled into alertness: The morning sun is a smear of red on the horizon. I woke when I flinched, when I felt the old nun touching my hair. I woke up thinking of the small brown girl who had to be there. If I could see her again –

Yesterday's mail in my lap: Dear Sir, I am writing to tell you how much your interpretation of the Fauré means to me. Dear Sir, I was moved to hear your most recent views as expressed at the conservatory. Dear Sir, may I have your autograph?

The radio comes to life with the national anthem. It is an uninspired tune and there is the problem of the lyrics. I would prefer it if we had another anthem. May I recommend Oscar Peterson's "Hymn to Freedom," just the music, in order to confound the solitudes: loud sites.

We should be content to hum . . .

Eyes gummy, shirt sweaty. Letters in my lap, pushed aside by the needs of the morning. The old men in the bush camps call it a piss hard-on. I stand on guard for thee. Hmm hmmm hmmmm . . .

My head is clear for the first time in days, and I am very hungry. A good sign. I will bathe, then I will eat salami and eggs and toast with blackberry jam and drink a pot of coffee, and read the papers. I will not listen to the news. I will play until noon.

And I will call Paterson, Carol, again.

Note: The convent story is news to me.

No flies on him this morning. He is on his way to another coffee date with Carol Paterson, girl news photographer. Does he intend to fit her into his schedule along with . . . ? He is nothing if not cold-blooded.

Why hasn't he gone to see Singer?

Tape, October 5:

[On the sidewalk: a heel dragger, a cane tapper, a woman with a limp, a baby bawling in a rolling baby carriage. A twist on the usual refrain: "Spare change for beer?" A newspaper swatted on a thigh, a scrap of art school talk: "The chalk at Gwartzman's is cheaper but –" And, if you will, the clang-clang-clang of a trolley. Shift to coffee shop interior:]

"You're late."

"You're early."

"You brought the rest of the photos."

"May I smoke? An espresso please. Do you want one? I thought not. I can't live without a – mmm. If only it were healthy."

"Where do we begin?"

"These are the shelter pictures. I took these over a period of a couple of years."

"Such faces. How many of these people are still alive?"

"This man is dead. Her, I saw her last week. People come and go. You see them or you don't."

"Why did you take pictures like this?"

"I know them. I like them; I like some of them, anyway. We ignore them, and it makes us smaller when we do."

"Tell me about these shots of Singer."

"I have breakfast in this café most mornings. I keep my camera with me all the time. Many of them eat here, especially early in the month, when the welfare cheques arrive. The food is not particularly good, but it's cheap and the portions are generous. So are most of the people who come here, actually. Anyone who happens by, if he has a pack of smokes, he will share it."

[Scrape of match, the feathery puff of its extinction.]

"This guy, Singer. Not long after I saw him play at the Mission, he started coming to the café. Look at this. The way his eyes are closed, in anticipation of the smoke. I had my Leica on the counter. He asked me for a cigarette. I gave him one and pressed the shutter as I flicked the lighter. I thought he wouldn't notice what I was doing, but he heard. He covered his face with his hands. He wouldn't speak to me. He was quite upset."

"Has he seen this? Surely, if he's seen it, he's forgiven you."

"He didn't say anything, not for a long time. A week or so later I gave him a small print. He put it in his shirt pocket without a word. The next day he said he sent it to his daughter.

"Later in the week, someone broke into my car and stole my equipment. Two cameras, three lenses, my portfolio – a year's worth of work. The photos of my mother. Everything I shot in the café."

"But how did? Surely you had the negatives?"

"No, they took everything. I was stupid. Never again. The next time I saw him, I wasn't sure if I should say anything. But he knew something was wrong. He could see it in my face. He asked. The first time he'd ever asked me a direct question. I told him what happened. He laughed."

"But that's . . . He laughed? He must have . . . You must have been devastated. Were you covered? Do you have insurance?"

"For the cameras, yes; for the negatives, no. I have no way of recovering those photos."

"Why on earth would he laugh?"

"He said, 'I have lost everything in my life. You have lost everything in your life. Now we are equal.' And then he invited me to his apartment."

"You went?"

"I wanted to get to know him. While I was there, his daughter phoned. From Johannesburg. He let me talk to her. She agreed to return the photo I had taken of him. I was able to make copies. Eventually, I took this series of him in his room. I've given him many photos; he always gives them away. I think he's proud of them, of the attention.

"You want to know why I take these pictures? No one notices these people. They are everywhere. They have lives, they have families, they live all around us but we don't see them. It's a shame. He got it right, this old man. We are equal, in a way. You never answered my question the other day. Why do you play?"

[Half a minute is not a long time, but half a minute of silence is a long time when you're listening to audio tape with earphones, and all you hear is a spoon rattling in a cup, soda being squirted in a tall glass at the counter, the chuckle of eggs being fried, hash browns being turned on a griddle, and burgers sizzling as they are heeled.]

"Does it matter?"

"There has to be a reason."

"I don't think so. I'm not sure it matters."

[An odd pause in the background, almost as if the entire diner is straining to hear what she is about to say.]

"You're ducking the question. You must think it matters. Otherwise, why bother? If you don't want to talk about it. . . . Do you want another? Thanks, another espresso, please. I'll tell you what matters to me. I'd like to shoot your hands."

"You want to shoot my hands."

Notebook, October 5:

So, Singer has moments of lucidity.

Before she left she showed me a photo of an old man on his back in a narrow room, on the nearest of four beds, the others empty, the metal frames lined up one after another along one side of a long wall. High windows, a shaft of sunlight falling on his face. His mouth open, his eyes closed, every bone in his body is visible, the cords of his neck are stretched tight, there is a patch of stubble on his chin.

What does music do for him? He hears nothing.

I hear nothing.

I'm looking for a key that may not have a key-shape. A key that may not fit any lock.

Note: He says he sees nothing of what he hears.

There is a problem with the metaphor: It is real and symbolic at the same time – choose the meaning at your peril.

I took a walk around the neighbourhood tonight. Listening to the tapes is a strain, but it is training my ears. I heard everything around me. Driblets of Polish. The sough and sigh of hydraulics, pneumatics; leather heels on cement; internal combustion. The scrape of plastic milk crates along the sidewalk in front of the Korean fruit stand. There's too much sound, too loud.

But my ears – and Dom's, I'd guess and bet – are less sharp than those of the average South American peasant who hears nothing louder than wind and water, campfires and thunder, frying meat and the grunt of animals at night.

I remain confused.

❧

Note: The telephone startled me from sleep. I lay still and let the answering machine kick in. "I'm not here right now. You know what to do." The sound of my voice is always a surprise.

I am under the impression that I am thoughtful, considerate, confident, and reflective. But when I hear my recorded voice, I hear a man who is tired, who is rushed, who struggles with caution, and who cannot hide a measure of disappointment.

What does Dom hear when he listens to himself?

It was my editor, offering an assignment if I wanted one: Would I like to go to Sudbury and write a feature on the status of the city – talk to the miners and the scientists, sail on the lakes, find out if the boys still get stinko and the girls still play bingo on a Sudbury Saturday night? No rush to make up my mind. I could call when I'd recovered from the trip.

Stompin' Tom doesn't interest me. Stompin' Dom does.
And so to work.

Notebook, October 6:
I await the ministrations of the tuner.

There are not enough good tuners. The world would be a better place if ten per cent of the pianists currently playing would quit the stage and learn to tune, learn to voice. I do not suggest this lightly. I am not the only one to suggest this. Brendel: blender of sense and common sense.

Note: Margie?
"You've really never heard of him? You ought to open your ears."
"If I told you how much my ears hurt –"
"Brendel, Alfred. A smart player and a smart writer. He's written a couple of books and a very clever article, 'Coping with Pianos,' published in Hi Fi Stereophonie, 1974. To which your man refers. He didn't put a percentage on it but said the concert situation would be improved if more tuners knew how to play. Speaking of playing, Brendel was a big Beethoven boy. A big Liszt boy. Get some of his records and I'll like you more."

Notebook, October 6, cont'd:
An art gallery at night exhales the deep slow breath of history; there is no more eloquent silence: one lilt sequence. I suppose I could compose with silence: a minute from the top of an outpost along the Great Wall; a minute from the Campo in Siena at 3:00 a.m.; a minute from a classroom in the conservatory on a Sunday night; a minute from the inside of an old man's coffin; and so on. Murke's collected, and so on.

Or this, as a performance: A piano *sans* pianist, with one hundred men and women seated on hard chairs in a concert hall – the first row filled with people who have runny noses; the second row filled with those who have coughs; the third row filled with those who have been instructed to cross their legs in unison at timed intervals; the fourth row filled with those who wear pagers or carry cellphones. No more absurd than the concert for one hundred metronomes.

Sound occurs in and out of sequence according to a random pattern.

At this moment, for example, I can hear the noise of my fountain pen, the whistle of breath escaping my nostrils, the white noise of this quiet place. It makes as much sense, musically, as any of the mathematics poor Gould dreamed of.

He sought safety in symmetry – as far as I'm concerned, that's a sign of mental illness. He was neither auteur nor artiste, but a combination of the two – he was an *autist*. I suppose if he'd lived, he would have been a man entranced by fractals. And he'd have felt justified. "Aha, you see – I told you so!"

There is no need for me to be here tonight. I know which piano I've chosen. I know this will be a losing battle. It's a question of what I might hear here. The hall is muffled. I am muffled. Not much the tuner can do. The way the piano sounds in an empty room is not the way it sounds when the room is full. This is a dull room to begin with.

If he could tune the audience . . . And if I could see the colour of the notes I hear . . .

My minder peers around the corner, smiles and waves. My minder does not mind. Unless of course I should feel the need to slash a painting, in which case I am certain he would mind very much. I have no doubt he would – in an instant – throttle me. He is thick-handed, hard-shouldered, short-haired, obviously capable. I bet he was recently mustered out of some middle-European army. And yes, the world would be a better place if ten percent of the world's armies stood down in order to mind art.

A performance note: I will be facing the entrance to the European Gallery, where they hang the big fat portraits in the big gold frames: rich courtiers with their best feet forward, handsome women with rosy nipples, chubby children, decaying flowers, ripening fruit, and wicker baskets of fish.

When I look up I will see – beyond the heads of the black-tie crowd – St. Paul the Hermit, staring at a raven.

Thirteen ways of looking at it.

I do not know which to prefer, the beauty of inflections or the beauty of innuendoes, the blackbird whistling or just after.

Note: The reference is to Wallace Stevens, "Thirteen Ways of Looking at a Blackbird." Margie: "He cites the fifth way."

And "Murke's Collected Silences" is the title of a short story by Heinrich Böll. An editor at a radio station collects snippets of silence from various taped interviews and so on, and splices them together on a reel. She also told me that a Canadian sound artist – she used the term lightly – recently recorded a day's worth of BBC radio and cut the silences and saved them. The BBC was not amused.

Tape, October 6:

"Pleased to see you, maestro. Do not, like the last time, be alarmed. You remember I am Radev, Lec. The name on the tag, it looks like Leck but is pronounced another way to rhyme with frets, bets, Stan Getz; Lec. As for me, I do not fret or bet. As for Stan Getz, I can take or leave him."

"Yes, but can you take or leave St. Paul the Hermit?"

"To us the saints were forbidden. No God, no angels, no saints. Which of course meant forbidden fruit. Paul of Thebes. The curator's explanation – he was the first Christian hermit. I think he was the second. It doesn't matter. Like the begats, it is of interest only to the begetters and the begotten. Paul is ducking here some persecution. He decaves because he hears the raven. The bird has bread in his beak. This gives Paul an inkling that company is coming, but he had not sent invitations.

"Don't tell my bosses, but here they are wrong – it says the visitor is St. Anthony Abbot. Hah! He is Anthony the Hermit, and Paul was his disciple. You see I am right in what I said before, Paul was not the first. So. Anthony is about to arrive and the two old hermits will catch up on old times. Eat the bread of the raven, talk about the life of the caves, and then Paul will die. If it was Bulgarian bread in the beak of the raven, maybe he died of heartburn. You laugh. You have not eaten our bread. Anthony will wrap Paul in his cloak. Two lions will dig the grave. You can't see the lions. They are out of the frame –"

"Enough of hermits. What is that up there?"

"Maestro, an explanation is in the corner. It is a kind of art. Well, I have studied art. But not art like that. Read the inscription and you will know as much as I do."

"You are very well informed. Do they pay you to be?"

"Very little is what they pay me. No matter how little they pay, they will never pay me as little as I will work for them. I do not work. I walk and I look. For the most part, it is a pleasure. A bit of money in the bank. But I must go now and punch the clock. You are expecting Mr. Mazur, the tuner. I will send him to you. If you have other questions about art, please do not hesitate to call me."

Notebook, October 6, cont'd:

Scratch a Bulgar, find a man who knows hermits. Scratch a man who knows hermits, find a security guard with a gimlet eye for modern art.

These words, in red, run high around the walls of Walker Court: Ojibwa Iroquois Petun Ottawa Neutral Nipissing Huron Algonkin. A paragraph of explanation is stencilled in the corner. I'd never have noticed if it weren't for Lec.

"The decorative frieze spells out a catalogue of tribal names that instantly evoke cultures and places violently at odds with the classicism of Walker Court. The viewer is inevitably reminded that many of these people have been ruthlessly wiped out by the Old World's greed for land and power. Though grief is solicited, so is action against injustice and inequities in the present context."

A sprayed "fuck you" in an alley is as eloquent.

The only real difference between this and street graffiti is typeface and location. Why are the letters in red? The red man? Most artists have the intelligence and the attention span of horses. It is fatuous to presume anyone would be at odds with Walker Court. A pianist, perhaps. A native pianist might possibly be doubly at odds. Frankly, if there were any Ojibwa here tonight, I'd bet they would be warm and dry and at odds with nothing but this pretension.

In any case, as far as the environment is concerned, most tribes were children of a nature red in tooth and claw: Head-Smashed-In-Buffalo-Jump. I rest my case. And if native people did not overpopulate it was certainly not for lack of trying. And if they had no electricity, they like lights fine now. It is romanticism to think others are better or worse or more noble than us.

We, too, are the stuff of nature – we are that part of nature with the ability to make tools. As unnatural as it might appear – pin block, back posts, soundboard, keybed, strings, and hammers – there is no instrument more natural than the piano. Because we devised it.

Where do I aim the sound?

It doesn't matter. The room is oddly shaped – tall and long, with proportions of a salt box – similarly proportioned to the dying room at Seaton House. This, however, seems to be a room with no purpose; it is unconnected to the rest of the gallery. Although it is a perfect place in which to lay a coffin.

I clap hands: a child pans the acoustics, which are as bad as I remembered. Worse. Lec came at the sound of my clapping. I stopped and shook my head. He stopped and shook his head.

Where is the tuner?

At least I do not have to pay admission when I play.

In any case, echo is not always an impediment; there are portions of the *Pictures* that will be enhanced: hen dance. "Ballet of the Unhatched Chicks."

Worth noting: Off to the side of this room there is a wall hung with empty frames, finely carved and glowing with gilt. They frame no art, but are examples of the framers' trade. A gesture of postmodernism. I presume the texts are a kind of irony.

"What is the place of the frame. Does it have a place. Where does it begin. Where does it end. What is its inner limit, outer. And the space between the two limits" – Derrida, 1975.

If it were possible to dismiss a thinker out of hand on the basis of a single paragraph, this is the thinker and this, the paragraph.

Let's see if it can be transposed: What is the place of the keyboard? Where do the keys begin? Where do they end? What are the keyboard's inner limits, outer? And the space between the keys?

The size of keys and space between them is actually a matter of the dimensions of the human body: We are neither elephants nor ants. And if we played only with our feet, there would be fewer keys and they would be larger and lower and we would have a simpler music, with fewer chords and more slurs. And if we had smaller hands, shorter arms, and fewer fingers, then we would not have eighty-eight keys. The space between notes – these are potential energy. Ask anyone who has ever played seriously about the tyranny of potential energy.

That first note waiting to be struck.

The Russian who said he felt like a trained seal performing for a pack of noisy monkeys – that's not stage fright, that's the purest and most brilliant contempt. It is the musician as critic.

In a way, that's what Buddy did. He walked away.

As for us poor saps who continue, perhaps we do so because we prefer not to hear questions for which there are no answers; we pretend that playing is an answer.

"Pictures live housed within their frames" – Ortega y Gasset.

This seems perfectly obvious:

Music lives housed within the frame of composition.

Piano music lives housed within the piano. A score lives housed within the margins of the page; the page lives housed within the margins of the book.

A score comes to life in the hands of the pianist.

An implied limit in any case.

The thing about music: It exists in a perpetual state of disappearance. Once it's done, it fades, it goes away, it ceases to exist except in memory. As for recording, that's not performance; it is a sketch of a duplicate of a photocopy, a forest minus the sound of the birds, the smell of the trees. How can anyone stand to hear music unless it is heard as it is being played?

Recording = embalming.

Music dies in the ears of the listener. It sounds so lifelike. You'd swear it was alive. It never sounded better. It dies as it is played. It leaves no trace.

"The violence of framing proliferates. It confines the theory of aesthetics within a theory of the beautiful within a theory of taste, and the theory of taste within a theory of judgment" – Derrida.

I suppose a violence of music proliferates: Metallica, etc. There would certainly be violence – anarchy, at least – without the tyranny of the score. Presumably, Derrida means the form of a framing device – a theory of harmony, contained within a theory of taste, housed within a theory of judgment.

Derrida, the deep thinker. He'd have saved himself a lot of trouble if he'd said, "To each, his own." Or, "You pays your money, you takes your choice." But that's not fancy enough for philosophy.

The piano is not moving. The pianist must not be playing.

All non-black things are non-ravens.

All non-black keys?

Still no tuner.

Note: Margie: "Your boy is certainly widely read. Here he hops from Stevens's 'Thirteen Ways of Looking at a Blackbird' to Hempel's Paradox."

"?"

"Let me make it easy for you. All ravens are black. Suppose you see a parrot. Because it's green, you know it's not a raven. According to Hempel, a green bird confirms the blackness of ravens."

"I see."

"The hell you do, handsome."

She is right. The hell I do.

Notebook, October 6, cont'd:

I dreamed I heard a man assembling a piece of music note by note – a musical carpenter – and the notes were spikes and the carpenter had a bag of them, and he dumped them onto a long white sheet of music, and was tacking them into chords for a Missa Solemnis, or some such music devised to accompany the manufacture of a crucifix. The carpenter – the executioner? – drove the notes home with his hammer until he was satisfied that each one was firmly in place.

I could hear him making the cross. I heard him pinning the hands. Get it right, right, right. Driving spikes through the instep of some saviour. I felt the sound moving up and down my spine, I felt it in the meat of my shoulders, I felt it in my hands and feet.

"Jesus!"

"Not Jesus, sir."

I sat up, suddenly. The voice was behind me.

"Jesus would be a miracle too large on a night like this. I am not even one of the Magi. I am Frank Mazur, a tuner. No more, no less. Speaking personally, I did not wish to disturb you, but if I don't tune this, it would disturb you more, yes?"

I agreed it would.

Tape, October 6, cont'd:

"One must make a little noise. Or a lot. I have to hear not just the note but the note as you would have it played. For which I need your attention. But should you wake a man from sleep if you think he is better off sleeping? It is the question for the ages. Or a question for the aged. I am aged. Should we startle each other at a vulnerable moment?

"What if, when you woke, you were not you but someone else. Claudio Arrau. No matter. You are safe. Surrounded by art. Listen."

[a single note struck three times in succession]

"Okay? That is okay? We will get to the nuances in a moment. Unless you have any special instructions."

Notebook, October 6, cont'd:

I was covered in sweat. I felt as if my head had been peeled open roughly, like an orange. I had fallen asleep on the floor. On my back. With my arms spread wide, and my fingers splayed. I took a deep breath. My skin prickled. I sat up, shaking – cold.

Note: The remainder of the tape is conversation, accompanied by the modern and – to my ear – utterly musical sound of tuning:

Tape, October 6, cont'd:

"I think it's not too bad. I tuned this recently. A couple of weeks ago. I have studied your tendencies. You want a clean sound. This one has a sweeter voice than the Yamaha. Can you guess what I am playing? I didn't think so. An ancient Chinese love song. Written centuries ago by the composer Tu Ning. Ha, ha. Get it? Tuning.

"Are you thirsty? It's not late. Would you like a coffee? Or, considering this is Chinatown, perhaps tea. Lec will let us out and he will let us in again. Let's ask. I know a place where we can get something other than the yellow piss – excuse me – usually served to round-eyed customers. I mean real chai. No?

"Here is an idea for you to consider. I have often had this thought. This is good, yes? A bit more? Yes? Okay, now it is good.

"Suppose it were possible to take a composer out of commission, remove him from the public ear. Of course it can't be done, we have records at home. But suppose the CBC and the major concert halls were to put a moratorium on Handel. No *Messiah* – not even at Christmas; especially at Christmas – for let's say ten years. Radical, yes? No? You frown. I don't see you frowning. I hear your frown.

"My point is this. Familiarity has bred content. We are not pleased with music because it no longer sounds new. We have lost musical freshness. Forgive me, but most music is old hat. Glass is transparent when it is Philip. Part does not stand apart even if it is Arvo. Anyway, the best tunes have been taken long ago.

"Let me provide you another example. Upstairs is a burlap bag filled with dried shit hanging from a rope at the end of a balance beam. Forgive me, that's not art and it's not novelty. Novelty was the Italian who canned his shit when the war was over. On the label was printed the list of ingredients of what he ate before he shat. Once is novelty, twice is repetition, three times and we're bored stiff. This is good, yes? Good? Okay. Better? Yes.

"Painting, too, has lost its punch because of reproduction. The currency is debased. A work of art in a book is often more pleasing to the eye than the original. The colour, for example, is often better. We might take the Group of Seven out of view for a while. Okay, like this? Like this? Just give me – there.

"Who would it hurt? There isn't a single piece of music – or a single piece of art – with the power to make me gasp. I've seen it all before, I've heard it on the radio. Don't mention advertising – ad men have strip-mined the symbols and the songs for more than they are worth."

Notebook, October 6, cont'd:

Mazur's not wrong about the repertoire.

I have a small one. Richter had a larger one. Who cares? Music is not heard, it is remembered, badly. The predictability of an idea – a melodic line rattled off at a particular tempo, *crescendo, rubato, sustenuto ma non troppo* – tonight, thanks to my tuner, it all seems too obvious.

Surprise me.

He surprised me.

It wouldn't hurt to cull the repertoire. I touch the border of an empty frame. Improvisation provides the illusion of freedom. To do what Gould did to Beethoven: toss in spurious notes, alter the rhythms, break chords into separate notes and ignore slurs – a man so easily slighted should not ignore slurs.

The question is, why bother to play Beethoven at all? Take him out of circulation for a while.

Might as well draw a moustache on the Mona Lisa. Might as well put your money where your mouth is: G. ought to have composed what he wanted to hear, or perhaps what he thought Beethoven – had he been born within earshot of a television set and a diesel engine – would have wanted us to hear. Instead of distorting what B. intended.

False to do otherwise.

Note: Margie says this is a reference to the Sonata in F-sharp Major, op. 78 – the interpretation, she said with brisk confidence, is a mess – legato for staccato, soft for loud; Gouldish, ghoulish, peculiar, wilful. The overall effect neither as sweet nor as witty as B. intended.

How could she know witty or sweet intent?

"Witty is as witty does," she replied. "Ditto, sweet. It's in the score."

I said I'd take her at her word.

She said I should be so lucky.

Flirting.

Notebook, October 6, cont'd:

I think of the accordionist in the subway station. As if he were to play "Hey, Jude" in the manner of a polka, substituting "Joshu" for "Jude," and throwing in a reference to kishka.

On the other hand, that might not be such a bad thing.

To give GG his due (reluctantly): How many times can you pull a piece out of a keyboard – or hammer it in – before it goes stale in the ear? Perhaps as many times as the number of peaches you can eat before the smell of peach turns your stomach. No more, but no less. And different for each of us.

This is an experiment best avoided out of season.

Distance, a necessity. Is this why my ear is dead?

"Keep talking," I said to the tuner.

Note: The phone interrupts before I can rewind this tape and insert the next one. Margie: "I'm turning the tables, calling you. I have to log these questions, you know. You could spell it out for me a bit better than you have."

"I can't, not yet."

"Well, you might hurry things along. I'm taking a few days off next week. I thought I'd let you know. Because you aren't likely to find the others around here as, shall we say, sympathetic to your needs."

Hmm.

Tape, October 6, cont'd:

[The tuner continues to make his way across the keyboard.]

"The easiest way to shock the listener into attention is to take liberties. Like a certain genius whose name you know. He cut and pasted, used the modern studio tools. Why not? Anyone can buy a record but not everyone can see a concert. But for my money, what he did was so much quilt making. Okay, we are done.

"What I said earlier – why not put some of the repertoire aside? Return to it when we forget it. Let me tell you a story. You have seen the Moore sculptures? I attended the opening. I was captured, not by the sculptures but by the drawings, the charcoals, hundreds of them. Londoners asleep in subway tunnels during the Blitz; also sheep and clouds in the countryside. I dislike sheep but the drawings are brilliant. You can almost smell the mutton in the paper. Stupid creatures. My disgust extends to the smell of wet woollens. After an hour of looking, I couldn't find the exit. I was wandering in circles. Like a sheep. No Lec to lead me, lots of strangers hemming me in. I turned a corner and there was Tom Thomson in my face. I nearly wept. If I had, my tears would have been falling from my face like autumn leaves. After all those shades of grey, pure colour floored me.

"Now, back to music: How to hear the way I saw? I suggest an abecedarium of absences. Away with Albinoni. Bye, bye, Beethoven. Chop Chopin. Demote Debussy. Forgo Fauré. Go, Grieg. To hell with Hindemith. Here is a good one – jettison

Janacek. Put the kibosh on Khatchaturian. Lose Liszt. I lose lists anyway. Make no Mozart. Off with Offenbach. Pooh-pooh Puccini. You get my point, yes? And you can see I have too much time on my hands. Now sir, will you play this for me? Tell me truly, what do you think? Is it satisfactory?"

Note: Dom plays various bits and pieces – at first, I thought he was just taking a test drive around the piano, but Mazur began to laugh. He laughed as long as Dom played. A curious reaction.

I got his number from the gallery – I don't know what it is with those people, you'd think they were dealing in state secrets; I had to pretend I was working on a piece for Saturday Night, *on the tuner's art, or some such nonsense. In the end, I dropped my editor's name and mumbled about a deadline.*

Mazur was not surprised to hear that I knew the details of a conversation a year old, which had taken place shortly before Dom's disappearance, on a night when no one else was present. I think he is one of those old men for whom everything exists in the present.

I asked him why he had laughed.

"Can you believe it? I was tuning, we were talking, I rattled off the names of some composers in alphabetical order, more than a dozen, some well-known, others not. I said we could take them out of circulation so their music would not be so familiar. I finished tuning, he sat down to play. I was expecting the Musorgsky. There are one or two places where the music makes specific demands, where he requires the instrument to . . . At first, I didn't know what he was playing. Then it hit me, he was giving a few measures of each of the composers I had named, in the order I had named them. I've never heard anything like it. A parlour trick, yes? But a trick from the parlour of a virtuoso."

Was there anything in Dom's behaviour that night which, in retrospect, might have held a clue to why he walked away? Was he taking himself out of circulation?

"No, no, no, all was normal. I came in late, he was sleeping on the floor. Among artists such things are normal. Not for you or me perhaps. No matter. Mostly I talked as I tuned. He lay on his back, eyes closed, listening. Now and then he'd make a note in one of his books. Or fiddle with his tape recorder. An intense man. Observational, sensitive, alert. But no, I remember nothing out of the ordinary. Apart from his playing."

"How would you explain the disappearance?"

"You will have to ask him."

"Have you spoken to Dominic since that night? A note, a call, any kind of communication?"

A quick and firm reply: *"No, nothing. What have you heard?"*

I ducked the question and asked Mazur again if he had any idea why Dom would disappear.

"Maybe he needed a rest. If you are asking whether my suggestion about the absences had anything to do with . . . Excuse me, I don't believe so. It's silly. Perhaps he needed some time to refresh his ears. He plays a limited repertoire; maybe he went away to learn some new music. If I may be bold, what do you think is the reason?"

I said nothing. Called Margie, asked her if she'd like a drink at the Plaza after work. It was, she said, the easiest question she'd had all day.

A hint of snow in the air, the sky as grey as concrete. She took my elbow as we made our way along Bloor St. I like walking next to her, the way she moves her hips, as if she were paddling a canoe. She cannot help it that she does.

"Why the drink?"

A down payment, in return for answers to future questions.

"The shortest way to my heart is a question whose answer is 'Scotch on the rocks.' "

I spent the night at her place. Her gentle snore was a relief after the tyranny of the tapes. She was up and showered and gone before I woke. A note on the night table: "Lock up. Call me when you can."

I left a note beneath her note: "Count on being called."

I took my breakfast – eggs over – at the Daily Planet, at the counter, next to a couple of kids with spiked hair, dog collars, pierced chins, nostrils, eyebrows, and ears. They put out their cigarettes in their plates. It was a shock to see as I was eating, but the greater shock was that I could hear the crackle of the butt in the grease on the plate, and the squeak of stubbing.

There is more sound around me than I am used to hearing.

❦

Notebook, October 7:

Bumped into Charlie Wilson late last night. Literally bumped. I was not paying attention. I was thinking about my good fortune in meeting Mazur. It is rare to run across a man who knows what he's doing with a tuning wrench. In any case, I rushed to make the elevator and hit Wilson with my shoulder; frightened him.

He is an older man and he dresses very well: camel hair topcoat, houndstooth jacket, yellow silk shirt, summer flannels, sockless in his loafers despite the cold – English tailoring, bespoke from top to toe. He seemed frail; there was less of him than there should have been, and the loss seemed recent.

He clutched at my forearm to regain his balance. I thought his head too big for his neck. His cheeks are veined, and there seemed to be a milky sadness in his eyes. He was frightened, then furious, and then curious – this, in a split second – until there was a glimmer of neighbourly recognition. "You are the pianist." I nearly laughed. This is one of the least endearing habits of the powerful – a tendency to present a statement of fact, rather than pose a question. A powerful man assumes he is right at all times. I replied in kind. "And you are the newsman."

He winced and I remembered: Control of his empire had been wrested from him some months ago; the move had been guided from the inside by his son; betrayal rising on its hind legs in the best of families. I have no pity for him; he is still one of the richest men in the country.

"Not the newsman I once was, I'm afraid. Out of the business. Let the young people have their day and so on."

The doors of the elevator closed around us on that note. He looked uncomfortably up and I looked down at my shoes.

As we neared my floor, he asked if I wouldn't mind joining an old man for a whisky and soda. An old man. He'd been one of the most influential men in the country. The elevator doors opened. Without thinking, I held the door and said, "I am going home to practise. I am preparing a small recital. Perhaps you'd prefer to have a drink with me. If you don't mind listening while I rehearse."

"I've always wondered what your piano sounded like. I don't know a damn thing about music, but I'd be glad to join you."

He said he'd heard one or two of my recordings, had attended one or two recitals. He knew about this one. He ought to know. His paper is a major sponsor.

Note: No need to call Margie for the dirt on Wilson.

Until recently he was the owner of a chain of medium-market daily newspapers, including a small but influential national magazine whose cultural influence was, at one time, considerable.

I have earned some of his money. Why be modest? I have earned some money for him.

His empire had been stripped away from him in a series of arcane financial moves by a multimedia conglomerate bent on acquiring various properties in the electronic marketplace. Convergence, in newspeak.

At the time of this meeting, Wilson fils – the one who had helped depose the old man – had gone missing in Tibet and was presumed dead. The old man had exhausted himself using back channels and all the clout he could muster; no word of the son.

There was a daughter-in-law, the marriage a scandal; she'd been a maid. And there was a grandchild. All of them waiting nervously for confirmation of the worst.

Old man Wilson would have been feeling a double loss in the elevator and would have been reminded of it. Dom is roughly the same age as Wilson's son.

Tape 2, October 6:

[Starts cold; he's obviously talking as he switches it on.]

". . . if you don't mind; it's a habit I have. I play, I tape, and I listen to what I've played. This isn't the most comfortable room in the apartment. I don't notice; comfort is not a consideration. I don't want to be comfortable when I play. The absence of discomfort is good enough. Make yourself at home. The whisky; help yourself."

"You always record your rehearsals?"

"Errors creep in quietly; before you know it, a path is worn that is rather too easy to follow. I have to keep my guard up at all times, especially when it comes to something I'm preparing. No matter how well I think I know the piece. I hear as I play, of course, but there are times when I tune out. A kind of automatic pilot. The piece plays me. Does that surprise you? I'm spoiling an illusion. For the listener, there are differences in the way you hear, depending on the circumstances – if you are preoccupied, if you are ill, if you are in the midst of some unpleasantness. Or if you are wildly happy. For me, when I play, these things are not a consideration. I'm sure this is all quite boring. Do you know much about Musorgsky?"

Note: Dominic places the accent in the Russian manner, on the first syllable. I called Margie for a bit of verification. I could hear her blush over the phone; the thought of last night.

According to her reading, the name derives from "musor," a Russian root word for "garbage"; it can be traced to the ninth century; is reckoned to be the legacy of an ancestor with a famously dirty mouth. This fact is thought to have delighted Musorgsky. As for the spelling, take your pick, although he was registered at birth as "Musirskoy." He was introduced to the piano by his mother. Not unlike Dom.

Tape 2, October 6, cont'd:

"What I know is only what is broadly known. The work is meant to represent a critic at a gallery opening, as he walks along from one picture to another."

[Dom grunts, seats himself at the keyboard; pulls his seat forward, plays a few idle exercises in order to get the feel of his own piano. The ice in Wilson's glass is audible, a cold and not unmusical slurry. There must have been several microphones placed around the studio. A nice contrast – the piano creamy, the ice in the Scotch both soft and brittle.]

Tape 2, October 6, cont'd:

"Not quite. Musorgsky was a friend of the architect Viktor Hartmann. They drank together, and so on. That's what got Musorgsky, by the way. He was a drunk. I've never quite understood. I guess it's a Russian thing. He and Hartmann were in the vanguard of the Russian nationalism of the time. Think of Douglas Cardinal chumming with Harry Somers, trying to come up with a new way of thinking about the country. Hartmann died young. Unexpectedly. An aneurysm. A year or so later his pals mounted a show of his sketches and drawings and – forgive me, do you mind the lecture?"

[Dom plays almost jazzily with the opening "Promenade"; the music continues under their conversation.]

"Not at all. Please continue. I'm happy to hear a man talk about what he knows with certainty."

"These were the drawings that inspired the music. Musorgsky and a few other musicians looked to the folk tradition. Radical, because the music of the day was German. Musorgsky was a good documentarist. Like Dvořák, with the "New World Symphony." He used what he heard – folk tunes and so on – things he remembered from his childhood. He wanted to break with tradition. A bit like the Group of Seven in that regard, looking for a new way. . . ."

Note: Dom is probing. He knew – everyone knows – that Wilson owns a magnificent collection of Canadian art, the best private collection in the country, including a number of major works by

*the Group of Seven, some of which are on permanent loan to
the* AGO.

Tape 2, October 6, cont'd:

"We have a way of painting, thanks to them. They gave us a
definition, a before and an after. I'm not telling you anything new.
As for music, we have very little traditional music, per se. What
we usually think of as traditional is from England, Scotland, and
France, across the ocean and into the bush, and out by way of
Edith Fowke. Fowke songs. Gould may have flirted with nationalism in his thinking – he was on the right track with that radio
stuff, 'The Idea of North' for example – but he went quite wrong.
Veered off into . . . well, never mind."

"You didn't like Gould, I take it."

[Dom continues to play swiftly, lightly, humorously breaking
into the "Ballet of the Unhatched Chicks"; the lightness of the
music is in marked contrast to his voice, which is slow and dark.]

Tape 2, October 6, cont'd:

"If his neuroses hadn't been so strong. If he'd had the courage
to test his ideas in composition. Give me Harry Somers any day of
the week. The trouble with Gould – I am aware that not everyone
thinks there is any trouble with Gould – is that he played well
enough to think he knew best."

"Isn't that a prerequisite for excellence?"

"Yes and no. Doubt is an intellectual asset. Playing the piano
is a physical skill. Just because you play well doesn't mean you're
bright, or right. He seemed to think his gifts as a player trumped
those of the composer. Not to mention the conductor and most

recording engineers. He was a superior player. End of sentence. Back to Musorgsky. Almost immediately after seeing the show, he began to write this. It took him twenty days. A staggering outburst of creativity."

"Did he get what he was after?"

"That's the question. Do you ever? I think he came close. If you have seen the drawings of Hartmann – once you know what the various pieces represent – for example, it's impossible to hear this –"

["The Market at Limoges"; half a heartbeat slower than Richter's 1:18, although that could have been the speed of my machine; a full three seconds faster than the young Pogorelich.]

"– as anything other than 'The Market at Limoges.'"

"Reminds me of Kensington in the days when you could buy a live chicken. Not that I ever bought a live chicken."

"Well. Perhaps. But I think if you were to compose with Kensington in mind, it would have to sound different. To my ear, Kensington is slower and there are fewer kids running around. If you listen to what Musorgsky wrote – if you let the music take you from start to finish – then I think you cannot separate his intentions from the intentions of his friend. I've seen the Hartmanns in St. Petersburg. The exhibition must have hit him hard. Musorgsky drank too much, his friend was dead, he had a Russian sense of his own mortality, and then after a year he went to see . . . But I talk too much. Let me just . . ."

Note: Dom hesitated for a moment; stopped playing, in fact. To gather himself. Or – and this is more likely – he stopped because it has occurred to him that Wilson's son was still missing. On tape, you can almost hear him thinking.

He then plays the first few notes of the pure and stately "Promenade," and what follows is a complete run-through. Like the best music, it is very nearly a conjuring act:

There is nothing, and then there are twenty-eight minutes of legerdemain, followed by the decay of the final notes, and then there is nothing again. Nothing but memory, and the notion that something has forever changed. It is breathtaking.

Tape 2, October 6, cont'd:

"I cannot thank you enough. It isn't often that one hears a private recital by one who is – by a performer as gifted as you are. I am profoundly moved. I'm sure you are used to praise, but this has been a comfort to me, to listen to you play. I don't often, any more. Listen to music, I mean. Not any more."

[A longish pause]

"I can't recall when I did not listen to music, to sound. How's your drink? May I get you another? There is no respite from hearing except deafness. Even when I block my ears I hear the repetitive pulse of my own blood, although – would it surprise you if I said there were days when I don't much care for music?"

"There are days when I don't bother to read the papers. Why is that, do you think? Overfamiliarity?"

"That's part of it. I suppose I could play this backwards if I had to. But I sometimes wonder if . . ."

[He plays a trill like falling water.]

"Yes?"

"The magician wants to be surprised by the magic. How would it be if, instead of pulling a rabbit out of your hat, you pulled out a snake that burst into flames. There is a bit of this feeling at a concert if you haven't heard the music before – you don't know what to expect. That next note – it ought to contain some magic, some almost inevitable surprise. Provided the person next to you isn't sniffling or whispering. But I find there are no surprises in what I play or what I hear. Not for some time."

"Not at all?"

"Afraid not."

"Does this concern you?"

"Yes and no. Yes. I have the ability, I think, to play what is required. That is the virtue of the score. It is a map. There are signposts and speed limits and so on. But there are times when I would like to hear what I play more clearly."

"It's not enough, then?"

"What is not?"

"The fact that those of us who listen are moved by what you play?"

[Dom pulls himself up short:]

"How did this take such a philosophical turn? I'm afraid I am not a very good host."

"Not at all. I see you like the Group of Seven."

"Oh, you mean this. A poster I had framed. I don't see it when I sit here. And I always sit here. But I've always thought if we were ever going to have a Canadian music, it ought to hit the ear the way that little sketch hits the eye."

"I don't mean to . . . I'm sure this will sound . . . The original panel is in my study. That is Wolf Cove. On Baffin Island, not far from Iqaluit. Jackson went there one summer on a supply boat. I've been there, to that very spot. He got it right. If you want to see it – the original, I mean – I'd be more than happy to show it to you any time you like. But I'm afraid you must excuse me now. I'm an old man, and it's been a long day."

Note: Was the seed of the idea of destination planted during this discussion? Did Wilson suggest he go? Did he have contacts there? I assume Dom is still in the North, given the postmark on the package. You work with what you know. I called Wilson's office to ask for an appointment.

I was surprised when he answered his own phone. How the mighty have fallen. I'd never have reached him so easily if he were still a full-time newspaper baron. At the mention of Dom's name, he agreed to see me at my convenience.

Wilson's office is in a handsome old building on King St. He was well-dressed, well-mannered, comfortable in his own skin. Clearly, he had reconciled himself to a life of directorships and philanthropy. There are worse ways to live.

"If I may come to the point, I understand Dominic Amoruso played for you in his studio shortly before his last performance. Not long before he disappeared. I believe you and he had drinks."

"Has there been word of Mr. Amoruso?"

"Not exactly –"

"What the hell does that mean, 'Not exactly'? You are a newspaper man. You have heard from him or you have not. You had better not straddle the question in my company. Back up a step. How do you know if I or anyone else had drinks in his studio? Are you implying something?"

It looks harder on the page than it was in person.

He was at ease – it was hardly worth breaking a sweat over the likes of me. At one time, he used to buy and sell journalists by the dozen.

He sat, not behind a desk but at an elegantly proportioned table with the usual discreetly rich appointments: a leather-lined blotter, a fountain pen, a pad of notepaper, cream-coloured, expensive. One or two slim files. A small gold clock, a polar bear made of dull-black soapstone. On the wall behind him hung a small collection of work I recognized without really trying: two pastel horses by Harold Town; a York Wilson abstract; two David Milnes, worth a small fortune. That's what I saw from where I sat.

If he looked past me, which he imperiously did, he saw an enormous canvas by Eleanor Bond; grey, unframed, a paper mill – perhaps it had once supplied newsprint for his dailies – straddling a swollen river in the midst of the wilderness; it was there, I suppose, to remind him of the grandeur of his former station. Or to make his visitors look small.

I didn't want to argue. I dissembled, based on what I knew from the tapes and notes.

"Forgive me. Dominic was – is – a friend. I've known him since childhood. We talked a couple of times a week, usually by phone, often late at night. He told me he'd invited you in one evening after running into you. I think he said you met in the elevator of his building. He played, he talked, and you listened. I'm curious to know if there was anything he said that might seem, in the light of what seems to have happened . . ."

After a long moment, Wilson said, "Perhaps this is something: As I was leaving, he said there were days when he didn't care for music. That's how he put it. He didn't care for it. I must say I found that more than passing strange. How can you do a thing well, and not care about doing it? Is that why he quit? Who knows why anyone does anything. Where is he now? How the hell do I know."

Another pause. He sat quite straight and kept his eyes on me. Finally, he said "A kind of selfishness. The need to go off like that. In search of something. I have no idea. A foolishness. There is risk enough in crossing the street these days. But there was nothing out of the ordinary that night. I don't know him well. He seemed pleasant enough. A bit on the artistic side, but then he is an artist. I assumed he was thinking about his performance. He played and I listened. We spent not much more than an hour together. He was – I'm no expert, but he was obviously in better form that night than on the night of the recital."

"Where do you think he might have –"

"How the hell do I know where he might have? He did not confide his travel plans to me. I barely knew him. Saw him in the lobby now and then. That's it."

"He was curious about the North. He –"

"I'm sure he was curious about many things. He is an intelligent man. He had an A.Y. Jackson sketch in his studio. A cheap poster. It caught my eye because I own the original. I suppose that is a coincidence. Place called Wolf Cove. An old whaling station. Might he have gone there? Your guess is as good as mine."

"Is there anything else that –"

"He mentioned Gould."

"I'm sorry, did you say he –"

"Gould. That documentary thing. 'The Idea of North.' Dismissed it out of hand."

Note: Wilson saw me to the elevator. He walked stiffly, like an old bull driven out of the herd. No longer potent, and wearing the bruises of his last battle. I was tempted, briefly, to feel sorry for him. The elevator arrived and by the time I'd elbowed my way onto the street, all traces of pity had evaporated.

∼

Note: This next tape, and the accompanying notebook, are a deviation from the norm: There are no dates but it makes sense to put them here. At one time, the tape was labelled "Tuning: various" – a record of the work of Mazur at the gallery or perhaps of the visits made by the Remenyi tuner to his piano. But that label has been scratched over, and replaced by this:
"1. Singer 2. Carol 3. Claire"

Tape, Singer:

[A slurry of voices speaking low and all at once, a dark sound that ebbs and flows like the ocean surf on a calm night; the voices are layered over each other, rising and falling back. There are other, softer sounds: the turning of newspaper pages, the shuffling of feet on the floor, and the rustling of – what else can it be? – plastic bags. The luggage of the homeless. Now and then, a shouted greeting pierces the din.]

Notebook, Singer:

A hundred men on chairs – blue plastic, stacking; ten rows of ten each. A dozen or more men sitting on the floor. These are men who haven't washed. The smell is a rank blossom unfolding in the heat of the room. In addition to the alkies, the addicts, and the crazies there are several immigrants and, surprisingly to me, women of all ages, shapes, and colours; what is common is a blank stare: tears of the hopeless homeless.

In the front row, two men and one woman rock back and forth in their seats, uncontrollably, compulsively. I've read about this – schizophrenics, suffering the effects of their meds. Or lack of meds. People do refuse to take them.

One of the women in the room – I can see her out of the corner of my eye – is plainly pretty. She sits with her legs spread on the floor in the posture of a child at play in a sandbox. She is wearing several skirts and sweaters, and is surrounded by plastic bags jammed with clothing. A smile frozen on her face. One of her teeth is black. Her gums are liverish.

Three pianos in a row along the wall.

Near the first is a tall man with a shiny face. He wears neat clothes, has excellent posture, and carries a briefcase stuffed so full of newspapers he can't snap it shut. It's tied with a piece of rope. He talks in two voices; some kind of a dialogue. One of his voices is pitched high, like a girl's; the other is deep and confident – this must be the way he hears himself. Who's he talking to? His wife? His students? An employee? From the look on his face, he has this conversation daily.

No one pays him any mind. Sir, I know the feeling.

Even I can spot the wolves in this crowd. Hard cases, wiry little addicts and bottom-feeders. They are sizing me up, watching me make notes, watching me react to what I see. I am a new face. I have clean fingernails, good shoes, and clean pressed pants. Perhaps they think I will be easy pickings.

I suppose if you didn't know any better – I look no one in the eye, I am intent on my notes, I know no one here, and I keep to myself – you might think I'd only recently gone off my rocker.

I have no visible signs of wear and tear.

Not visible, not yet.

Note: He has taken Carol Paterson's advice.

The Scott Mission is a plain building tucked in the middle of a short block of Spadina between a seedy bar and a funeral home – the block, a kind of strip mall for the indigent.

The Mission is privately run, church-supported, with the usual amenities: simple meals, some nursing, warm clothes, hot water and soap.

God on offer, but not a lot of God.

Tape, Singer, cont'd:

[Three taps on the microphone; a puff of breath.]

"Can you hear me? All right. Is this better? Good morning, everyone. If I could have your attention for a moment. Today is Thursday. The Latino AA group will meet downstairs at noon. The coffee shop will open tonight at seven o'clock. We'll be handing out bag lunches at the counter at 2:00 p.m. and once again at 8:00. Before we sit down for the noonday offering, if we could take a moment and give thanks. . . . Father God, we turn to You in difficult times. We remember that it is You who has created all – the air we breathe today, the sunshine this morning, which is very nice to see – and the food we are about to eat. Amen. Thank you, gentlemen. Now, by row if you please."

[Chairs scraping on the floor, more shuffling. Then a deep voice, speaking loudly, with an oratorical inflection:]

"*. . . it is as clear as the nose on your. No, I AM TELLING you. It's not as if you were the first who ever thought of it. FOR CHRIST'S SAKE. I want to hear the – YES, WHAT IS IT!*"

[A second voice, quiet, non-threatening:] "John, if you'd care to . . . We had the piano tuned yesterday. Some of the men were wondering if you'd like to play while we eat . . ."

"BUT OF COURSE."

[D:] It's him.

Notebook, Singer, cont'd:

It is him. It must be him. If not him, who?

He takes his cue from the staff and moves the first piano away from the wall with – there is no other word for it – humility. The tall man engaged in the imaginary dialogue continues to speak loudly, in both voices. Without looking at him, Singer tells the man to stop talking and take a seat. He speaks with authority. The talking man sits down, stops talking, busies himself with a knot in the rope around his briefcase.

Singer continues to move the piano until he gets it right.

There are scars on his cheeks, a tribal thing; his teeth – the ones that remain – were filed into points long ago. He is built like a barrel from the waist up and he is skinny from the waist down. He is shorter than I remembered. One of those fisherman's caps on his head – has he gone bald? The laces on his sneakers are undone. He is wearing baggy, mustard-coloured corduroys and a sweater with a snowflake pattern. His leather jacket – the colour of a cup of coffee with double cream – matches his skin. His goatee, the colour of tobacco.

Note: *Margie to the rescue in the nick of time: She tracked down an article by Anton Kuerti in an old issue of* Piano Quarterly:

John Maisela Singer, b. 26 July, 1946, in Johannesburg. Father a gardener, mistaken for an intruder and shot to death by a Boer in 1948; no charges laid. Mother a housekeeper. According to the story, she took her baby with her to work. My Singer – that's how he was known – was made to sit quietly in a corner while she cleaned. He listened while his mother's employer gave piano lessons to her children. One day, young Singer crawled up on the piano bench and began to play while his mother mopped a floor. He'd learned to play by listening.

His mother's employer, in one of those rare acts of white-black generosity, arranged for further studies. And so he eventually became Lupo's star pupil – fearless as a child, striking sparks off the keyboard, playing with the impression of utter spontaneity.

But he left Siena suddenly.

There were no recordings. There are rumours of a tape made during a concert, the Tchaikovsky Piano Concerto no. 1. It is supposed to have been made at a miners' rally in South Africa. Two thousand miners sitting quietly for the performance. One of the miners with a tape recorder.

The rally was broken up brutally. The tape is supposed to include, under the music, the snarl of attack dogs, the rising up of the miners, truncheons on skulls, and the crack of gunshots.

Sixteen men died. Singer was arrested and imprisoned along with hundreds of other demonstrators. He was charged with illegal political activity and beaten while in jail. His captors were clever enough not to break his fingers; they broke his forearms instead. Singer is supposed to have been haunted by guilt – had the miners not sat still while he played, perhaps they might not have been taken by surprise.

After three years in prison, he was released and spirited out of the country by missionaries. He went back to Italy; gave two recitals in Milan. They were politically remarkable, but his touch at the keyboard was gone. Lupo sent him to Toronto, to study with Boris Berlin in the hope that Singer could be, as Lupo put it, rebuilt.

Berlin arranged an apartment on campus and a temporary position in the music department of the University of Toronto. There was talk of an operation to reset the bones in his arms, which had healed badly.

Singer would not hear of any operations. He refused to show up at the university, declined to teach, and would not stay in his room. Eventually, he found a place in a rooming house, ended up on welfare, was hospitalized several times for mental illness, and disappeared from view.

He was forgotten.

Tape, Singer, cont'd:

[Dominic whispers:] Who else if not?

[Singer's playing is tentative, at times unintelligible. Fifteen measures of Mendelssohn, then a pause. His voice is a thick and private mumble: "There were concerts. I remember very well. The women wore white. The men took gin and tonic." A few bars of music: "The Baby Elephant Walk." A few bars of music: "Do You Know the Way to San Jose?" Then the Chopin, Etude in F, op. 10, no. 8.]

Notebook, Singer, cont'd:

Evidence of technique remains. The music is a pure expression of his mental state. He plays the way he speaks: choppy, disjointed. He plays the way I feel.

After a measure or two, he stops and whispers to no one, or to everyone. He wags his finger as if giving a master class; a familiar gesture.

The way Lupo wagged his.

Tape, Singer, cont'd:

["Chopin. A fuck a suck. Paderewski. A fuck a suck. Of course he was an old man then. A fuck." The opening measures of the *Hungarian Rhapsody* – he plays it perfectly, but only for a moment – and then he plays something else I don't quite recognize as music at all.]

Notebook, Singer, cont'd:

He can't hold it. The music breaks down, he becomes aggressive, incoherent. He curses like a man with Tourette's syndrome. Now and then he repeats a single musical phrase. I swear he mimics an old recording of Lupo's: Scarlatti, the Sonata in B Minor – the same touch, almost as if he were quoting. He finishes with a flourish. Stands. Nods his head. And walks off –

Tape, Singer, cont'd:

"Thank you, thank you all, you are too kind –"

[Dom's voice:] "My Singer. John Maisela Singer. It is pleasure to see you again. I don't know if you remember, but –"

"I KNOW WHO YOU ARE!"

"I studied with Lupo in Siena –"

"LEAVE ME ALONE! DON'T COME NEAR."

[Muffled noises; a scuffle?]

Notebook, Singer, cont'd:

He clearly has no idea who I am. This rage must be how he fends off people he doesn't like, or who he fears may harm him.

His face, his manner and technique – he is halfway between the certain smoothness of Lupo and the sewing-machine precision of Gould, the music feather-light, almost wispy, fluid, and – when he's actually trying to say something – beautifully accurate. The piano is a packing crate with strings and there are no acoustics in the room, but still he managed to achieve some sort of communication, even when he was playing off his rocker. Was he the better pupil?

I scared him off. No idea of what I wanted to say. I should have had a plan. I ought to have thought it out. I wanted to acknowledge his performance. And perhaps remind him of what Lupo had said: *He plays with his own voice.*

He certainly does now. But he's clearly beyond conversation. I don't know him well enough to sneak past the barrier – whether the barrier is meds, or meds and madness. He may not want reminding.

I honestly don't think he knows who he is any more. The piano must be some sort of anchor. He pushed past me, walked out of the shelter.

Why does he play? To hear an echo of who he was? He may hear the way he used to play. He may hear Lupo. He may think he is playing a superior music. Clearly, he knows what he was at one time capable of doing. It is a madman's monologue.

I noticed his hands. The tendons prominent – signs of arthritis in the joints – knuckles swollen, the tips of his fingers bent. It must hurt like hell to play.

As he made his way to the door, he noticed a newspaper on the floor. He stopped, but he did not pick it up. He spread his legs, bent forward at the waist, and read the open pages with his hands behind his back. "Singer first; the rest, nowhere" – Lupo.

Note: Amoruso, somewhere . . .

Tape, Carol:

[After the scuffle with Singer the cassette goes cold; there is a gap of five seconds and then there are two voices – Dom's and Carol Paterson's:]

"Whenever you're ready. Just pretend I'm not here."

"Would you like me to play anything in particular?"

"Anything you like. It doesn't matter. I just want to get the sense of your hands at work."

[As he plays:] "I saw Singer today."

"You did?"

"He played. He played like a man off his rocker. It's as if all the keys were there but somehow they'd been rearranged. But there were hints of what he could do."

Note: Dom begins to play – even I recognize this – the same peculiar snatches of music Singer had played. Then he segues smoothly into the Moonlight Sonata, *cuts it short and plays two little Chopin rondos with a couple of brisk variations. His playing is swift, darting, almost fluttery – like a field of flowers in the wind.*

I do not defend this description very strongly. But the way he moves the music forward – there is an aspect of his technique that is similar to Singer's. I'd say Lupo was an influential teacher.

The music is punctuated by the cock and click of the shutter of her camera. She shoots his hands; he hums faintly as he plays. There's not a word between them – just the music, her clicks and whirrs, her short deep breaths, his humming.

I called her studio: "Have you heard from Dominic Amoruso by any chance? In the past few weeks?"

"Why would I hear from him?"

"I understand you took a series of photos last year. Just before the recital at the AGO. *I thought . . . It occurred to me that you might have . . ."*

"Who told you that?"

"I'm working on a magazine piece, and I'm talking to anyone who saw him shortly before he disappeared. It's been nearly a year, and –"

"I went to his studio and shot six or eight rolls a few days before the recital. His hands, mostly. I haven't heard a word since. You? What have you heard?"

I ducked: "I have no idea where he is or what he's doing or why. But I'm doing this piece and maybe there's a way to help each other. You have photos of his hands. I'll let my editor know – he may want one or two for the article."

"Yeah, maybe."

"Can I see what you shot?"

"Come over now if you can."

She left me with a loupe at a light table.

His hands are supple and strong, almost square; his fingers, short and thick, almost spatulate, with well-tended nails; half-moons present in the nail-beds of his thumbs.

The backs of his hands are richly veined, like a river delta. There are two neat scars cut deep into the webbing between the thumb and forefinger of each hand; they look surgical. I've known him forever. I've never noticed these. . . .

The impression, overall, is one of tremendous strength.

In some of the pictures, his fingers are a blur of motion, rushing over the keys like water; in others, his fingers are so contorted they seemed inhuman.

One picture struck me more than all the others: She had shot along the keyboard, the focus in the foreground. The white keys reminded me of ice. The tips of his fingers seemed frozen to the keys.

Had she noticed anything unusual that night? She said that, as she packed up her gear, he sat at the piano and rubbed his temples. She thought he was tired. She said he was curt.

Notebook, Claire:

Claire said she would not be able to attend the recital. Said I should break a leg and not a finger. Offered the view that my prowling among the indigent – her terms: prowling, indigent –

was a waste of Time and Talent, as if I were no judge of the uses of my T and T. She offered the view that I might be unwell, in which case was there anything she could do?

Me, unwell; well.

I hung up. I was not well; my head –

Tape, Claire:

"Hello."

"You're home."

"You can call me back and I can let it ring through if you'd like."

"Don't be smart, not tonight."

"What's the matter? I mean apart from –"

"There's really nothing wrong. There's nothing else to do."

"When did they say?"

"I just found out. I go in that evening."

[pause]

"How did?"

"It happens. And when it does, you deal with it."

"Like a sore tooth."

"You have a gift for the perfectly wrong metaphor. Simile. Whatever."

[pause]

"I wish you'd told me when you were here."

"I didn't know for sure when I was there. Edward thinks I'm having a bit of cosmetic surgery. Which, in a way . . . It's really not a problem. There's nothing to it. It won't be –"

"Am I supposed to –"

"You aren't supposed to do anything but play. There is a development: It's going to be filmed. A documentary about health care. The failure of. I know the producer, a friend of mine, she needs a clip. It isn't always easy to get permission from a stranger. No one will know it's me. But things sometimes get around. I wanted to warn you. I know you hate surprises."

"This is one of those. Is there anything I can do?"

"It's sweet of you to ask. One thing."

"What, anything."

"Play well. I'll be thinking of you as you play."

"Will I see you before – ?"

"Are you home this evening?"

Notebook, Claire, cont'd:

Not my business and not my decision. No different from the one I'd have made if I were her. In a way, it is a relief. A great uncomplicating. The death of music . . .

What I want is for her to visit, for us to eat takeout, and for me to have warm hands and a clear head. Which tonight I have not got. Which it seems I have not had for weeks now.

(Later) Claire arrived with red beans, rice, and ribs. I knew it was her – three double buzzes. Again. Again. Again. The sound, enough to burst my eyeballs. I didn't buzz her in. I couldn't move. Why she brought the food, I'll never know.

An irony: maternal instinct.

She had a key. The sound in the lock, too loud. I heard the tumblers and the turning of the knob, and the silence of the door as it swung on its hinges. My drugs do not always mask the pain; they did not mask it then.

I had lost sight and appetite. I can play if I can see. I can see if I can hear. But what I heard when she rang was loud enough to burst my eyes. No colour, but a flash of white –

She found me sitting on the floor. She asked if she could help. She said she'd call a doctor. I said no. Yes, she could close the curtains. Quietly. Because the light hurt. Yes, she could put the food away. Because the smell was making me ill. Yes, she could lower her voice. Because a whisper is too loud.

She covered me with a blanket. I pushed it away. The sound of the wool on my cheek was as loud as a rake over gravel.

She brought me a glass of water. I drank it. I asked for the wastebasket. She brought it. I threw up. She wiped my face. She stroked my hand. She smoothed my forehead. I pushed her away. My skin hurt.

I slept. Or I passed out. She was in a chair with a book when I opened my eyes. I had a foolish thought: If she stayed in that chair for seven more months, not a long time in the scheme of things, there would be some sort of revenge in some sort of cradle. And all sorts of hell to pay.

She brought me pills. The smell of tap water. I kept the pills down. An act of will. I said I was sorry. I wanted to help. I didn't know how. She said there was no doubt, she was right to do what she was about to do, she'd done it before, twice actually. Not my fault; no one's fault. I said I wished it was me in her place. She said, "There, there, you're quite delirious." I said I was no such thing. She laughed her soft silver laugh: "That's precisely what a delirious man would say."

I said her laugh was too loud. She led me to my bed. Helped me out of my clothes. Covered me with the blanket. Turned out the light. The light switch snapped like a tree branch.

She asked if there was anything I wanted her to do.

I said she should give the food to Abdi. He could take it home for supper. He would say, Thank you, ma'am. No idea if he eats pork –

Note: No wonder Claire was brisk with me. She thought I knew she'd had an abortion. Thought I was going to use it against her somehow. I'd say she did the only thing she could. She cut her losses.

Now: The remainder of these entries were made after a gap of several days, as will soon become clear. Which makes this as good a moment as any to recapitulate:

His migraines were on the increase; crippling, knocking him out for days at a time. Are they symptoms of a more serious illness?

The failure of his synesthesia. He never spoke about it, as I recall, but he is clearly troubled by it. He feels that his performance, in the days leading up to the recital, has been impeded.

There are hints that he intended to tackle the question of Gould by starting a composition – "The Idea of Here."

Singer. Carol Paterson. Burnout?

What follows is in his impatient hand. These notes were made several days after the recital. And these days will be lost until he reveals them, unless he does not remember. He has flown, and has come to land on a cold perch.

＜

Notebook, October 14:

As for the rest of what happened, I am now going to try to reconstruct. Or deconstruct. The ways in which I am so extraordinarily – no other word for it – fuct.

Never mind where I am at the moment. I'm in a room – smelly, flimsy, noisy, unfamiliar.

Of this I am sure – I've had sufficient drugs now. I will try to restore some sort of order. The matter at hand. Or shall we say, the matter of hands: mine.

I slept for a full day. And woke, I thought, refreshed. Light-headed, not unusually so. At the very least, if not ready to play, then not groaning, not vomiting, not staggering under the pulse of the blood in my temples.

I ran a bath, took the pumice stone from the medicine cabinet, and sat on the edge of the tub. Pumice stone looks like weath-ered bone, mine at least. It is stained from previous buffings, the stain of my skin.

Filled the bath and worked the tips of my fingers, the outer edges of my thumbs, humming as I buffed and sloughed: pum-pawm pum, pum-pim-pom . . . not unlike my Musorgsky. Hello, I'm Modest. Who is not immodest in his bath?

I took a few preventive pills.

The tips of my fingers are, at the moment of this writing, bright red. One of the side effects of drugs on an empty stomach – espe-cially when I double the dose – is cold hands. And lucidity.

All non-lucid things are non-cold.

In spite of the damp heat in this room, I am so lucid I can't stop my hands from shivering. Of course, I am not properly dressed.

In my left hand was the warmth of friction. In my right hand, the honeycomb sharpness of the pumice. A pleasant numbness when I was done. I had not pumiced for quite some time. I recall the familiar, faintly flooding sensation: a wetness of feeling rushing in. It is, or so I have read in the worst and therefore most pleasing of the pulp novels, a safecracker's trick – a way of heightening the sense of touch, dating from the days when a safe could be opened with the twirl of a dial. Do safes have dials these days? I think all combinations must now be digital. I suspect a falling off of the sale of pumice stone to thieves. And an increase in sales of plastic explosives. LED. QED. *Boom.*

It didn't matter if it was true – buffing makes my fingers slightly painful – that's the point. A little pain is a tool in the regulation of the attack. I can play towards the sensation or away from it. Any shaving of the distance between the music and the self is not a bad thing.

I am not concerned that I do not know how I got here. Perhaps I ought to be.

I turned off the taps and tested my hands on the edge of the tub, tapitty-tap. The porcelain ledge, a long white middle C. I am at sea. It may be frozen but it is still a sea.

I stepped into the bath and, adjusting to the shock of the heat, lay back and let my arms float freely. Me, Ophelia. Is there a masculine?

Ophelium.

In tubbium.

Note: Margie, without having to look it up: Ipi 'n Tombi – *a Zulu musical, popular in the seventies, scandalous at the time for bare black breasts and bare black nationalism. "Is your man stoned, then?"*

If he is not now, he was so then.

Notebook, October 14, cont'd:

When in the world, I am most comfortable in black. But when I am in my world and there is no one else with me, then I am most comfortable in a white tub of hot water, with nothing to do but soak.

I remember this quite clearly: pale white floating pinkish arms, looking as if they belonged to someone else. I, still as a corpse. The only motion, that of the water. A corpse with tingling hands. Title for a book?

I shudder at the thought of damage to my fingers. It is the dark fear of every musician, and quite possibly of every dentist and typist. I flutter my fingers now, as I fluttered them then. I thought of the fetishists whose concern is amputation.

Nadia, close your eyes.

Note: Margie, now fully caught up in the game, advises that the reference is to Nadia Salerno-Sonnenberg, dark star of the violin, who severed a portion of her pinky – on the hand she chords with – in a moment of carelessness with a very sharp knife; parse that word, carelessness.

It was nearly the end of Nadia's career.

She was lucky there was a surgeon, a specialist, in a nearby, etc. She learned, afterwards, not just to play again, but to play as well as she had before. In fact, she learned the better lesson. She learned again to love to play.

Notebook, October 14, cont'd:

There are men and women in Toronto – rumours of them, anyway – willing to spend large sums of money for the surgical removal of fingers or toes, hands or feet, arms or legs or ribs. They seek amputation at the hands of quacks, addicted medics, self-taught weirdos, and failed medical students – those with a requisite lack of scruples and the requisite possession of the proper tools. Or at least a willingness to improvise with the tools at hand. Who can be trusted within reason – within reason! – not to botch the job. The cutters do not advertise, except by word of mouth.

When I first heard of this, I imagined what it might be like: prick of needle, flood of numbness; cut and scrape; dab and staunch of the warm red spurting; the hum and buzz as bone is zeroed to and through the marrow. Zero at the bone – not exactly Emily Dickinson's intent.

The thump of chisel as it chips an inch of digit. The tug of a flap of skin tucked and stitched tightly over what is not-there.

Unlike those who use their skin as a canvas, or who turn themselves into pin cushions with rings or hooks or studs – *my little blonde schoolgirl, where are you now?* – or who brand themselves for decoration, apotemnophiliacs (there's a word calculated to disgust a pianist) do not seek adornment; they seek the subtlety of subtraction.

The erasure of the self.

A choice that, oddly, confers power over the self. That's the logic of Derrida – and peculiar enough to be the subject of a talk show: men who cut their fingers off, and the women who love them. *I can't quite put a finger on it, Sally Jessy, but now that there is less of him to love, I love him all the more.* What's sought must be delicately suggestive in some sexual way – desire not denied but thwarted.

Perpetual absence.

It used to be – or so I'm told – that the people who sought this sort of thing were fashion models willing to sacrifice small toes for the sake of skinny shoes, or to spare the shortest ribs for the curve of haute couture. Or bondage freaks, cinching wasp waists even waspier. So powerful is this urge that it is unstoppable. Or so I am told.

There are means of inflicting self-harm in such a way that amputation is the only remedy. The self-inflictors print and publish their results in *samizdat* manuals. Or so I am told.

I cannot imagine. Not true. I can imagine, and it makes me nauseated.

Some of these poor souls, with the aid of surgical tubing, will in a pinch tie off a finger, cutting the circulation until necrosis sets in.

I actually used to do this in grade school. I would wrap an elastic band around the tip of my forefinger until it turned cold, numb, blue. The pleasant painful pulse of blood. A gathering red prickle. And then full sound and colour in a flood of feeling rushing back when I snapped the elastic off.

The trouble – I'm guessing – with self-amputation is that good surgeons can reattach almost anything they choose, and these days they often choose to do so just to keep a hand in. Pulling out the stops for penises, hands, and thumbs. A doctor I know once showed me a set of pictures illustrating how Chinese surgeons went about the business of replacing proletarian thumbs with toes.

The notion of bathwater warm and oily, red and viscous and swirling down the drain – a C-sharp major vortex. The notion that while I was bathing, Claire was draped and sedated and . . .

There is no bath in the room I am in now.

I am far from my own room. I am in an unfamiliar room. There is an upright shower stall, yellow and rusted, instead of a bath. The walls are thin. Light leaks through the jamb of the door. I can hear the hiss and dribble of my neighbour's piss.

If he listens, he hears mine.

Back to the night of the recital.

As I lay in the bath, I remembered the way I'd felt on first noticing the old Finns on the streets of Port Arthur. I was, for a time, sent north to Mrs. Ojala for lessons. I seem to have sent myself rather farther north this time. Port Arthur, where the streets were haunted by white-haired, wispy bush workers – retired plain-sawyers, cross-cutters, and mill workers – in their green twill work pants and long underwear; they owned no other clothes except the good black suit saved for Sundays, for the burials of friends, and for that one last burial. One must cut a figure in the coffin, after all.

They smiled rummily, ginnily, and even radiator-fluidly at boys like me who gaped at them. The very idea of the loss of a limb was as shocking as the first thoughts of sex: *Is this a thing that happens?*

They shuffled along, smelling of sour milk and alcohol, onions and sweat, licorice and tobacco, stopping to lean against parking meters on the sidewalk. The sight of the first partial hand made me blush with shame. I can't explain it: a stump, a nub, a knob, a node – it trumps all else, it draws the eye, it is always the first fact. I could not stop looking.

My own hands have always been soft. Everything I touched as a boy felt new and sweet. A recurring nightmare: my fingers sliced at the tips like quills or the stems of flowers in a vase.

Drops of blood instead of sap.

I lay in the water, remembering individual hands. One sliced on the bias, three fingers missing. One nothing but a pruned thumb, and the half-lumps of knuckles. And a pair of hands, minus the right and left forefingers. Because I listened I knew some of the stories:

A man who, in the lazy heat, closed his eyes to the cool breeze and lost his forefinger in an instant to a sawblade. A man who caught his pinky in a drive belt; he was trying to flick a piece of torn rubber. And a man who tore the ring finger off his left hand – he'd been working on a hydro pole, holding a guy wire for balance; he finished putting up a sign and he jumped, and while he was in the air it occurred to him that his wedding ring was snagged on a frayed strand of metal; a moment of disbelief. His ring remained snagged. His finger was lost.

Most afternoons after music lessons – I spent three scant months with Mrs. Ojala, who taught me to appreciate counterpoint and to dislike the smell of boiling milk – I went to the Hoito restaurant to wait for my ride home. I kept an eye peeled for anyone who pinched his utensils awkwardly, reached shyly for the handle of a cup of coffee, clutched the sugar dispenser between his wrists, fumbled awkwardly for cigarette papers, rolled crude smokes, sat turning the pages of the daily Finnish paper with an improvised sleight of hand. It seems important to note this now.

It seems an age ago but, in my tub on the day of the recital, at the thought of the wounded hands, I shifted uneasily. Opened my eyes. Wiggled my fingers and toes. All pinkly present.

Note: These notes begin to make a first-rate case for nervous breakdown. Here he is, a few hours before a performance, with a belly full of pills and a vision of missing fingers.

I told Margie, who said unhelpfully: "Forgive the phrase, but he's losing his grip. Although he is more or less correct about apotemnophilia."

I mentioned the scars in the webbing between his thumb and forefinger. She said that she had heard some pianists used to have it done in order to increase the span of their hands; it was not a modern practice. In Dom's case, if that's what had happened . . .

I have no idea.

This may or may not be related: The summer before he left to study in Siena, his cousin lost an arm in a mining accident.

I know Rocco Amoruso casually. He was trying to earn some money for university. Underground at the mine in Shebandowan (old Finn, identifying the fast woman who stole his wallet: "She ban de one!") when an ore car jumped the track. Rocco decided to show a bit of initiative. He tried to right the car by himself. He was rocking it back and forth, trying to set the wheels back on the rails. The cart rocked back too far. It tipped and fell on him. His arm was pinned, snapped, crushed.

He lay in the darkness, passing out and waking up, passing out and waking up from the ebb and flow of the pain. His screams were masked by the chatter of drilling equipment. He was not rescued until someone noticed that there had been no cars rolling down the rails from his section of the mine. He nearly died from loss of blood.

The doctor on duty in the mine clinic applied a tourniquet, stabilized him with splints, shot him full of painkillers and tranquillizers, rigged him up to a saline drip, and sent him off in an ambulance to McKellar General in Fort William. The mine doctor ought to have cut his arm off. It would have saved him ninety minutes of agony in the ambulance.

His elbow was completely pulverized, as was a large portion of the upper arm. They amputated at the shoulder. For years, Rocco said he suffered pains in his missing hand. He told us once, after several glasses of wine, that he would see the rail car tipping in slow motion in his dreams, as if he'd been given a second chance to get out of the way, and yet he would be unable to move. He would wake up covered in sweat, trying to keep the dream-car from falling with an arm no longer there. . . .

He used to kid Dom, saying he was going to take piano

lessons. He'd learn to play "Chopstick." The joke, such as it is, was on him.

Dom noted – a bit stiffly, I thought – that there was an extensive repertoire of one-handed compositions, including works by Ravel, commissioned by Paul Wittgenstein, concert pianist and brother of the celebrated philosopher, who lost an arm in the early days of the First World War.

Notebook, October 14, cont'd:

Brief dizziness.

If I had lost a hand, would I play music in my dreams? Would it be equal to the music I have played, or would it be as evanescent as the music I cannot remember when I awake after having had a migraine?

Perhaps it would be more real.

I remember opening my eyes and splashing water on my face; I can see the droplets of warm water, rising and falling in slow motion; the pain beginning. This memory is surprisingly accessible: I sat up, pulled the plug and, hands on thighs, ran through a few bars of "The House on Hen's Legs." Wishing that the pain in my eyes would flow away as easily as the water running down the drain. Was it the flash of Paterson's camera? The stab of the strobe.

I fret about lateness on the day of a performance, but I had five hours and ten minutes to spare. I reached for my shaving brush; a gift from Claire, as was the Roget & Gallet shaving soap; together, they make a plush lather that holds heat and moisture and turns the act of shaving into a pleasure. I do not have that pleasure now. The best I can expect are disposable razors, lather from a spray can.

There was a dual and duplicitous reason for Claire's gift: It was the same soap, the same scent her husband used. Because if, after an afternoon with me, Claire's cheek held traces of R & G, what harm was there in that? His preference, her prudence, my pleasure.

Lather to stubble; straight razor stropped.

I have at this moment not shaved in a week. My cheeks itch. I ought to have cobbled together a kit. Panic produces many little errors of inconvenience. On the other hand, if I hadn't stood up and walked off stage, I might now be somewhere under sedation – a rather larger inconvenience than stubble on my cheeks. . . .

I remember drawing the blade down my jaw and up my neck, whistling through my teeth, angling the razor with sharp straight strokes, scraping carefully under my nostrils. The scratch, scratch of the blade.

I rinsed the soap from my hands and from the badger brush, I dried and folded the razor, I ran the tap until the water was cold and splashed my face. The pulse of cold water on the tips of my fingers.

Of such pedestrian attention is art made: Clip a nail, file it smooth; push the cuticle, inspect, adjust, move on. I was about to remove the barest sliver of nail from the third finger of my right hand when the phone rang. Once.

I looked up and held my breath –

After a moment, I was sure it would not ring a second time. Who would have phoned and thought better of phoning on the afternoon before a performance? A misdial? Claire, from the hospital, making sure I was all right, or to tell me she was so. I clipped.

The nail flew at my face.

It might not hurt to have a bite before I dressed, is what I thought then: toast, egg, tea, a continuation of codeine. I should not have let Carol use the flash.

Not much food; it is always better to play with a little hunger. But a sufficiency of drugs.

I detest performing with a migraine. When I am in pain, the softest music is too loud, it makes me nauseated, it hurts.

It must have been the flash.

I began to compose an imaginary picture of those who might come to the recital. This is a matter of no small consideration, and something that until then had always been part of preparation. It helps to know. Helps me, at any rate.

I imagined, because of the Hartmanns, that there would be a handful of emigrés swooning in that lovely Russian *nostalgie*. Plus the usual stuffed shirts of commerce, and the old-money members of the gallery board, and the most deluded of all the saps – the lovers of art.

I had been preparing a Musorgsky a bit different from the one I'd recorded. I was ramping up the fireworks a bit, while still playing it with crisp clean lines. I intended to drop a couple of the "Promenades." Carter wouldn't know, hadn't asked, didn't care.

An air, spilled into air.

I set a pot of water on the stove, took the tea from the cupboard, the eggs from the fridge, the knife from the drawer, the bread from the bin. I cut a slice and dropped it in the toaster and was about to cut a second slice when I glanced at the pot on the stove and –

I stuck my forefinger in my mouth a split-second before it had a chance to hurt. I licked and winced; felt the roughness of my tongue. A little flap of loose skin; no taste of salt.

I did not want to look. Sucked in a breath of air. Hoped for the best. Withdrew my finger from my mouth. Small scrape, close call, dull knife: fun killed. The toaster popped. It startled me; my hand flew up in front of my face. I could feel the tide of my blood. I touched the countertop. Inhaled and held my breath. Tapped sharply. More pain than I was used to.

No choice but to endure.

If I relied on the pad of the finger, if I used more arm and less wrist, if I played with a somewhat uncupped hand. Hadn't Kuerti, when young, played his big bright Beethoven with a thorn from one of his roses piercing the flesh of his forefinger? Or am I imagining things?

I began to run through the score in my head, making a series of mental adjustments as I did so. "The Great Gate of Kiev" requires to be closed with considerable force. It loomed.

There are gaps in what I remember.

You will forgive me if I do not finish – a small joke.

I suppose it might have gone like this:

I cabbed it over to the AGO, tuxed and topcoated, and found Carter and his minions smilingly unsure of whether to speak to the Artist.

Me, not wanting to be spoken to.

I paced back and forth, not nervous; anticipatory. Kept hand in pocket. Was shown to a makeshift green room. It happened to be painted, for some reason, the red of Scriabin. I sat in a wing chair. It was green. I got up to pee. I looked at one or two paintings, suitable for hanging behind some fat Regency sofa. I paced awhile. I sat and closed my eyes, listened to the patrons cooing and taking their seats. I peed again.

Nothing to worry about.

Not counting the silliness with the bread knife, attention had been paid. Every nuance, sustain and diminuendo, every commitment to every key was well in hand. Even if the forefinger of one hand had come near to harm. Given the acoustics in that room it might not have mattered if I played with the tip of an umbrella.

Note: Margie: "You do come up with questions. You make my day. You provide me with much-needed relief from questions about 'The Sound of Music.' The umbrella, that's Hindemith. About whom I have already spoken. As for Scriabin, he imagined C-sharp major as a particular shade of red. Not unlike your man, it seems."

Note: He recounts the events of the recital. Make of it what you will. This is his version of the facts, after the fact. I have no idea how much time has passed since the recital and the time of this writing, but whatever came over him has dissipated – or at least settled into something manageable. But there is no way to confirm anything he says here, since whatever happened to him happened only to him.

Notebook, Recital:

Here is, as near as I can remember it, what happened:

Introduction, applause, and my usual brisk strides to the piano. Grey industrial carpet underfoot, not quite clean, loosely laid over the wooden staging. Careful now: tuxedo pumps lack tread. It would not do to trip; no Victor Borge, me.

The piano's glossy black wing was up. I turned and noticed in the distance, on the far wall, the painting of Paul the Hermit – the raven, glossy wing up – and shut it out of mind.

A crisp bow to modulate the applause. For what it's worth – applause, on such occasions, is meant to honour not the player and not the music, but the audience itself, happy to be gathered in its own company: Aren't we all so clever to be here?

It is best ignored.

No hint of anything amiss. All well in the world. Except for the finger. Except for the lingering effects of camera flash. I sat at the keyboard. Shrugged my shoulders to loosen the muscles. A rubbing of the hands, mindful of the close shave of my finger.

The keys – it never hurts to look at them for a moment – are a blank sheet. Wait. Let the sitters settle. Let them cough and fidget, give them time to wiggle their bottoms, wait for them to turn and smile and whisper, roll and fold their programs. That man seated off to the side, trying to find that one last satisfying cough – let him find it. One.

Two. Three. Until they begin . . .

Four. To wonder if there isn't something . . .

Five. Wrong with . . .

Strike.

1. Promenade: *allegro giusto, nel modo russico, senza allegrezza, ma poco sostenuto,* B-flat major.

The first thirteen notes, brisk and confident. I let my mind drift, and began to hum. I occasionally do so; not as loud as Peterson the porter's son, nor poor Gould bent and tangled on the chair his daddy made; but I do hum. It is a way to fall into the stream of the music, a way to cut free of a performance, a way to drift above it.

A picture emerged: Musorgsky's shoes, old, soft, polished, comfortable. He'd been a soldier and knew the value of footwear; he was a minor noble on his uppers, and so he knew humility; he was a drunk, and so he knew chagrin, remorse, and the throbbing temple; above all, however, he was a friend in mourning, and so knew sorrow.

A minor miracle or a stroke of luck: The worst fear had not come to pass. No problem with the finger. And the spilling of the sound without, for the moment, seeing –

I've never been able to explain how I play.

If I knew. I told Claire once that, at times, I felt as if the music were playing me. That I felt it as a wave. That I saw sound as colour, that I felt wave after wave of colour washing over my chest, that it pulsed from my hands. She snorted, or paused to consider. She was absent, as was colour.

An empty seat next to Weller in the front row.

Hard not to notice. What did he know? What did he know about me and the fact that Claire was at that moment in a private room in a hospital down the street and around the corner from the gallery, a short walk from where he and we sat in Walker Court?

There was, at that very moment, less of her to be absent than there had been yesterday. I let my hands find their way through the music, unaware – perhaps not unaware enough – of my ever-so-slightly-pared finger and my ever-so-slightly-pared her.

2. The Gnome: *sempre vivo*, E-flat minor

And so now *snap* the audience to attention. The gnome is a wooden toy designed by Hartmann to hang on a Christmas tree, a gimp, a limping dwarf come to life. I played with the pulp-cutters in mind. As I did, my hands seemed to belong to someone else – to a man who hummed, a man who looked like me and happened to play as well – the man in the window of Fran's.

If I had lost a finger –

3. Promenade: *delicatezzo*, A-flat major
They were straining in their seats to hear me now.

I played carefully. And tried not to pay attention. If I listen too closely, I tend to reconsider the possibilities inherent in the structure of the chords. I can get lost. No stumbles in this prom-enade. Not warmed-up, but warm.

4. Il Vecchio Castello: *andantino molto cantabile e con dolore*, G-sharp minor
Do not play this as architecture. Do not play it as the Dane who sees the ghost. Play this as the thought a man might have if he were alone at night in a castle made of doubt.

5. Promenade: *moderato non tanto, pesamente*, B major
Freshening the sound is what Gould said he did – adding and subtracting at will, speeding up and slowing down according to the whims of his arrogance, ability, autism – as if a fixed piece were an automobile whose seats required new upholstery any time he drove it.

"That's the way I play early Beethoven." Arrogant little – Jesus, how did he get in here . . . ?

6. The Tuileries: *allegretto non troppo, capriccioso*, B major
The fierceness of children playing marbles, or putting hapless ants in paper boats and launching them in the curbside river after a brisk rain. *Nianya, Nianya* is not, as some interpreters would

have it, *Nanny, Nanny*; more likely, it is the universal taunt that needs no translation: *Nyah, Nyah* . . .

7. Bydlo: *sempre moderato, pesante*, G-sharp minor
    A rumbling cattle cart comes along and scatters the children off the street; the cart pulled by a brace of stinking, stupid, heavy cattle, with a dull-witted driver singing a Ukrainian folk song. My accordionist with his metal tooth.

8. Promenade: *tranquillo*, D minor
    Sparkly, hesitant, this time it is anticipatory –
    Oh, poor Gould. The Beethoven crack – that's the way I play, etc.
    I wrote an open letter to the *Globe* taking him to task, and he cracked back in kind and I replied. We had an old-fashioned call and response that lasted a week, GG penning a histrionic defence of his genius self and I, scribbling on behalf of the composers. Helped, on the sly, by the clever, studious Kuerti. We won; which is to say, GG and gg tired of the game and left the field.
    Outside musical circles: "Cat fight."

9. Ballet of the Unhatched Chicks: *scherzino vivo, leggiero*, F major
    If you've ever seen twittering chicks, or children dressed up in eggshell ovals, twittering like chicks . . . I detected a smile on one or two faces in the front row, and a tingling.
    GG called me at home one night. In his whiny voice, he suggested we collaborate on an opera; he had some absurd notion about the Mafia trying to take over the whale hunt in the Arctic. It was late. I was tired. My head was, as usual, splitting.

He said, "Oh, sure, it's the same old story. Not tonight, you have a headache."

And I said it: *Va a fa 'n culo!*

We never spoke again.

10. Samuel Goldenberg and Schmuyle: *andante, grave energico,* B-flat minor

Two old Jews, one rich and one poor. Hartmann walked through the ghetto of his wife's hometown, rubbernecking and sketching those who were kvetching. Musorgsky was somewhat less anti-Semitic than others of his class. He was drawn to Jewish folk and religious music, even if only to pick a pocket or two. I looked up. And saw St. Paul the Hermit gaping at the raven.

St. Paul's gnarled hand –

11. Promenade: *allegro giusto, nel modo russico, poco sostenuto,* B-flat major

This is often skipped by *Pictures* players – Horowitz, for example. I had planned to drop it. At the last moment, I changed my mind.

We live in a small, silly world. Once, during a tricky bit of Borodin, I was reminded of something familiar in a sequence of chords and was startled – several minutes later – to hear Tchaikovsky intruding on my reverie. I had no idea how long I'd been proceeding along these lines; it took all my improvisational skills, and more than a little sleight of hand, to turn one Russian back into the other; it was exhilarating, and no one seemed to notice, least of all the critics. I felt like I'd picked pockets.

I began to feel indifference.

12. The Market at Limoges: *allegretto vivo, sempre scherzando*, E-flat major

A panorama, long since lost. The description remains: Two women quarrel in the market; a man finds his lost cow, and wants to tell the world; a woman shows off her porcelain teeth; a bibulous man bemoans his red and bulbous nose. The music, not particularly difficult, not at all like Kensington, where it was possible to buy a live chicken and take it home minus the best part of its neck, bagged and bloody and –

13. The Catacombs: *largo*, B minor; With the Dead, in a Dead Language, *andante non troppo, con lamento*, B minor

In which a top-hatted Hartmann, along with one of his Paris friends and a guide with a lantern, explores the catacombs; a gloomy little watercolour, not much more than a minute long.

14. The House on Hen's Legs: *allegro con brio, feroce*, C major

This is also part of the AGO show – Hartmann's clock, ornate, ormolu, shaped like the house of the witch, Baba Yaga.

During the first notes, my left hand – more particularly the tingling one with the knife-familiar finger – slipped on the corner of a key while I hammered out the fury of the tick-tock folk-witch clock.

A peculiar sensation, inexplicable and distracting. As if the keys were greased. . . . The notion jarred me. I was aware of an urgency in what I played. I fought the urge to look at my hands.

I thought of Claire. I thought of red.

I stared at the lid of the Steinway: Concentrate – it is lacquer-black, black as Paul the Hermit's raven's wing, as Toby's arse, as coal tar and Stalin's moustache – what did Dzugashvili make of

Musorgsky? Play on. Black as sin or printer's ink, as oil under the fingernails of a mechanic. Play on! Black as a hearse, as the wick of a snuffed candle, as the bottom of a grave dug by a lion. Play on.

15. The Knight's Gate at Kiev: *allegro alla breve (maestoso con grandezza)*, E-flat minor

A Nihilist struck a blow at Tsar Alexander, who survived and commissioned a gate, the competition for which resulted in this sketch, which so moved Musorgsky . . .

Who is the composer? Musorgsky? Hartmann? Tsar Alexander? The Nihilist? Or me? I played on and I looked and I saw white shirts and black tuxes, white gowns and black shawls, black shadows and white lights; and roses, red as drops of . . . Look away.

A rustling in the seats.

The tips of my fingers, red – red notes, red ivory, red dots on my shirt front, roses in lapels. I shivered, halted, shivered – stopped.

Left hand high. And did not move. Could not bring myself to nail the next notes into the gate. Someone coughed. Someone whispered.

Someone rose from his chair.

I can't, at the moment, explain because I don't, at the moment, know. There were murmurs. A voice or two. "Play on!" Play on? A whisper from the wings. "Are you all right, sir? Is there anything we can do? For god's sake, what's the matter?"

I could not describe the matter. It did not, does not matter.

I squared my shoulders and –

"Maestro, may I?"

Lec, my saviour, from the wings. I gasped for words. Couldn't find and couldn't feel my legs, my arms limp, my hands weak –

was there a red light coming from my finger? I was not aware that I was walking. Only that I was tired and happy to be led.

"Finished." A whisper, a whimper.

The director of the gallery – this I remember clearly, his program was rolled like a spyglass in his hands, he was an admiral ready to go down with his ship – reached for my hand.

I would not let go of Lec.

Carter looked me in the face, studied me, turned on his heel and walked out on stage.

"Get me out of here," I said to Lec. "For the love of god, now."

Lec said, "Let's go."

"Ladies and gentlemen," said Carter.

Note: Carter, I recall, was deft:

Something like this: Mr. Amoruso has been taken ill. It isn't serious, but we are taking all precautions. There are, as you know, doctors in the house – which netted small and nervous laughter. He launched into a brief essay about cross-fertilization in the arts – for example, the pictures on display tonight, the music we have just heard, Hartmann's architecture. He was talking blather, for all intents and purposes. I am not convinced by art talk.

"And now, if you would be so kind as to join me, let's go look at a glass of champagne and listen to some pictures."

Notebook, Recital, cont'd:

Funny, what happened. Not ha-ha. I played the piece according to Musorgsky – spare, straightforward, unadorned. I held a note at the gate, I sustained it until it drained away, I held it until the memory of it was gone and silence took its place. And I walked out before I was finished.

I don't know why I am embarrassed – perhaps because I have trained myself not to care – but the memory of what happened causes me to care.

I betrayed myself.

Someone began to clap, a signal. A cue, a rescue. The room began to fill with applause. I gasped for air. None came. No words.

Lec was there.

"Finished."

Note: Back to the scene of the crime.

A pleasant day, in contrast to the tension in these notes. On Dundas St., dry leaves and scraps of wilted bok choy swirled in the wake of passing cars, along with briefly weightless plastic bags, Asian newspapers, and napkins from the Second Cup across the street. In the crisp air, the fat salt scent of barbecued pork, orange peels, soya, and star anise.

Inside the Art Gallery of Ontario, off to the right, a prim young man sat behind a counter minding his nails and the switchboard:

"I'm sorry, sir, I cannot page a staff person while he is on duty. No, sir, I cannot tell you where he is. You may call personnel. I'm sorry, sir. A guard cannot leave his post during his shift. I'm sorry. Now, if you will excuse me, I have calls to attend to."

Perhaps the gallery has a permanent supply of these types, or perhaps snottiness is a condition of employment. For all I knew, he was the one who'd intercepted Dom. I left him sitting on his stool and entered the gallery with my membership pass.

Looked up at the Moore: Draped Reclining Woman.

Her thighs, Claire's? Eyes of the beholder; thighs of the beheld. I never thought of her that way before; I will never think of her again, except that way: knees drawn up, legs slightly spread, anticipatory, about to undergo a dilation – Dom would have turned that into "I laid not" – and curettage – would he have added "get at cure"?

A turbaned guard, with a wordless nod, headed me towards the Canadian collection and watched my back as I went on my way.

A black guard – a blaggard? – with a pink and upturned palm showed me to a small room filled with David Milnes. There, in addition to a dozen priceless paintings and several sketches of low bushes heavy with snow, was a solid, stolid guard standing with his legs spread and his hands clasped behind his back. He was gazing at a filigree of Milne birch trees in a white landscape. He had thick hands and short fingers. His hair was silvery, brush-cut. Who else?

"Excuse me. Lec?"

"Let's what, kind sir? Let's talk art? Let's spend the day in quiet contemplation of this magnificent painter? Let's play twenty questions?"

"I mean your name is Lec."

"So it is, and so you have the advantage over me."

"My name is Joe Serafino. You were working here on the night when the pianist Dominic Amoruso disappeared. 'The Art of Music' fiasco. You were working here. He is – well, no one knows where he is. I am writing about the incident that occurred that evening, and I have one or two questions, if you don't mind."

He pursed his lips and made a calculation.

"It was not a fiasco. It was, overall, not even an incident. Let me also correct your other assumptions. I am Lec Radev. But I was not here. I was there." He pointed with a sweep of his hand to another section of the museum. "A fine distinction, but an important one. Also, I was not working. I am familiar with the Musorgsky. I wanted to hear him perform. I came of my own *accord. You raise an eyebrow. An evening for patrons. I cannot afford to patronize. But I have a uniform. No one notices a guard in a museum. So. I came. Finally, he is not like a tree in a forest."*

"I'm sorry, but I don't understand."

"You said no one knows where he is. As if he is nowhere. The world does not depend on your knowledge of it in order to exist. Consider: Suppose, when I leave this place, these paintings cease to be. You enter a moment after me, thus restoring Milne to splendour. If, a moment later, you go out, is Milne erased again? Useless and exhausting. What kind of world is that? Amoruso is not here. That does not mean he is not, at this moment, somewhere else."

"Let me start again. . . ."

"Permit me to allow you to buy me a cup of coffee. I am due for a short break. We can talk about the maestro and that evening. You may have tea if you prefer it, although neither beverage is what it ought to be in this place."

He confirmed that he had been in attendance that night.

He'd seen Dominic in the makeshift green room – a small alcove off Walker Court containing some of the AGO's collection of European paintings – overripe flowers, fruit in bowls beset by bees, baskets of limp-necked dead ducks, and centuries-old fresh fish.

He said there were several gallery attendants, art girls, hovering around Dominic, dressed in white shirts and black skirts.

"They looked to me like a living piano broken into bits, dumped in a bag and shaken into lumpish, or rather girlish, life."

He said Dom seemed distracted; his hands were fluttering; Carter shooed everyone away, and asked Dom if there was anything he could –

There was not.

As for the recital, Lec couldn't tell me much more than I already knew since I, too, had been there.

"You wrote in the papers – I remember – that he looked like a small boy confronted by a big black dog; very good. I will tell you something you don't know. I heard him run through the Musorgsky several times when he was rehearsing here. He played those nights as well as Richter. How do I know? I was in Sofia in 1958. The famous recital. You might say I participated in the recording. My father was a sound technician. I was pretending to assist. I had a cold that day and was sucking a lozenge. A blackberry lozenge. And I swallowed wrong. Listen to the record – you will hear three small coughings and one big coughing at the start of the second "Promenade." That is me. So. When I say he played as well as Richter, I am telling you as one who knows first-hand. As for Mr. Amoruso, I have no idea why he walked out. It happens. It is not such a big thing. It happens a lot to piano players. I saw him. I took him in hand. Come with me, I will show you where."

The little snot on the switchboard pretended not to notice as we made our way towards Walker Court.

"Piano was there, on a platform. I was exactly here. Maestro walked off this way towards me. His face was blank, as if he saw nothing and heard nothing. He was tired, maybe sad, also fragile. There was hubbub in the audience. I took him in hand. I know where the alarms are. 'Maestro, follow me.' I led him here; please to follow."

I did as Dom had done. I followed. He led me down a corridor, around a corner, down another corridor. The AGO is not a large building, but I lost my bearings very quickly.

"No one was following us. People were a bit shocked. How to react, and so on. Not every day does such a thing happen. I disarmed and re-armed the alarms. This way leads to the room with the Eskimo things. I left him there. 'Don't move,' I said. He didn't. It is a shame. I had a surprise for him, I was going to give it that night – a copy of Richter in Sofia, reel to reel, from the original of my father. I was going to present it after the recital. I did not. The wrong moment.

"I said he should wait and give time for the crowd to go. He didn't say one word. Was just sitting on the floor, holding his own hands and staring at that."

Lec pointed to a large Inuit carving – a man holding a bone knife in one hand, facing a polar bear; the bear on its hind legs; murder in the bear's heart and murder in the man's, by the look of it.

"Did he say anything?"

"He wasn't talking. He was trembling. I have seen it before. It was nothing. People were shocked. But it is a miracle it does not happen more frequently. I left him alone and went over here. To stand on guard, not for thee but he. It took a long time. A lot of people, don't forget, had come to see the exhibition, which, frankly, was not so good as it should have been. Never mind. It is my opinion. So. When the coast was clear, I showed him out of the gallery, hailed for him a taxi, and said to him good night."

"That's it?"

"You have heard something? But of course you have, why else would you be here? Tell me, please."

"No, I don't know a thing. I just wanted to ask. I don't know why I never thought to ask you before. He sat here. What time did he leave?"

"*It must have been close to midnight. Forgive me, but I must get back to work. I have now to guard a sack of dried shit hanging from the end of a pole by a rope. Why, I don't know. Who would want to steal a sack of dried shit? I think you have heard from him.*"

"*I haven't heard.*"

He knew I'd heard. I tried to imagine what it might have been like as Dom sat on the floor staring at a stone man with a bone knife, aware of Claire in the hospital, thinking perhaps also of Singer, a prisoner of some inner madness, his own head aching, his hands tingling . . .

Having walked away.

The cold air keeps my neighbours off the street.

So much the better for me – it is much easier to work when there are no low conversations on the walk below and no traffic save for the streetcar grinding on slow wheels as it rounds the corner.

Instead, I am distracted by smaller noises: the creak of the walls as the temperature drops. Closed doors echo and locks snap shut. My neighbour, the old man in the apartment over-head, goes to the bathroom. I can hear the stump-thump of his dull heels down the hall; after a time I will hear the flush of his toilet. I will hear him again in two hours. Nine steps.

We nod but do not speak when we see each other in the hall. He is retired. He has never, as far as I know, been married. He receives no visitors. He is an old Pole who drinks in the after-noon at the Staropolska Bar. His presence there makes him a pun – he is an old Pole in the "Old Poland." He has no idea what I do for a living. He doesn't read the daily papers. He wouldn't *know my byline if he saw it. He reads only the Polish papers. Given this neighbourhood, this building, his age, and the unpredictability of my comings and goings, he probably thinks I'm a drug dealer. I know, from the sad thump of his heels, that he is an old man with a swollen prostate.*

A concert pianist has a hallucination.

If he was taking the fiorinal plus amnitol, with deltrex, it would be unnatural not to hallucinate.

The next tape was made in the Dorval airport in Montreal. It shows how he got on the flight north – pure chance, I think – and it speaks to his pre-flight state of mind, which is shaky.

As for the corresponding notebook, it is significant enough that I am wary. I am no expert on handwriting, but this much seems clear: These entries were made in a single sitting. My guess is that he made the original notes on the fly in the hours, the days immediately after he walked out of the recital.

He may have scribbled notes on scraps of paper and compiled them here, so as not to lose them. Or he may have used a notebook and decided, on reflection, to dress his remarks up a little. In any case, the handwriting is consistent all the way through.

An aside: If the notebook was recopied, I am convinced this tape was mixed in a studio from a combination of tapes; at one point, for example, it cross-fades from one segment to another quite professionally, and seems cut together like a documentary. I ought not to be surprised. He had studio skills. I am sure he had access to a studio.

Actually, I'm not sure of anything.

I know he played at the AGO. *I know he stopped playing, got up, walked away. And I know he disappeared. That's as far as I'm prepared to go for now.*

Tape, October 18:

[Two voices; the first is that of an older man, a native man, a northerner. The second voice, although strained and higher-pitched than normal, is Dom's. The ambience is hollow. It's late at night – the only announcements now are of flight arrivals.]

"You look like you need a smoke, mister. Want to smoke?"

"I'm sorry. No. Thank you, I don't –"

"It's good to smoke. It helps you think. I like to smoke. I have plenty of tobacco in my pouch. I can roll one for you if you like."

"No, really –"

"I will roll one for you anyway, *kabloona*. To keep my fingers busy. You can smoke it now or later. Eeela, tell me where are you going in those Pingu clothes."

"I have no idea where I'm. I don't even know where I've. Pingu clothes? What do you mean?"

"Pingu. A little penguin on TV. In the cartoons. We watch it all the time, it is very popular in the North. You should watch it too sometime. I was thinking to myself that in your suit, you look very much like Pingu, very much a little bit."

"You used another word . . . *kabloo* – ?"

"I am a person from the North. An Inuk. You are a *kabloona*. *Ka-bloo-na.* A person from the South. Where you going dressed like that, anyhow?"

"I really don't know. I can't even tell you how I got here."

"Here is the smoke. Take it, take it. If you don't know where you are going, you might as well smoke. How did you get here? It doesn't matter. You are here now. I think you are maybe going to Wolf. Go on, take this. If you don't want it now, you might want it later on."

"Where is Wolf, exactly?"

[Flip-chink of Zippo lighter lid; a scratch of flint; the lid is chunk-shut and slipped into a coin-filled pocket; an inhaled sigh, exhaled; silence until a gob of thick spit is hacked up into a tissue.]

"Pretty far away. Very north of here for sure. This place where we are sitting is the asshole of the airport. Just us Inuit come here. When we want to go home to the North. Sometimes there are miners and teachers also, government workers and so on. There will be miners on the flight tonight. Right now, they are drinking in the bar. I seen them. But I don't drink. Not any more. They will drink until the plane is ready to go. Mostly it's just us Inuit here. You can get a ticket from the Nordair counter if you want one. If you want to go to Wolf. That woman in blue, ask her. There's still time. Me, I was in Florida. I went to the Disney World. You been there? I liked it very much. I took my little nephew. We saw that dolphin, Flipper. He looked very good to eat. Oh, yes, we eat those things. I was looking at him and it made me hungry. There is no country food down there. No caribou or seals or whales except for that Flipper. I miss country food very much. I'm going to have some when I get home."

Notebook, October 18:

An object of curiosity in an airport is a man in a tuxedo talking to an old man in a parka. I am short of breath, wide-eyed, wild of hair, carrying nothing more than an overnight bag full of my pretty drugs, a tape recorder, some cassettes and notebooks. I seem to be on the run.

I am in danger of losing control.

A man in a tuxedo ought not to appear in danger of losing control. It lets the side down. A man on the verge of losing control is not capable of composing a list. So, a list:

The man across from me is wearing sealskin boots and a parka with a fur-trimmed hood. I am a man in a tuxedo. I used to have gloves and a scarf. I had an overcoat. He has heavy mitts attached to his sleeves with bright red idiot strings. His mitts dangle.

He is heavily tattooed – there is a cross on his forehead and there are animals on his hands. I have no tattoos. I don't want to stare at him. He sees me not staring.

There are several thick scars on his hands. I have small scars in the flesh between the thumb and forefinger of each hand. I never think of them as scars – they are my octave makers.

I have an overnight bag. I am making notes. He has a pouch of tobacco. He is not making notes. That does not mean he is not making observations.

His name is Etulu. What kind of name is that? My name is Amoruso. What kind of name is that? Suppose I'd had a child with Claire. Suppose this old man was my best friend. Suppose I named my child after my best friend. Etulu Amoruso.

Soon we will be on an airplane.

I have no idea how I got here – a mildly frightening thought. All the way to heaven is heaven. Catherine of Siena would be hard-pressed to include Dorval airport among the many paths.

Excusez-moi, je cherche la route au paradis – ou est-il? Alora, dove u paradi? I am being stared at by pilgrims. *Ici, on parle pellerin.*

Io, pellegrino.

A second list: Things one might conclude from the sight of a man in a tuxedo in an airport in the winter making notes: That the man is an important person. That the man has attended a ceremony in his honour. That the man has won a prize. That the man is a politician, or the head of a large corporation, and he is scribbling in a book because he has important thoughts. That the man is dressed this way because the weather is of no concern to one who is used to being met and driven.

A list of things one might not conclude: That the man is on the run. That something went somehow wildly wrong for him. That the man has no idea what he is doing. That the man has a satchel full of drugs. That the man is very hungry. That his head is splitting. That he can play piano. That the keys he played ran red with . . .

According to the clerk at the counter, there is a flight to Wolf Cove two hours from now. I bought a ticket. It will take us three hours to get to Kuujjuaq – wherever that is; there will be a short layover to unload cargo and take on new passengers; weather permitting, it will be two more hours to Wolf. That's what the clerk calls it. Wolf.

I have the urge to vomit.

I am a lone wolf.

Note: Here, he makes a cross-fade on the tape – the scene shifts smoothly from the airport to the inside of the airplane:

Tape, October 18, cont'd:

[Old man:] ". . . as soon as I get off the plane . . ."

[Stewardess:] ". . . but in the unlikely event we have to make a landing over water, you will find a life jacket under your seat.

We will be serving a hot meal in about an hour. Tonight's menu is a choice of chicken or beef. For those of you who are interested, I'll be coming with the bar cart as soon as we reach cruising altitude [applause and shouts from some of the travellers]. Settle down, boys. It's a long night. We are scheduled to arrive in Wolf Cove at 4:15 a.m. On behalf of the captain, I wish you a pleasant flight and a pleasant night. Thank you once again for choosing Nordair."

[The rising roar of the jet engines on takeoff and a new voice, his seat companion, from the sound of it. A man whose deep voice has the anomalous delicacy of a lisp.]

"You don't mind my asking, where you going dressed like that?"

"Wolf Cove."

"Me, I'm going to Nanisivik. You're going to Big Bad Wolf. You know why they call it that? You'll find out when you get there. You don't know what you're in for. Shit, I'll tell you anyway. Every spring the towns in the Baffin get rid of their scum; they kick out the drunks, the drug addicts, the glue sniffers. Rapists and whatnot. Anyone they can't handle. No place for them to go but Wolf. Only town on the island that isn't dry. Wolf gets the dregs of the Baffin."

"I see."

"You'll see if you're up there any length of time. I seen you in the airport in that suit. Buddy, you're hard to miss. I'll tell you, if that's the only clothes you got, you'll freeze your ass off there."

[No response from Dom except a sigh.]

"You get a parka or you won't last a minute. I'm not kidding, it's really fucking cold."

[Another sigh and a slight change in the drone of the jet engines.]

"My name's Ed Stucky. What's yours?"

"Dominic Amoruso."

"Pleased to meet you. Eye-tie, huh? Don't take offence. I'm a bohunk. You don't mind my saying so, you look like you just got married. Or maybe was gonna get married and got cold feet. None of my business, but I got to ask."

[Dom's answer – the slick and furious flipping of the pages of the airline magazine.]

"Oh, well, don't mind me. I been married. Just the once. One time too many if you ask me. What happened was I smacked her. Just the once. I got fucked harder by her lawyers than by her. That's why I work north. I got the big alimony." [A clearing of throats.] "I seen you got that notebook. You pull it out. I seen you write. I could write a book. About getting screwed by lawyers. Bet I could."

"Yes, I bet you could."

"You like that Walkman? Me, I don't like Walkmans. I stick those ear things in my ear, it hurts. I got the big ears, but I got the little earholes. Anyway, I'd rather listen to live music. In bars, like. Who you listening to?"

[pause; cough, sigh]

"Gorecki, Symphony Number Three."

"You're shitting me."

"Excuse me?"

"Fucking Gretzky. He wrote a symphony?"

"Gorecki, not Gretzky."

"Oh."

Note: It is a measure of his state of mind that he did not laugh. Or perhaps it is a measure of the menace of his seatmate.

Here's a question: Why did Gorecki spring to mind? Is the Pole a straw he clutched at? Or was he sticking it to Stucky? Margie provides no clues except: "The Symphony no. 3 is the deepest expression of Polish sadness. There is no sadder sadness than that of the Poles. They wear sadness like a flower in a lapel. Did you know his mother was Polish?"

I did not. I had never thought of his mother as having any nationality other than "married."

And did I know that the Gorecki no. 3 made Margie weep every time she heard it?

I did not.

Tape, October 18, cont'd:

"Something from the bar, gentlemen?"

"Not for me, thank –"

"Two Scotches, double doubles on the rocks, one for me, one for Gretzky here."

"No, that's all right, I really don't –"

"Nope. You got no choice. My treat. Not to worry. I got enough cash to keep our whistles wet until we get to where we're going."

"But I wasn't –"

"There you are, gentlemen, double doubles. And some peanuts. Enjoy. Can I get you a blanket, dear? It's cold in here tonight."

[Torn snack-pack cellophane, crisp as tinder. Laughter and low conversations hover under the drone of the airplane engines. The talk is easy, familiar – most people on this flight seem to know each other. No surprise, I suppose – small towns make familiar neighbours.

The *fissst* of soda poured over ice in plastic cups.

Dom's seatmate, an open-mouth chewer.]

"No blanket, thank you. Not now. Maybe later."

"Tell you what, Gretzky. Her under a blanket any day of the week. Ass like two bunnies in a bag."

[Swirl of ice at the bottom of a plastic cup.]

"You know that shit about a picture's worth a thousand words? I got what, must be half a million words in my briefcase. I'll show you after supper. Blow your fucking mind, excuse my French."

Notebook, October 18, cont'd:

Stucky is sleeping now. He has the aisle seat. I am stuck with him. The plane is full, there are no other seats. I refuse to tape his snore. I am still not sure how I got here. There is a gap as big as . . . It may come back; it may not.

I remember making my way through late arrivals at Dorval. Which means I must have flown to Montreal after the recital. No memory of that. I have stubble on my cheek, enough to suggest three days without a shave. Did I go to Montreal immediately? No memory. The idea of lost days would frighten me if this flight didn't frighten me more. All things are now divided into before and after. Before the recital, and after this flight.

I still don't know how I got to Montreal.

I remember coming to, if that's the word, in Dorval airport, stumbling over a hockey bag on my way to a water fountain. I remember walking in circles until I found a place to sit. When I had calmed myself – deep breathing, orange pills, and a splash of musty fountain water – I noticed a smell: thick, sweet, rank but not unpleasant, unlike anything I had ever smelled.

I saw him then – a compact, well-muscled man, leaning forward, seated with his elbows on his knees, dark skin, thick black hair, indeterminate age. At the moment, he is across the aisle from me and two rows up. Now and then he turns and grins at me. He is hard to miss. You cannot mistake him. There is a crucifix tattooed in the centre of his forehead.

I suppose it takes confidence to know that, as soon as others see you, they see indelible stupidity. And it will be the first thing they see all the days of your life. Get used to it? I don't suppose I would. But it is a gauge, in a way. I am sure he reads other people by the way they react, or try not to. We sat in silence in the airport. I watched him and he watched me. He did not move, although the arms of the cross tilted when he frowned or squinted. I made no effort not to stare. I observed: his fingers thick, sinewy, and crimped at the ends with hard black nails; the hood of his parka, trimmed with fur; soft grey, knee-high sealskin boots on his feet. That was the smell. Him, in sealskin.

This whole plane smells like sealskin. And, for some reason, Kentucky Fried Chicken. Fuck it, a bucket. I have a right to be frightened. I want to throw up. I have no idea what I'm doing. Stucky snores; the plane shudders.

The old Inuk seemed unconcerned in the airport, as if he sat across from frightened men in tuxes all the time. After a while he walked over to a potted plant, coughed, and spat into the soil. He looked at me, and spoke a few words in what I presume was Inuktitut. I did not respond; no idea what he'd said. He spoke again, this time in English. His voice was deep, thick, rough at edges.

He said I looked like Pingu in my tux.

Apparently, that is some sort of cartoon creature. He gestured with a pouch of tobacco and offered to roll me a smoke. I shook my head. He rolled one for me anyway. And he said something else in Inuktitut. The language is a tumbled mix of glottal stops, gutturals, and saliva. I have no idea what he said, but I swear it sounded like, "Emmy Lou, Glenn Gould he cleaned your clock really good, ah."

Of course he didn't say that. But that's what it sounded like and there was no stopping him; he placed a thatch of tobacco in the palm of his hand, folded a leaf of flimsy rolling paper over it and rolled it into a cylinder with efficient delicacy. He licked it, sealed it, pinched shreds of tobacco from each end, and handed me a perfect cigarette.

I tucked it behind my ear.

He offered me his Zippo. I declined with a shake of the head. The smoke fell from my ear. I plucked it out of the air with my fingers and tucked it back behind my ear again.

Dexterity, or a fluke?

It didn't matter. He smiled and lit his smoke with a thick flame. He sniffed and snorted, sighed and swallowed, expelled white plumes of tobacco. Eskimo: I smoke. That word, *kabloona*. He explained it meant bushy eyebrows; me and all the others like me. Eyebrows like the Scottish whalers. Furry as caterpillars. *Kabloona*.

He wanted to know where I was going. I told him I had no idea. I don't know if he believed me. If he thought I was being rude, he took no offence. He squinted at his cigarette; spit-wet at one end, ash-tipped at the other, soft as silk. And suggested a place for me to go.

I could have stayed put.

It's bad enough that I walked off stage in mid-chord. That's what I did. I stood and walked away. That is not an explanation, it is a description. Bloody fingers, bloody keys . . .

When the world ends, go to the end of the world.

North: The idea of.

There was room on the flight to Wolf Cove.

A quick check: I had wallet, credit cards, and cash. A bag full of tapes, drugs, and notebooks, possession of which must mean that I'd gone home, ignored the ringing phone, loaded the bag with black books, red-jacketed plastic tapes, and a polka-dot array of blue-and-white pills, orange pills, red and yellow pills. . . .

I seem now to have a destination.

There is something familiar about the tattooed man – something in his posture, his attitude. I will remember or I won't, but I worry because at this moment I can't. I make notes so as not to forget.

The other passengers are mostly men, miners by the size of them and the way they joke and drink and swear. There are also one or two mothers with babies. A blind man could tell there were babies on this plane; they cry as one. A blind and deaf man could tell there were babies on the plane; they fill their diapers as one.

The old Inuk turns and grins at me, he gets up and leaves his seat, walks down the aisle to the washroom, stops to ask if I'm all right. I am not all right. If I were all right, I would not be here.

Amoruso and Etulu. Miners and mothers. Babies and me. And Stucky overflowing his seat. He is sleeping; he is snoring; he is drunk.

We are stuck in this together.

I make these notes to pass the time. No sleep for me.

We talked. No, Stucky talked. I killed the recorder and put the bud mics in my bag. He might have asked to listen to the tape. To see how well Gretzky played.

"You fucking taping me?"

He works in a nickel mine. Three months in, three weeks out, and if he isn't lying through his teeth, then last year he made more money than I did. The camp is dry; he drinks as much as he can on the plane because the drinks have to last him a long time.

For supper I had cubes of chicken in what was supposed to be tomato sauce, served on a lump of gluey noodles. Stucky had cubes of beef slopped on the same gluey noodles. I hardly ate. He ate his supper, cleaned his tray, drank his wine and mine, and had two more Scotches. By the time the trays were cleared and the coffee poured, he was not talking, he was grunting.

He wiped his greasy fingers on his shirt and took his briefcase from under the seat. He flipped the latches with his thumbs and retrieved a manila envelope. He handed it to me and said I should take a look, and keep it to myself. The envelope was filled with photos, glossy black and whites, taken in a hotel room.

A table, a bed and him on it.

In the first photo, a slip of a girl kneeling between his fat white hairy legs. She with milky skin, skinny arms, black-ink tattoos – a bird with one wing spread over the rise of her left breast, and a claw poised to clutch her nipple; thorns or perhaps barbed wire circling her right thigh; and above her pelvis, a Gothic "Glenn" – her boyfriend, or her pimp.

Too bad Gould is dead. I could have told him about the hooker with his name on her belly. *"No, no, no, I don't want to hear it."* He'd have covered his face with his hands. He was sufficiently a prude that he is supposed to have shielded his eyes when, late at night, driving back from a session of studio work in New York, he passed the live nude girl neon of Times Square.

I am no prude, but I should have blinkered mine.

The photos showed the girl on her knees and on her belly. There was a photo of her on her side with her legs apart, not unlike the Moore of Claire except she was not a draped reclining woman, she was a raped, declining woman; no, not old enough to be a woman. There were photos of her breasts, her feet, her hair. Photos of him in her, on her, over her. Photos of him spreading her, pinching her, kneading her, splitting her like a fig. Her eyes staring dully at the camera.

On the wall next to the bed was a dim oil painting of a stag standing by a mountain stream in the middle of a forest clearing. . . . I am stoned at the moment – warding off the usual. Suppressing the usual. Calming the unusual. She must also have been stoned. She couldn't have consented without the help of drugs.

She probably did it for the drugs.

He is still snoring, elbowing me, leaning on my shoulder.

Did he fall asleep on her? He gave me the photos without embarrassment or explanation, he took them back with a grunt, resealed the envelope, snapped the briefcase shut, and fell asleep. He is now dreaming; presumably, of her.

As, presumably, will I. My arousal disgusts me.

What in god's name am I doing?

We are delayed in Kuujjuaq.

As if I know where that is. Somewhere in Northern Quebec, apparently; I had no idea there was this much North. We are sitting on the tarmac, besieged by the wind. Stucky slept through the landing. Eleven people got off. The plane is rocking on the runway.

There was no snow in Montreal. There is much snow here, and it looks as dry as sand. In Montreal – I remember this quite clearly – the trees were still thick with leaves, and there were flowers in hanging baskets along the broad avenues.

I seem to have flown from early autumn to the dead of winter.

It is impossible to see much, other than the frosty yellow shafts of light leaking from the terminal. A few faces at the windows staring at the plane. Snowbanks along the runway. Half a dozen trucks half-hidden in the shrouds of their own exhaust. . . .

It must be very cold. Must be, shit. It is.

We waited for an hour. They would not let us off. I am swaddled in the blankets provided by the stewardess. Moments ago, eleven passengers in parkas boarded the plane and raced for the empty seats: more old people, more laughter, more babies, more packages wrapped in cloth and tied with twine, jammed in the overhead bins. Every one of the eleven looked down the aisle at me. Word must have travelled: Pingu on the airplane. The new passengers brought in the cold with them. I shiver. I cannot stop shivering. Stucky snores through it all.

I have no idea what I'll do when we arrive.

I don't know where I will stay or what I'll do if there is no place to stay. The prospect is slowly becoming terrifying. According to Stucky, I am stuck. One flight in or out each week.

He offered his hand as I got up to leave. I hesitated for a moment. He had slept with his hand between his legs. I didn't feel as if I had a choice. His skin was hot and curiously soft – a good thing or a bad thing for the girl in the photos? Given what he'd done to her, I don't suppose she was grateful. He told me to buy a parka.

We arrived in darkness.

There was no warning, other than the gradual descent of the airplane. Nothing visible from the air. All the lights are blurred.

I am unstoned enough for an observation: It is possible to arrive in any city in the world with no notion of the lay of the land and no knowledge of what you ought to do or where you ought to go, and yet still find your way. Because even in a country where the language is not English, there are pictograms directing you to the washroom, the coffee shop, the city bus, the taxi stand, and so on; anywhere in the world. Not here.

In Wolf Cove there is no kiosk, there are no signs, there is no airport coffee shop, there is no taxi stand, and if this is a town, it does not seem to have any downtown. The terminal is a hole in the wall through which luggage – I have none – rolls frostily. I pretended to have luggage. Stood with my hands in my pockets, peering at the suitcases and the strapped wooden crates and the cord-tied boxes as they rolled by.

I did not need to pretend I was anxious.

On the walls of the terminal are posters of a polar bear, an iceberg, some tiny Arctic birds and flowers, and a printed warning not to take any meat or ivory down south without a permit. I promise. . . .

If you have not made arrangements, as I had not; if you don't know where you are going, as I did not; if you have no real reason to be here, as I had none; then, to borrow an expression from my seatmate, you are royally fucked. No one just drops in on the North.

But I have done so. And I am at a disadvantage. Not just because of my tuxedo, although the tux is bad enough. I have paid the price of panic a thousand times over. I am unready. I – a man who prides himself on readiness – might easily have changed clothes, and might have done more than sweep a few things into my flight bag.

I might also have gone south, towards warmth.

Everyone but me knew what to do, was properly dressed and had friends waiting at the terminal. Helplessness is uselessness; a useless man is a burden. I had hoped someone would size me up – "Hey, look, here's a guy who doesn't belong here, let's see if he needs a hand" – but everyone, including my friend who smelled of sealskin, took their bags and boxes and disappeared into the blistered darkness.

I walked over to the desk and asked the attendant – gold hoops in her ears, orange lipstick, gum in her mouth, blue uniform with red scarf knotted at her throat, blonde hair in a bun – where I might find a place to stay in town, and where I could get a taxi to take me there. She looked at me with curiosity – is this guy kidding me? – returned to her paperwork and said in a monotone, "Taxi through the door to your left if one's not there it will be there soon unless they think they've got everyone but you could call there's a phone over there you could call the transient centre it's cheap but I hear it's full or maybe try the Wolf Cove Inn. Now I've seen everything."

This last, under her breath.

I walked to the door.

Metal frame, dented and scuffed, frost as thick as velvet; fragments of refracted light trapped in the glass by the cold; the doorknob burned my hand and the night air burned my lungs. White breath, black air. A single truck idling.

The airline clerk with the gum in her mouth looked at me like I was an idiot when I told her I didn't know what number to call. She let me use her phone. Dialled for me. This is a place so small it takes only four numbers to use the phone.

A cab came quickly.

Wolf Cove Inn. Best Rates in Nunavut. Satellite TV. No Drinking. No Fighting. No Drugs. Check Out at 11:00 a.m. No Exceptions.

I asked for a room. Reached into my jacket, pulled out my wallet – I know how to do that – and put my credit card on the counter. It is the universal language, plastic.

"No credit cards; cash only; how long you plan to stay?"

"I don't know."

"You don't know how long you're staying?"

"Let's say a week."

"That's $700."

"I don't have that much cash."

"How much do you have?"

"$450."

"Then you can stay four nights. Longer if you can get some more cash. That's up to you. Here is your key. Your room is on the second floor, top of the stairs to the right, halfway down the hall. There is no drinking in the room. There is no drugs or parties in the room. There is no loud noise in the room. There are no non-smoking rooms. Sign here."

I signed there.

The room is simple enough. A metal cot with a thin mattress; a plywood desk with a wooden chair by the door; a brown plastic radio screwed to the top of the night table; a gooseneck lamp screwed to the night table; a portable black-and-white TV with rabbit ears, screwed to the top of the chest of drawers.

There is no mini-bar. There is no chocolate on the pillow. There is no room-service menu offering a post-recital omelette, a basket of fresh fruit in season, and a glass of wine. There is no bath with thick white towels. There is no crisp white linen on the bed.

There is a plywood floor covered with chipped grey linoleum. The walls are stained. The sheets on the bed are thin and sour and I don't have the nerve to ask for clean ones in case this is what passes for clean up here. The room is thick with cherry air freshener, old tobacco smoke, human funk.

Did someone laugh? Did a cellphone ring? Did I black out?

It seemed as though I might have. Did something go wrong with the drugs? Was there or was there not wet red blood on the keys? My fingers, apart from the nick, are unmarked.

Who knows, who cares now?

The old man in the airport was familiar.

I was sitting on the floor of a room in the gallery feeling like a fool, staring at a carving of a man with a wild grin on his face and a knife in his hand. The man with his knife held high. Facing a polar bear. Stone drops of blood on a white bone knife?

My old man with the cross on his forehead. That's who he looked like. The rest is a blur.

There is a party down the hall.

So much for the admonition about liquor and guests and noise. It is 5:15 a.m. Someone is pounding on a hollow door down the hall.

"Hey Billy open the fuck up I got the fucking ice."

"About fucking time. What took so fucking long? Get the fuck in here. I'm dying of thirst in here."

A conversation from the room next door:

The man says "You fucking rat, come here." The woman whimpers, sniffles, says "Don't call me rat. I'm not a rat. I'm an Inuk."

I have no blank tapes at the moment. Just as well. Someone has just tried to get up and has fallen back on the bed. A squeak of bedsprings and a grunt. The remote control for the television is attached to the night table with a twelve-inch length of wire cable, as if somebody might walk away with it. I picked it up and pointed it at the TV. Pressed On. Nothing. On. Nothing. On. Nothing.

The man tells the woman to get him another beer if she knows what's good for her. She gets the beer, but she does not seem to know what's good for her. The beer is on the other side of the wall. I can hear her fumble for a can. I hear the snap-hiss as she opens it. Maybe she is praying he'll pass out.

I turn the television on by hand. A knob, you pull it. The screen blinks twice; white noise is a blotter of noises. I won't guess what they are doing next door. No need to guess.

The picture on the television fades into snow when I am not standing next to it. No matter how I spread the rabbit ears. Volume up: the familiar news, the familiar news reader. His bald head, his pursed lips, his oddly nasal "Kyanada."

Peculiar – why is there news at this time of the morning?

An item about the decline of the dollar. An item about the decline of trade with China. A feature report about the decline and fall of the health care system – an advocate says it is next to impossible for women to have certain procedures in some small-town hospitals, except in an emergency; the situation is not much better in large towns. Cut to an operating room; the sound of suction; the doctor in a calm flat voice asks the patient how she's doing. Her drugged voice. "Fine." Her bare knee.

"Turn that fucking thing down!"

I did as requested. Her drugged voice. "Fine." The knee – a shift of the white sheet draped over a fleeting shooting star? A woman with her legs spread, and a doctor speaking calmly. Claire?

Unlikely. Likely. Unlikely.

I am here and she is there.

And I have heard her voice when she is tipsy and I have heard her after sex when her voice is low and throaty and I have heard her when she is curt and cross with me but I have never heard her drugged.

It could have been a thousand women. It was one woman. I closed my eyes and thought of her knee and watched the image flicker.

To be attracted to a woman while she is in the midst of her dilation and her curettage . . . My tux, and – how ridiculous – my French-cut vest hang on the chair nearby. My empty shiny shoes. My lifeless socks.

"Turn that fucking thing off, for fuck's sake!"

The walls are so thin he could punch his way through and turn the TV off for me. Pills are my salvation; two more won't hurt.

Measure my wealth according to the coin of codeine and I, with my bagful, am Croesus with a splitting head. Everything I touch hurts me.

The party down the hall shows no signs of slowing down. Or maybe it is starting once again.

Of course it was her.

The smell of this room grows more complex as I thaw out: Under the cherry funk is the smell of steam heat, overheated drywall, wet wool and urine, cigarette smoke, and the smell of – Jesus, there it is again, the KFC from the airplane. It is an invasion of privacy.

I do not have privacy any more.

No one knows me here, but everyone here must know by now that I, in my tux, am very much here. And I know no one except a man with a tattoo in the middle of his forehead.

The odd man out is me.

I turn the TV down. *That*, apparently, *is more fucking like it.*

I am disoriented, not because the pills haven't sent me to sleep as they usually do. I am disoriented, not because of the smell of this hotel, which disgusts me. I am disoriented, not because I recognize the voice from the room next door – it is the man who yelled at me through the walls last night. Why do I find this reassuring? Continuity.

I am disoriented because I seem to have lost a day.

Notebook, October 21:

Events, as follows:

I have been here seventy-two hours now. Or more or less. I must have spent twenty-four of these hours in bed. Call this the return of hope, or the entry into civilization.

I will – under influence of the last dribbles of a bottle of San Gimignano, a good and giggly wine – expand:

After I got up – whatever day it was – I walked down to the hotel lobby and asked the woman at the desk if there was a clothing store in town. She – glorious and sleekly fat, her straight black hair hanging around her shoulders and shining like a tent lit from within – did not look up. She was counting receipts – licking her thumb and turning the corner of each yellow slip of paper with methodical intensity.

I sensed that, if she did look up, she would have laughed at me. She said nothing. Several men in filthy parkas, some northern and some southern, were smoking cigarettes and milling about near the entrance. They were on their way to work, or waiting for – what? I have no idea but I am certain one of them said, "Look at the fucking penguin."

As if there were only one joke in the whole of the North and the punchline is a man in a tuxedo, and here I am. The woman at the desk continued not to reply so I went to the hotel coffee shop and sat at an empty table.

The noise – laughter, conversations, stirring of spoons – died. As it would in a movie. Upon my entrance. So I sat at a table and made notes. *Nota bene*. Pretending all was normal.

Note: This last part of the account – the part written in the hotel room – was originally written in a Hilroy scribbler. I recognize the familiar blue lines and red margin. He has cut and pasted the pages into one of his regular notebooks, although nothing is regular for him now.

I pretend to look at murals on walls of the hotel dining room; they are crude, but vigorous nonetheless: a team of dogs pulling a wild man on a sled, the wild man lashing them with a whip; a man dressed in skins peering at a hole in the ice, his harpoon raised high; a polar bear standing on its hind legs, surrounded by six huskies, one of them bleeding along its flanks; a man with a rifle following three caribou over the tundra. All that's missing is a man dressed in a tuxedo standing on an ice floe, pursued by a raven.

It helps. These observations. Pretense of control. A man in a tux in this place is no more strange than a man in skins in the south, although the tux is the less practical garment. I will hear whispers until I find suitable clothing. I should have insisted on playing in my leather jacket. I'd be, if not warm, then warmer than I am at this moment.

My finger, my single-digit stigmata, smudging the ivory as if it were a bingo-dauber – somehow all of that has disappeared. There is no red on these hands. Not at this moment.

The key to sanity: There may be blood in the past; there might be blood in the future; there is no blood now. In fact, apart from the ketchup in bottles and the lipstick on the waitresses, there is no trace of red in this room. I pretend to be fascinated by the murals; making notes about them gives me something to do.

A man with something to do is a man with a purpose.

I am like the crazy man who talks to himself as he walks down the street, feigning involvement in the world. The waitress pays me no mind; deliberately so, I think.

The air in the coffee shop is thick with the blue salt smell of smoke, the hot fat smell of fried eggs, the limp brown smell of buttered toast, and for some reason, liver and onions – a smell not unlike the old man's sealskin boots.

I place my hands on the table and look down at them. The tips of my fingers are as they should be.

Except for the nicked one.

I am trying to appear normal in the face of the gathering silence and the unsubtle craning of necks in my direction. The waitress is otterish and could easily be a twin of the woman thumbing receipts at the front desk – the same tiny shapeless breasts, the same shiny tent of hair, the same ripe skin and wet black eyes. She is avoiding me. Not because she does not see me.

Everyone in this room is breaking his neck trying not to see me. She does not know what to do.

I just waved a hand at her. She ignored me. And then I coughed and she, her hips aswivel, came over because she could no longer avoid doing so, watching me as the others – construction workers? – watched her.

I asked for a menu and we started a tennis match.

"The menu's on the blackboard."

"What blackboard would that be?"

She aimed a dimpled chin at the wall behind her.

"It is there for everyone to see."

"I see. I mean I didn't see it. Two eggs over easy, sausages and toast, and a cup of coffee, please."

"Breakfast is over for the morning; it says so on the board. There is no breakfasts after 9:30. Right now it's after 10:00."

"I see."

"No, mister, not really you don't."

"You're right, I don't."

She pointed to another blackboard on the other side of room. As if to say any sensible person would have not only seen it, but would also have known there is a time of day when breakfast is served and a time when breakfast is not.

Where the fuck do you think you are, fucking Bloor and Yonge? Fucking College and Spadina, maybe fucking Fran's? No fucking coffee until lunch. Okay, when is fucking lunch? Fucking noon; delete the fuckings. They are my own invention, assertion, insertion.

I see. I saw. I say.

"Let me try this another way. Where can I get a cup of coffee now?"

"Down at the coffee shop, but the coffee shop is not open yet. If you want to get a coffee now, you have to wait till noon."

I may have thought for a brief moment not long ago that I had red light or red blood or some sort of C-sharp major plasma leaking from the tips of my fingers, but I'm no idiot – if I have to wait for a cup of coffee, that means I cannot have it now.

"Okay. If you cannot give me eggs and a cup of coffee, maybe you can give me some information."

"Such as what kind of information?"

"I need some clothes – a parka, a pair of boots, some mitts or gloves. Is there a clothing store, a place where I can get a parka? Or do I have to wait?"

"Northern Ventures."

"I'm sorry?"

"You will be when you get there. Northern Ventures."

"Northern Ventures is . . . ?"

"A store where you can get some clothes. Where you can get them. Clothes. It costs a lot of money there. If that's what you want to get."

"How do I find – ?"

"Out the door, turn right and follow the ring road."

"Follow what?"

"The ring road."

"What's that? No, wait, I get it. A road in the shape of a ring."

"You got it, Pontiac." Giggles.

"Follow it until – ?"

"Until you see the sign."

"What sign?"

"The one that says Northern Ventures. You better take a cab."

"Is it far?"

"It's not far. But you won't get anywhere the way you're dressed like that because it's very cold." Giggling, jiggling as she walks away.

And she will tell the story all day long.

There was snickering, and the conversation in the room began to swell before the doors had closed behind me.

Did you see that?

Can't believe my eyes.

Etc.

Not what I would have said, but it's what I would have thought if I were them. The men in the oily parkas were still blocking the hotel door. I excused myself and they parted, but only just barely. I headed out the door and the cold slapped me in the face. A cold slap, not a cold snap.

This place had snapped cold a long time ago. Whereas I snapped only recently.

Might as well have been midnight. There was a row of beige taxis, cheap Russian things, Tinkertoys with plumes of exhaust pinned to their tails. I took a deep breath, hailed a cab, and coughed. You have to breathe slowly here. I'm learning how to breathe. I thought I knew how. It is so cold, you gasp. No cab cut loose from the rank.

I picked one, the nearest, it was too cold to be choosy. I jumped in and slid my cold bottom across the seat. The driver grunted, put his car in gear and waited. The smell of seal, alcohol, vomit, coffee with milk, and of course cigarettes.

"Northern Ventures, please."

He scraped a peephole in the frost on the windshield, gunned the motor, slipped the clutch, backed up and fishtailed until he was turned around, then sped out of control, out of the parking lot and down the ring road, across a small bridge over a ditch, around the corner and into the trees – except there are no trees here, and the road is nothing but one continuous corner. There are black rocks, and there is white snow.

Northern Ventures was where the woman said it was.

I paid the driver cash – the fare for the quarter-mile was roughly equal to the price of a bottle of good wine – and got out. And sidled carefully up the steps – the tux is bad enough, but pumps are ludicrous on ice – and pushed my way through frost-whitened doors. Not before I'd burned my hands on the cold railing.

A small grey man with curly hair, mutton-chop whiskers, and a thin and downturned mouth looked at me askance and, antsy, asked, "Who in bloody hell are you? No, don't tell me. Let me guess. You want to know how to get to Carnegie Hall. Practise, you silly bugger. Or else go back out the door, turn right, and head south for eighteen hundred miles. Start now, you might get there by spring."

"I need a coat."

He stared hard at me.

"You need more than that. You need a coat, scarf, hat, pants, wool shirt, wool socks, good boots, and warm gloves for your hands. Unless you brought luggage, but I hear you're travelling light. In your case, maybe you want mitts. Better for the hands is mitts. You'll find coats on the rack over there. Boots in the bin, in back of the rack. Other things are elsewhere. Feel free to look around."

I walked up and down the aisles in a state of grace or wonder.

I might not be able to get coffee at the hotel but for as long as I am here and I have money I can buy a jar of seedless raspberry jam and a packet of biscuits covered with Belgian chocolate. I can buy capers in brine and smoked meat in packets from Schwartz in Montreal. I can buy a box of sea salt from the Brittany coast and a tin of motor oil from Pennsylvania. I can buy sour cherries from Poland, olive oil from Bari, and all the caviar I want from the Caspian Sea. Not to mention wool sweaters, snare wire, and egg timers.

Along the far wall, I saw the parkas. I inspected a dark brown one with a fur-trimmed hood and was trying it on when the grey man walked up to me. "You want forty-two regular. That is too small. You don't want snug. Try this instead." He helped me put a slate-grey parka on and zipped it up for me as if I were a child. Two layers – an outer shell and an inner duffel cloth liner. I was warm for the first time since I arrived.

"You'll want boots. What are you, a ten? Rubber boots with insoles and liners. And I have these hats. Freeze your ass if you don't have a hat on your head." He pointed to a cardboard box of brightly knitted, tasselled caps. "And you said you want the mitts, rather than the gloves. If you're worried about your hands, you better have the mitts."

I hadn't said. He had said. Why would he think I was worried about my hands? The crack about Carnegie Hall when I walked in.

He gave me pause.

"Now, unless you intend to run around town in that monkey suit, you want a pair or two of pants. I'd say you are a thirty-two waist and a thirty-four leg. And flannel shirts. Not stylish but warm. Help yourself to briefs over there. Get a belt. I'll throw in socks and handkerchiefs for nothing."

He took what I had gathered, hauled it over to the cash register and rang it up. The bill came to nearly a thousand dollars.

I took out a credit card.

He cocked his head. "You can't use a fucking credit card in here. Cash on the barrelhead. These people would go nuts if they had credit cards. They do not understand the concept of the timely payment of bills. Untimely nonpayment is more like it. If you have a cheque, I'll cash it. Otherwise put these on – you can change in the back – and then go across the street to the bank, open an account and bring back a fistful of money. If you need help, I will vouch for you."

I must have looked drop-jawed.

"You're not going anywhere. There's only one plane in and out of here a week. No place to hide. In the sticking-out department, you are a sore thumb. Never mind. I expect you for supper this evening. I'll pick you up at your hotel. You are, if I'm not mistaken, in room 223 of the lovely Wolf Cove Inn. Don't look so surprised. This is a very small town. A shithole, if you like. But we are all in it together. And I am the mayor. There is nothing worth knowing that I don't know. Do your banking. Come back and pay me. Then take a walk around town, get to know the lay of the land."

I must have gaped.

"I know who you are. You disappeared a week or so ago after a performance in Toronto. No need to worry. Your secret is safe. You could be Yehudi bloody Menuhin for all anybody cares. Nobody in this godforsaken place knows a thing about music but me. It's all country and western, even on the fucking CBC. I had to browbeat them into letting me play classical music on Sunday nights. One bloody little hour –"

"Who, if I may ask, are you?"

"Arthur Parsons, at your service. I know everything and everybody in this town. The only thing I don't know is how long you intend to stay, Signore Amoruso. And that is what I plan to find out at supper tonight."

Note: Dom's writing style is conversational – he writes as easily as if he's talking on the phone – by which I mean this is precisely how he sounded whenever he talked to me on the phone.

First Wolf Cove Tape, October 21:

[He is now narrating; his voice is casual.]

Until I can place an order for new books, I'll rely on this machine. Luckily – thanks to Arthur Parsons and his marvellous store – I have access to audio tape.

[He clears his throat; his giggle, replaced by a yawn.]

Dinner tonight – his town, his place, his show. I could hardly refuse. The notion of other people's cooking gives me the creeps, but this was a pleasant surprise. I don't know where I would have eaten otherwise.

Parsons lords it over this town like a feudal prince. He lives in a rather large house a mile or so on the outskirts. The road – it angles off the ring road like the tail of a comet – is narrow and has three dark ruts where tires have worn the ice down to the gravel. A car going east or west has easy going; but when two cars approach, there is a mutual slowing down until one driver chickens out and unruts. All northern roads are like this. It comes from hugging the centre.

Good advice, that: Hug the centre.

The house overlooks a bay. That is, it overlooks a bay when there is daylight, of which there are two hours on average at this time of year. Arthur Parsons built, he says, the house himself.

Expensive, and improbable: German windows, Italian hardware on all doors and cabinets, American solar technology on the roof. He has a sunroom filled with flowering plants. Not that there is sun at this time of year; but he has lights and generators, and generators to back up his generators. He has lived here for thirty years, in this house for twenty.

Parsons, in summary: left Liverpool as a boy, shipped out with the merchant marine, got a job on a supply boat to the Arctic, jumped ship here – he has no idea why except he thought it was a good idea at the time – took odd jobs, worked hard, saved his money, now owns half a dozen properties including an office building, a coffee shop, and Northern Ventures; was elected mayor two years ago.

From the outside, the house is plain. Inside he has: a silk flag from the Snail quarter of Siena, a sketch of a woman examining the hair between her legs. I peered at her, peering – a Picasso, real by the look of it – and professed surprise; he rolled his eyes and asked me if I liked that sort of thing. I wasn't sure if he meant Picasso, or women. The drawing is worth a small fortune but he says no one would steal it because no one knows or cares about Picasso in this godforsaken place.

He has eight heavily carved mahogany chairs with plush red velvet seats arranged around a dining table, seventeenth-century Spanish, maybe fake and maybe not. He has a blowpipe; the shell of an armadillo; Inuit prints and several good carvings; a brass sextant; two old rifles; a narwhal tusk; Armenian rugs on every floor.

It feels a bit like the McCord Museum.

His Bang & Olaf is newer and better than mine. He has four speakers, the size of small refrigerators, in each corner of the living room. A wall of records, tapes, and CDs. Impressive,

eclectic, quite a lot of opera. All the pianists. Two of my recordings, pulled out for my benefit and sitting on one of the speakers. Was there anything I wanted to hear? He didn't wait for an
answer. Gould, *La Valse*; the prick.

I wasn't sure if he meant it as a taunt. He jacked up the
volume and handed me a cold bottle of San Gimignano and a
corkscrew with a scrimshaw handle. He apparently brings it in
by the case from Italy, don't ask me how, he didn't say, I have a
hunch I'll find out.

He left me in an easy chair and disappeared to prepare supper.
Half an hour of banging pots and cursing produced two plates of
impeccably poached Arctic char with lemon sauce, roasted potatoes, Brussels sprouts in browned butter, and an apple tart – the
tart boughten, he said, *boughten*, plus espresso and calvados. The
first meal I can remember since the airplane.

He said – I think this is pretty much verbatim:

[Here Dom mimics an English accent]

"I trust you've enjoyed supper. I am out of good cigars at the
moment. I have some Cubans coming in next month. Try one of
these. Hondurans. I'll bet you can't tell the difference. Now. I'll
come right to the point. We get the papers up here. We get them
late, but they do come in. You walked off the stage in Toronto.
There's a search on. Did you know that? The airline agent knows
you are here, but he doesn't know who you are and has never
heard of you. He wears loafers because the tying of shoelaces
requires mental effort. Others are not so stupid, mark my words.
If you want your whereabouts to remain secret for more than
the time it takes the Mounties to make a phone call, then just ask
me. I'll call the sergeant. I'll have a word with the airline people.
I know the president. He used to work for me, years ago.

"If you've done nothing wrong – I trust you haven't, apart from spending too much time on the Russian repertoire – the sergeant will be happy to keep his gob stopped, and will stop other gobs.

"The Wolf Cove Inn is not what you're used to. You are welcome to stay here if you like. I have plenty of room. I'd welcome a diversion. Intelligent company being in short supply and so on. But perhaps you prefer your privacy. If you like, I can arrange a place for you to stay. There are vacancies on civil servant row. Government accommodation. Beggars can't be choosers. You are, at the moment, a beggar. If you plan to stay here longer than a week, I might be able to get you an apartment. Public Works owns most of the housing. All of it subsidized. Nobody will build or buy in this town as long as they can suck on the government tit. That doesn't concern you. In any case, you won't get a subsidy; you aren't a civil servant. It will cost you an arm and a leg. Freda Kuntz is in charge at DPW. She owes me favours. Life up here depends on favours. I scratch hers. She scratches mine. We scratch yours, and you – when you get the chance – will scratch mine."

What else? Oh, yes – he had advice:

[The English accent again]

"It's no good staying here and doing nothing. You'll go crazy. There's a piano in the school. You can use it at night. The senior music teacher is an ass, but the woman who teaches the kiddies is a nice young native tart. Perhaps you're not interested in tarts. Or natives. None of my business. Do as you like. But the piano is there. The head of the music department, Ken McCardle, I don't trust him. You want Geela Ashevak. She works with the younger kids. Teaches music in Inuktitut."

It's not that he was too polite to ask. He is many things but polite is not one of them. He put it bluntly. He asked when I planned to play again. I said I didn't think I could, I didn't know, I wasn't sure. He asked if I had stage fright. I said I thought it was a bit more complicated. He said nothing is complicated. There is a thing to do, and you do it if you like, or you don't. I wish it were as simple.

He made a proposition: "I have much too fucking much to do. Run this town and run my business. The Inuit are lovely people but they get up when they want to, bless them. The ones with more than a pinch of brains are working for the native organizations; they make far more money than I can pay. I have a sullen little bugger named Sam Willy – Sam Won't is more like it – who helps me at Ventures, but I need someone who can actually do a day's work. I can't pay much. Can you get up? Note, I did not say can you get it up."

I felt like I was falling through the looking glass.

Yes to government housing, whatever that is. Yes to the job, not for the money; he's right about the benefits of diversion. He gave me a ride back to the hotel. Where I am now, and where I am pleasantly drunk and pleasantly tired and where I am minus, for the first time in days, a splitting head.

I asked Arthur about the news on TV.

He says they feed features overnight by satellite to the station in Yellowknife. They do it in the early hours of the morning, when nobody in their right mind is up. That's how he put it. In their right mind.

I am up. And I am out of my right mind.

The party has started up again. I don't care. There is noise from the room next door – rat this, bastard that, don't you hit me, don't you hurt me. I don't care. The television is unavailable for some reason. The radio sputters. I don't care. Last week I was on stage in a tux at a piano playing for a roomful of idiots. And then I was running for my life.

Tonight I am huddled in my new parka at a desk in a room on the second floor of a sealskin-smelling hotel in a small town on the west coast of a frozen northern island, and I have a job at minimum wage.

I have no idea how I got here.

Or how I got to Montreal.

Never mind the red blood on the keys or the drops of blood on the black lapels.

He knows who I am. He wants to know how long I'll stay. How do I know?

✦

Note: He must have bought fresh batteries. He has also bought a scribbler, the same size but obviously not the same quality as his French ones. Given the closet full of wonders that is Northern Ventures, he could probably find a way to import them by the case.

Notebook, October 22:

Freda Kuntz of the Department of Public Works is six feet tall, matronly and masculine, abundantly warm, and could snap me in two if she wanted to. Not a woman to be trifled with. She has a thick Swiss-German accent. Her apartment is overheated, smells like ginger cookies, and is overdecorated in the Black Forest style – ornamental cuckoo clocks, dark wood panelling, heavy furniture. She eyed me up and down as if I were a piece of salty meat at dinner.

"You'll have tea, ya?"

Left me alone in her living room while she went to put the kettle on. Lime green carpet on her floor, lace doilies and embroidery samplers on every surface. A serving tray with six gold-rimmed glasses resting on a brass-bound chest. A cabinet filled with crystal, a polar bear skin on the wall, and a birdcage shaped like the Taj Mahal, whose occupant is a small white hyperactive lovebird. Not a book in sight. But, like Arthur, she has an incredibly good stereo.

Tape, October 22:

"So. I pour you a cup. You take sugar, milch or lemon, help yourself. Arthur says you are needing a place. He says you like piano music. I have over here these *Goldberg Variations*. Gould is too cold for me but many people like him. You do not? Arthur said you did. No matter, I don't play nothing if you don't like to hear nothing. So. I have one unit of white row housing available. It is furnished. There are –"

"White row housing? Row housing for whites?"

"Ach, that's a good one. I got to tell that one to Arthur. Row housing with white siding. It comes with pots and pans and so forth, we furnish everything. It cuts down on the moving costs. It is temporary, you understand this? If someone is sent here to work from Yellowknife, you have to move. I cannot make no promises about how long this place might be vacant. We don't usually give white row housing to bachelors. But there is no demand right now. It's getting pretty soon Christmas. So. A month. Six months. A week. The new year. Who knows? Read this form and sign it and give it back to me and I will give you the keys. This is what we call the March-In."

[Spoons circling in hot tea in bone china; the frenzied chirps of a small bird scratch-pecking at the door of its cage, the sound like furious tiny typing.]

"You want to see something, I'll show you. I'm just going to open his little door and let him out."

[Gasps, laughter – his surprised and hers, companionable; she's seen it before, clearly – the flutter of tiny wings.]

"Look out!"

"Watch he doesn't –"

"*Dio madonna*, I've never seen anything so . . . Look at the way he's just gone for the bear, he just dives right in. I never thought I'd see a little bird attack a polar bear. He must think – what? – he thinks he's protecting his mate."

"Come to momma, pretty Snowball, there you are, pretty bird. Aren't you my pretty little Snowball. He sits on my shoulder like this and picks my hair. His mate died a month ago. They were a long time together. This is a problem for lovebirds. They mate for life. I thought he was going to fade away to nothing, maybe he was going to die, so I ordered a replacement lovebird sent from Montreal. I put her in the cage with him. He pecked her to death. It was horrible. I went out in the evening and came back and she was lying in the bottom of the cage, with her lovely feathers all red and bloody. It is because of the memory of his mate that he killed her. But he's not trying to attack that polar bear. He's trying to make love to it."

"You mean he's –"

"Ya, he is attracted in a primitive way to the colour white."

Tape, October 22, cont'd:

[He is still in the hotel. He has placed the microphone near the wall of his room. The tape detects the merest nasal country music. "– *all the night spots, dance, drink beer and wine; if you got the money, honey* –" snap of the tab of a beer can, tab skitters on the floor – "Shit!" – squeak and shift of mattress. "– *I've got the time.*" A friction of rubbed hands and a cracking of knuckles; four. He sighs.]

Note: My ears are much too sensitive now. When I remove the headphones, everything I hear seems twice as loud as it ought to be. I sigh, and with a sigh, recap:

He fled to Montreal.

I suppose I could track it back if I wanted to, and learn if he went there straightaway or took a panic-stricken circuit. In any case he remained in Montreal a couple of days, no more, no less. I'd like to think he was, as Buddy Keane suggested, busking. But it is unlikely. He would have recorded it and I would have heard it by now. Then again, he may have kept some tapes from me. I have no way of proving otherwise. Just as I have no proof he sent these.

He may have been on the move and came to his wits only to find himself between planes at Dorval with nothing to do.

Having talked to a tattooed Inuk who smelled of sealskin, tobacco, and sweat, he bought a ticket and found himself on the way to Wolf Cove, looking at photos of a skinny drug addict performing sex acts on a miner in front of a still camera. Add the continuing vision of drops of blood, and the allusions to a penguin –

Have these people got their poles in order? There are no penguins in the North. Pingu is a southerner.

I suppose the joke, if there is one, is that he's really lost.

*He then walks into a general store, buys a parka, has supper
with the mayor, gets a job, meets with a bird with the hots for a
polar bear skin, and finds a place to stay.*

I'm not making any of this up. I'm transcribing it.

Notebook, October 22, cont'd:

Note: A form letter, folded over, and pasted in a notebook.

P.O. Box 400
Wolf Cove, NWT

March-In Procedures:

If this is your first time in the North, we at Public Works Canada
(your landlord) welcome you and sincerely trust that your stay
here will be a pleasant one.

Because housing in Wolf Cove is at a premium, we regret that
we are unable to give you a "choice" of homes, but rather we
match the size of your family with whatever home we have vacant
at the time your application is received.

There are some things you cannot do in your new home, i.e.

- have a pet (see attached memo re restrictions)
- attach wallpaper or mactac without written permission
- paint any part of the unit without permission
- construct or demolish any part of the unit
- erect antennae, build fences
- use crawl space for storage areas

Most housing units DO NOT have adequate storage space for
such items as bikes, canoes, boats, Ski-Doos, lawnmowers, etc.
We suggest that you inquire about this from your Department's
Housing Officer.

If we can be of assistance, please visit our office.

The appraised rent for your unit is $2,200.00 per month.

The net square meters of your unit is 120.2.

We look forward to meeting you.

Freda Kuntz
Northern Property Manager
D.P.W.

Note: He must be losing his grip. Or he is caught in the throes of a boredom so colossal –

There is no point in transcribing this next tape; in fact I still can't believe I wasted the time it took to listen from start to finish, and I don't know why he bothered to send it. He has narrated a single game of solitaire.

He set the microphone on a table somewhat clumsily – thunk – and recorded everything: the dumping of three cubes of ice in his glass; the pouring of a long drink of what I presume is liquor; and the shuffling of the deck of cards – old cards, from the feathery sound of the shuffle. And then there is the painfully slow dealing of what is apparently a hand of klondike. He calls each and every card as it is turned over.

I suppose it would be possible to reconstruct the deck as it was when he dealt it, because it's all there – the cards atop the tableau, each third card turned up from the deck, and the subsequent moves – ace of diamonds on the foundation, six of clubs revealed and moved under the seven of hearts, and so on, and so on, and so on.

I'm not sure what the point is. In any case, he lost.

There is a gap in the tapes and notes. Several months are missing.
I presume he has been working in the store. I presume he is still
in white row housing. I presume he has learned his way around.
But whatever hit him in the AGO – if it was more complicated
than pills – has hit him again.

Notebook, January 7:

Sunday evening. I am on edge, on the edge of the sofa. As of
now, the air is thick and smells of sweat; of waste. Arthur gave
me a bottle of gin for Xmas. I am reading an article in an old
National Geographic magazine about the sense of smell, including several scratch-and-sniff squares, and a chart to help test the
acuity of the reader-scratcher-sniffer's nose.

I spent all day pricing rubber boots and stocking shelves
with ammunition, stacking kilo bags of Greenland shrimp in
the freezer. In my nose: rubber vapour, lead and brass and wax,
plastic: it claps. I have a perpetually splitting head.

The magazine is dog-eared, a year old. The smell test is un-
scratched. I shall test myself.

The first square is odourless, as far as I can determine.

The second square is a flower of some sort; I can't quite tell
what it is, the scent will come to me in a moment.

The third is musk, disgustingly pungent.

I once went to the supermarket and, as I shopped for groceries,
I brushed past a woman who had doused herself in patchouli. I
walked up and down the aisles, past the lettuce and the laundry
soap, crossing and recrossing the trail of her scent; now and
then one or two bubbles of musk would burst in my nostrils;
repugnant.

The fourth square is not cinnamon; synthetic cinnamon.

The fifth square, rotten eggs. For a moment I felt like throwing up.

A reminder of summer afternoons when the wind blew over the neighbourhood from the paper mill and my father in his underwear, in his easy chair idly staring out the front window, cutting a deck of cards with one hand over and over again, drinking beer and smoking his pipe to kill the stench.

The last square, a generic floral scent, the sort of smell Americans spray in their bathrooms or their kitchens. A smell to kill all other smells.

The air in the apartment is thickening.

I cannot get the taste of sulphur out of the back of my mouth. I sniff the second square again; the vague memory of flowers. It occurs to me that I am sweating: waste gin.

Except I have done nothing more strenuous than draw breath. The heat in the room is oppressive, but it is too cold to open the window and in any case the window is glued shut by an inch of ice.

A moment ago, I opened the tap: apt. Nothing. The water is unaccountably turned off. That happens here; the water lines freeze and burst. If there was an announcement on the radio, I missed it because I can't bear the sound of the radio.

A moment ago there were two pills in my hand. I cannot recall taking them from their bottle. I tried to swallow them without water because there is no water. They stuck in my throat. I retched them up and immediately retrieved them before they melted – waste not, want not. I got an apple from the refrigerator, chewed a mouthful and swallowed the pills with the apple. This time, I kept them down.

I disgust myself.

I can feel the heat pulsing from behind the walls. My hands are cold.

There is a bitter taste in my mouth. For the sake of argument, suppose that the room is not shrinking.

It is, I am certain, shrinking.

Or it gives the appearance of shrinking. And I am losing my mind. And I don't know who to call. I know it is physically impossible for a room to shrink. But if this room were somehow getting smaller – I'm not actually saying it is; just suppose it were – then there is nothing stopping me from picking up the phone. I could summon help.

I could call Claire. And tell her.

She would say airily, practically, matter-of-factly – and has, as a matter of fact, said – "Don't be silly." Would add, in this instance, "Rooms do not shrink. Bank accounts shrink. Heads are shrunk in the hands of savages and psychiatrists. Hemlines do not shrink, they rise or they fall according to the whims of the season. Violets, on the other hand, are reputed to." That was the second scent square: violets.

If I replied, "I suppose you're right," then it is possible that I might, having said it aloud, believe it to be true.

But I cannot call her, not in this state. We have not spoken for a couple of weeks now. She may think I am ignoring her. She is impatient with me because I have yet to tell her precisely where I am. Better not to call. Not tonight. Her impatience would snap me in two like a twig.

If I assume this room is not shrinking – if I *entertain the notion* it is not – then I might be able to pretend it to be true for as long as it takes to fall asleep. But I don't trust myself asleep. The walls might crush me as I slept. It would be too late by the time I felt them. No way to escape. To take a sleeping pill at this point would require the nerve of a suicide, which tonight I have not got – neither sleeping pills nor nerve.

I am staring at the phone. It is a squat black toad.

The phone stares back. It doesn't matter what is true. If I think this room is shrinking, then it is. And I have a bottle of gin. And I have a drink, a double with no ice. There is enough ice outside. I will not have it in.

The gin is hot. The room is warm. And the walls are nearer.

I am trying not to look. I am staring at my glass. There is a country song coming from the house next door – someone is smoking cigarettes and watching *Captain Kangaroo*. Don't tell me I've nothing to do. Look at the walls. Count the flowers on them; violets.

The walls are nearer. If I had a tape measure, I could determine by how much. If the toad of a phone were to ring, I would not be able to say hello without weeping.

A ticking in the air. The heater. The walls creeping in.

I have just lifted the receiver to make sure the phone is still working. Because if the walls are moving, it could be that the telephone wires have pulled free from their connections.

It is a way of telling.

There is a dial tone. Peculiar, to my ear. Not the usual flat grey buzz; this time, a tinge of yellow. It might be a ruse. It is the sort of dial tone the machine would send when the walls were moving – in order not to alarm the occupants.

Do you understand how close I am to cracking up?

I have recorded the dial tone for reference.

I have recorded the voice of the operator telling me, in English-French-Inuktitut, to please hang up the phone.

I have recorded the silence after she did so. And the subsequent loud alarm. And the silence after the alarm stopped ringing. Then I hung up. And then I picked up the phone to hear if the dial tone returned. Because someone might have tried to call while I was ... And if the phone was not ... The smell of the scent squares lingers in the air.

How much more of this?

Note: *The tape with the sound of dial tone and the voice of the operator is missing, or has been erased.*

Notebook, January 8:

I slept, I woke, I vomited. After which, I took more pills and turned off all the lights and curled up in a ball on the couch and fell – thankfully – asleep again. It is now mid-morning, cloudy and cold, the light as thin and as grey as it always is on cloudy days.

It feels stupid to write it, but it's true: The walls did not move.

There is a flight south the day after tomorrow, if the weather holds. I could buy a ticket, I could put on my tux and put an end to this.

If I don't take the next plane, I will have to wait another week until the next one. . . .

At the moment I am supposed to be cleaning the storeroom in the back of Arctic Ventures: piling cardboard boxes filled with used junk, old clothes, unsold toys in boxes corner-soft from use and use again. Making room. I will instead make notes.

I left for work, frightened by the thought that I might not be able to go back to the house, for fear of cracking up. I counted dogs on the way to NV; fifteen of them during the course of a five-minute walk, of which nine were mongrels on the loose – nervous, jealous, snarling, ready to attack but afraid of being beaten – and six were sled dogs snapping at the ends of their chains. There were ravens on the hydro line – five wires, thirteen birds, as if the opening notes of the Musorgsky had been inked in air. . . . The birds flew off as I neared.

Am I Paul the Hermit? Is this place a desert? Ought I to find a cave? I found three disposable diapers, two of which had been torn open and stripped of their contents by the hungriest of the strays; one diaper unripped because empty of anything edible.

And there was blood along the footpath – bright red spots.

There is always blood on the ice in this town – ribbons, welts, and gouts of blood, strings of blood, specks and drips and drops of blood. People quarrel easily here. Alcohol dulls prudence, heightens the perception of slights, blunts the fear of fists or knives. A trail of red dots, growing redder as I walked.

Not blood from a split lip or a torn ear, it seemed too thin, somehow. I looked up and found that I had been following a short man who was – aha! – coughing and spitting. Every few steps, cough and spit. Tuberculosis?

White clouds of his breath in the air. I had escaped being crushed in my room, my head had not burst apart, I had managed not to lose my mind, but I was inhaling the breath of a man with tuberculosis.

I thought I ought to tell Arthur. He would ask who it was. And so I took note of his parka and the way he walked. That's how you tell who's who around here – by the fit of their parka, by their posture and their gait, and by their hats if they have them. This man had a bit of a limp; there were three round blue Hunter & Trapper patches sewn onto his left sleeve; on his head, he wore a knitted blue-and-white toque. Arthur would know and he would tell the health nurse who it was.

When I arrived, the door was unlocked and the lights were on and there he was at the counter. Immediately, last night's apprehension was swept away by his brusque good cheer:

"For Christ's sake, look at you. A case of the vapours, is it? Mustn't let it get you down. Cabin fever. It hits everybody up here, even the bloody Inuit. Usually in the spring. Hit you sooner than most, apparently. Nothing to be done. We're all in the same boat. Why should you be any different? Clean up the back room, there's the lad, and I'll buy you lunch when you're through."

I nearly wept with gratitude.

I told him in a rush about the spitter. He looked at me with a mixture of mirth and pity. "You poor bugger, you haven't been here very long, have you? That was Petaloosie. He sucks on cherry cough drops. Addicted to them. Buys them by the case. I order them in bulk just for him. He goes through a box a day. It wasn't blood, it was spit."

Towards the end of the afternoon, Arthur left Sam Willy in charge of the store. He said he had a surprise for me and I should come with him.

Sam Willy glowered and said nothing. He doesn't like me because Arthur likes me and has given me more responsibilities. No one calls him Sam, it's always the double-barrelled Sam Willy. Except for Arthur, who calls him Sam Won't to his face. Sam Willy swore under his breath because I was getting a break. Tough luck, Sam Won't.

I pulled on my parka and followed Arthur out the door.

The trucks in this town run all day long, are always frosted on the outside and overheated inside, and they always smell of cigarettes, motor oil, cold tools, and pine air freshener. I presume the pine serves as a reminder of trees, of which here there are none. Trees: reset.

Arthur drove. The tires of the truck, after standing idle for a mere two hours, were squared on the bottom. As we rode along, I felt like a finger being dragged across a keyboard. "You'll enjoy this," he said as he pulled into the parking lot of the school.

He left the truck unlocked, and opened the side door of the school as if he owned the place. He smiled at the kids, waved at the teachers, and led me to the gym. A small boy, not much bigger than his basketball, was shooting hoops; trying to.

"You, there – little Kunuk – where's the bloody piano?"

"In the bloody music room, mayor."

"Arthur, I said I didn't want anyone to know –"

"Never mind that. Nobody will know who you are. I just thought you should see the piano. The music room is out that door and down the hall. Room 123. You'll be surprised. Don't you like surprises?" Spurs rise.

"Mayor, when is bloody Wolf Cove Days?"

"Don't say 'bloody.' Do you know when Easter is?"

"Yes."

"Wolf Cove Days is after that."

"Oh, that's too bloody far away. Can't we have it earlier?"

"We can't have it until the ice breaks on the river, you little scamp. And watch your mouth or I'll wash it out with soap. I'm the only one who can say bloody around here. Who taught you to talk like that?"

"You did, mayor. When is the ice going to break?"

"Go ask your father."

To me: "His father's a very good hunter. Go on, have a look at our piano. I have to talk to the principal for a minute. Anybody asks what you're doing, say you work for me."

"But I don't –"

"I'll meet you back here in half an hour."

The door to the music room was closed. No light showed through the frosted glass of the door – frost indoors up here. No sounds of practice. I tried the handle; unlocked. I swung the door open on a tall, slender man, standing with his back to me. By his side was a sullen little boy, perhaps eight years old, with a porridge-bowl haircut. I startled them.

Not true: I startled the man.

The boy seemed clenched, closed, withdrawn, far from being startled. On my entry, he turned away from the teacher, jammed his fists into the pockets of his jeans and stared at the floor. The teacher began to gather his papers from a desk near the piano. He made a show of it. As if that's what he'd been doing when I opened the door.

Along the top of a blackboard on the far wall, I noticed the alphabet in syllabics. And on the near wall a map, curiously inverted, showing the view you would have if you were standing astride the North Pole, looking south at the rest of the world.

The clock read ten past four.

"You can run along now, sonny. I'll see you again tomorrow after class." The boy walked away without looking at either one of us. "Tomorrow, after class," the teacher called. The boy shrugged, shoved the door hard and let it slam shut.

"The Inuit have a gift for music. That's Pootoogook. He's very strong-willed. Both his parents died in a fire last year. Alcohol, don't you know. But I have hope for him. My name is McCardle. How can I help?"

He offered a hand; pale, soft, moist. He has sandy hair, a patchy beard, skinny lips, and yellow teeth. He was wearing a blue ski jacket over his sport jacket. The air in the room, thick as the smell of orchids.

I said I hadn't meant to disturb him during a lesson, I'd thought the room was empty, there were no lights, I'd come to look at the piano.

I don't know why I apologized. Perhaps because it didn't look like there had been a lesson. The fallboard of the piano was closed and secured with a cheap padlock. McCardle turned to face me now, holding a sheaf of papers; mimeographed sheet music, the notes purple instead of black. He smiled and stroked his beard but he didn't mean the smile.

"You are Amoruso. I've seen you at Northern Ventures. There is a pianist of that name, in Toronto I believe. Oh, we are aware of Toronto, even though we are remote. Are you a relation, perhaps?"

"No relation, not really."

Tape, January 8:

[His sleight of hand with the tape recorder more than a match for the teacher:]

"Arthur has told you about our little piano, then, has he?"

"He hasn't really told me much at all."

[Zip of briefcase, rustle and shuffle of papers, rezip; case closed.]

"A Steinway. Are you surprised? These little things were made for the American troops during the war. There was a DEW Line base here for years – you've seen those buildings on the hill behind town – they left the piano when they pulled out. Do you play?"

"A military piano? I had no idea there was such a thing."

"Nice to know we have something Toronto doesn't have. Are you sure you wouldn't like to play? I'll unlock it if you like, and you can see for yourself how it sounds. Let me. I must be. I have a meeting to attend. I'll just. It's a bit out of tune. We have a man who knows how to tune, but he's down south for a couple of months. I've never learned. I'm quite hopeless with my hands."

[Unlocking, unhinging, the knock of the fallboard, McCardle's proprietary stab at middle C.]

"There you are. Close the door on your way out."

[His footsteps receding. A door opens and closes with a pneumatic sough. Dom stops the tape recorder.]

Note: It is impossible to know if he played. A guess is useless. My eyes refuse to focus, my poor ears hurt, my back aches, and my hand is cramped – minor annoyances.

My tape recorder is out of batteries; my printer is out of ink – major annoyances.

If there's an urban equivalent to cabin fever, I have it.

I quit –

(Later) I spent the afternoon at the Revue with a box of popcorn in a seat close to the screen. A seat with broken springs. An old war movie shot amid blazing dunes, with camel charges and small brown men screaming and falling backwards with red wounds in their breasts. Useful, straightforward, guts and glory. More to the point, an escape.

I returned home to the ringing of the phone: Margie. She'd come across something I might find interesting. Was now a good time to bring it over? As good a time as any.

What she thought I might find interesting was a double order of churrasco – grilled chicken bathed in salty hot sauce, a tub of bland rice, another of roasted potatoes, and a tomato salad. I like a girl who eats with her hands. I like a girl who drinks beer out of the bottle. When we finished eating she put on her coat, reached into her handbag, and dropped an envelope on the table.

"You might want to take a look at this."

In the envelope were photocopies of articles on the subject of stage fright. She'd highlighted passages about prodigies who had burned out early and disappeared; the names of leading therapists with leading theories. There was an article about Victor Borge, whose on-stage schtick was developed as a response to the jitters, and a short piece about the guitarist Julian Bream, who suffered from stage fright for years. And this quote, from Stephen Fry, who walked out of a play in mid-performance and hid for several weeks: "I can only offer cowardice, embarrassment and distress as excuses for such absurd behaviour."

On a yellow sticky: Did I want her to follow up on any of these? No. I'm not persuaded Dom had stage fright. It isn't just that Dom has more nerve than a sore tooth, but he has never, to my knowledge, been afraid of anything in his life. If I had to guess: All this red blood, white keys, black tuxes, white shirts, black shawls, white gowns, and red roses – and this business of the shrinking room – is either a reaction to an unwise combination of his drugs, or a cover of some kind.

He could be making things up. This whole package might be an elaborate false trail. He might simply have been seized by an overwhelming pointlessness. Who among us has not wanted at some point to turn our backs without a word of explanation?

As for the drugs, I have no idea what Dom was taking – or, rather, what combination of things he was taking – or what *happens when you mix one thing with another. Dr. Capek is cagey. So far, I suppose, the easiest explanation is some sort of drug psychosis. It's a relief to have written that down.*

There was a cassette in the envelope.

Margie is a clever girl. She had made me a copy of "The Idea of North." It is what Gould called an exercise in contrapuntal radio.

He recorded several people – a geographer, a sociologist, a nurse, a surveyor, and a bureaucrat – talking about the North. He mixed their voices and their thoughts over the so-called basso continuo of the Muskeg Express running north to Churchill.

Gould's subjects talked in stiff, self-conscious voices about their impressions of the North, and how ill-prepared they were when they arrived; how they see themselves in the landscape and among the people; and the problems of a policy conceived a world away in the South, and inflicted without much compromise on the people of the North. On some level the documentary was, so Gould said, an analysis of solitude – the myth we have in Canada, not of a Wild West but of a frozen North. Gould was entranced by the notion of a place pure and white, cold, clean, and spacious – his sensory metaphor for loneliness and for quiet isolation, the wellsprings of his creativity.

It may have been daring radio – certainly, a concert pianist trying to communicate in a medium other than the piano was daring in 1967 – but the documentary, if that's what it is, is snobbish, stiff, unoriginal, and hard to listen to. Plenty of references to Shakespeare and Pirandello, Eldorado and Utopia, Prospero and Caliban. There are no native people. Not a word in Inuktitut.

The flaw is typically Gouldian. There was nothing in his North to show how northerners might view southerners. In addition to which, the device he used of overlapping voices was a contrivance, an annoyance, an impediment.

Are these tapes – and was Dom's flight north – a journey towards the limits of Glenn Gould Thought?

Notebook, January 8, cont'd:

Sam Willy was still stocking the same tins of stew on the same shelf he'd been stocking when we'd left. Arthur sent him home. He left without a word.

Arthur, to me: "What do you think of that little prick?"

"Sam Willy? *Testa dura.* Always does things the hard way. I don't know why –"

"You're right about him. I meant McCardle."

I said I thought there was something just past ripe about the man. Nothing I could put my finger on. A smell, a hunch, a suspicion. I told him that there was a boy in the room with him and the door was closed and there was no sound of a lesson. I felt I had interrupted something when I walked in.

Arthur said he had his suspicions. He said there was talk in town. Nothing more. Just talk. About kids – and there are no happier kids than Inuit kids – who became sullen and withdrawn when they reached the fifth grade. Who dropped out of school early. Who started sniffing glue, who started to drink and fight. For no apparent reason.

Sam Willy – had he studied music with McCardle?

Arthur finished stocking the shelf.

Note: Apart from a singularly vivid bout of cabin fever, he has chosen not to acknowledge the effects of the long black northern darkness or the long white northern silence. He has jumped over

winter . . . I presume he has simply packaged and sent whatever
tapes and notes he considered germane.

I should presume nothing, and pay attention.

—

Notebook, April 19:

Wolf is laid out like a wheel, with an igloo-shaped church at
the hub. Small streets fan out like spokes along which live the
government workers, the civil servants, the nurses, teachers, and
professionals. The ring road forms the outer rim of the wheel.

From the top: Wolf Cove Regional School; Lutaliaqvik Public
Health Clinic; the RCMP station; the Wolf Cove Inn; a Ski-Doo
dealership; the Hunters & Trappers store; T-One – Arthur's coffee
shop – so-called because it was the first Temporary Government
Building; the Nunatsiaq Co-op; the Royal Bank; the transient
centre; a garage whose sole purpose seems to be the repair of taxi
cabs; a machine shop; several warehouses; Northern Ventures.
None of the buildings have signs, and none of the streets have
names. There are no sidewalks. The people who live here know
where everything is. You are an outsider until you stop asking for
directions.

Between the town and the beach the Inuit workers and
hunters live side by side with the town's drunks and glue sniffers,
the unemployed, the unemployable. They live in five-twelves –
houses that are 20 ft. x 26 ft. and contain all the amenities, such
as a bucket for an indoor toilet. Such as a space heater and a gas-
canister stove. Such as windows covered with plastic. Drinking
water, delivered weekly by the town. Some of the five-twelves
hold families of eight. My piano studio is 424 sq. ft.

I am no longer considered unusual in this place. No one stares. That I arrived in a tuxedo is the merest rumour. There is no more whispering. It is unclear to me if Wolf Covers know who I am – apart from that man who hasn't been here very long; that man who came by himself; that man who works at Northern Ventures. I am that friend of Arthur's.

Who I was down south doesn't matter here, because this is not down south. There are, however, a few things I consider unusual: There is no neon. There is no bookstore. There is no fresh food. There is no alcohol, except at the Legion. Most people order their booze from the territorial liquor store in Yellowknife. It is as if you lived in Montreal and had to order drinks from Vancouver.

I am learning to find my way. I have yet to learn not to stare at the wreckage of Ski-Doos and sleds, the tangled skeins of rope, the rusted oil drums and random antlers, the skins on home-made stretchers, and the dogs – dogs on leashes, running loose, or lying on the roadside, idly chewing bones or eating dirty diapers.

Earlier today, I took a walk to the beach. It is spring now; still cold but daylight is returning and the sun is sharp as acid on the snow. Although the harbour – perfectly protected, with a wide flat beach – will not be open for some time, sheets of ice like giant shipwrecks have been crushed and pushed up by the tide below.

I was making my way past the five-twelves when I heard music. Not the ululation of the dogs, which is constant. This was something both unexpected and familiar, snatched away in the wind and then returned to me from over there, from where, from there. I slipped as I walked, straining to listen, following my ear.

Tape, April 19:

[The siren songs of staked dogs howling, the whisper of his parka as he walks, the nasal keening of the singers and the tinkle of a guitar and a mandolin. Margie instantly recognizes the Louvin Brothers. I did not ask how she knows, or if she has cowboy boots and a gingham dress in her closet. A girl with depth. I digress.]

"You got some new clothes, Pingu."

"Well. I haven't seen you since the airport."

"I see you working for Arthur now."

"I don't see you. You don't shop at Northern Ventures?"

"I buy from the Co-op. Or the Hunters & Trappers. Arthur don't need my money. You want a smoke?"

Notebook, April 19, cont'd:

Etulu was sitting out of the wind, beside his house, on a sofa cushion, on a sheet of plywood on the ground. He was carving what seemed to be a woman with the body of a fish, or a fish with the head of a woman. He wore dusty overalls, a parka with the hood up, cotton gloves, and rubber boots. He sat on the cushion, not for comfort but to protect his ass from the cold. He held the woman between his legs, leaned forward, turned her this way and that, moved around her with a rasp, soothing and smoothing her, talking as he worked. Clouds of breath and cigarette smoke; puffs of dust from the stone. The stone was mottled green. He took off his gloves and laid down his tools. His hands – the anchor, the rabbit, a heart in blue ink.

The cross on his forehead.

Tape, April 19, cont'd:

"I forgot. You don't smoke. I remember from the airport now."

"Do you mind if I?"

"You taping this for the radio?"

"No, I'm just . . . It's not for any . . . I'm taping it for myself."

"I don't mind."

"I have a question."

"*Kabloona* always have a lot of questions."

"Well. Can I ask you about the tattoos?"

"The tattoos."

"How did you? When?"

"We were kids. A long time ago. Nothing much to do."

Notebook, April 19, cont'd:

I have never been tempted to get a tattoo. But I am beginning to understand what "Nothing much to do" means here. It means you kick some gravel, get a pizza-pop at the Co-op, wait for the plane, drink a cup of coffee at T-One, watch the weather; not much else going on. You give yourself a tattoo.

Perhaps, if I stay here long enough . . .

Tape, April 19, cont'd:

[The sound of the rasp on the stone; short, rapid strokes and then a pause, and Etulu spits; he rubs the stone with his bare hands, and then grunts lewdly, like a man about to come.]

"They like that, eh – touch their backs like that."

"You made the tattoos yourself? How did – ? If you don't mind my – ?"

"You take a needle from your mother when she's not home. You look at yourself in the mirror. You break a ballpoint pen and dip the needle in the ink, and then you stick it under the skin. Or sometimes a bit of soot from a candle."

"Didn't it hurt, to do that?"

"It hurt a little."

Notebook, April 19, cont'd:

While he talked, he worked on the belly of the woman with his file – a scuff, a brush, a rub. Her breasts were small, her body was thick, her tail was a fish's. The tips of his fingers were red and raw from rubbing, smoothing, filing. The piece was coming along, the work seemed to be going fast. He'd caught her in mid-gesture, swimming in stone. The cross on his forehead was indistinct, covered with dust.

Tape, April 19, cont'd:

"You know who this is?"

"A woman?"

"Sedna."

"Who?"

"The goddess of the sea. The mother of the sea creatures. It happened a long time ago. Her family wanted her to marry a shaman. He lived across the water. She didn't want to but her parents forced her to. They were going across the water in a boat and she was crying because she didn't want to go. A storm came up. They got afraid. They threw her over the side. She tried to climb back in the boat but they wouldn't let her. She was clinging to the side. They chopped off her fingers with an axe. Also her hands and her arms. She fell back into the water. Her fingers became the fishes, and so on."

Notebook, April 19, cont'd:

He punctuated the story with his rasp.

I suppose it makes sense. It is as good an explanation as any, and better than most religions. If we are the origin of the fishes, then we are God. I was acutely aware of my own fingers as he talked. What would it be like if someone were to cut them off? I imagined the blood in the water billowing like a curtain of red music, and that familiar split-second's worth of absence before the recognition of pain.

I thought for a moment of Claire.

Tape, April 19, cont'd:

"That's a good story."

"We have many good stories – we have the two giants who were fighting, we have the woman who fucked the prick of the lake, we have the man who – ah."

Notebook, April 19, cont'd:

It happened just like that.

He picked up the woman, held her in his hand, thought about what he still had to do, turned her over for a better look. Her tail snapped off. Rotten as chalk. A flaw in the stone. I wanted more than anything to rewind the tape, to catch the snap of the broken tail and reverse the moment. I held my breath.

He stared at the stone woman. His face was set and without expression. He didn't move. I didn't move.

A heartbeat later, he reached into a pile of broken stone at the edge of the sheet of plywood, grabbed a fist-sized chunk that resembled the head of a bird. It must have snapped off a previous carving.

He looked at the woman, and the head.

"*Taima*," he said. It will do.

He filed the neck of the bird until it was smooth; he filed the broken edge of the seal-woman's tail. When both were smooth to the touch, he drilled and pinned the bird-head to the fish-woman, turned it, found the attitude he wanted, glued it in place, smoothed it where it joined, worked some stone dust into the glue, carved some more and then, as if he'd planned it all along, there was a bird where the tail had been.

I wouldn't have believed it if I hadn't seen it for myself:

With a hunter's knowledge of anatomy, and an artist's nerve, he turned disaster into tour de force. The carver set the fish-woman on the spindle and rolled a smoke.

"Wait here, you."

He returned from the house carrying a steaming tub of water and a tin of floor wax. He took off his parka, rolled up the sleeves of his shirt and bathed the carving in the water, letting the stone soak in the wet heat; when it was warm and clean and smooth he dried it off and began to rub it with the wax.

Taima; done.

Tape, April 19, cont'd:

"Want to buy a carving, Pingu?"

"How much?"

"How much do you think?"

"I have no idea. Tell me how much and I'll pay you."

"A hundred dollars."

"That's all? Surely it's worth – ?"

"A hundred dollars, that's how much I need. You can get it."

"I don't have any cash on me. I'll pay you tomorrow."

"Eee. Very good. I'll come to Ventures and you can pay me there. You want some tea?"

[A clatter of tools dumped on plywood, hands slapping at dusty trousers, a soft dull thump – a lump of soapstone kicked aside? The two men cough and clear their throats, spit and stamp their feet. A door squeaks and slams double-shut; a match scratch, pants unzipped; thick splatter of pissing, a satisfied sigh.]

"You still don't smoke, eh? You should learn. It's almost as good as pissing. Help yourself to some tea on the stove. Don't wait to be asked. We help ourselves up here. Did you know I killed a man?"

[There was a silence of fourteen seconds on the cassette; an eternity. Count it off if you like. Sit with a friend and, in the middle of a conversation, stop talking; fourteen seconds is an eternity.]

"I was drunk one time. I used to drink a lot. One night I came home late. I found my old woman fucking another man in the bed. That man, he got mad at me when I came in. It was very hot. The room began to spin. The man who was fucking my wife, he stood up and changed into a polar bear. I got very afraid. I was going to run away but I couldn't move. I heard a voice telling me what to do. It was like in a dream. The voice said I should get my knife and stab him in the neck. I stabbed him many times. My old woman was hitting me on the head. I was stabbing him. I stabbed her too. And then I went to sleep. When I woke up there was blood everywhere on the bed, a lot of blood. I walked over to the Mounties and gave them my knife."

Notebook, April 19, cont'd:

He was no longer Etulu, the old carver. He was a man who had killed another man. He had put the head of a bird on the tail of a seal-woman. He had used his knife to kill a polar bear-man. I said nothing. I drank my tea. I stared at his hands.

Tape, April 19, cont'd:

"I went to jail in Yellowknife. I stayed there a long time. I got very sick. I don't know why. You can't put an Inuk in jail. We're not made for that. They gave us country food but I couldn't eat. The judge found out I was sick. He told the boss of the jail he didn't sentence me to death. He told them to give me some tools and he sent some stone for me. I didn't want to carve at first, and then I couldn't stop carving. I made many carvings of the bear who was fucking my wife. The judge bought all the carvings, a lot of them. He bought many carvings. This was the first one I have made since I got out of jail that was not a bear."

Notebook, April 19, cont'd:

It occurred to me as soon as he said it. The blood on his hands. The thought of blood on mine. I had nicked my finger with a knife, not seriously, not enough to bleed, I was no Nadia Salerno-Sonnenberg – although I'd put her wounded finger in my mouth if I had the chance. But I had drawn no blood. I'd only thought of it.

And thought of Claire, the curettage, the scraping and the suction. A picture painted with my drugs. No less an explanation than if a piano turned into a raven.

Enough.

Notebook, April 19, cont'd:

I checked with Arthur. Every word is true. He showed me a catalogue of Etulu's work. On the cover was a photo of a carving – a bear on its hind legs, its arms spread wide, its mouth open, and an Inuk with a knife in one hand, his eyes wide in horror. It's the carving in the gallery. I'm sure of it.

Notebook, May 21:

We have come out of winter. The wind has stopped and the clouds have disappeared. Some ice has melted. Some rain has pelted. My pants are belted. Each day is longer and warmer than the one before. People are covering their windows with aluminum foil so that they can sleep at night.

I am trapped in euphoria. I feel as if my face is drinking in the light. Everyone is smiling. We have forgotten the darkness. We forgive each other. I say we, as if I were one of them.

The absence of wind, the presence of quiet.

For the first time in weeks the smoke from the chimneys rises straight up and all the houses, even the five-twelves, seem suspended from the sky by strings.

I called and asked Arthur for the day off.

He grumbled, but could not deny me. He owes me a day because I open the store for him in the morning and lock it up again at night. I do not take a break for lunch. I pick up stock from the warehouse and from the airport. I load the truck and bring it to the store and I refill the shelves. I remind him when to order shrimp from Greenland, olives from France, pilchards from England, and for some reason – he likes it, it's his store, the hunters find it useful out on the land – corned beef from Argentina. He owes me a day because I listen to him rant about the Inuit, the airline, the town council, the federal and territorial governments. He owes me a day because I get along with Sam Willy, which no one else can do. Sam Willy is lazy, wild-eyed, and aggressive; he spits when he talks, he doesn't brush his teeth, he smells like ammonia. He owes me a day because I pick the music for his radio program. There isn't much to choose. It is the same music over and over.

He needs no script. "You're listening to the Sunday Symphony on CBC Wolf Cove. I'm Arthur Parsons." Followed by sixty minutes of cuts chosen for no other reason than to fit the time available, and then "You have been listening to the Sunday Symphony Show from CBC Wolf Cove. I'm Arthur Parsons. Good night."

It is as good a premise for a classical music show as any. Why call it the "Sunday Symphony Show"? Why not call it "Music to Fit the Time Slot"?

How did Arthur get along without me?

He owes me a day. A precious calculation.

Sam Willy can pick up the slack.

Tape, May 21:

[A sniffle, a thick cough, the dry-stick crack of a distant raven's call; the rubber heels of dull boots thumping up a wooden staircase; his wet swallow, his short sigh; six short strides across a floor to a door with rusted hinges; silence, the echo of a squeak, and silence.]

Notebook, May 21, cont'd:

I am sitting on an empty blue cable spool in an abandoned room with a cup of rapidly cooling thermos coffee. Dry snow and bent nails on the floor.

It isn't hard to imagine this room full of crew-cut men in army fatigues telling jokes, ragging each other, chewing gum and playing cards and writing letters home: "Dear folks, it sure is cold up here. . . ."

I came in Arthur's truck along a series of switchbacks up the side of the hill behind town. When I could go no farther – I could have gone farther but I found a place where I could turn around without backing up; this road is slippery, no point in taking chances – I got out and walked up to the base. It is what's left of the DEW Line. It is where the piano was.

There is a sign on a gatepost, warning me to keep out. At one time, there would have been a chain link fence around the perimeter; now all that remains are the metal posts. Not just the fence has been stripped. The entire complex – the control tower, radio shack, two generator huts, the barracks, a kitchen, and a mess hall, at one time enclosed and interconnected; no soldier ever had to set a needless foot outside – is now gutted, the roof breached, the windows smashed or stolen, most of the doors, including their frames, carted off by scavengers. Not much here at the moment except my presence, and the echo of my presence in the narrow corridors.

Note: He is correct – there is an echo in this tape. It sounds as if he is walking by himself in the transept of an empty cathedral. I don't know how it's possible but I swear I can hear the cold.

If he thinks this is summer . . .

Notebook, May 21, cont'd:

The plumbing fixtures have been rooted out and carried off, the light switches are gone and there are ragged holes in the walls, as if hyenas had torn them open and ripped the wiring out like guts. I should have brought a camera.

The end of the world – not with a bang, not with a whimper – with a shiver. I can tell how cold it is by how long the tape recorder lasts until it slows and stops. It is ten below at the moment, maybe colder. I scribble wearing half-gloves.

Most of what's been stolen from the base has been hauled down to the beach and put to use in the beach shacks. There are sheets of the missing chain link fence all over town, nailed to the wooden frames used for drying sealskins and caribou hides.

I'm afraid I might meet someone.

The creepiness. Bear or dog, I am too cold to defend myself. Because of the parka, I am unable to move easily. My hands – if I ever had to hit someone, or shield my face . . .

I stepped outside what must once have been the mess hall and waited in the warmth. That's how strong the light is. Even at ten below there is warmth in the light. I poured the last of the coffee. I was about to drink. A shadow moved. Then two more shadows moved.

And then a herd of shadows moved towards me – a dozen caribou, their patchy thick coats the colour of the tundra. I could see them nibbling and pawing at the snow to find what it conceals: moss, grass. I eased over to the corner of the building, stood still, held my breath. I was downwind; they could neither see me nor catch my scent. I could hear them lowing, jostling each other with a half-frozen, nostril-dripping stupidity. They smelled ripe, almost sour, not unpleasant. I heard their breathing, grunts, and moans.

On impulse, I stepped out from behind the shelter of the building. For a moment, the herd continued to browse. Until one saw me. Raised its head and grunted. Two of them reacted slowly. Three, and now the rest of them transmitted the alert like an electric current, plumes of white breath snorting from their nostrils, chins now pointing upward, until one bellowed and bolted and they all bolted roughly, wheeling in the dry snow, shouldering each other to gain sure footing. And then they were gone behind the hill.

I could have killed any four of them, if I'd had a rifle and knew how to use it.

Note: There are no more pages in this book. But if I have this next taped sequence right, he has just driven back to town in the truck and is warming up in T-One. The sound on the tape is slow and thicker than usual. I'd guess the recorder was also warming up.

Tape, May 21, cont'd:

[Scratch of match, throats cleared of phlegm, chairs scraped back from tables; the voices of two women deep and wet and rich, and babies bawling richly in the background.]

"Last night, I seen the prime minister."

"Seen him where?"

"On TV."

"I didn't see him myself. Two teas, please."

"Coming up."

"Last night."

"I didn't see him."

"He's been staring at me."

"Who?"

"The prime minister. He's been looking at me through the TV. I can tell by the way he looks right at me. Spying, like. I wrote him a letter. I put it in the mail. They said at the post office you don't need no stamp. You can send him mail any time you want for nothing, he's the prime minister. I put in the letter that I was going on a hunger strike. No eating until he stops staring. Even if I die of starving. That's what I said. I know he's been staring. He's got to stop."

"Two tea, there you go."

"A hunger strike. You mean no food?"

"No food. Just some lemon juice in hot water. That's how they do it down south. When they go on a hunger strike. I read about it. Lemon juice, hot water, cayenne pepper. If you don't do that your eyes go blind. Eee. You got to have a lot of liquids on a hunger strike. To not go blind. I have to see if I can get some cayenne pepper. Hey, you. You got that cayenne pepper over at the Northern Ventures, huh?"

[Dom:] "We got it if you want it."

"I'll come and get some. You save some of it for me."

[The two women resume:] "Lemon juice and pepper? I think you'll get very hungry."

"I might take some caribou tea and maybe pilot biscuits."

"That's food."

"No, it isn't. It doesn't count. It's not like a meal. I think I should go tell them at the radio station that the prime minister is staring at me. If he makes me starve myself to death, that's going to be news."

"Maybe instead of a hunger strike, you should eat a lot, a really lot. Maybe if you get more fat than you already are, then he won't stare so much."

[D. coughs, is overtaken by coughing, is masking a fit of helpless laughter. A pause. The tape starts up again with white noise and then a dozen rubber boots on ice, and the tap and slap of hockey sticks on frozen gravel, the laughter of kids pushing each other off the puck and the drone of a jet aircraft so close.]

Notebook, May 21, cont'd:

I heard a steady, growling thunder as I was coming out of the coffee shop. The noise was deep and hit me in the chest. Ha, I am now an old northern hand: It was the first flight of the spring schedule. We get afternoon arrivals now, instead of flights early in the morning. I walked to the fence that marks the edge of the runway and watched the airplane descend.

(Later) I poured a drink and listened to the tape.

There is a layer of sound within the sound. Under the jet engines, I could hear a dozen or so Ski-Doos like a swarm of mechanical bees, buzzing over to the airport to pick up supplies, or to meet relatives returning from hospital down south. Nobody got off in a tux. If anyone had, nobody would have raised an eyebrow. Oh, we got one of those already. But it struck me that I hadn't quite noticed the Ski-Doos; I'd been paying attention to the plane. The noise of it hit me in the chest. But I also heard the small sounds hidden in the larger sound. A monstrous metal monster at bay on the tarmac. The Ski-Doos, like so many fleas in its fur.

I have recorded things that I never in my life imagined I would hear: water dripping from sheets of ice thrown up on the beach; the scrape of a boat hauled across a stretch of gravel road; the scratch and ratchet of a wrench in the guts of a truck; the barking of the dogs and the barking cough of a carver; an off-key gospel choir whose songs pour like light from the windows of the igloo church; the sullen giggling of glue-high kids on their way from Northern Ventures; the groan of the tide beneath the ice.

Natural rhythms, disparate chords, and the multiple layers of almost-music. The sound within the sound. This is the real idea of North.

Gould never imagined any of this. He never got his hands dirty, never ate raw seal – not that I recommend raw seal or dirty hands – never sat next to a nickel miner who handed him an envelope stuffed with pornographic photos and the admonition, "It's a long winter, you better take a good look, there's no women up there." He met no men on the run from wives and families or themselves. He met none of the men who have lived in the North so long they are afraid of the South, who no longer go South, not even for a holiday; this town is full of them. Nor did he, at breakfast, sit next to drunk white men who call their Inuit girlfriends rats.

Gould, deaf to the North.

Arthur, the night I first had supper at his house: "Half this town is on the run from something. You'll find most people prefer to mind their own business because they don't want others minding theirs."

Notebook, May 23:

The morning began clear and cold, but even I knew there was a storm on the way. A sharp division in the sky – blue overhead but in the distance a bank of low slate-coloured cloud stretching to the horizon.

Late morning, the wind began to blow and the temperature was dropping sharply. Just after lunch, the loose snow on the ground began to fly through the air. Arthur: "You'd better get home. I'm closing up. Take some candles and some matches. And you better take this." He threw a flashlight across the aisle in a looping, lazy arc. I caught it without thinking. Everyone outside was scurrying home under the dark sky; the schools and the offices closed early. No one stopped to talk. I did not go straight home. I was exhilarated as I walked. The dry snow needled my cheeks but I breathed the cold air as deeply as I could. There is no purer sensation.

A foolish thing to do, walking in a storm.

The wind bit into my skin. I froze the tips of my fingers. Not badly; they are tingling now. My cheeks are blotchy red and white, not numb but burning. This is reckoned to be the reason the Inuit are short, with tiny feet and small noses – less exposure to the cold. Unlike the Masai, who are long and lean, therefore more efficient in the heat. Although both are people of the desert. According to the *National Geographic*.

I put the kettle on for tea; before it could boil, the power went out. Half an hour later, one of the men from the Department of Public Works knocked on my door: "Open a tap or two. Let the water drip in the kitchen and the bathroom sinks. Don't forget the tub. We don't know how long the power will be out. We don't want the pipes to freeze."

I went to the Legion for a bite to eat the next day, when the worst of the storm was over and the power was returned. While I was eating I saw a man with a native girl on his lap. He was drunk – so much so, his face seemed on the verge of melting. Without warning, he dumped the girl on the floor and confronted a man at another table.

They had words. The drunk man picked up a glass and smashed it and pointed it like a jagged knife. He was too drunk to do much but wave the broken glass. The Mounties came and took him away. He was frog-marched out; blood leaking from his knuckles.

Claire at the sink with the wineglass. A breathtaking image – no one in a thousand years would imagine her standing in my kitchen with a delicate wineglass in her hand – the swell of her skirt below the hips, the knot of a tea towel at the small of her back, the length of her calves, the wisps of hair behind her ear, the fury of her elbows; shards and tendons.

The girl who'd been at the centre of the squabble – her name is Susie, she wears her hair in a short straight bob, she has thick glasses and thick legs – got up off the floor and dried her tears and went to sit on the lap of someone else. I don't know who, I don't know why, I don't want to know. I ate a caribou burger with my soup, drank my beer and walked home. The wind came up again, the temperature dropped.

Trouble with my key at the door. Hands numb, fingertips white. Ran my hands under the tap.

Tingling . . .

～

Note: Sometime last spring – the date lost, who keeps track of such things? – I woke in the middle of the night to the sound of the telephone. I rolled over, opened my eyes, looked at the alarm, heard nothing more, closed my eyes again, unable to distinguish between the room and a dream in the room. I fell asleep; an instant later the phone rang again.

I lifted my head from the pillow and, helpless, let it fall back. On the third ring, I reached for the receiver. I didn't get a chance to say hello. Whoever called hung up.

I thought of Dom. I can't be sure, but I have a hunch this tape was made the same evening that he – if it was he – called and hung up. The date is approximately right.

A second voice: Claire's.

Tape, June 1:

[six rings]

"Who is this?"

"It's me. You'll never guess what happened. I mean didn't happen. Are you alone? Have you got a minute? You've got to hear this, Claire. I was out last night – early this morning –"

"What time do you think – ?"

"No, please, just listen. You know they shoot the dogs here in the springtime. How could you know, you've never been. You really should come for a visit, bring Chinese. There are hundreds of dogs here, sled dogs, pack animals, they're all half-wild. Some get off their chains, they run around in packs and they breed – old dogs, young dogs, puppies on the loose. When things get out of hand, they shoot them."

"Are you all right?"

Note: I know his tone of voice; the rhythms are conversational, but his panic is barely contained.

"I'm fine. Right as rain. I don't know what that expression means. There is hardly any rain up here. Never mind about that. I'm trying to tell you about the dogs. When they run in packs, they are a danger to the children. Kids everywhere. The way these people have kids. I'm sorry. I didn't mean to remind you. Are you all right?"

"Of course I'm all right."

"Good. But listen. About the dogs. The mayor put a notice on the radio last week: It's time to shoot the strays, any dogs you want to keep you better tie them up. They do it early, so the kids don't see. I'm not sure why – I mean, if I were a kid and heard gunshots before I'd had my cornflakes, I'd wake up and – Oh, Jesus, I must have got you out of bed. I'm sorry. I'm sorry. I'm sorry. But you have to hear this. I don't know who I'd tell if I couldn't tell you."

"I'm wide awake. Fascinated. Get on with it."

"Okay, so I was trying to sleep. There's almost constant daylight now. I heard a rifle go off outside my bedroom window. I sat up. I heard footsteps. I rolled off the bed onto the floor. You never know here, everyone has a gun, it's not unusual to –"

"Where are you now, right now?"

"In the living room. In a chair. You wouldn't believe how ugly this place is. The walls are fake wood panelling, the curtains are orange and green plaid, the chairs are maple, varnished, also plaid to match the curtains, very ugly. They should shoot the chairs. Stop asking questions and listen. I get down on my hands and knees. I crawl across the floor and peek through the curtains. Nothing in sight. Clear sky. Lots of stars. Cold as hell. It's –"

"How cold is it?"

"It's so cold you won't let me finish. Twenty below last night. I saw a man with a gun prowling between the houses. I wondered if I should call the cops. You know, maybe he's drunk. He gets back in his truck. He pulls away slowly, with the gun poked out of the window. Leaning forward like he's looking for something. And then it hits me. He's the dog killer. Kid named Malachai. His father is a carver.

"I get dressed. You should see my parka, I look like Nanook. I thought I should get the dog hunt on tape. I just listened to it a few minutes ago. The air here is just so pure. Where was I? The guy in the truck. A young guy, Malachai. It's very biblical up here. Guys named Junah, girls named Ooleepeeka – that's how they say Rebecca. So I go out and wave at Malachai. He's a very good hunter. I bought a carving from his father. Malachai isn't sure if he should stop or not. Maybe I'm in favour of animal rights. They hate Greenpeace up here. But he –"

"Why for heaven's sake do they hate Greenpeace?"

"Because the price of seal pelts dropped from forty-five to seven dollars overnight. After the Newfoundland thing. People lost a lot of money here. Don't interrupt. Okay, so Malachai has a gun but I'm a white guy. I could be a boss. He stops. I ask him if I can ride along. He shrugs. I hop in, and right away we see a pup. It runs under the house next to mine like it knows nobody's going to shoot at a house. Malachai stops. He sneaks around a corner with his gun. I get out, I'm slipping off my gloves, I'm trying to get the tape recorder going, and the pup comes running up to me. Cute little thing, a mongrel, mostly husky.

"Right away, it's trouble. If I shoo it away, Malachai's going to see it and bang! The pup is panting, his tongue is hanging out, he's jumping around like he wants to play, he's trying to bite the microphone. I'm scratching his ear. And then I see a big dog. From the way she's watching, I know it's the mother. I'm scratching her pup, somebody's shooting dogs. She waits. She watches. And she makes her move, trots along the side of the house. I'm thinking, if I swat the pup to make him go away, she'll think I'm hurting it and she'll come after me. She's big enough to rip my throat out. If I do anything stupid, I'm dead. I stay on my knees, scratching the pup's ear. And praying. The mother dog is coming closer. I can see her out of the corner of my eye. I don't know where the hunter is. I can hear her paws on the ice. I don't move. Not a muscle. She's behind me now. I close my eyes. She leans her shoulder into me. I don't move. I don't know what to do. Then she takes my wrist in her jaws and moves my hand off her pup. She looks me in the eye. She starts to squeeze, hard enough to let me know she could take my hand off if she wanted to. But she just holds my wrist in her mouth. Her tongue is hot. Her teeth are hard. I can't breathe. And then she drops my hand. Just lets me go. Looks at the pup and off they trot together.

"I'm still on my knees when Malachai comes back. He looks at me like guys are kneeling on the ice at four a.m. all the time up here. He doesn't say anything except 'Let's go.' It would kill him to ask. People don't ask a lot of questions up here. They figure if you have something to say, you'll say it. Like asking is rude. I can't get used to it.

"I told him what happened. He said if I had got down on all fours and shown her the side of my neck she would have licked my face. I said I wasn't about to let her rip my throat out. He says no, it's a sign of submission. Like I was admitting she was superior. She'd have licked me. You still there?"

"Still here. Is there more about dogs?"

"No, that's all. You can go back to sleep."

"How long do you plan to stay up there?"

"I have no idea. I need a favour."

"What favour?"

"I need more notebooks. The black ones, from Laywine's. A box. Also number nine leads, HB, for my Rotring. Ask Peter. Just tell him you want the ones I use, he'll know. And if you can figure out how to pack a tea-smoked duck and a barrel of pho and a prosciutto – ?"

"Have you played since you – ?"

"No, I have not. There is a piano here. I don't know if I will. Or when. I actually like not playing. Can I ask you something?"

"Ask anything."

"Are you sure you're all right? I mean after the –"

"Oh, for heaven's sake. It was nothing. Less than nothing. It clearly upset you more than me. You mustn't think of it. What you should think about is putting an end to this exile, whatever you call it. People want to know you're well. They want to hear you play."

[The tape ends abruptly.]

Note: She knows where he is. I know where he was.

Where is he now?

Tape, June 1, cont'd:

[A truck idling throatily – there is a hole in the muffler. Chunk – a truck door slammed. Clump and drag of boots on gravel. "Eee-la, there." A careful click – the safety slipped. "I got you now." Crack, crack. Two rifle shots, their echo in the air. The whimper of a dog. Crack. Another shot, its echo, and then footsteps tramping across a layer of silence. The thump of a limp, still-warm carcass tossed in the back of the half-ton.]

Note: There is nothing more on this tape.

⟞

Notebook, June 4:

I retain a library of sensations: taste touch sight sound smell – the sensations indexed, cross-filed, and ready to be retrieved.

A moment ago, I caught the scent of the split pea soup on the stove at Mrs. Ojala's house – a whiff of clove, of peas burnt to the bottom of the pot. She fed me occasionally, after lessons at her house on Egan St. in Port Arthur.

The trigger? Sam Willy let the door to the storage room fall shut behind him. The sound as it closed, *ka-bunk*. The same *ka-bunk* as her door. The sound, and then the memory of taste. Other examples? Chocolate cake brings back the pretty little "Traumerai." Because chocolate cake is what I had for dessert the night before I left to study in Siena, and "Traumerai" is the piece I had played for Boris Berlin, who on hearing me play made good my escape.

I no longer yearn to play. I have not yearned since walking out of the gallery. A bit of hysteria, utterly suggestive; who knows? I could no longer sense the presence of colour; the path from sinews to fingers to keys was blocked. And then, on the night in question, it is likely that the red I saw – or thought I saw – had something to do with my meds, or –

Guilt, pointlessness. The winding of a cheap watch.

An apple is rare here. They arrive overripe, bruised, on the sick-sweet edge of rotten. The essence of the apple is red. A field of stars, the colours of the spectrum – I used to feel that as I played. The colours flowing from my hands onto the keys, the sound blinking from star to star in the sky. The hue of tone and overtone, the northern lights.

I will not play again until I sense it.

All rhythm derives from the beating of the human heart.

The way the Inuit have taken to the fiddle and the accordion, you'd think they had Scottish hearts; some do.

For the past three months, I've eaten nothing but frozen sausages cooked in a skillet with onions. I have boiled potatoes, and I eat third-rate oranges for dessert. There is, however, olive oil. It is worth every penny. Sam Willy is baffled by my need for it. Curiosity overcame rudeness, and he asked why I was willing to pay so much for something that seems useless. I told him it is what I require instead of seal fat. The answer seemed to satisfy him.

Etulu came into the store today. He bought tobacco, floor polish, steel wool, and sandpaper. He lingered for a while. We talked – the weather, the increasing daylight, when the ice might break. He asked me if I was Italian, and did I make wine, and without waiting for an answer he told me he used to make wine, too. I said it must cost a fortune – grapes are expensive up here, and if you could get juice – at $3 a kilo for freight, it's prohibitive.

"Oh, I never used no grapes."

"What, then?"

"Potatoes and water. You add some yeast and raisins and leave it by the stove a day or two, it's pretty powerful."

Note: This begins with a simple narration – call it an audio letter.

As if he knew he was going to send it to someone. As if he were planning to send it to me.

That may be a presumption. I suppose, based on the familiarity of the conversation he had earlier with Claire, that he has, in a way, been conversing with each of us all along.

Tape, June 11:

[Scuff of boot on rock, skid of heel in gravel, a splash, a grunt, a sigh, a zipper's snug ascent. The unscrewing of the cap of a thermos bottle and a splash of clear tea in a metal cup; these sounds within the rush of river water. And this:]

The weather is easing up.

The ice on the river broke last week and the force of the water cleared it quickly. You'd think I was an old hand. I have no idea what quickly is in this place. But that is what I am told.

I was in the store when it happened, stacking frozen char like lengths of cordwood in the freezer. There was a sharp report, like the crack of a rifle shot. And the strangled ring of the bell on the ice. A curious association. That line – ice cod bell or stone.

Ellesmere is a long way off.

Everything is.

Note: Something familiar here.

A quick consultation with Margie – she calls to tell me it is a quote from the Earle Birney poem "Ellesmereland." Of which I have a vague recollection from high school. Dom has a superior memory, and clearly a fondness for Birney. In full:

Explorers say that harebells rise
from the cracks of Ellesmereland
and cod swim fat beneath the ice
that grinds its meagre sands
No man is settled on that coast
The harebells are alone
Nor is there talk of making man
from ice cod bell or stone

An aside: In the days when the CBC *could afford the luxury of staff announcers, this poem was required to be read as part of the voice audition. You sat before a microphone. You were handed a sheet of paper with the poem. The way an announcer handled those last two lines – they are deliberately elliptical – was the key to the test. These days the idiots who read the local news have never heard of Birney. I digress where I ought not to, given what follows.*

Tape, June 11, cont'd:

Break-up is a floating civic half-day holiday in this place.

Most people buy tickets at Arthur's – a sort of lottery: An iron bar is driven into the ice and tied by a rope to a bell on shore; the rope grows taut or snaps tight of a sudden as the ice breaks up; the date and time of the ringing determines the winner.

I was nowhere close.

It came suddenly and everyone in town dropped what they were doing and raced to the water on ATVs, on foot, in trucks – even the village bus took a load of people. Arthur joined in; he has to, he's the mayor, he pretends to be gruff but if he didn't show up, he wouldn't get elected next year.

He dragged me along and had me throwing hard candies from the bed of the truck to the kids on the rocks near the edge of the water.

[Dom, in mimicry accent:]

"Careful where you toss the jawbreakers. No use having the little bastards falling in the water and floating off, it upsets the parents, mustn't encourage them to go on making more."

[He resumes his normal voice:]

It's still cold, and there is still snow on the ground – actually, it isn't snow any more, it's ice pitted with gravel – but there is a spine of warmth in the air.

[Crunch of footsteps, rush of water, clatter of loosened stones.]

Okay. I am out of the wind. There is shelter among these rocks. You can't actually see the water until you are almost upon it; nothing gives its presence away except the sound.

The water is green in the middle where the river must be deepest; it is opal along the shore. There is a small waterfall, and a chorus of whispers a hundred yards from me – froth like milk – that's what you hear first. The banks of the river – not banks, really, they are more like heaps of broken stone – amplify the sound until it is a choir of whispers. I have scraped my precious hands crawling down.

[He hums.]

Note: His voice is warm and goofy, loud and clear; the tune is that of the "Promenade." He sounds slightly drunk as he continues:

The rocks form a natural corridor. The water rushes over the falls, the sound rushes along with it. Half a mile or so down from here, the river widens and slows and spreads into the bay. Above the falls is where Jackson made the sketch. It seems so long ago.

I should score the sound of this river for a choir. Let's say forty voices, thirty or so humming a low slow basso continuo, and maybe ten altos – *I wish the river ran forever in the air, the river there; I wish the river ran forever in the air.* I'd need a few sopranos to cut into the heart of the murmur. Me and Philip Glass. It seems to me that I. Oh shit, what is . . .

[A long pause; nothing on tape for twenty seconds except the sound of the river in the air, the water there, and the brush of Dom's parka as he presses against the rocks.]

Christ. I thought it was a bear. I thought I was done for. Oh, my god, he's going to. Look at him go. Come on. Look at him go. Malachai, hallooo!

[Another pause; nothing but the river in the air and then a whisper.]

Come on now, come on . . .

Notebook, June 11:

It must be on the tape. The sound within the sound. I have listened to it again and again. It is there, even if it's not.

I saw something moving above the falls. White and slow-moving, slope-shouldered – perhaps a polar bear – scrambling over the rocks. I held still until it occurred to me that no bear, not even a bear in a legend, has ever carried a kayak on its shoulders. My eyes were teary from the cold. I blinked and then I made out the form of a man. He wore a white canvas anorak. The hood was down. There was a bright red balaclava on his head. He bore a kayak on his shoulders. He stopped and set his burden down and looked around. It struck me as extraordinary, how far I could see.

Malachai, the hunter of the dogs. He hadn't noticed me. How could he? I was in the rocks, hidden from the wind.

I saw him pull down the front of his pants and take a piss. I saw him hitch up his pants again and disappear from view.

I cannot stop seeing him.

He came out from behind a boulder onto the flats and set his kayak in the quiet water. He tied the bowline to a stone. He stood and steadied himself and adjusted his clothing. He lowered himself into the kayak, held tight to the shore, buttoned the splash cover and then he pushed off.

He windmilled with his paddle and was sucked into the current like a matchstick. He was going to shoot the falls.

I lost sight of him, then I saw him again riding hip-high in the spray. If he had not had the correct line, he'd have been smashed to bits. I lost him and then the little sliver of the kayak pierced the standing waves and he was riding in calm water.

He dipped his paddle and steadied himself and began to carve his way to the middle of the river, and he saw me then and he turned his shoulders as he sat, he turned towards me and he raised his paddle in triumph. I stood up and held the microphone above my head.

He shouted as he waved at me, and the kayak rolled easily in the water and did not right itself and I thought it was a trick. I smiled at the foolishness of it; he was showing me an Eskimo roll. Even the Inuit call it that. But he stayed down.

"Come on now, come on."

It's there on tape if you wait for it; a whisper above the water. What he said is there. He overturned and disappeared as if that were the most natural thing in the world to do and he stayed under and did not come up and then he was gone out to sea. Malachai, his breath bursting in his lungs and his heart on fire, and the river, rising. I lost sight of him.

He was carried out towards the bay. I went to get help. It was too late to get help. I looked back at the falls, at the white spray of the river. I looked back to make sure. Not a sound of him, not a trace.

Note: This, cobbled together from his shaky notes:

Dom hurried back to town. He saw no one along the road. He stopped at the first house he came to. There was no phone and the people inside the house were asleep or drunk and the dogs were barking, but he could not rouse anyone. He found a phone in the second house and called Arthur and told him what he'd seen, and the mayor called a rescue party together. Men from town rushed to the water's edge and jumped into their Cape Islanders, men who lived near the beach ripped the cords of the outboard motors and pushed off in their freighter canoes, and men with ATVs tore along the icy shore to get to the mouth of the river.

Notebook, June 12:

I have played the tape over and over again. The moment is there, it must be there in the sound of the water. His whisper under the rush of the river. I have played the tape until I can't stand the silence.

He disappeared without a trace.

Notebook, June 14:

They found him yesterday. A mile and a half from the mouth of the river. The kayak had managed to right itself in a small bay west of town. He was sprawled, half in and half out, with one arm caught in the bow rope. His right foot was bare – he'd kicked a hole in the bottom of the kayak in an effort to free himself; in doing so, he'd lost his kamik. His balaclava had fallen over his eyes; the men said if it happened like that, he might not have been able to see in the water. He would not have seen the light. He wouldn't have known which way was up. That's what they said.

Not that he'd been drinking. Not that he'd been on the water too early in the year and alone when the river was cold and swollen. Not that he'd made a foolish error. Not that he'd been showing off. He'd had an accident in fast water where anyone could have had tipped. He knew how to right himself. He'd been blinded by his hat. That's why he died. That's what they said.

And they would, according to Arthur, construct a lesson from that for all the young men of the village, a kind of Inuit coroner's report: Don't go on the cold water in a kayak with a balaclava on your head.

I had been there. I had seen it. I had it on tape. I had caught his attention. He turned to wave at me. And then he overturned and went under and he drowned and the kayak drifted for three days in the current, not quite afloat near the floe edge. Malachai, limp in the water below the wheeling of the gulls, above the idle schools of fish.

There was fresh sign of wolf along the shore near where he had come to rest and there was also sign of bear. The rescue party said if they hadn't found him when they did they might never have found him.

―――

Notebook, June 16:

The igloo church was filled with mourners; the keening of the choir high and shrill and off-key; unbearably sad. Tears streamed down all faces, and voices broke freely. I have the songs on tape.

I thought of giving my tape – the sound of the river, the last silence of Malachai and the song of the choir – to his father. But Etulu would not look at me. I was the last person to see Malachai alive.

Note: It is now quite late.

I don't know what Dom was thinking, but I know what I'd have thought – that I'd had a hand in the death of the young man in the kayak. In spite of the hour, I called information, got a number, and rang the RCMP detachment in Wolf Cove.

They were polite, but not forthcoming; yes, there had been a drowning, it was deemed accidental; it was a long time ago. They seemed more interested in who I might be and why I might be calling than in what I was calling about. Cops are the same everywhere.

There was no private listing for the mayor, but I got a number for Northern Ventures and, after five rings, an answering machine kicked in.

"Not here now. Leave your message at the tone."

The message I wanted to leave depended entirely on who might check the machine in the morning. I blurted, "Dom, for god's sake if you're there . . ." I was not sure how to finish the sentence. The longer it remained unfinished, the more difficult it became. I hung up and had a drink – somehow, I made my way through half a bottle of brandy – and went to sleep. When I woke, I called again. A gruff hello.

"Excuse me, is Dom there?"

"Are you dim? Do I give a damn? Whoever you're after, he's not here. Now fuck off and quit bothering the working people."

Notebook, June 16, cont'd:

I can't stop listening. I hear the river suck him under. I can see the spume of light-tipped notes, the refraction of the sun – Malachai carried along for an instant – and then carried away. His last breath, a song beneath the ice.

Notebook, June 17:

The taxis are not moving, there are no trucks on the road; even the dogs are silent. The whole town is in mourning. Malachai was Etulu's son, Nipisha's husband, father of the infant Josipee. He was the dog-killer. He was half-brother to Petaloosie with the bad leg and the cough-drop grin. He was cousin to the pregnant and prickly Elisapee and the clever placid Monica; he was uncle of the little bird, Ooleepeeka, and best friend of Junah with the big voice who worked at the radio station. There was a thread connecting him to everyone in Wolf Cove. Because he was young, and had died in a kayak he had made by hand, it was as if some portion of the past and future of the town died with him. I didn't know him well.

I don't know anyone here well. Not even Arthur.

He hired Malachai once.

Sam Willy slept in/got drunk/didn't bother to show up for work and Malachai needed money for supplies – he wanted to go seal hunting. Arthur offered him a box of bullets and some gas in lieu of wages for a half-day's work. We inventoried a planeload of dry goods on cargo pallets in the warehouse at the airport.

He was tireless and uncomplaining of the cold and damp, phlegmatic about the lack of coffee breaks, the awkwardness of the boxes, and of Arthur's air of perpetual annoyance. He went hunting early the next day in a freighter canoe. He was gone for a week. He stopped by the store and offered to sell me a skin. I paid more than it was worth. I knew its value from Arthur, who bought skins now and then.

I thought, if I do not remain here, then I am unlikely to return and so may never again be in a position to buy one; therefore I paid cash and didn't quibble. He was a northerner levying a tax on me, a southerner – what of it?

He is dead and no one can think of anything but the funeral; no one is in the mood to celebrate Wolf Cove Days.

No one knows I have the tape. His last moment in air.

Arthur led a discussion last night at council. Preparations for Wolf Cove Days had been set aside while the search for Malachai was on. No one seemed to have the heart to continue. A vote was taken. Cancel Wolf Cove Days altogether this year? All in favour? Unanimous.

Until Etulu cleared his throat at the back of council chamber. He said he wanted Wolf Cove Days to go ahead anyway. There was silence. He cleared his throat again. In a thick voice: "Malachai died like a real Inuk. In a kayak on the water. We should go ahead with Wolf Cove Days. Nobody should think it's dangerous to go out on the water. It is not dangerous to do the things Inuks do. If we don't do those things we are not Inuks. The games and races should go ahead. The concert should go ahead."

Arthur called another vote. Unanimous, again.

Note: I called the Nunatsiak News, *one of the few papers on Baffin Island, to find out what I could. Another error of omission – I should have done this days ago. The reporter I spoke to ducked my initial questions about Dominic. I can't believe she doesn't know him. She told me what she remembered about the death of the young man on the water: There was an autopsy; he had been wildly drunk.*

She also told me about Wolf Cove Days. It was a way to break the mood of winter and release the demons that build up over the course of the long darkness. Happy to have someone down south to talk to, she chatted merrily about the seal-skinning contest, the good-woman contest, the rifle-shooting and harpoon-throwing contests, the blanket toss, and the feast in the school afterwards. She insisted she didn't know anyone named Dom.

She must be new.

Tape, June 19:

[Arthur, on the phone. Apparently he has caught Dom off guard, because the tape begins in the middle of a sentence.]

". . . to make things worse, McCardle has gone missing in medias fucking res. Been gone since the day Malachai – Who knows where the shifty bastard is. Wheels falling off the fucking wagon. The principal says he heard one of his students say he thinks the music teacher might have gone snowmobiling. That's as much intelligence as you'll find in this bloody place. Somebody thinks somebody said somebody might have gone somewhere. My guess is – it doesn't matter what I think. Here's the problem: We have not got any seals because the hunters are involved in the search for McCardle. No seals, no feast. As if that's not enough, someone broke into the school last week and – I can't believe this, even as I say it – went after the piano with a hammer. As if a piano ever hurt anybody."

[The breath of both men whistles through their nostrils. The mayor's frustration is apparent; from Dom's end, I get a sense of dead-level calm.]

"What about the piano?"

"Oh, do we care about pianos now? I am no expert in musical instruments, the demolition of. Principal thinks it can be fixed. Janitor scared the little bastard off before he could do much damage. A few dents in the wood is the extent, but it's badly out of tune. If there was someone in this town who knew something about pianos, he might be able to put it right. I don't know who that would be. A person in this town. Who knows about pianos. If you get my drift. Concert on the twenty-second."

[A pause]

"I'll take a look."

"Bloody right you will."

Notebook, June 20:

Wolf Cove School is modern by northern standards, made of bright white fibreglass modules trimmed with red. Seen from below the cliff, it resembles a wolf's head; apt. Inside, there is a specific northern school smell: a cloud of wet wool, floor wax, magic markers, cleaning products, seal fat, and the hormones of teens. One of whom politely asked what I wanted and then pointed me towards the office.

The principal is a hearty man. Curly Craine, the nickname presumably derived from his steely, close-cropped, curly hair. Wide shoulders, white-blue sled-dog eyes. Wearing a porridge-coloured jacket and a red tie covered with white wolves – the school tie, no doubt – and flannel trousers tucked into well-worn kamiks. His hand, strong as a mechanic's.

Tape, June 20:

"Follow me, please. I'm glad you can. . . . We just don't know where the music teacher has gone; it's not like him to disappear. These things happen in the south, too, I suppose. Kids misbehave, teachers don't show up, everything goes wrong at the wrong time. We don't have the luxury of. . . . Well, we do the best we can with what we have. It's wonderful to be human. You never know what's around the corner. You're Amoruso; isn't there a pianist by that name down south?"

Notebook, June 20, cont'd:

I ducked another reference to the famous Amoruso. Instead, I feigned interest in a soapstone carving at the intersection of three corridors outside Craine's office: a life-sized hunter, bent at the hips, his massive chest resting on his massive knees, his head cocked to the side, listening closely at an imaginary breathing hole, one short strong arm poised to drive a very real harpoon into the flesh of an incautious and imaginary seal. An eternal wait, by the look of things.

Tape, June 20, cont'd:

"Who did this?"

"That's Etulu; our most famous carver. One of the first high school graduates in the North. You may have seen him around town. You wouldn't forget him. He has a tattoo on his forehead. He made this before he went away to Yellowknife. That was his boy who died on the river."

Notebook, June 20, cont'd:

Craine left out the reason why Etulu went to Yellowknife – a nice bit of discretion. He led me down the hall, past the trophy cases and displays of student art, past the rows of grey metal lockers with their stench of running shoes and rotten sandwiches.

The auditorium floor is a blur of red, white, yellow, and green lines for basketball, volleyball, floor hockey, whatever. I have never been athletic; I have no idea which lines are for which sport.

At the far end of gym, a stage and curtains of sky-blue duffel cloth; the curtain embroidered, and pulled open.

Stage right, in the shadows is the piano. I hadn't noticed them before. A glossy decal glued to one side: a wolf with its head raised, howling – symbol of the school as well as the town.

The front of the piano is painted with a northern scene: a hunter standing on the runners of his sled, his dogs splayed out like the fingers of a hand, and the man's whip snaking wildly through the air – a frozen arabesque. One dog, obviously a slacker, is looking back in fear, about to feel the sting. The fallboard bore fresh dents where it had been worked at with the hammer.

Tape, June 20, cont'd:

"Our man Joanassie was polishing the floor when he heard the noise. Whoever it was snuck in through the side door. Joanassie came running at the sound of the first blow. His father did this painting; the old man worked at the base as a handyman. Good thing we keep it locked at night, or the keyboard would have been smashed to bits. I'll leave you to it. There's a kit, tools and so on, in the workroom. I'll have someone bring it over. If there's anything you need . . ."

"Can you get me a telephone? I may need to consult with someone while I look things over. I'm not a trained . . . There's a man I know down south who tunes and repairs pianos. If there is serious damage, or something I can't handle, it may be a long call."

"You're the expert. I don't care if you call Mars, just as long as you can help. The phone. There's a jack in the corner. I'll see to it right away."

[Three rings]

"Yes?"

"Frankie. I need a favour. Tell me this: Can you listen to a piano over the phone and walk me through the tuning and a few repairs?"

"Dominic, is that really you? Where are you calling from?"

"I'm up north. On Baffin Island. It's not important where I am . . ."

"Baffin Island? Tuning a piano? Perhaps you have taken up a new line of work? I tell you from experience there is not much money to be made from the tuning of pianos. I wouldn't wish on anyone the abuse you have to endure from pianists. I shouldn't imagine there are so many pianos among the Eskimos that you can make a living –"

"Quit kidding, Frankie."

"You call me Frankie, you must want something nice. But you won't tell me where you are. Okey dokey. Baffin Island is good enough. By which I mean it is very far from here and you have been gone too long, dear boy. You know I didn't mean for you to take yourself out of circulation, Mr. A for Amoruso. Tell me what kind of repairs, please?"

"No idea, not yet. I'm hoping minor."

"Well, whatever it takes, I will be glad to listen. I am home all night. It will be a novelty. I have never worked on a piano over the phone. It will be like working blind. Perhaps I should have done it like this with Gould, yes? At a distance. The son of a bitch. Over the phone. Never mind. All I ask you to remember – there is minor you can fix it and there is minor you can't do nothing at all. Tell me first – have you come down off your high horse? Are you fixing to play again?"

"Don't ask. . . ."

"You ask me, but I shouldn't ask you."

"You'll help?"

"I will do whatever I can."

"Give me a few minutes to get organized. Keep the line free and I'll call back as soon as I know what I'm dealing with."

[Half a ring; some satellite echo; obviously later]

"Yah, hello, is it you?"

"It is."

"I am bating my breath; shall we proceed? I am impatient. Describe the patient, please, for me."

"Okay. A small upright. A little Steinway unlike any you've ever seen. It looks more like a packing crate than a piano."

"Have you looked inside?"

"The bass strings aren't copper-clad; the metal's grey, it looks –"

"For heaven's sake. An ODGI."

"As a matter of fact. How did you know – ?"

"The strings. There was a shortage of copper during the war, so they wrapped the bass strings with iron. You want more?"

"How much more?"

"All night it won't take. Steinway converted to war production. Made rifle butts and coffins – an irony, yes? Something for the rifles, and something for the dirty work of the rifles. But somebody had a bright idea to keep the older workers busy. They made a few little pianos. The company persuaded the War Office to send a few overseas so the boys could make music. They turned out very popular. Shipped in crates with tuning wrenches and sheet music. It is easily carried by two men. There should be handles on the side. A few thousand only were made. Most of them are disappeared. There is supposed to be one in the Smithsonian, still in its crate, but nobody I know has seen it. Personally, I doubt if it's there. Do you have the tool kit, by any chance?"

"I have some tools, yes."

"Okay. Let us proceed. Tell me what you see."

"Some kid took a hammer to the fallboard. It's a bit banged up but it was locked, he couldn't get at the keyboard – that's the thing you'd want to smash first, I suppose. Keys, action, strings. Apparently, he never thought about going in through the top."

"Tell me, how did it get there?"

"Apparently it sat in Thule until after the war. Then it was shipped to the radar base here. When the Americans pulled out, they gave it to the school. As for the crate, it's probably a kennel for someone's dog."

[Pause]

"Play me something."

[D. walks his fingers up and down the first notes of the "Promenade"; the piano is quite out of tune.]

"Hopeless, but not so very hopeless."

"Frank, I'll call you back. There's someone here. I'll call you right back."

"Okay, but –"

"Hello, who are you?

"Geela Ashevak. We never met. I teach music a little bit. The principal said you were here. I thought you might like a cup of tea. Do you play a lot?"

"I have played."

"Can you fix this?"

"A friend will help me. That was him on the phone. An unusual piano, this. It's not really damaged. I think it just needs to be tuned. Tell me – do you have a nail file?"

[Her laughter is instant and rich.]

"No, not for me, although I have used them. I mean for the piano. Also I need some needles, three if you can, good strong sewing needles and something to – a cork if you have one – something I can stick the needles in."

Notebook, June 20, cont'd:

Geela Ashevak is a cousin of Malachai. Everyone here is related, but there is no sign of inbreeding. Thanks, at least in part, to the whalers and the Bay men, the explorers and the anthropologists, and the nomadic nature of the people. A toughness, a hybrid vitality.

I pulled the keyboard quite easily; Geela said she had never really looked at the action before. I struck a note; the hammer rose and fell back helplessly. She said it reminded her of a fish taking the bait. Just so. A single note lingered.

Here, I said, play any key. She stabbed the same one I had.

Tape, June 20, cont'd:

"This is an old instrument. Over time, the felt gets hard. I'll prick it to soften it up. Hear this? If I jab it with the needles, like so, it makes a softer sound. Listen. I'll play a little of the bottom end – here here here, hear it? Whereas this – here here here – can you find me an eyedropper and some glycerine? Maybe there's something in the chem lab."

Note: Dom had no real need of Frank Mazur. He knew very well how to tune a piano. He'd made a point of learning. Just in case. This was the very case. . . .

Notebook, June 20, cont'd:

I thought I ought to do it right, and play a little. Not on the school's piano bench; too slippery. The notion of falling off a chair – however amusing, and however privately – is not and never was my act. Did I have an act? It seems I had both act and affectation. My leather jacket, the linen shirt underneath.

I miss them now.

In any case, I had no intention of horning in on poor old Victor Borge, even while alone. Surely he'd done that more than once – slid off the end of his bench like he was the carriage of a typewriter cut loose from its moorings; *whee!* The Inuit would be amused; they revel in slapstick, the slappier the better. For example, the day after Boxing Day I was picking Sunday's music for Arthur. One of the CBC announcers came in with a mug shaped like a pale white breast with a long, pink nipple for a spout. A gag present. I saw him fill the mug with coffee and raise the nipple to his lips – his eyes closed, his eyebrows raised at the prospect of milky coffee-titty bliss. There were snickers. He stopped drinking; he stared at the mug, puzzled, as if something was not quite right. Aha! – he added more cream, suckled once again, nodded his head, smiled, smacked his lips. To the delight of all. Odd: the shape of the teat, like Claire's.

The thought of it makes me shiver. Ridiculous, really. A trail of associations leading from a piano bench to Victor Borge to an Inuk with a coffee mug, to the stirrings of . . .

Where are there chairs in a school? In a classroom, idiot!

I prowled the corridors, whistling as loudly as I could. The resonant echo, a pleasant effect. Live notes piercing dead ones. I peeked into the ninth grade; all the chairs were winged. I followed my nose, drawn on a beacon of scent; archaeologists, a thousand years from now, will discover in these ruins the aroma of french fries. Beef tallow, stronger than the sweat of adolescence. But here in an overheated room, in a school on the top of a cold white world, I caught the smell of something more powerful than beef or hormones – the thick, almost muttonish scent of seal fat. You can count on the fingers of one hand the number of schools in the world that serve, not just seal for lunch, but three kinds of seal – harp, ring, and bearded – three different ways: fried, boiled, and roasted.

Plastic chairs, blue and yellow, had been overturned on refectory tables, their skinny metal legs pointing up, like insects pinned in place. I pulled one off and sat on it; too low, and it wobbled. The height of a chair is not a serious problem. It is a question of the angle of attack; where are the elbows, where are the wrists; is there sufficient freedom; and how are the shoulders held? The second chair also wobbled. The third chair seemed solid enough; I dragged it off to the gym.

And played. For the first time since. Sitting hunched with an ear near the keys.

Tape, June 20, cont'd:

"You play good. As good as on the radio."

"Oh, you frightened me. Thank you. I play. I used to play good. Did you know there was a Bislama word for piano?"

"I got your needles. What is Bislama?"

"The common language of the native people of Vanuatu. A kind of pidgin English. There were pianos like these there during the war. If I remember, they say – *Wan big fella blak bokis hemi got waet tut mo hemi got blak tut supos yu kilim smol hei singaot gud.*"

"What did you – ?"

"A big black box. More white teeth – keys – than black ones. Kill him small, I guess that means smack him – which is to say, pound the keys – and he sings out good. As if there were a creature inside, and when you strike him, he will – well, you get the point."

"Why are you telling me that?"

"What?"

"You think I am a native person, so you can say a native thing, no matter where it's from, and I'll just sort of get it."

"Oh, Jesus. I didn't mean to – I'm sorry if that's what you – it never occurred to me – I just like it as a description is all."

"Here are the tools. I'll leave you alone."

"What are you going to play during the concert?

"I'll accompany my kids. Are you going to play?"

"No I'm – I don't think so."

"Why not?"

"It's a long story."

"You think us Inuit don't like classical music?"

"No. It has nothing to do with – I stopped performing quite a while ago."

"Are you afraid to play?"

"Maybe I'm afraid to find out."

Note: She leaves him alone. He plays for an hour. I offer this with caution – his playing is fluid and light – it's as if, with nothing at stake, he feels free and therefore so is the music free.

Margie: " 'The Well-Tempered Clavier.' You ought to know it by heart, you should be able to whistle it while you work, I can't believe a man who pretends to be educated doesn't –"

I cut her off with the promise that she could listen to the whole tape when she got off work, provided she promised to keep it secret and brought supper with her.

Notebook, June 20, cont'd:

One string stayed dead.

I thought there might be a problem with the sustain pedal. Peered inside, nothing. Opened the foot plate. Curious. An envelope, brown paper, letter-sized, taped to the inside of the plate.

The tape, dry and curled, came loose as I played. I opened the flap. And sealed the envelope again.

A photo of the music teacher and Malachai – a younger Malachai, a boy Malachai – and McCardle, naked. Even as I write this – what to do?

Note: He has pasted a page over a page in the notebook:

Notebook, June 20, cont'd:

It's late. I put the envelope back inside the piano. An instant decision, unregretted. The death of Malachai is a shock, but it is not up to me to braid the strands of grief. Bad enough I have his death on my tape recorder. I have to get out of here.

It suddenly seems too complicated.

After the concert, after a merciful few days more, I'll get the plane out of here and leave word with Arthur and he can tell the Mounties where to look for the photo – this is his town, not mine. But I'll bet it was Malachai who broke into the school. I'll bet he was looking for the photo.

Was his death a suicide?

How did the teacher disappear?

And are there other boys and other photos?

—◗—

Notebook, June 22:

The hunters have given up the search. They returned without any news of the music teacher, but they brought back many seals, a hundred seals, dozens of seals, eight big fat seals.

The games, subdued, went ahead: Women raced for kettles,

raced back, lit twigs and boiled water for tea; teens were thrown high in the air by the blanket tossers; pop cans skittered like popped corn across the ice, propelled by hot shots with .22 repeaters; and so on. Ribbons were awarded, smiles returned to faces in spite of grief.

An elder spread some groundsheets for the climax of the day, the seal-skinning contest. We gathered near the entrance to the school. He was in no hurry. He was enjoying himself. A tailor-made dangled from his lips, and his belly fat poked out from under his parka.

The assembled us – teachers, nurses, civil servants, hunters and their wives, the ragged, mongrel-tough girls and boys of town, and me – gathered in a circle, jockeying for a good look.

The elder lined up the seals on the groundsheets – the little corpses were glistening torpedoes with yellow plastic ropes threaded through their nostrils.

Seals have surprisingly long, almost feminine eyelashes, and comically long whiskers on their snouts; not so comic when dead. The elder made a show of inspecting, grinning, and joking – look how small this one is, eee. Anyone could skin it in a minute if he knew what he was doing, eee. Look how fat that one is, just as fat as the man who shot him, eee. He called the contestants, eight men chosen who knows how. They took their places and stood still, legs spread, boots unlaced, white puffs of breath and tobacco smoke rising in the air – casual, careless, anything but eager. As if they did this every day. They probably do.

The old man spoke Inuktitut; the crowd cheered. Not true; the Inuit cheered; those of us who spoke nothing other than English or French kept mum because we had no idea what was about to happen, except for the fact of the skinning.

The old man held his hand high. We shushed.

He let his hand fall and just as quickly fell seven knives. The eighth man dropped his and began giggling, bent over to pick it up and farted as he did so, and was helpless and giggling and so lost any chance he had to win.

I kept an eye on the skinner nearest me.

He cut easily from snout to tail in a straight line, baring a layer of snowy fat, working in an easy hurry, running the blade along with short deft slashes, loosening the skin, flensing around the shoulders, making little snicks to free the skin from the flippers, peeling the last of the grey hide from the head. A skinless head; the mouth a rictus.

I saw Etulu walking along the edge of the crowd, with a stern look on his face. And the skinner I'd been watching stuck his fingers like hooks through what had once been nostrils, made two more sharp cuts with his knife, and raised the sealskin high in the air.

It takes longer to tell than to do. The skin in the slippery air was wet and heavy. The carcass was little more than a rib cage, two slabs of fat, the dark strings and knots of bubbled guts, a bulging stomach, and a few gouts of black and ropy blood.

Time elapsed: one minute, seventeen seconds. The time it takes to play "The Ballet of the Unhatched Chicks." . . .

It was not long before the other men were done.

The winner made a mocking face, pretending to gloat as he wiped blood off his knife. He made a jibe and drew a good-humoured jeer – oh, you only won because you got the smallest seal. The man who dropped his knife when he farted was still giggling, holding a private conversation with those nearest him.

The winner motioned for silence. He pointed his knife at the carcass he had just skinned, and he spat out a string of thick

Inuktitut. He bent and – *oh!* – he carved a milky orbit from the skull of the seal and – *eee!* – he held the eyeball up for all to see. A long warm grey nerve dangled in the air. The woman next to me – from Quebec, she worked for the telephone company – shuddered as if she could not believe, and did not want to see, what we all knew was going to happen next.

The man threw the seal's eye in the air. It rose, in slow motion, as if it were taking one last look at those of us who'd watched the skinning. We followed its high flight, the orbit of orb and string.

A handsome woman, pregnant, wearing a bone-white baby parka with red and green embroidery – the prickly Elisapee, I'd seen her at the radio station – shot out her hand and plucked the eye from the air. The nerve wrapped around her wrist like a snake.

She showed off her prize like a bridesmaid who's caught the bouquet. And then she popped the eyeball in her mouth. And worked her jaw. And the jelly burst and aqueous humour dribbled from the corners of her lips. She bit off the stringy nerve. I did not see her cast it aside. I do not know if she ate it. I watched her eyes. They shone. "*Eee!*" cheered the crowd. The woman next to me clutched at my sleeve and vomited in the snow.

Afterwards, we moved slowly into the cafeteria, those of us with any appetite. We lined up with our plates and our trays. One of the cooks smiled as if to say, You're in for something, mister; we'll see what sort of *kabloona* you are. She gave me a broiled hand – I suppose more properly a flipper – of seal. Also a mug of caribou broth. A lump of raw caribou, I declined. Boiled fish, I accepted. Wieners floating in grey water, I declined. Instant mashed potatoes, I declined. White bread, what the hell. And an oatmeal cookie from a box.

Another smell inside these smells: Kentucky Fried Chicken.

Tape, June 22:

[He taped the feast – knives forced across difficult meat, forks stabbing plates, spoons dropped on linoleum, hot tea and broth sucked from cups to ease, not so much the chewing, but the avid swallowing – it makes me want to clean my ears.]

"Sam Willy, tell me something."

"What's that?"

"Did you take music lessons from the teacher?"

"The fuck you want to know for?"

"I don't want – Can I ask you another question?"

"What's that, *kabloona*."

"I smell KFC."

"Yeah, so?"

"Why would anybody – you have char, you have caribou and seal and so on – why bother to bring in the Colonel?"

"You can't get it here."

"Come again?"

"It's a delicacy. You can only get it in the south. You gotta bring it with you on the plane. There is no KFC here."

"I see."

"Who gives a fuck what you see?"

Tape, June 22, cont'd:

[Dom, obviously with his bud mics on, shuffles helplessly in the midst of a stream of people talking, coughing, telling stories, and scraping chairs along the floor; babies suckle, women coo and chuckle, and kids call to their friends as if they haven't seen each other in ages. His narration is *sotto voce*:]

I am leaning against the wall at the back of the gym. There's the waitress from the hotel. She has a baby in the hood of her parka. When she turns her back to me, she seems to be a short fat woman with an infant's head – like one of Etulu's carvings, utterly natural and abnormal at the same time. I see her bare brown shoulders and her back. Mother of the child? Not necessarily.

The idea of North is not an idea. It is real and it is in this room; in the tobacco sweat of men and the yeasty sweat of women; in the bad breath, the sealskin, and the farts; the smell of coffee from an urn and a bright pink note – Petaloosie is here, his cherry cough drops – also in the smell of milk dripping from bottles and leaking from teats onto clothes; and above it all I smell it in the ammonia urine of babies. Oddly, it is not unpleasant. And in the air, the absence of Malachai.

[The noise in the room moves like a restless animal until someone thumps a drum and there is a hush. Dominic continues to whisper in his play-by-play voice:]

A movement behind the curtain now. Gym lights flicker off and on and off again, the room is dark, the stage lights come up slowly.

Eee-la, here it comes, shut up you, the talent show is starting now, shhh, be quiet!

A small head peeks out from stage left; giggles, disappears. Now the curtains open with three short sharp pulls –

Oh, look at that, look at those kids, they look so nice!

The grade threes, two rows of them, fuss, fidget, and elbow each other in the ribs; a girl scratches her head, puts her hands behind her back, looks up at the ceiling. Rows of boygirlboy in white shirts, black pants, white blouses and black skirts – the children are a line of ravens in the snow.

[The speaker is unidentified but he sounds like Curly Craine – he clears his throat with a series of heh-heh-heh bursts, a machine gun of a man. He speaks alternating lines of Inuktitut and English:]

"It is nice to see everyone here tonight, students and teachers, parents and guests. We have come to celebrate not just Wolf Cove Days – we celebrate the life of Malachai. He is not with us here – not in person – but I can see his face and I know you see him too. He was a young man in the prime of life, a good hunter, a good son, and he was becoming a good father. He was a graduate of this school. He built his kayak in our workshop. And now he is in a better place. He would have wanted us to be here tonight. It is the wish of his father that we continue. And so we dedicate this evening, and this concert, to Malachai."

[Painfully soft applause. Dominic whispers under his breath:]

Old women waving to their grandchildren. Can't help themselves. The kids from the house next to mine. The backs of three hundred heads.

[On stage, a chorus of Inuit voices; an iambic chant.]

I have no idea what this is. Inuktitut with the rhythm of – oh for heaven's sake, "The Shooting of Dan McGrew." *Strange things done* . . . As for Dan McGrew's furnace, Arthur says when the missionaries came north they painted such vivid pictures of the fires of damnation that the native people prayed they'd go to hell when they died. In the darkness – it is hot as hell in here – there is Etulu, his eyes are wet. It looks like he's been drinking. I see heads bobbing in time, small boys bossing their little sisters, babies squirming and sweating in the heat, old men smoking cigarettes, toothless and happy. There has never been a place like this for smoking.

[The first set of kids is shuffled off the stage, replaced by a rhythm band marching to the sound of little sticks beating plastic buckets, tambourines jingling, kazoos buzzing the line of the melody, and someone pounding toy vibes as if administering discipline. Dom continues to narrate:]

A "Für Elise" such as never was. Here comes some kid in a sealskin jean jacket dotted with silver studs – skin-tight sealskin jeans – his mother must be a seamstress.

[Karaoke Elvis Presley]

"Jailhouse Rock." In Inuktitut. The only word I understand is "jail."

[Wild applause, as if it were the real Elvis. A pause in the narration; then, a capella and charmingly off-key: *Teetoo, teetoo, teetoo ree* – or words akin to it, repeated over and over with great energy and charm. Dom shouts to the woman next to him:]

"What's that song?"

"They're singing, those kids."

"Yes. I know. What is that song about?"

"Have some tea."

"That's it? That's what it's about?"

"It's a song about you visit, and you come into the house, and you help yourself to some tea."

"I see."

[Cackled jokes and coughs, empty pop cans rolling on the floor in the background. The principal introduces the grade five boys and girls' junior choir. Dom continues:]

Okay, now we'll see if Geela can play. She herds children centre stage, lines everyone up. Black pants, white shirts, a triple row of keys. She takes her place at the piano. The picture still taped inside. Geela's kids are mute, without expression, hands clasped in front as if they were shielding themselves. She opens the sheet music, waggles her bum on the chair, straightens her shoulders – the classic gestures of beginning. [She stabs middle C – once and once again.] I have a future as a tuner if I want one.

She looks over her shoulder at the choir. Kids open their mouths, stand on tiptoes in readiness. Her hands are poised over the keys.

"I'm sorry. I can't. I can't play this."

Notebook, June 22, cont'd:

I have had some experience –

To refuse to play is to offer another kind of music. I had no idea whether hers was defiance or defeat. The audience sat and listened to itself. The choir began to fidget mutely, unsure and worried for their teacher, caught in the hands of a rising stage fright. *What's wrong with teacher? Why isn't teacher playing? What should we do? Is teacher okay?*

I could not see her face. A woman with a baby in her parka spat on the floor. Etulu said something harsh. Another man, a hunter, stood.

This was too familiar. Etulu reached into his parka and retrieved a mickey. He drank. He drank again. The sweet smell in the air. His eyes, liquid and unblinking in the darkness.

I have listened to Malachai on the river. Again and again. I have seen his face – his broken tooth, brown skin, white smile, dark eyes. I see him in my dreams at night.

I waited and Geela struggled.

And then it hit me as clearly as I ever have heard anything: Malachai in the water, the song beneath the ice – Scriabin, Sonata no. 5, op 53. Cold oily chords, the spray of the silver-tipped notes, the refraction of the white light on water, until there was nothing but the calmness of the water and the wet slow spreading of the river pouring into the bay. Geela sat with her head bowed, her hands in her lap.

She was then as I had been.

Tape, June 22, cont'd:

[A boredom verging on ugliness is audible in the background noise, and an urgency in Dom's voice: *Excuse me, I'm sorry, if you could please let me get by. I'm just coming through. Sorry, sorry.* Then in a hot whisper:]

"What's wrong?"

"He taught the kids I taught."

"Who did?"

"Every kid in this town who learned music got help from me. And I sent them to study with that man. I know what's in this piano. I saw you take it out and put it back."

"What do you see? How did – ?"

"I stayed. I watched you. I listened. I saw you put it back."

[A new voice. The principal:] "Geela, what's wrong? The children –"

"I won't play this thing."

[I can't make out what Dom says but the bench scrapes on the floor of the stage.]

[Craine:] "Just give us a minute, ladies and gentlemen. We have a change in the program tonight. An unexpected surprise."

[Geela:] "Eee, I'm sorry, I'm very sorry, Mr. Craine."

[Dom:] "Let me just –"

[Whispers, the shuffling of shoes, a little girl crying. Someone yells at Dom – I can't make out the words. He sets his tape recorder on the piano – dull thump of the microphone – lets out a deep sigh and rubs his hands.]

Note: *He hasn't played in months, not for an audience. I can almost see him turn to the audience to say – what?*

The first notes are single notes, and the sound is bright as a trickle of water dripping from the lip of the shore ice in the springtime. I don't know what to think, except I have listened to this several times, as many times as he listened to the tape of the young man on the river. It seems to me, as the music thickens and grows more complex, that he is making a music of all he has seen:

The furious taxis slipping over the curve of the ring road and the howling of the dogs at night; the hesitant steps of caribou on crusted snow and the throaty roar of an airplane in a slow descent. And his voice under the music now, like the grunt of a bear rising on its hind legs in a small close room.

The coughing, the spitting, and the crying of the babies falls away and there is no sound now but the breathing of the people like the rushing of the great river in the spring, and then there is a light and sharp and darting note, like a kayak in the water or a shard of ice before it melts and is swallowed in the thick hot air.

And now the concert pianist Dominic Amoruso – for that is who he is again – begins to ring the clear strong bells in the tower of a mighty church, announcing the end of the day and the burial of the dead and the closing of the great gates of the city for the night.

Tape, June 22, cont'd:

[Curly Craine:] "Ahem, ladies and gentlemen, I don't. Ahem. I have never heard such. I'm sure Geela and her pupils, all of us would agree. Just as I'm sure Malachai, if he were here. Ahem. I think we can safely say Wolf Cove Days is now officially over. Thank you, students and teachers, thank you parents. And Mr. Amoruso. Thank you, maestro." The principal applauds; one or two people in the gym join in, but the applause is not unanimous. As if what Dom has played has fallen flat and has not, in this audience, left a trace. There is milling and shuffling as the gym empties.]

Note: *This next tape, the one I played when I first opened the box, now makes sense:*

Tape 2, June 22:
[A whisper of white noise; cold air, warm breath, and the squeak of footsteps on snow; the call and response of two barking dogs; the drone of a distant ATV; and now a hesitation in his step – I hadn't picked this out before. A door opens and closes with a pneumatic sigh; his sniffle and his cough.]

Note: *I was right about what I heard. It is evening, after the concert. But there has been a shift, one that I could not possibly have detected. It is after the death of Malachai, after Dom found the picture in the piano, after the disappearance of McCardle, after Geela refused to play.*
It is after Dominic played.
He re-enters the school by an unlocked side door.

Tape 2, June 22, cont'd:
[The hiss of the tape overwhelms, it pulses. I imagine him looking down a long corridor – waiting, watching, listening. And then a single voice, far off, rising and falling, punctuated by the echo of a hammer on wood – a hollow blow and another and another. He hurries towards the sound – the beat of his running steps. The voice is louder, now audible, it is guttural, coughed up and spat out. Another hammer blow. Dom's voice – "*No!*" Him, running.

And then a single, massive syllable of anguish, otherworldly, as if the piano were a living thing choked by the dark hard hands of a strangler.]

"Etulu, stop."

"You can't stop me, *kabloona*. Help me."

Notebook, June 22, late evening:

Broken bits – hammers, dampers, felts, and jacks – flew across on the floor. I picked up an undamaged key and put it in my pocket. A souvenir. The notes poured from the frame of the little piano like blood rushing out of an open vein. . . .

I was afraid to go near him. Etulu had the envelope. The picture of his son. He was drunk. He was talking to himself. None of the words he said made any sense.

Tape 2, June 22, cont'd:

[Breath and footsteps.]

"What the hell are you doing, Amoruso?"

"My hands, Arthur – they feel as if they're on fire."

"You won't put them out in a puddle of water. Get up off your knees, you silly bugger – your hands are your fortune. There. Now brush yourself off and tell me what the hell is going on in that school, then?"

～

Note: Margie dropped by earlier this evening, as I was listening for a final time to the concert in the gym. She didn't ask to hear it. I didn't offer to play it for her. She arrived with groceries and took charge.

"You didn't call back. I was worried. Which is to say, I'm not worried. You're a big boy. But you don't get out enough. You should. I mean, get out. You need some air. You need some greens." She stocked my fridge with fruit and lettuce.

I shut off the tape and closed my eyes.

I could hear her in the kitchen. She washed a head of lettuce at the sink and whirled it dry. She peeled and sliced an onion on the cutting board. She pitted olives with a little knife, she dropped the pits in the sink, she filleted an orange – I could hear it as I smelled it.

She gathered the pits and the peels and dumped them in the garbage. She whisked oil and vinegar and mustard in a cup. She filled a pot with a rush of water and set the pot on the stove. She rattled around for my best pan, heated some olive oil, slivered all my garlic and threw it, with a sizzle, in the oil. Aglio olio before I knew it, with a salad and a glass of wine.

"I have a bit more information for you if you want it."

"Information such as . . . ?"

"Such as don't talk with your mouth full, it's not polite. Anyone would think you hadn't eaten for days. Such as one manuscript exists. Of the Pictures. *It is – and you can see how this might appeal to me – in the Saltykov-Schedrin Public Library in St. Petersburg. It consists of eight double sheets of manuscript paper. The sheets are sewn together. A title page, and twenty-five pages of music. Your Musorgsky was a lush –"*

"He's not my Musorgsky, he's Dom's."

"Whatever. He was a lush, which makes it fitting that the slurs in the score are kind of blurry – it's hard to tell where they begin and end. Or so I'm told. But I am told there are plenty of slurs, and they are plenty slurred."

"Who told –"

"I am a librarian. I made some calls. We librarians look after each other. Many of us speak English. The one I spoke to in St. Petersburg said Musorgsky pasted fresh paper over certain sections when he changed his mind, rather than start afresh. She said there is no record of a public performance of the piece in his lifetime. Apparently his pal Rimsky-Korsakov worked on it briefly – smoothed out a few bits here and there, fiddled with the rhythms. No recordings until the forties. Ashkenazy's is the closest to the score. Except for your man. The one who isn't here."

I said he was here. I pointed to the tapes. She wiped her lips and raised an eyebrow. I finished the story for her.

"Do you want to stick around and hear the rest of it? Not much more, by the look of things."

"I'd love to but."

What do you mean, but."

"I'm taking next week off. I'm going to Montreal in the morning. Be gone for a couple of days. I have to go home and pack."

"Bring me bagels."

Notebook, June 23:

I feel as if I have been holding my breath for a full year. And now I can breathe. I have been over it several times. It was not as if I was making up the music on the spot; I played a continuation of what I have been thinking and what I have been hearing – the basis for all music surrounds us. Thorn of Idea: Idea of North.

Tape, June 23:

[Footsteps on icy gravel; the voices, his and Geela's:]

"Wait up."

"Hello. Are you okay?"

"That was very kind."

"What was kind?"

"What you did."

"What did I do?"

"Last night at the school."

"I played."

"It helped. It helped me."

"It didn't help the piano."

"It was good that you played. Nobody can play like that except on the radio. Arthur said he found you with your hands in a puddle of water. I've heard of hot playing. You must have been really hot."

"It's not funny."

"No. It was funny. Last night, parts of it were very funny."

"What was so funny?"

"When you were sort of doing throat singing; men don't do that."

"Men don't –"

"It's a woman thing."

"I made a fool of myself, then."

"No. It was a relief, like a kindness."

"How did you know about the envelope?"

"I stayed after I brought you the needles. I wanted to listen to how the piano sounded after you used them. To see what difference it made. A way of learning something. I saw you reach inside and take it out. I saw you put it back. You were thinking very hard. After you left, I went to the piano. There were always a lot of rumours about that man. The kids, all of them were always a bit afraid of him."

"Malachai? Tell me, was he –"

"He broke into the school the first time. The night before he died. He was drunk then. He must have wanted to get the picture. I guess he couldn't find it. He was still drunk when he went in the kayak the next day."

"Why did Etulu smash the piano?"

"If it was your son, what would you have done?"

"How did he know?"

"Malachai must have told him."

"Will you tell the police?"

"There is no photo any more."

"What do you – ?"

"Never mind about that. What are you doing right now?"

"Nothing much; I was just walking."

"Do you want to come down the bay with me? We can make the tide if we go now. I have my father's boat. I have a lunch and some tea. I can show you something, maybe you'd like to see it."

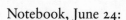

Notebook, June 24:

I still have no idea whether I have done the right thing.

I am now a man with a secret.

She had me untie the ropes. I jumped in the boat awkwardly; the deck was greasy and I landed on my ass. She pretended not to notice, reversed engines, swung around and we – she – headed into the channel:

Oil tanks on the hill like silver-painted pill boxes. A few stray icebergs. She watched me swallow a pair of blues, dry. And I took something for my stomach – no sea legs, me. The first pills in more than a week. Force of habit.

She pretended not to notice and she opened the throttle.

The wake was a white collar curling on the green water. I could feel the power of the engine rising up through my feet, into my legs, my hips; the vibration, almost sexual. Not almost.

I couldn't hear what she was saying. I read her lips: "We'll get there soon. We are running with the tide. It is now eleven. We have to be back tonight by seven or we'll miss high water."

Useless to tape. The drone of the engine too loud.

The cold air cut through my clothing and clutched at my throat. I could feel it wriggling in my jacket. I can still feel the rocking of the boat as it nosed through the waves.

"Look over there, do you see!"

I saw nothing – the water was so cold it seemed like oil. In the distance, a low line of black mountains, the peaks as sharp as broken bottles; in between their jaggedness, the tongues of white glaciers licking at the water.

"There, can you see them? Seals."

"Where?"

"Over there, a hundred yards."

"I don't see them."

"You have to look at the water like an Inuk. Keep your eyes open and don't try to see one thing. Try to see everything and nothing all at the same time. When you get used to looking that way, anything unusual will stick out. Keep your eyes open, that's all you have to do."

The whole bay before us. I could see the water, she could see what the water held. My eyes welling, blurring. And then I noticed ears and a blunt snout break the surface. A twitch, a sniff, and the seal ducked effortlessly under.

A program I saw on television: Two hunters in a small house, smoking and drinking tea, the camera recording every sip and drag. After a time, they got up and hauled several pack sacks and boxes down to the water's edge and loaded them into a freighter canoe. The camera got it all: the stowing of the gear, the pulling of the cord again and again to start the motor, and the journey across the water.

The man in the bow stared patiently with a rifle in the crook of his arm. The program was shown in real time and seemed to take forever. After a time – a long time – the bow man stiffened and shouldered his rifle. He sighted along the barrel with both eyes open and his cigarette clenched between his teeth, and the rifle was rising and falling with the rise and fall of the boat. And then he became still and the rifle shuddered; fifty yards away the nose of a seal exploded with a red slap and the man at the stern gunned the motor, wheeling the canoe around as sharply as he could, and the two men raced to retrieve the animal before it sank.

It occurred to me that the program was not as pointless as I'd thought. The Inuit had no paper but they had stories that they told the same way over and over again. The program, like the stories, was a map: Turn right when you clear the mouth of the river. Past the second glacier, you will come to a rock like the face of an old woman. Keep going right, and a few minutes later you are going to be where the good hunting is – where we are now.

I kept my eye on the spot where the seal had disappeared. Twenty yards farther on, the little head popped up again.

"There it is again. A harp seal."

I suppose I could have shot it if I'd needed the meat. No, she could have shot it if she'd needed the meat. I briefly imagined her hauling the limp dead creature from the water; she would have cut it open on deck and eaten the liver while it was warm. I could have killed it for her if, instead of playing the piano, I'd been hunting on the water since my childhood.

"Harp seals, more of them."

I have seen the hides scraped and tied to wooden frames or to metal stretchers on balcony railings or on the chain link fence near the airport. I've seen an eyeball eaten. I had harp seal at the feast. Could I shoot and gut and eat what I shot? Too late for me: fool tore meat.

Geela steered towards open water, far from the rocky security of shore. She said, "Take the wheel. Hold it steady. Aim for that point of land over there." I did as I was told. That's what you do when you are out of your depth. You do as you are told.

She reached into her backpack, pulled out a thermos, poured cups of black tea with sugar and gave me one. She asked if I wanted to keep steering the boat. I did not. I was unsure of myself. No idea what to do if something happened, if we hit pan ice on the open water, if there was an unexpected shoal, if we saw a polar bear swimming towards us. Or if the seal-woman rose up to take revenge for Malachai.

I held the mug and let it warm my hands.

Geela remained quiet. She seemed content to say nothing. That's not my idea of oral culture. The Italians have an oral culture. I drank my tea. I wanted to talk. I felt the urge to tell her the whole of it – what had happened at the gallery that night; how I'd lost the sense of colour, how my fingers had lost the sense of light and sight; what had happened in those moments just before I stopped playing; how I'd sat and stared at the carving of the man with the knife. I said nothing.

After half an hour – I'd stood next to her for warmth, and she'd leaned her hip into me – she throttled back and took her bearings. She slowed the boat and steered towards a tiny opening in the rocks, a narrow channel. I'd never have seen it on my own. I'd never have been there on my own. And I'd never be able to find it again if I had to.

She steered between the flat, low-lying rocks, shelves of them in the water. An illusion – as if the rocks were floating. There was ice in the water, a few bergs unable to catch the tide and escape into the sea. I could feel them as we passed; they seemed to breathe as they melted in the air.

Geela said they were dangerous – the taller ones became unbalanced as they melted; they were prone to roll without warning. I imagined it in slow motion: the heaving and the rolling of the ice, and the boat raised helpless and high on a crest of water – and then a moment when the boat tipped sideways under the heavy wave; death would come suddenly; the shock of the cold before we drowned: down, red.

Malachai.

An incident one afternoon in Toronto, coming back from Serafino's place: three boys racing down the stairs to the platform of the Lansdowne station; one of them holding something in his hands. The other boys poking his arm, trying to make him drop it.

A train approached. The boy bent and placed a mouse, small and grey and stunned, on the platform. He timed his kick as the train entered the station. It would be like that.

A shock and a rush and a swift exhilaration, the rising and the helpless falling. I shuddered with pleasure at the thought of the iceberg rolling over. I can't explain why.

We came to a place where the shore was level with the water and it seemed as if the sea were about to spill over the rim and flood the world. I was aware that my feet, in the boat, were actually lower than the surface of the water. Geela pulled up to the shelf of stone – a perfectly natural dock. The boat bumped heavily against it, and made a hollow sound.

No wind, no waves, no birds.

I jumped ashore and she threw me a bowline and told me to loop it around a rock. This rock? No, that one! Like this? No, the other way!

She cut the engine, threw her pack on shore, and took the lines fore and aft. She made the boat secure. She led me inland. After a few minutes – tiny black flies buzzed and bit my ears until they burned; they didn't seem to bother her – we entered a small meadow, protected on two sides by low rock walls.

"Look," she said. There were small stones in the dry grass. It took me a moment to notice the pattern they made – a circle of stones. "That is a tent ring," she said. "A long time ago this was a summer place for a small family, not too many people. There is a lot of fish here. Whenever you want fish you can get them; also a lot of seals and birds." I tried to look at the land as if I lived there – an absurd notion.

Nearby there were two large stones, covered with a lace of orange and white lichen. "This is a place for drying a kayak. After hunting, you bring your kayak here and put it on these stones." I'd never thought about this before – not that I'd had reason to – but there was a time when a kayak was made of skin, not fibreglass or plastic. You couldn't leave it wet, or it would rot. She took me by the hand – hers was dry and cold – and led me to a place where the earth had been torn open. It looked as fresh and raw and dark as if it had been done yesterday.

"You see the pattern, like an igloo."

I saw it as soon as she said it. A straight entrance a few feet long leading to a circular, dug-out pit containing some flat rocks, a few large bones, and a jumble of small ones.

"This is a summer house. People lived here. They dug into the earth like this. You see those bones?"

They were white and brittle, as long as I am tall, and slightly curved. "The ribs of a whale. That's what they used to frame the house. They covered the bones with walrus skins." I reached for one of the bones.

She stopped my hand.

"This is very old. A thousand years old. Maybe four or five hundred years. A very long time. You should not touch them."

Nearby, there were more bones, a midden, the remains of ancient meals – thighs of birds, ribs of seals, the breastbone of a whale, and the head of a creature that instinct told me was a walrus; all these bleached white, and the grass around them lush. A drop of blood, a scrap of cartilage, a hundred years of growth. Or so she said.

"What's that?"

I pointed to a mound in the distance, a heap of stones a farmer might make when he cleared a field. It was the size of a small car.

"I'll show you later. Come here now."

She led me to the shelter of the rock wall. She spread a blanket and took out lunch. Sandwiches, the flask of tea, a box of apple juice. The sandwiches were smoked meat on rye. Not all Inuit eat seal at every meal. She also had a box of Belgian cookies from Northern Ventures.

I asked her what would happen to Etulu.

She said that after I'd gone outside he had tried to burn the picture. He was so drunk, he couldn't light the matches. Curly

Craine would not press charges. I asked her what would happen to McCardle. She said she was certain he was gone and maybe that was the best thing. After lunch she looked at me as if she were trying to make up her mind about something.

She stood and offered me a hand and pulled me up and at the same time she opened the front of her jeans. And she pulled at my belt.

Her hands were rough and cold and she said what she wanted me to do in clear, almost mocking terms. "Come on, what's the matter with you. Are you afraid of an Inuk?" And she turned her back and I leaned into her and I braced myself and placed my hands against the warm rough stone.

"I want to show you something. It's why I brought you here. Come with me." I was still breathing heavily. She was calm, and the sun had come out, one of those things that is simple and natural and no marvel at all.

She led me to the stone cairn.

"Be careful where you walk. Try not to disturb the grass with your boots. There is not much soil here, not enough to dig a grave. A long time ago they put their dead under piles of stones like this, so no animals could get at them. There are not many of these cairns. They are protected. If you go close, you can look inside."

"There's a body in there?"

"You go and look."

I peered in the cracks between the stones.

When my eyes adjusted to the light, I saw a wizened corpse in a skin parka, sitting with his head bent and his legs pulled up, arms around his knees, kamiks on his feet. He'd been sitting there, summer and winter, since these stones were placed. I could see a few wisps of hair on his head. A Thule-culture corpse. His sunken eyes, his open mouth, the dry skin stretched over his cheeks. The wind blew through the cairn. He was perfectly preserved. He had been there hundreds of years. I could hardly breathe. I wanted to speak. If I'd had anything to say, it would have come out as a whisper.

I was about to turn away when the clouds shifted and the light changed. Next to the old man in the skin clothing, I saw – I thought I saw – a second body, the collar of a blue ski jacket, the glint of a zipper. The Thule people had no ski jackets, no zippers.

She said, "You played the piano very well. It was good you played like that. It was good you left the photo where you found it. You did the right thing. We know how to take care of ourselves up here. Things heal slowly in the North. I don't know what you saw in that cairn. I'm not going to ask. The man who did those things to Malachai and the other boys is gone. He is not coming back. And you will go home soon, too, I think."

She turned away and headed for the boat. I followed her. She said, "Arthur told me why you came here. He told me who you are. I couldn't touch that piano, it made me sick to sit there. To put my hands on it. Maybe it was not easy for you to play any more. But you played. So I showed you this place. Come on. We have to go. If we don't leave now, it won't be safe getting back."

Tape, June 23, cont'd:

[Thirty minutes of the sound of a diesel engine, and the hard lapping of water on the hull of the boat.]

A final note:

I am almost embarrassed to admit this. No, I am completely embarrassed: After I finished auditing the tapes and editing the last of the notes, I thought I'd stow everything back in the original box. For safekeeping. And I shifted Dom's tape recorder to make a bit of room, and there was a tape cued up, ready to be played. I'd been so blinded by the package and my own eagerness that I hadn't bothered to look where I should have looked first. It is his voice.

Tape, undated:

I am sure you will know how to make use of this material. I no longer know what any of it means. I've given up trying to decide. You have my permission to use it as you wish, with one or two qualifications.

I know that there has been some curiosity about what happened. When you listen, you will learn most of the answers. Telling the story will profit us both, although in different ways.

A word about the contents.

The tapes and my notes are as close to a linear record as it is possible to get from the time I stopped playing until I played again – and I have played again, as you will discover – but for reasons of my own, I have kept some notes back and I have done some discreet editing of the tapes. Trust me, what is not included is of no real consequence.

I have a couple of requests.

First, above all – you may transcribe the tapes, but you may not broadcast them. I have plans of my own. They are my idea of north.

Second, I know you could easily bankroll a trip to Wolf, to search for the elusive me. Not hard to do. Search for me, that is.

Don't. This place is an isolated village on an island; it's easy enough to get here – I proved that – but once you are here, there's nowhere to go, no hopping in a car and driving down the road. The road ends where it begins. It is the snake that swallows its tail. And so, in a way, is Wolf Cove. You won't learn much. People here mind their own business. But in any case, I am not here now. By the time you get this package, I will have gone somewhere to work with the tapes I've kept, to get my hands back in shape, and to prepare a return.

Let me clarify what the tapes may not make clear – and if you do not understand what I am about to tell you now, then you will by the time you've finished listening: Two hours after I played in the gym, the piano was destroyed. It was not an act of music criticism. It was an act of cleansing committed by an old man with a broken heart. What he did taught me a lesson:

Music neither soothes nor heals – it simply is, and then it disappears. As does the spoken word. One does what one can. I can play, and that alone is reason to. It doesn't matter what you hear. It only matters that you do.

As for what I saw or did not see in the cairn – and if you go through these tapes, you will discover a cairn – it's quite possible I caught a glimpse of two bodies, and I may have seen the collar of a blue jacket and a flash of something silver, perhaps a zipper; of course, it's also possible the wind blew something in my eye.

The young Malachai is dead; there's no bringing him back. His last breath is caught in the hissing of the tape.

The music teacher is gone. No one admits to knowing where he is. And if he is in the cairn, I could not find it again if my life depended on it. A missing persons bulletin has gone out across the North. No one misses him. Let it rest. I've said too much already.

Arrangements have been made with the help of an anony-
mous donor to have a new piano flown in. The principal of the
school will hire a new music teacher in the fall. I have it on good
authority that she has been taking lessons from a very good
player. I have it on equally good authority that she is a quick
student. You don't know what I'm talking about, not yet.

Note: Well – I know now.

Tape, undated, cont'd:
The little Steinway was a total wreck. The man who destroyed it was so drunk he couldn't talk, but he did a very good
job of it. People up here know how to fix things; as a result, they
also know how to smash them. When you see me next, ask me if
I raised the hammer and struck a blow myself.

The Mounties came and found the old man sitting amid the
wreckage with a stone carver's hammer by his side and a torn
photograph in his hands. He tried to burn the photo. He was
too drunk to light a match. He spent a night in jail.

The remains of the piano were hauled off to the dump the
next day; improbably, since almost everything here is used and
used again. I told a man named Sam Willy that I thought it
would make a fine sealskin stretcher. A first for Steinway, I'll bet.
He shrugged and spat and grunted. You have never seen such a
place for spitting and grunting. Not the answer I was looking for.
I pressed him a bit. I said I thought the strings would be good for
snare wire. He said he wouldn't kill anything with those strings.

You will think the real story is that I stopped and walked
away and found myself again. I suppose that's true.

The people of Wolf Cove took me in, no questions asked. I
was the man in the tuxedo. I was the penguin, I was that man

who worked at Northern Ventures. I have no illusions – I did not rock the boat while I was here – if I had, they'd have found a way to push me over the side and cut off my fingers. Or they would have left me buried under a heap of stones.

I think the real story is this: I was the last man to play that piano. And I have a better idea of North now than Gould ever did. I will play again, and seriously, and soon. There are a few things I have to do first. I want to use the tapes to make a step, so to speak.

For your information, I have not been entirely out of touch. I have made calls. I didn't call you because I wanted to keep you as a clean slate. Forgive me, it was for the best. You will be pleased to know – as I am pleased to tell you – that I have not had a headache in some time. I may have made a mistake with certain of my drugs. But I have had no drugs since I went out on the boat.

A last word on the subject of the recital:

In the right light, if you have taken the right drugs, if you do not focus your eyes, and if you stare into the middle distance, then a row of patrons dressed in formal wear looks remarkably like a keyboard, black and white.

Just as a rose in a lapel looks like a drop of blood.

An afterword:

The tapes and notebooks, along with Dom's tape recorder, remain boxed in my closet. Two cassettes – unlabelled – contain material I will neither transcribe nor describe in detail except to say they are of a frankly sexual nature. Margie has gone to Montreal. She might have been shocked had she heard them. I certainly was.

I had a call yesterday from Carol Paterson. I played dumb and asked her if she'd heard from Dom. She played dumb in return; complicit from the beginning, as were the others. She told me that Maisela Singer had a stroke last month; he has lost the use of his right arm. She was arranging to have him moved into a small private nursing home, one with a piano. She would not tell me how she managed to get this done, or where the money came from. From the man who bought the piano, is my guess. Why tell me? By way of reply, she wondered if I'd heard from Buddy lately. I said I hadn't. She told me to phone him, and broke off the call.

I met Buddy at Dai Nam, one of Dom's old haunts. We ordered and chatted idly until I lost patience and asked if he'd heard from Dom. I knew he must have been in touch; he'd called the others, he must have called him. By way of reply, Buddy smiled and pushed a small package across the table. He said I looked like a guy who knew what to do with a package. I tore it open. No notes or tapes; a composition for the left hand, clearly meant for Singer. "An Idea of North." Dom's writing. Nothing more than this.